I0818193

PRAISE FOR FADED FRAGMENTS

Mandi's world-building is immersive and emotional, blending magic, love, and danger. All in one!

— JESSE

A great start to a debut series, with flawed and wounded characters in intensely interdependent relationships and an ancient Egyptian curse gnashing constantly at their heels!

— SHAYLA

The story keeps you entertained and you never know what is going to happen next.

— LORINDA

Mandi writes in a way that is both compelling and emotional—this is a book you won't be able to put down.

— PETA

Faded Fragments is one of those books which is fun, fabulous and fast paced. It'll keep your interest the whole way through.

— KYLIE

ONE OF THOSE BOOKS I COULDN'T PUT DOWN!!

— SETHMI

A beautifully written tale of friendship, family, loss, love, battles, mystery, and respect.

— STEPH

The characters came alive for me, and I found that I came invested in the outcome for each. The way that mythology is seamlessly blended into a modern story makes it such an enjoyable read.

— CLAUDIA

If you're not into brilliantly written, highly compelling fantasy novels then keep scrolling. But if that is your cup of tea, welcome to Faded Fragments. You won't regret it.

— WC

Being transported into Lucy's world was a treat with Egypt as the background was amazing

— NICK

The twists and turns woven into the plot kept me on the edge of my seat all the way until the final page, and my mind is racing with all the possibilities that Mandi has left open for exploration.

— CHEYENNE

ALSO BY MANDI KONTOS

The Nexus Series

Faded Fragments

Published by Dreaming Fully Awake Press
https://dreamingfullyawake.com

Paperback ISBN: 978-0-6459077-3-5
Ebook ISBN: 978-0-6459077-4-2
Hardback ISBN: 978-0-6459077-5-9

Edition: 1
First Printed: 2025

Trigger warnings include: gore, murder, torture, kidnapping, and allusions to rape.

Edited by Brittany Bitossi from BLD Editing
Proofread by Ramona Mihai
Cover Design by Miblart
Formatted with Vellum

A NEXUS SERIES NOVEL

MANDI
KONTOS

To Peter.

Who taught me what being a brother was like and inspired Devin's nurturing spirit.
I take back telling Mum that I wanted a sister.
Because having a brother shaped who I am.

AMP

CHAPTER ONE

Devin
Mechir 2017
Melbourne

A STEADY STREAM of lights flickered as the whole city was alive and thriving—an unusual sight for it to be so open, so full of people at that hour of the night, but White Night was in full swing. The City of Melbourne was open to the public for one night only, as if it were the middle of the day. Art museums, the library, concerts and installations of light thrown onto buildings. You name it, it was on and open. My watch vibrated as it hit midnight, the sky erupting as fireworks brightened the night. Loud cracks masked any other sound, faces in awe, and I zeroed in on the one I'd haunted—the one whose dreams I slipped into to warn him that I was coming for him.

David Gagliani. Thirty-two. Three kids. CEO of Gagliani Industries.

He took over the smaller companies and expanded them under his own image. He was at the top of his career, a doting father with a hotter-than-anything wife who was only twenty-seven. He had it all, but someone wanted him dead.

And someone was paying me a lot to do so.

They'd called on me, the Dreamwalking Assassin, to end his life.

I should mention that he was a werewolf too.

A deadly one.

His real crime was selling Lupos—its street name was W. It gave takers unparalleled strength and healing abilities that were out of this world, almost as if the user were a shapeshifter. I'd nearly have been all for it if it weren't being used negatively and causing users to have adverse reactions to it, robbing service stations, holding people for ransom and shooting up schools. It was a derivative of werewolf blood, and it was mixed with other deadly drugs because werewolves didn't willingly give up their own blood unless they had nothing to lose. Colour shot through the sky and lit up the path across the buildings, showing the concrete maze for what it was: a playground of jumps, leaps and twists that led me to the exact spot that would be the perfect place to end Gagliani's life.

I scaled the ledge and jumped to the next building with ease, my bow slung over one shoulder with my quiver full of arrows. I was old-school when it came to kills. Guns were too easy and took the fun out of the kill.

As I settled into my spot, I watched Gagliani usher his young family along the path, trying to get closer to the action while he kept a keen eye out.

He knew I was coming for him.

I'd visited his dreams for weeks, taunting him with countless versions of his death over and over again, but this wasn't one he would have ever imagined. He was so sure I would never come at him with his family, but that's where he was wrong. That was where he was least safe.

He had bags under his eye, and for a werewolf, that was a hard feat; they almost always look perfectly pristine and always on point. But not then. I gripped the bow with an easy hold and grabbed an arrow from the quiver with my free hand. It clicked into place like a key opening a lock, and I pulled back steadily. The string rested against my cheek as I took slow breaths to steady the thumping in my chest.

I let go of the arrow, the string making a slapping sound as it snapped back into place. The arrow sailed through the air and sank into Gagliani's heart. His eyes widened, and he searched wildly for the source of the arrow. His eyes found mine in his last seconds before he crumpled to the ground. His wife screamed and pulled him into her lap, her eyes scanning the buildings as I ducked down, out of sight.

Only a few ever locked eyes with me before their life was stripped from their bodies. Gagliani joined that selected few.

Keeping low, I stashed my bow and arrow in a nook. I'd come back for it when the city was tucked into bed in the early hours of the morning. I pivoted on the balls of my feet, keeping low as I moved across the rooftops of the buildings close by to get to the one that mattered the most: Ankh, the club Travis owned—my twin sister's best friend. My fresh stash of clothes was lying in a bag in the top penthouse above the club, along with the rest of my belongings.

On a hunt, there was no need for ID or money. Currency seems petty when one was taking the life of another.

As I slipped through Ankh's back door, I made my way through the throng of pulsing bodies, covered in alcohol, sweat and sex. The flashing, coloured lights and vibrating bass thrummed through my body as the thrill of the kill, still pulsing through my body, made me giddy. I stole a drink on my way up the stairs from a patron too drunk to notice. I probably did them a solid by taking it off their hands. I caught Travis' gaze and winked as I turned around at the top of the stairs. I could feel his eyes on me the whole time, but then again, I had a sixth sense of supernatural beings.

The room was cool, a respite from the sweat and heat that was unconventional for Melbourne. And with the extra bodies of White Night, it was going to be a long walk from Southbank to The Wheeler Centre.

My flashing phone caught my eye, and I picked it up and flicked it over to voicemails. I had three, and they were all from Lucy.

'Devin, you're *late*. Again. You know, being older than me by three minutes doesn't give you the right to always be late for everything. Get your arse down here before Hunter walks out on me. I *need* you.'

And like that, the buzz of the kill wore off and a switch in my brain clicked into place. The Dreamwalking Assassin left the building, the drink I had was forgotten and I changed into my street clothes. Devin Ryder, older, caring brother, replaced the shell of the warrior I was so used to being.

My sister was pissed at me, and I would rather have faced another three years in The Camp than go up against Lucy. And I'd almost rather have been a monster than a disappointing brother.

I would have preferred to take the cyanide capsule than have to face the wrath of Lucy Ryder.

The walk from Ankh to The Wheeler Centre was normally short, but that night, when the City of Melbourne was flooded with bodies, it was three times as long. I made my way over the Yarra, past Flinders Street Station and the clocks and followed the straight maze down Swanston Street, weaving between Melbournians laughing, chattering and oblivious to the underbelly that lay between the cracks.

With every step, I felt the way the city bustled with energy, people excited for a glimpse of what their favourite hangout looked like in the dark. But the shadows were where the real action was. In my peripherals, I caught scattered glimpses of the metaphysical world, trying to hide at a time when it would be their natural hunting ground.

Too many humans around, too many chances to be seen, too many reasons to be thrown in a cell with no way out.

Beneath the thrill of going into the museum and night, the artwork lights projected on the town hall and the line to get at the state library. There was a quiet panic. It settled into the depths of the city.

I did that. All of the members from The Camp did that on the regular, but that night … That night was different. The hushed whispers of gossip that would turn into reality flittered between the conversations, but that wasn't my immediate problem. Not then.

As if there was a switch, I stared at Lucy, my twin sister, who nervously walked down the side street where The Wheeler Centre was situated, her hands gesturing as her lips moved. She was memorising the talk she had to give about her book and the time she spent in Egypt. Her wavy brown hair trailed down her back. I knew it would be annoying her, but she knew she looked good with her hair down. And Lucy liked to make a good impression. Her floral dress looked like it hung effortlessly on her frame, but I could tell her movements were far from that. I crossed through the sweaty bodies on the other side of the street, and just as my foot hit the path, she looked up. Her stormy grey eyes—irises that mirrored my own—caught mine, and I watched as her shoulders relaxed, and her hand gestures stopped as she pointed at me. I felt like I'd done something incredibly wrong, and she was calling me out on my bad behaviour.

'Devin!' she yelled, and I slipped out of the Dreamwalking Assassin and into Devin Ryder, brother and friend. I felt a hint of warmth touch my heart as the persona became an entity of its own volition. Lucy was a soft spot of mine—as any sister would be. There was no limit I wouldn't go to. Perhaps that was why I was who I was.

'Luce, what are you doing out here?'

'I've been calling you for ages. You know how I feel about you not picking up your phone. Where were you?'

I sighed and caught myself before I rolled my eyes at her. The last time I didn't answer my phone, I was taken to The Camp, and was missing for close to five years.

'My phone was upstairs at Ankh. I only realised the time when it was almost too late. I'm sorry. Where's Hunter?' I asked as I guided her back down the side street and to the stairs that led into The Wheeler Centre.

'I'm here,' Hunter said as soon as we entered the building. It was full of writers, fans and everyone in between.

'Were you eavesdropping, Wyatt?' I asked as we bumped fists.

'No way, but I can only imagine that if you had to save Lucy outside, it means you would be wondering where I was. You know, you're obviously here to see me.' He grinned, and I shook my head. Hunter loved to play with fire.

'Hey!' Lucy said and elbowed him in the ribs.

'Watch out, Hurricane Lucy is in the house,' I joked. Her scathing look would have scared me if she wasn't my sister, but Hunter wrapped an arm around her shoulders, which forced her to relax into him.

Hunter and Lucy's relationship seemed so easy in those days. Well, in comparison to when we were teens and before I was taken. I never knew if they were on or if they were off, and I never pried because I didn't want to know about the relationship my best friend had with my sister. Back then, it had been weird, but after killing to survive and learning how to hurt someone without even touching them, it suddenly felt normal for me.

'Miss Ryder … Uhhh Lucy, there you are. I've been looking everywhere for you. You're meant to be in the green room, and you're here. We need to mic. Oh. *Oh*—' Lucy's new assistant, Freyja, looked my way and flushed.

I grinned at her, thankful for her presence distracting Hurricane Lucy from digging for the real answer to her question outside. I didn't want to have to lie to her about killing Gagliani—easier to avoid.

'Hello, Freyja. It's good to see you again. You look great.'

'Dev,' Lucy hissed.

I stepped closer to Freyja, careful to avoid the elbows that were out in force. I'd seen her dreams, and they were most definitely wicked.

'Um … yes … Hi, Mr … Devin. It's nice to see you again. Uhhh.'

'Freyja, *Freyja*.' Lucy clicked her fingers to get her assistant's attention. I just smiled at her and looked past her to Hunter, who rubbed his top lip to hide a smile behind his hand. I could see the laughter in his eyes.

'Yes. Sorry, Lucy. Hi, what was I saying?'

'You were looking for me …?'

'Oh! Yes! Everything has been set up and ready for your talk. Your computer is ready, here's your clicker and I have to mic you up. You're five minutes out.'

'That's my cue to leave. Will you guys make sure you behave yourselves? Drinks are on me after,' Lucy said as Freyja attached the microphone to her dress. Once she was done, Hunter kissed Lucy on the cheek and whispered something in her ear before the girls disappeared through the sea of bodies.

'So where were you?' Hunter asked. He was harder to placate than Lucy, but Hunter could also see through a lot of the shit my sister was oblivious to. He didn't know anything about the extracurriculars with the whole killing people thing. I hated lying to my best friend, but it kept him safe, like it did Lucy. Hunter had always been there when I needed him—even when I didn't want Lucy to see me like I had been. He'd been there to step in and make sure she was shielded from who I'd become as I tried to slip back into the 'real' world.

'I was at Ankh and some chick spilt her drink on me. Travis wanted to see what I could do to help him out with the club. You know how it goes.' I shrugged.

We moved out of the foyer and into the main room in The Wheeler Centre, where we hung back and stayed close by the door. There were rows of chairs on either side of the room, a centre aisle to move through and book signing tables set up at the back. We moved to Lucy's table and manned it—it was the only request she had asked of us. On the stage, there were three chairs, a podium and screen. I could see Lucy to the side of the stage, deep in conversation with Freyja, but I could feel her nerves through our twin bond—one I was learning to lean into again. But things were different than they had been. I'd had it closed off for so long that having that channel open to her again felt like I was drowning in emotion that I didn't know what to do with. She was more freaked out than she let on, and I took a steady breath and pushed that energy to her.

Lucy was a grown woman, and I couldn't save her, but her shoulders did relax.

'I don't buy it. You're so careful. Who is she?' Hunter asked.

'No one, man, seriously. Travis will vouch for me. You know he's good for it.'

'Yeah, like he's going to tell me anything. You know how he feels about me.' Hunter leant against the wall and folded his arms over his chest. He didn't like talking about Travis because of the history between him and Lucy, but that was something they had to deal with. I had no problem with the guy.

'Oh, well, there's only so much you can do.' We were silent as they introduced Lucy and her achievements. It was eerie to hear it. She'd been working on her book for years, and there she was … giving one of many talks to promote the book she wrote about the worst few years of her life.

'Have you seen how crazy it is outside? I can't believe someone actually thought this up, although I kind of get how cool it is,' I said quietly to change the subject.

'I know. White Night is a cool concept, although I'm not sure why Writers Victoria thought it would be good to have a writer talk after midnight …'

'It's because they know she doesn't sleep,' I joked, but it wasn't really a joke. 'She's stopped dreaming.'

'The nightmares are back again, and she's throwing herself into writing her next book. Luce thinks that if she can crack that, she can get the images out of her head.'

I sighed. The book she was promoting was a biography of what had happened in Egypt three years earlier. She was tortured by a mummy, ancient gods and found out that our older sister, Destiny, and I weren't dead. Lucy had also killed for the first time. All things considered, she was holding up okay, but there was a cap put on the memories to help her cope. Sometimes, though, the mind just needed to cope all on its own.

'The anniversary seems to fuck her up with sleeping, and the closer we get, the harder it is.'

'We're nearly th—' I was interrupted by a voice on the PA system.

'Attention, patrons. There has been a situation in the city, and Victoria Police have put a lockdown on the area. Please take care when exiting to the dedicated lockdown building. There is nothing to be alarmed about. This is a security measure. The nearest security point is to the left, at the state library. Please make your way there.'

Hunter and I reacted quickly, snaking our way through the panicked crowd to Lucy. Her eyes caught mine, and while the killer inside me wanted to stand back and watch the chaos, the brother in me needed to protect her because I hadn't been able to three years earlier.

'Gagliani is dead,' Lucy said as she threw the paper down in disgust. 'That sleaze can't even get on the front page without making me need a shower.'

I looked past my coffee and knew I needed to react, but my brain couldn't decide whether it wanted to react as Devin, Dreamwalking assassin or Devin, doting brother. So, instead of choosing, I shrugged and gulped down half of my coffee.

'He looks like an upstanding man, but there was more to him. Did you know he was a werewolf?'

I choked on said coffee and stared at Lucy. *How ... How does she know that?* I didn't remember mentioning it anywhere, and I was extra careful about all my files.

'What?' I finally sputtered, my face devoid of the emotional turmoil happening in my head.

'Yeah. The last time he was at a party, he let down his shields, and I saw it. It was for like, half a second, but it was more than enough for me to get it. I asked Travis ... and he didn't deny it either.'

'Did he confirm it?' I pulled the bowl of cereal closer to me to give my hands something to do and keep my tells from showing Lucy the truth.

'Well ... no ... but he did a little show through our Bond to tell me he knew it.'

The Bond that Lucy had with her best friends, Liliana and Travis, was both perplexing and weird to me. If my bosses knew something like that actually existed, they would probably kill it off before it even started—or maybe they did know about it, and they let it go. Their triangle made my head hurt. Being direct descendants of Nefertiti made our lives difficult, but Travis was a direct descendant of Nefertiti's husband, Akhenanten, and he was a werewolf. Lili's line was a little blurrier to me, but she came from a line of Watchers who made sure that the lines between Nefertiti and Akhenanten never crossed again—almost like they were keepers of the flame or some shit like that. *Maybe that's why Karrept built an army ...*

Lucy pulled me out of my thoughts with the frantic waving of her hands.

'What? What did I miss?'

'You were deep in thought. Anything I should know?' She jutted out a hip and raised her eyebrows at me.

The sister who was so innocent when I had left was long gone. I liked the woman she'd become. She had really come into herself, and I wished I had been there to see it.

'Yeah, that you're prying. Shoo,' I said, and shoved a spoonful of cereal into my mouth.

Lucy laughed and shook her head. 'Is that a defence mechanism? Did they teach you at The Camp?'

Her words were so nonchalant when it came to The Camp. I knew she was trying to make the situation lighthearted, but without Hunter, I wouldn't be alive. I couldn't be alive. I didn't tell her that because she was my little sister, my twin, and that made it harder to acknowledge how close I had been to not being there.

'Yeah ... You know, along with all of the other survival tactics. Is Hunter coming over today?' *Change the subject and she'll drop it.* She was good like that.

'It's like you read my mind, Dev,' Hunter said as he walked into the kitchen. He high-fived me, and I smirked.

'Did you know he was coming?' I asked Lucy.

She shrugged. 'I felt him come up the driveway about ten minutes ago. He got stopped by Dad.' She smiled at Hunter and motioned for him to go over to her with a finger. He obliged. Luce giggled, Hunter whispered something I was glad not to have heard and they kissed. I looked down into my cereal. It still weirded me out, but I thought it was more because of their whole fated situation. Lucy had tried to explain it to me, and I just … tuned it out. It was their love story, not mine.

'That bond you have with him is weird, but whatever. What are the plans today?' I asked, hoping it would break them from their PDA.

'A picnic. We're going to enjoy this weather while it's here because, you know, Melbourne weather is so fickle. You're cool to join if you want,' Lucy said.

'And be a third wheel? No, thank you.' I spooned some cereal into my mouth and looked at Hunter, who stared at me while Lucy was busily gathering supplies.

'How are you going?' he asked. I knew he was doing that because he cared.

I had a flashback to when they found me. The scratches that covered my body, the pain in places that were new and the animalistic tendencies that were now buried deep.

Without Hunter and his unrelenting presence, non-judgemental attitude and really annoying reliance to just show up every day, I wouldn't be there. And as I began to heal and feel more human, he was the reason I wasn't still going through the motions and remaining shut down. It took a whole year to feel some semblance of whatever normal felt like, but I was standing there because of him.

'Yeah, not bad today. I'm sorry you got caught by Dad.'

He waved that off, but I knew he was only saving me from what was to come. 'You have to give him an answer soon enough, Dev, and you know he's not going to take no as an answer.'

'I know.' I sighed. Taking over the company was the last thing I wanted to do.

'Are you sure?' he asked, and I wanted to wave him away, but I knew I couldn't. He wasn't Lucy.

'Yeah. I'm working on it.'

'Better work harder on it, Dev. Dad's on his way.'

That was my cue to leave. 'I'm going to work out. Enjoy your picnic.' I picked up my cup of coffee and left the cereal. I knew someone would clean it up, even if it was Dad. But I couldn't risk seeing him or talking to him because I didn't want to get dragged back into it.

It was inevitable. I knew what I had to do.

CHAPTER TWO

Acionna
Mechir 2017
Melbourne

Ninety-four days, twenty-three hours, fifteen minutes and thirty-three seconds.

It had been that long since I'd felt the cool rush of water on my skin as I dived beneath the depths of the surface. The ancient power of the sea called to me in the confines of my human flesh. The hints of salt on my skin were a tease; the brush of water against my toes tormented my soul and pulled at my heart. I wanted to strip out of the human husk that covered my body and join my sisters, my family and my friends. Instead, I was landlocked, cursed to capture the same picturesque sunset day in, day out—a torment and a reminder of what I had done and where I'd done it.

I yearned to join the sea dwellers again, but I couldn't, not until I had my pelt back. And it was in the hands of a conniving witch.

I rubbed my eyes. The summer breeze, light and fresh, wrapped around my body as I waited. There was a change in the air; autumn was on its way, and layers would soon be needed to keep warm and ease the chill that came with the shifting seasons. I held the camera steady and brought it up to my eye. I closed the other as I toyed with focus and metrics to get it just right. At the vibration of my watch around my wrist, a reminder of the exact moment, I snapped the image. The camera—a gift—was spelled to directly upload the image of the day to the cloud the witch had for my images. Not a single day was missed.

That day, the sky had pinks, reds and hints of purple in its palette, the golden halo of light from the sun almost blinding. But for the past ninety-four days, my eyes had become accustomed to its burning radiance. There was a haze in the sky, different from the day before, and that meant something was shifting. Just as the season was shifting, so was the world.

My body ached to frolic with the seals; kinsmen to my people, gentle beings who were bundles of pure joy, living each moment as it came. I always wished I could've been as carefree as the mermaids were, but selkies were the ruling body of the Undersea, making sure that order to the ocean stayed as it was. In the human world, neither selkie, seal or mermaid would have come to my rescue.

One misstep had cost me my future.

I was cursed to take a photo of the same landscape, day after day at the same exact time until I found a way to get my pelt back or I went insane. I could see which option would be the one I succumbed to first.

The repetitive nature of taking the same scene over and over again was getting tiresome, and being so close to the ocean and knowing what lay underneath its surface was torture. But the witch knew that; she used my weakness as a sore point she could push, knowing she'd get a reaction out of me.

I cradled the camera to my shoulder and took one last look at the setting sun before I made the hike over the soft sand and across the road to my house. The sharp lines of the house made it look out of place, but the softness of the circular windows was what caught my eyes in the first place. The house was soft but sharp, akin to the world

I lived in, but coming from the waters to the land made it make sense. It had balconies and was fenced off.

Sighing, I got to the road and took a moment to look over my shoulder. The memory of what happened came flooding back. I was landlocked—a term every selkie feared growing up. It ensured that we were unable to return to the sea. To our home. To *my* home.

Without the pelt that was a second skin to me, I was unable to get more than my feet wet. I could take a bath, but any moving body of water felt like I had to learn to swim all over again.

I was one of ten princesses and daughters to the Queen of the Undersea. I was not the oldest, but I was picked to be heir to the throne. Mother oversaw my education and training to ensure I would follow in her footsteps and lead with a strong grip on the Undersea, just as she and my father ruled. Selkies were matriarchal beings, unlike many other Undersea kin, which were patriarchal in their hierarchy. Mother and Father even had me betrothed to a man who was well-versed about the crown and had extensive knowledge about what his role as Consort would be like. I didn't love him back then. I still didn't. When I was cursed, I was only doing what was natural to us; leaving the safety of our kingdom to entice men and have some fun. I hadn't expected that I would be landlocked as a result.

It was interesting to see that my betrothed, Ian, hadn't come to the surface to visit me. I wondered if it was because he was sworn against it or if he was just scared that my landlocked nature might be contagious, and he could be stuck as well. After our Matching, he had made sure I knew that he was always there.

The ocean in the background was angry. It roiled with every crash of water against the sand. I was trying to find the witch to break the curse. I didn't have the resources to find her, to coax her out of her safety, but I was going to. I was going to take my pelt and my life back, no matter how long I had to wait.

I turned my back on the ocean. For the moment, she would be there, taunting me, but I would be back beneath the surface where I belonged.

As I opened the door to the house, I was greeted by the smell of the ocean yet again, but this time, my mouth watered. Janice was efficient, and I wondered whether she worked for my mother or had been sent by her. She somehow knew exactly what I needed before I even did. It made me nostalgic for home. And that was so challenging because, since being landlocked, all I could think about was how indecisive I really was. Without rules and stipulations in place or a schedule to follow, I was lost. It was a freedom I'd never had.

'The ocean looks like it's about to revolt. Did anything happen while you were out there?'

I shook my head. 'Nothing but the usual internal emotional outburst about how I wish I was back … home.'

I caught myself before I could give anything away that would make her question who I was. To Janice, I was a wealthy photographer who was pretty level-headed. Even though I felt like she was someone who could be an ally, I didn't want to trust that Janice would actually help me. She hardly knew me.

'Was the ocean nicer where you were?' Janice asked.

There were no real words to describe exactly what it was like under the sea. Everything was warm, like I was always being encased in a hug. It was both loving and supportive, and I always knew where I had to be and what I had to do. Being on land was so different. I'd been around for small periods, but I always had a place to go back to. Being on land with no support to help me study, tell me how to wear my hair or even attempt to get me dressed was surreal.

'It definitely was. It was quieter.'

I looked at Janice and searched her face. It was like there was something she wanted to tell me but couldn't. That look lasted no more than a second. It was weird, but not the first time I had seen that expression either.

Every day, she reminded me that I could definitely see her fitting into my life at home—a home where there was everything and nothing happening at the same time.

The house I live in was furnished, and almost exactly the same way I had found it after I claimed it from the old owner. He was an older man with a stern jaw, but he had soft eyes. It was easy to coax it from him with my natural wiles. He'd said that he had a premonition-like vision that told him I would come for him, come for his home. He handed over the keys and vacated the property without much more than the clothes he had on. It was definitely one of the most bizarre effects I'd ever encountered. Janice had been a part of the house from the get-go. I didn't understand then, and I initially tried to coax her out, but she was resistant against my charms, and that was where it ended. Janice had refused to leave and still did, claiming that there was nothing and nowhere else she had to be.

For someone who claimed such a thing, she made herself really valuable. Janice went to the markets, the house was always clean and she always knew exactly what I needed. I was grateful for presence and her ability to just be there.

I tossed the camera on the couch. It was not one of my own. It was supplied by the witch who had my pelt to capture the moment of time day after day, so it was in no way going to get broken—she had made sure it was spelled against anything that could damage it. If it did somehow break, my pelt would be destroyed—and I would rather be dead than lose my pelt.

The gift I had with the camera came from my fascination with taking images of everything I could possibly get my hands on. Undersea was my favourite; using salt and a little bit of ocean magick, I managed to create pictures that lasted longer than anything above water. The images almost looked like they moved, but it was a trick with a little selkie magick and plain luck. My fascination went a step deeper, and I went to university to study it further. It was the only time I came to visit the shore. I liked to think I was pretty good at it.

I had a job that weekend for one of the richest men in Melbourne. He was having a fundraiser and needed some candid pictures.

My natural ability to see the moments others couldn't between those special ones allowed me to excel at photography, and it was a natural progression from student to entrepreneur. Observing was a talent that many misunderstood, and as a princess, it was all I could do—or did. I was always ready to learn about the kingdom and what I could do to change it, altering the DNA of what had always been. I never wanted the crown. I didn't want the responsibility. But I was the natural choice for my mother, though I could never understand why. I was a middle daughter. Agate was the better option for the job than me as she was the oldest.

I was too curious to be a ruler—too naive, too innocent. I called out bullshit in the kingdom, and all they wanted was a carbon copy of my mother to take over. That wasn't me. I could never be like her, and I thought that was definitely something I could now let go of. I wouldn't be going back to the kingdom any time soon—at least not without my pelt.

Selkies were mythical beings, and most of us were older than we looked, having lives spanning centuries. There was no record of what we were or even that we existed. It was better that way.

Selkies were a myth.

Searching the internet for our existence was fruitless, and an unwritten law was put in place that we couldn't bring attention to ourselves out of water and on land. With our pelts—which looked akin to a single scrap of fur when not moulded to our bodies—we transformed into human seal hybrids, allowing us to swim, breathe and live in the Undersea.

Selkies were prettier beings of the Undersea animals. Mermaids, as many expected, were not what they were portrayed as. I didn't want webbed fingers and a naked torso.

'Something came for you,' Janice said as she turned back to the kitchen and started to bring the food over to me. My eyes searched the room, and I found a vase of orange roses and poppies, yellow sunflowers, red proteas and purple and pink cosmos, perfectly arranged within the white ceramic vase. A picture was leaning against it as I stepped closer. A perfect sunset—much like the one that I had just taken a photo of—stared back at me. The only difference between the image and the one I took that night? There was a lot more red in the sky and less pink.

It was the photo from the day before.

On the back of the frame was a handwritten note.

I love this one. I think it's one of my favourites.

My chest tightened as a hot flash ripped through my body, and I couldn't stop the growl that left my throat. I dropped the picture like it was poisonous, and it hit the floor with a crack. Without thinking twice, I swiped the arrangement off the table, and it hit the ground, the vase shattering, scattering the blooms all over the floor.

'Miss Acionna,' Janice yelped, and before I knew it, she was there cleaning up the mess and shooing me away to make sure I didn't cut my feet. 'Be careful. You need to sit down. I'll attend to this.'

I wanted to help her, but I knew she wouldn't let me. Instead, I took the plate sitting on the end of the kitchen counter and scooped up one of the oysters. It was raw, fresh and tasted of the ocean. Every night, my body yearned to forage the Undersea to find fresher oysters—the kind one has to try and crack open with their teeth. Janice had to be some sort of spy because she always managed to know exactly what I needed. There was only so much human food I could digest.

'You shouldn't let her get to you. She does this as a ruse, and you know it,' Janice said as she dumped the shattered ceramic into the bin next to her.

I was caught by surprise. It was the first time she had spoken about what was happening in my life. She was paying more attention than I wanted her to.

'What? I ...'

'I know about the pictures. Every day, at the same time, there is someone who keeps you there. They are using your soft spots to get in deeper. You can't give her the satisfaction.'

I stared at her some more, then took a moment. 'You are a lot wiser than you look, Janice.'

'I know, but that's the best part.'

She smiled and continued to clean. I knew there was more Janice wanted to say, but she was going to let me sit with the fact that she knew more than she was letting on. *Go figure.*

CHAPTER THREE

Devin
Mechir 2017
Melbourne

RYDER HOTEL HAD a minimum of three different ballrooms that were used for weddings, functions and big events like the one that night. The walls were draped in white fabric, and there were shimmery lights that hung from the ceiling, twinkling with every subtle movement of the aircon. It was unseasonably warm in the city, so being inside was a much needed respite. Franklin Drisdale was an award-winning builder who helped many in that very room build their homes, businesses and anything else their minds thought of. He requested a masquerade ball—or perhaps it was one of his many mistress' ideas, but either way, we all had a mask that matched the decor.

'These things are always so stuffy,' Lucy muttered, a cocktail in her hand. She was wearing an off-the-shoulder maroon dress that sparkled. Her mask was a rose gold and looked like she was wearing some sort of lace on her face. Next to her, Hunter wore a black suit with a maroon tie and pocket square to match her. His mask was bronze.

'Always. Yet we're always at them,' I retorted as I scanned the dance floor.

How long is appropriate to be seen in the room before I leave?

I couldn't be there. The sounds were too much, the sights almost like an overload of what had been happening for so long. That feeling should have worn off. I had been back in civilisation for four years. It was enough time to get past the weird flashes, but something about slipping back into the facade of Devin Ryder, heir to the Ryder Enterprise, was too much to bear. If Lucy and Hunter weren't there, I wouldn't be, and no amount of begging from my dad would have made me go.

Hunter nudged me with an elbow. It was discreet but pulled me from my thoughts.

'I'm here. Sorry,' I said, and I was.

'Let's go and get a drink,' he said.

'Don't leave me alone,' Lucy said.

'You'll be fine, *agapi*.' He kissed her temple, and I looked away.

Their stable relationship made me uncomfortable at times. Maybe it was because I wasn't steady, but they were so different from when they used to be so tumultuous. Then again, they were sixteen when I left, so it was a typical teenage relationship.

Hunter turned, and we went over to the bar. The alcohol would keep flowing while everyone else stumbled home. I wondered what it was like to be able to drink without a care in the world. Or without wondering if I would be called to kill someone in the middle of a drink.

'Are you okay?' Hunter asked me as soon as we were out of earshot of Luce.

'It's just that sometimes, the flashes of this not being real come back to bite me in the arse. It's been a while since it happened, but something about tonight seems to have triggered it.'

'Do you need a quick exit?' Hunter joked.

'Don't tease me like that.'

He chuckled. 'You know, it's okay to feel that shit. I know you're all tough and macho now, but it's okay to not feel okay.'

'I know, but you know how Dad is with things like this. I would have skipped out, but I need to put on my face and work the room.' We got to the bar, and I ordered a single malt whisky from Starward Distillery. They were a small Melbourne-based distillery that had recently sold up their stock to the Tisianos and joined their corporation. They were slowly taking over all of Melbourne, and I wasn't mad about it in the slightest.

'I can get Luce to shadow you. You know how much she loves talking.'

My turn to chuckle. 'Yeah, as much as a hole in the head,' I retorted.

He smiled and shook his head as our drinks were put in front of us. I wanted to just down it like it was water, but I couldn't. I had to sip on it. It wouldn't take the edge away from the nerves, but little did in those days.

I brought the glass to my lips and took a sip. Looking out from under my lashes, I nearly choked as I watched the most gorgeous woman I had ever seen work the room, camera in hand. She wore a green dress that clung to her curves, her black mask dainty and lace-looking. Her brown hair was shiny under the flickering fairy lights. She moved with purpose.

I swallowed past the lump, the whisky burning the back of my throat, thanks to the sudden gulp I had taken.

Shit.

No one had made me want to be near them—not like she did. I couldn't take my eyes off her, and if we had been alone, there wouldn't be any distance between us.

'What are you looking at, Dev?' Lucy asked, and I reluctantly pulled my attention away from the photographer to my sister.

'Photographer chick in the green, yeah?'

'Shut up, Wyatt.'

'Aqua, actually,' Liliana piped up. 'It's one of my designs. Spring catalogue. Aptly named "Algae."'

'Where the hell did you come from, Tisiano?' I asked, spinning on my heel to look at Liliana. She was Lucy's best friend—one of them, at least. I hardly called her Lili because I'd known her brother, and it was a hard habit to break, using someone's last name.

'Across the way,' she said with a grin.

'Lils, you said you weren't coming until later,' Lucy said.

'I got out of the atelier earlier than I thought, and it was quicker to come here than go home. Luckily, I had dresses I could pull from.'

'Mask?' Lucy asked.

'Painted on.'

'Of course. You would have had that done in no time.'

'My assistant earned her pay rise today.'

I took that as my chance to zone out and watched Green Dress walk through the room. She stopped at my parents, who came together and smiled. They looked like they were so loved up, and it was always a wonder how they managed to always look like they were newlyweds while keeping everything so professional. No one would know how polar opposite they were. Subira Ryder was an Egyptian beauty who had married Matthew Ryder, a successful hotel mogul who, at the time, was just starting out. Dad had greyish blue eyes, reddish brown hair and a chiselled jaw, and Mum had brilliant blue eyes with caramel-coloured hair.

Dad looked up at me at that moment and nodded to come over. I shook my head and nudged Lucy through our twin bond thing.

Save me. Dad wants me to go over there.

Without pause, Lucy walked in front of me. 'You know, you have to stop hiding from him. Especially with all of the events you're about to start getting into. I've seen the calendar.'

I had to. That's what I was scared of, and I couldn't take it back because I was about to take on the biggest opportunity of running a fit-out of my first hotel from the ground up. I didn't want to do it, but Dad gave me no choice at all.

'I know, but tonight already sucks. Just give me a couple more drinks, and I'll be able to schmooze.'

'If you're drunk, Dad will kill you.'

'No, he'll kill you for letting me get drunk.'

Her jaw dropped, and I grinned and cheersed her, my glass in the air. There was a heavy part of me that wanted to do nothing more than to see how far I could push my twin sister. But on the other hand, she had been through a lot, and I didn't want to put her in that position. That was the hardest part.

Leaving Luce for five years had been too hard on her. She was different, and even after I was back, she still was. Lucy was a different woman. Stronger but more fragile at the same time. How she had managed to get through life without me was a worry, but then again, it was probably because she was so stuck in her ways. I wanted to be better for Lucy, but I didn't know how to give her what she wanted.

I took another sip of my whisky, winked at Luce and slipped away from her. I had eyes for one person, and I was going to take a chance. Did it matter that I could fall flat on my arse? Nope. I needed to do it. I would have to find a way to make it up to her.

'You know, the photographer chick is at least a high eight,' Josh said as he joined the conversation.

'Mate, you need to get those eyes checked. She's at least a nine and three quarters,' I said.

'He's dropped the "mate" and given her the highest score to date,' Hunter chimed in.

Now they are going to start.

'Who is this version of Devin? I don't think I've seen it before,' Destiny chimed in. I looked at my older sister, her skin a little too pale and her vibrant hair not as shiny. I gave her a look, and she shook her head at me. Destiny was lacking some energy. I could give her some just by thinking about it, but it wouldn't be enough to keep her going for very long. I wrapped my fingers around her wrist and let her have some anyway before I replied.

'Shut up. You're being childish. All of you.'

Destiny tried to discreetly yank her arm away from me, but I held on tight enough to bruise a human. Of course, she didn't have that luxury—not anymore. In my peripherals, I watched Josh's shoulders drop, almost like the tension he had been carrying left his body.

I let go of Destiny, and she stared back at me, tears welling in her eyes. 'Why do you do that?' I muttered. To everyone else, we were having a family chat, but anyone who was trained would see worried glances. But that was the beauty of humans; they were indifferent to anything that wasn't about them.

'I didn't get time to do it.'

'No. You didn't make time, Dest.'

She didn't say anything, and I didn't push further. Destiny knew what she had to do, and I wasn't going to let her get out of it any longer. We weren't in the desert anymore.

'You can't keep doing this to yourself. You and I both know it.'

'Leave it, Devin,' she muttered.

I couldn't. We were both back. There would be no saving our mother if Destiny was dead for good.

'No. I'm going to find someone to help, and if you don't want to help me, I'll get Josh to. And you and I both know he won't stop until he's found the answer.'

'Don't do that.'

'Don't make me, Dest.'

With that, I left her and walked towards the girl in the aqua dress. Maybe I could do some schmoozing now that I was ready. By even getting a chance to talk to her, I could leave that night happy.

I nearly gawked at her but caught myself. The way she walked away with such ... *Ugh, pizzazz?* No one said 'pizzazz,' but there was a pep that I didn't see often enough, if ever. I *had* to know her. I was going to find out who she was, one way or another.

'Devin, I'd like you to meet someone.' I heard Dad's voice over my shoulder and knew I had come at the wrong time. *Fuck.* I inhaled and relaxed my shoulders, stilling the excited beat of my heart with that single breath, and turned on the ball of my feet. I put on my game face and a grin. The boyish charm always won everyone over.

'Zaira, this is my son, Devin. Dev, this is Zaira. She's an important part of all we do,' Dad said.

I bet she is. I wondered what he did with so many women around him. How Mum trusted him after he cheated on her before we were even born.

Zaira held her hand out to me, and I took it. She squeezed my hand before the shake. I instantly felt a hum of power. She was not human, and while everything in my face kept that realisation blank, there was a part of me that itched to find out what she was. Figure out how dangerous she was and when her time to be a mark would come. She had long, ginger-coloured hair, a sparkle of freckles across her nose, deep green eyes and a wide smile. She looked like she was a nymph of some kind. Maybe the forest variety.

'It's a pleasure to meet you, Devin. I've heard a lot about you. Of course, you were dead at the time.'

I smirked. 'Everyone seems to be so surprised that I'm back from the dead. I think I look good for the undead.'

Zaira chuckled and let go of my hand. 'Charming, just like your father, I see. The next product is going to be a lot of fun.'

'Project?' I asked and looked from Zaira to Dad.

'You're going to head the next hotel from start to finish. It'll be the second one in Melbourne.'

Home turf. Almost like he was using it as a tester to see what I could do.

'Another one in Melbourne? Why?'

'Because we always need another. Perhaps one that is not so central, maybe even regional,' Dad said.

'Regional won't work,' I responded straight away.

It wouldn't have pulled in the same volume of clientele that hotel brought in, and Dad never did anything without reason or rhyme. It wasn't who he was.

His actions were always calculated, almost like he had already seen the outcome and moved with it.

'Don't be so negative. In Spa Town, it'll work. In fact, we've just acquired land there. Something about a TV show not being able to film there. So we took it over. Zaira is the project manager. You'll also meet Rhea, who will work with you to make sure everything else is in order for the decor and everything you need to pick.'

Is he fucking nuts? I didn't have a single bone in my body that allowed me to even get close to picking paint colours or making sure pillows and throw rugs went together. I wanted to gawk, but again, I held a soft smile on my face. 'Spa Town ... That'll be interesting to see.' I looked past Zaira and saw Lucy motioning me over to her. 'We'll have to resume this during business hours. I can see Lucy is needing some attention. It was a pleasure to meet you, Zaira. I'm sure we will definitely set up a meeting next week to have some time together.'

'Sister to the rescue,' she said with a wink. 'I look forward to it, Devin. We can break it all down and go from there.'

'Thanks.' I nodded at Dad, took a step around him and kissed Mum on the cheek. She squeezed my arm before I moved towards Lucy.

'About fucking time, I was dying there.'

'Dude, I was trying to get your attention for about five minutes. You weren't even looking my way. What happened?'

'I met Zaira.'

'Oh, project manager lady? She's a piece of work. She'll eat you alive if you're not careful—literally.'

'She's some sort of nymph, yeah?'

'Yeah. The variety that likes to suck on blood, but isn't a vampire ... Go figure.'

'Great. Now I'll need to make sure I have some sort of garlic on hand.'

Lucy laughed. 'Old wives' tale. Hunter will hook you up with a charm you can wear to help you avoid falling into her allure.'

'Will it work?'

Lucy shrugged. 'It works for Dad.'

'It'll work,' Hunter said as he replaced my empty glass with a new one. 'But you never have any faith in my magick.'

'You were fifteen when you tried to make a protection bag, and it turned out to be a voodoo bag that summoned a dead cat in your backyard that wasn't even yours.'

'Fair call. I *was* fifteen at the time.'

I rolled my eyes, took a sip of the whisky and locked eyes with the photographer. Those aqua-coloured irises swirled with surprise before she lifted her camera and snapped. I couldn't hear the shutter, but I could see her finger pressing on it, and the lens was directed right at me. I raised an eyebrow and grinned into my glass.

Could she be stalking me now?

CHAPTER FOUR

Acionna
Mechir 2017
Melbourne

THERE WAS something different about that party. I had worked many of them, but there was a sense of grandeur that was different to others. Maybe it was because it was Ryder Hotel and not the casino they were so commonly at, or because there was something so unique about the space. It had that old Hollywood glam feel, but it was definitely in a league of its own.

Sir Franklin had to be happy with what was happening. There was a room full of people who were there to celebrate his achievements and hide the mistresses in the space. His wife knew it—and they were all very aware of her—but she pretended not to notice. I didn't think I could be in that sort of relationship—where I had to turn a blind eye to what my man was doing. But then again, I wasn't the type to be with one person. Selkies weren't naturally monogamous, so it didn't really mean that much to me. Or at least, I couldn't quite understand the same way others could.

Through the lens of my camera—a Nikon D850 DSLR, the greatest on the market—I had the best seat in the house. I could see everything, the way people interacted, and capture it on film. A still, living picture in a fast-moving world. I loved taking images of people. It was almost like I could capture a part of them, whatever they were feeling, and it was all that mattered to me. The pictures I took always came with a price, but if someone was paying, I didn't mind. I was good at what I did. Between all of my time in the sea and on land, I made a practiced effort to study. It helped fund my lifestyle—or the one I'd had before it was all taken from me. It was hard to believe that so many months had passed, and I was still there. Still taking pictures of the rich and famous while a part of me was being held captive. Being there was a distraction, but not by much.

As I moved around the room, I smiled and nodded at everyone. I held up my camera, and most shook their heads. A shame, really, because they would look back on the night and realise they had nothing to show for it. They took their time getting ready, making sure their hair was right, their clothing, and even their masks and jewels, and there would be no record of what they wore for them to post on social media or even to show their grandchildren. Time would change, and they would be melancholic that they didn't get more stills of what had been.

I shifted on my heels, careful not to snag them on the carpet, and turned to see a couple who were older, whispering to one another like they were newlyweds. Their bodies were turned to each other, and while they were in a room full of people, they had eyes for no one else.

It simply took my breath away, and I had to get a picture of them.

I smiled. 'Good evening. Do you mind if I take your picture?' I waved my camera at them, indicating what I wanted to do.

'Not in the slightest. You just have to make sure you get my good side.' The gentleman grinned, and the woman rolled her eyes.

'You don't have a bad side, Matt,' she said, scoffing.

'You say that now, but wait until you get me on a bad day, and I haven't made the bed.'

I smiled at the bickering. It was refreshing to have it. Many didn't like to give much of themselves, but the more natural the picture, the better, I found. They were so perfect.

I snapped the first picture and looked back at it. They were mid-speech and looked like they were the easiest people to get along with. I wondered what it was like behind closed doors; if it was the same, or if it was all an act to show the world they were really just there to give them something exciting to look at. I took another one, and this time, they looked at me and grinned. I couldn't help but smile back because their level of fun was infectious. I'd never seen my mother look at a man like that before; she was of the opinion that men were there to procreate with, and that was it. I was one of the only ones of my sisters to believe that wasn't true, but I would never let her—or any of them—know that.

'Did you want to see the images?' I asked after taking another snap and holding the camera to them.

'Absolutely. It's not every day I get to see what the images look like before my wife picks out the best ones.'

'Matt,' she chided.

'What, Bira? You know I'm right.'

'Yeah, yeah.' She waved him off.

I couldn't keep the smile off my face, and turned the camera to them so they could see their image on the little viewing screen.

'Oh, my. I have never seen … Wow, you are seriously talented. Do you have a card on you? I'd love to book you for one of my parties.'

Honestly, I had enough work to last me ages, but there was something about those two that made me want to be around them more.

'Absolutely. I can give it to you before I leave.' The dress I had on clung to my body and gave me no chance of holding much else. I had the strap around my camera that was there just in case my hands got tired, but there was no place for a business card or my phone.

'That would be wonderful,' she said.

'Subira, you look wonderful. Have you heard from Heather …?'

And that was my cue to leave. I didn't want to know the inside workings of the rich. I had enough to worry about.

I searched the room for someone else to capture. There were so many people in the ballroom, all of them dripping with money. I could see it in their clothing and the way they held themselves. Every one of the attendees were there because they knew Sir Franklin or they wanted to know him. It was honouring his achievement, but they were all there for themselves.

There was a woman in maroon; her rose gold mask pulled her out of the crowd, but the part of her that was the most captivating was her eyes. They were grey, stormy and vivid. It was like they weren't real. Next to her was a man with whisky-coloured eyes. His mask and tie matched hers. They were beautiful together.

I pressed the shutter on the camera a few times. They were so candid. I could see the way the man supported her. He had a hand resting on her arm while she chatted to another woman.

'In many cultures, it's considered rude to take unwarranted pictures of others,' a voice said from behind me. I glanced over my shoulder and saw a man in a dark grey suit. His tie was blue, and his mask was akin to that of *The Phantom of the Opera*. His eyes were grey, cloudy and calm—very similar to the woman I'd just taken a picture of.

'It's probably because they are all camera shy. I don't seem to have taken enough.' I turned on the balls of my feet and snapped a photo of him.

'That's rude. I wasn't ready.'

'It's my job to take photos, not to wait for you to be ready.' I didn't bother to say anything else and walked away from him.

'It's also your job to make sure people are ready. You waited for my parents to be ready,' he said.

I stopped in my tracks, and he nearly walked into me. His reflexes were quick, and he sidestepped around me.

'Are you as important as they are?' I raised an eyebrow, but he couldn't see it under my mask.

'I'd wager I'm more important.'

'A son of a big shot doesn't impress me much.' I paused and looked over my shoulder at the couple I had just shot. 'She's your sister, isn't she?'

'Perceptive. How can you guess?'

'Your eyes.'

'I like it. You're a smart cookie.'

'I'm smarter than a cookie. That's an insult.' I wanted to see if I could get away from him. I didn't even know his name, and he was already a nightmare to deal with. I was hoping I'd never have to see him again—or at least not be that close to him.

He smirked, and I wanted to throttle him. *Why are all of the guys who come to these things jerks?*

'Sassy.'

'Can you let me do my job?' I finally said, and he just grinned at me.

'Am I bothering you?' he asked.

'Yes.'

'I must try harder then.'

With that, he walked away from me.

Who the hell is he?

As I pulled up into my driveway, the tiredness reached all the way down to my webbed toes. It was a lot to be snapping pictures of the rich and famous.

I had been in later, after the guests. And like all of my contracts, there was a clause in there that covered me from either disappearing or being late. Most clients never even looked twice, but I knew there were a few in the room who had wondered where I slipped off to.

Did I care?

No.

But what I did care about was the man with the grey eyes, hardened look and a fake smile. He looked through everyone who glanced his way, and not in a good way. It was like there was something that was missing from him. Like a piece had been stolen.

Opening the door and swinging my legs out of the car, I leant over and grabbed my shoes by the slings. My camera was safely tucked into its case in the boot of the car. As my feet touched the gravel, I sighed in relief. It was good to be home and on even ground again. Or not in heels. As soon as I had gotten to my car after the event, I took my heels off so I could drive and feel my feet again. Mr Franklin's choice of gowns was one I couldn't' even sneak in runner or a flatter heel in.

I shut the door with my hip and walked to the back of the car, popped the boot and grabbed my camera bag. I touched the button on the handle of the driver's side, and it locked the car without me needing to rummage around for my keys.

The front door opened, and Janice stood there, waiting for me to walk through the threshold. It was nights like that I was grateful to have her, but I always wondered why she was always just … there.

One day, I would ask, but it was not that day.

'Miss Acionna, how was the party?' she asked.

'Dreary, but I got some good shots. And no one got handsy with me at this one.' A huge plus.

'Perhaps Mr Franklin is getting better with his manners.'

I laughed. 'He was too busy keeping his wife and mistresses separate the whole night. Surely, they would know about each other.'

'I have no doubt the mistresses know who one another is. I doubt that Mrs Franklin would be so perceptive.'

Janice took my shoes out of my hand and ushered me inside. She shut the door behind us, and I looked over my shoulder as she locked it. Janice was more paranoid than I was. We walked down the narrow corridor to the open living room. On the table was a plate of food—crustaceans—and my laptop, charger and expansion card readers.

'Janice …' I said, walking up to the dining table. I put my camera bag on the table and unzipped it to grab the Nikon and extra memory cards.

'Hush, now, it was nothing. Eat before you start looking at the pictures of the rich and famous. You'll lose your appetite otherwise.'

She wasn't wrong there.

'Janice … Why were you just … here?'

She had turned her back on me and was making her way to the kitchen sink. Many times over, Janice had dodged the question like she was making me wait for the answer. *Perhaps this will be the same.*

'You would never have survived on your own, Miss Acionna, and I wouldn't have been able to handle that had I let it happen.'

Janice's standard answer to the question. I shook my head. 'One day, I'm going to get a better answer out of you because that never makes any sense.'

She chuckled. 'When you're ready for it, I'm sure I'll be here. Now, eat your food, and don't open that laptop until it's all gone.'

There was a familiarity about her that was so jolting because she felt like home. Like, under-the-sea home. She was more maternal than my own mother, but then again, selkie mothers had big broods, and they weren't always around to take care of us all.

The motherly figure was always something I appreciated, and while I wasn't ready for children—the call was there, but not as loud—I didn't know if I would be like my mother. I didn't want to be. But I also didn't plan on having so many babies.

I ate my very late dinner and opened my laptop, pulling the SD card out of my camera and sliding it into the computer.

The photos came through, and I scrolled right down to have a look at the few I had taken that caught my attention first—it was easier to work backwards because it made the ones that were a drag easier to deal with. The couple who were madly in love with one another … Her deep blue eyes that saw no one else, the easy smile on his face that made me think of sunshine. There was a level of devotion that went deeper than anything I'd ever seen, and it was rare to see.

I spiralled through the images. My finger was fast, and I took quite a few of them. Every image oozed love and it gave me goosebumps. But as I flicked past them, the image of the grey eyed dreamy man came up. He looked so familiar, but at the same time wasn't in the slightest. There was a darkness in his eyes. Like he had seen things that he couldn't comprehend.

Or he was hiding a secret.

But he was charismatic. I chewed on my lip, imagining all of the things he could do. And the banter ... *Who was that person that came out when I opened my mouth?* I normally didn't say much of anything to anyone, but I couldn't help myself. Under the suit, I could see the subtle hint of muscle. He wore no jewellery besides a watch, as if it were something he hadn't wanted.

It was going to be a long night if I didn't move on from him.

He just looked like home.

CHAPTER FIVE

Devin
Phamenoth 2017
Melbourne, 2.36 a.m.

THE BOLD LETTERS glared at me, and I realised I had been scrolling for details for far too long. Social media had made its way through everyone's life, and it was the one-stop shop for all the details one could want. People were perpetual overshares, and that worked fine when I needed to find out all I could about a mark. Don't get me wrong, I had a file that had all of the basics on the target, but that wasn't the same. I couldn't get more of what haunted them or what tormented them. Dreamland was always the best place to think about things like that because it meant I could see deeper into their psyche.

And I was in charge in my own dreamland.

It was later than I thought, and that would work in my favour—I didn't have to wait for them to fall asleep.

Taking a deep breath, I put my phone away and scooched down in bed. I pulled the covers up to my chest and folded my hands over my chest. The letters from the clock illuminated the room and were comforting. I no longer used the clock radio because I used my phone for both music and alarms, but the familiarity of having my childhood so close was a vast difference to the darkness at The Camp. I closed my eyes and settled into bed, letting it support my body before I slipped into a sleep-like trance. To anyone else, I would look like I was asleep, my chest rising and falling evenly, but I was anything but unconscious.

In my mind's eye, I could see the dreamlike threads. The tiny tendrils were attached to everyone who was sleeping, and different dreams had different colours. Nightmares were a vivid purple, happy dreams were a cheery yellow, stress dreams were a chaotic orange and sex dreams were red. Then, there were the white tendrils—they were the ones one had to look out for because their colour meant they had something to hide.

It was rare to have people who could hide their dreams. It took a different kind of person to be able to do that, and I only knew one who could. She had died years before at The Camp after they found out what she had done for me. Calla had been a one of a kind. It had all gone downhill after they killed her.

If I thought too much about her, I wouldn't be able to do what I was there to do or find the way to get to the dreamland I wanted to be in.

Pete Housing.

Thirty-six.

Retail Manager. High up too.

He was also a cu sith—a hellhound.

They were rare, but his whole family was one of the last rare breeds around. I had never come across anyone wanting a cu sith dead before, so when I read the file, I almost baulked.

Why is he on the list? They hadn't told me, but they wanted to make sure it was one of my specialty kills.

As I pulled on the threads of dreams, I could trace them back to anyone, like when I knew that Lucy was in a stress dream because she was in the room just next to me. There had been so much orange energy that if I focused on her energy for too long, she would latch onto me, and I would get some of her dream. Unintentionally, I would fall into it, and that would be it.

I was looking for Pete.

With his face in mind, I pulled through the different links between us. There weren't many, but I knew that by searching through them, I would be able to find my way. I pulled at the link of a friend of a friend who went to high school with him and waded through the mess of a red dream and straight into a purple nightmare.

Sometimes, the moments between are kind of like that door place from the matrix, and sometimes, I just arrive where I need to be. I looked around me and found myself smack-bang in the middle of an office.

Pete must take his work home with him.

The office was set up with rows and rows of desks, and a desktop sat on each. There was a shadowy figure behind every screen, tapping away mindlessly. Pete was sitting at his desk with his feet up and a phone to his ear. I stepped closer and could hear his words.

'What do you mean your mother passed away? You're still coming in, right?'

The words sent shivers up my spine. I never had a chance to work in retail, and I was grateful for Dad for that.

Pete was evil. He needed to have the life snuffed from him.

'Ohhh, Peteeee. Petey. Pete,' I said in a singsong voice.

He froze in his spot, mid-sentence, his eyes wide and his mouth open. His shoulders crept up to his ears, and I smiled.

'Peteeeee. You've done some very bad things, haven't you?' I called out.

He put the phone down, and I focused on the surroundings. The dreamland was my domain. I could do anything I wanted.

So I cut the power, just by thinking about it.

Everything went black.

Pete's chair creaked as I moved through the space. I was right behind him.

'What did you do, Pete?' I whispered in his ear before I returned to my spot.

'Who are you? Where are you?' he cried out. His hands flung out at his sides to try to find me. I couldn't stop the laughter that left my lips.

'You won't know me. No one knows me. But you will wish to know me.'

'Stop it,' he cried out.

This time, I moved faster than anyone could possibly see. Not that Pete could see me—it was pitch-black. 'No,' I murmured in his ear.

He tried to reach out again and found air. I turned the lights back on, and the room was devoid of anyone but Pete and rows of empty desks. His wide eyes scanned the room, searching for me. But he wouldn't find me. No one ever did. Not in that space.

I wanted to play with him more. It wouldn't take long, but I knew there was a limit.

Instead, I manifested myself in front of him. An arrow in my hand, I pulled him closer and shoved the weapon deep into his stomach.

He cried out, the arrow delving deeper into his body. 'This is your warning. You're going to hate what comes next.'

'Who are you?'

'I'm nobody.'

And with that, I let go of Pete. He dropped to the floor with the arrow in his stomach, blood spilling freely onto the carpeted floor.

I pulled myself out of the dreamland.

2.56 a.m.

That was all the sleep I was getting.

'Fucking hell.' I tossed in bed and rolled onto my back. *One of these days, these dreamland missions are going to take longer than twenty minutes.*

I ran my hands through my hair and closed my eyes. I had a meeting—one that was supposed to be important. But in the scheme of things, it didn't feel like one I should put my energy into. The only reason I was going to go was Dad. And if I wasn't there, he would rip me a new one.

Dad was kind to everyone, but there was something different

about him. Ever since I had come back, his demeanour had changed. And many times over, I saw something in his face that I cared for, but that was something I couldn't even put into words. He was never too much or too little. It was like he was always perfect.

'Dev, are you ready?' Dad asked me.

His words pulled me out of my thoughts, and I nodded. 'Ready.' *Or as ready as I'll ever be.* There was something off about that meeting. My gut was telling me that, and I'd spent years honing that intuition to make sure I could keep myself safe. But when was I ever really safe?

'Great. You're going to take point on this one, and I need you to be on your A game.'

'Dad, you're a walking cliché.' I had the folder of all of the decisions I needed to make in my hands. It had colour choices, floor plans, lighting, decor choices—details I didn't care for. But they were important to Matthew Ryder, so I had to make them important to me.

'Hmm?' He looked straight past me.

Dad was nervous. He tugged on his tie for the fifth time in the past three minutes. I would have loved to have let Lucy do it. She was the one who was supposed to take over, but Dad reminded me that I was older than her, that it was his legacy, and he was leaving it to *me*. I didn't want his legacy. He was a businessman. I was a hitman for hire.

I'd rather have had blood on my hands than sit in a suit and talk about paint colours and the way they looked on the wall. *Fuck.* It was going to be harder than the first few weeks at The Camp, when all I wanted to do was leave.

'Rhea, it's so good to see you,' Dad said, and shook the hand of a woman who didn't look a day over eighteen. *When did they make them so young?* 'This is Devin, my son.'

'Oh,' she said as she shook my hand. Her grip was firm, and her pastel pink hair bounced with her head movement. 'The prodigal son who was dead has risen again,' she said with a grin.

I chuckled and turned on the charm. 'Well, you know what they say, the best don't stay dead.' *Or were never dead in the first place.*

'They do say that about the greats.' Her eyes flashed yellow, and I had to swallow the lump that formed in my throat. She was a shapeshifter—some sort of cat shapeshifter.

Showing herself to me was dangerous, but I wasn't even sure if Rhea knew she had done it.

'I think I know why Dad keeps you around. If you flatter my ego this much, I wonder what you do to his.'

Dad cleared his throat and pointedly looked at the chairs by the desk. 'I try to make sure to build great rapport with my clients.'

'I'm sure you do. Take a seat, Rhea. Let's get started before we waste more of your precious time than we already have.'

She smiled. It was cute in a different way, almost like she was trying to put a spell on me. I felt a little bit of magick in that smile. I'd ask Dad later about it.

'This is a big project, and Matt said it was your first time taking point. I'm here to make your life easier so you can make sure you can bring your vision to life.'

Matt? I raised an eyebrow at Dad, and he shrugged. Mum was one of the few people who were allowed to call him Matt. He always went by Matthew. No matter who it was.

'I have all of the details for the lighting, decor and schedule.' I handed her a copy of all of the documents I had prepared for the meeting. 'As you can see, we're looking at a style that is totally different from what we normally do with each of the hotels. I want to start transitioning them away from what is expected.'

She flicked through the pages. I felt like I was back inside a classroom where I was getting judged and was about to get ripped into for not paying attention to the assignment. Ryder Hotel under Dad was old-school. Under me ... it would be different.

'This is ... edgy ... Wow. I have always loved what Matt comes together with, but this ... This is something different.' She looked up at me and switched her attention from me to Dad. 'He has something here. This is probably the injection we need to make sure that Ryder Hotel stand the test of time. There is luxury and then there is *luxury*. Devin, maybe you were definitely channelling something else when you were MIA, but this is something else. I didn't expect this. Not in the least.'

Dad leant against the edge of the desk with his hands folded in front of his chest. I could have sworn I saw a flash of a smirk before he stood up straight.

'How much extra is it going to cost us?' he asked.

I looked at Rhea, and she clicked her tongue as she flipped to the end page of the document I had given her. Her eyes widened before she looked at Dad.

'Not as much as one of your designs would ...' Rhea looked at me. 'How ... How did you swing that? Your dad has always managed to get the best prices, but this ... This is next-level.'

There was an unusual amount of pride in those words. I'd always thought I was immune. I didn't want anyone's validation, but part of me was still that young boy who wanted to have the approval of his father.

'I just have some great sources who said they would help out,' I replied. Lucy had them, but she was always willing to share. I knew that, after being back from The Camp, she would jump at anything to help me out. Part of her felt guilty about what had happened, but the other part didn't know how to understand me, and that was the hardest part for her to grasp.

I didn't know how to explain to her that I was a hired killer now. I couldn't. Lucy may not have been as naive as she was when I had left, but it was not something I wanted her to know about.

'Let me take a look over this, and I can put together a timeline that works. I think this is great, though. Matt, he really did the work,' Rhea said. 'Let me grab your number, and I'll call you if I think anything needs to be added to, or we can shuffle some things around.'

I couldn't help but smirk. 'Rhea, you just met me. Shouldn't you ask me to dinner first before you ask me for my number?'

'Devin,' Dad said. I ignored him.

'If it was the first time I'd met you, potentially, but I've known you longer than you would like to admit, Devin.' She didn't break eye contact with me, and I knew I was in trouble, but that was all it took to need her under me.

I pressed my lips together, the smile getting wider. I licked my lips just for show. 'Perhaps, but I'm a changed man, and this is the first time you've seen it.'

Her attention didn't waver from me, and I kept my attention on her. I wouldn't break eye contact. I didn't do that.

Dad cleared his throat, and Rhea looked away from me and to him. She rubbed the bridge of her nose and shook her head. I finished writing my number down on a piece of paper and slipped it into her pile of work.

'I'll get back to you as soon as I can. Matt, I'll see you at the 3.00 p.m. meeting for Port Douglas.'

'Thanks, Rhea. Let me know if Devin gives you any trouble.'

She stood up and collected her bag. 'If he's anything like you, I know how to handle myself.' She walked out of the room without looking back, and I raised an eyebrow at Dad.

'Is there another illegitimate child of yours around again?'

'Devin,' he warned.

'What? Kali wasn't enough for you?'

He didn't need to say anything, and gave me a look that any father would give to his son when he said something he shouldn't. The old Devin would have gone into hiding, but this version of me held my ground, and I squared my shoulders.

He just shook his head. 'I forgot how much you have grown in the years you have been away. Just try to keep things professional.' He shuffled some papers on his desk. And just like that, Matthew Ryder had dismissed me.

I left without saying anything, closing the door behind me.

Rhea looked up from her seat, and I bit the inside of my cheek to stop the huge grin that wanted to show itself. Sometimes, having the image I did was a little too much. I had to keep a stoic exterior.

I strutted out of the lobby without looking back, but I could feel her eyes on my back. *This is going to be fun.*

CHAPTER SIX

Acionna
Phamenoth 2017
Melbourne

The days always felt the same: get up, eat, putter around the house and then wait for the photo I had to take. It was so monotonous, and each day, the witch baited me. She sent the picture from the previous night with flowers or some other present. Each gift came with no return address, nothing to say—not where she was or how she was even getting those stupid things to me.

Time almost didn't have any meaning. I could get up at any time I wanted and not have to worry because I didn't have anywhere to be. I sighed and grabbed my laptop from the edge of the bed, where I had left it after falling asleep trying to edit photos, and lifted it open. I had a few events booked to shoot, and they paid well enough that I could pick and choose what I wanted to do.

I opened my emails and scrolled through them. Most were junk, newsletters signed up for discounts for the dresses I'd purchased for some of the galas. My eyes snagged on a name.

Subira Ryder.

It was familiar, but I couldn't remember why. I clicked on the email and read the first few lines. It jogged my memory. *The couple that had seemed so in love at Sir Franklin's event.* She wanted to hire me for her next event and was hoping I would be free. I looked at the time stamp, and saw that she'd sent it the afternoon before.

I picked up my phone and dialled the number she put in the email. I took a deep breath—talking was easier over the phone.

'Hello, Subira speaking.'

'Subira? It's Acionna. We met at Sir Franklin's, and you sent through an email.'

'Acionna, yes! My goodness, thank you for getting back to me so quickly. I didn't expect that.'

I had nothing better to do. 'I had some free time. When would work well for you?'

I heard rustling on the other end—like she was flipping some pages of a diary or something of the sort.

'Well … I have either today at two or time in two weeks. Today wouldn't happen to work for you at all, would it?'

I wonder what it's like to have such a booked-out schedule and still be able to make time to book someone like me.

'Actually, two is perfect. I can meet you anywhere you like?'

'Oh … Oh, really? I didn't think this would be such a quick appointment. I was sure we would be meeting in two weeks.'

I chuckled.

'Can you meet me at the hotel? Ryder Hotel?'

It was about a twenty-minute drive to the city. Then, there would be parking, the meeting would take an hour or so, and then I would have to drive back in basic peak hour traffic … I was going to be cutting it short for the night's picture. My stomach dropped at the thought, and I swallowed past the lump that formed in my throat.

'Is it possible to meet earlier? Like, say, one?' Pushing it forward would make it better.

Subira clicked her tongue, and I heard the faint scratching of a pen. 'Mmm … Actually, yep, that's perfect. I'll see you at one.'

'Great. I'll see you then.'

'I look forward to it. See you, Acionna.'

'Bye, Subira.'

I hung up the phone and stared at it for a moment. It was going to be an interesting meeting, and if their photos from the party were anything to go by, her event was surely going to be something else.

A flicker of excitement tingled in my chest—a feeling I'd forgotten — and there was a lightness, like I was going to be making a difference.

'Janice, I'm going out,' I called out as I pushed myself out of my chair and shut my laptop.

'Out? Do I need to make anything before you go?'

I looked over my shoulder as I hit the stairs to find Janice with a hand on her hip and a dish towel in her hand. She looked like she had always belonged there, a gleam of curiosity glowed in her eyes, and I could have sworn I'd seen that exact look—and those eyes—somewhere else. *Where?* I couldn't picture it.

'No, thank you. I've got a meeting with Subira Ryder at the hotel. I'm assuming she wants me to take some photos for her.'

'I'll get the albums so you can show her and get everything ready. Go and get changed.'

I nodded and walked up the stairs. I couldn't be meeting one of the most powerful women in Melbourne in bike shorts and a ripped tank. Even my own mother would have been horrified if she had seen what I was wearing. And I couldn't have that.

I had been the daughter named as the heir to the kingdom. I never understood why because I wasn't the oldest or the youngest of my mother's children. I was smack-bang in the middle, the one who was always the wild one of the rest—or that's how they wanted to make me out to be. I merely wanted to make sure that I was educated both above the sea and under its surface. If I had to learn how to be a princess, I wanted to learn how to live on land without being compromised in any way. My sisters didn't have any urges to do more than procreate and live their lives as they always had.

I knew there was something else out there, something that would take more of my time.

There was a different call for me.

I didn't know what it was, but I knew it wasn't all just living under the sea. I had a betrothed. He was a good man, but it was in my nature to have other lovers and move back and forth between the land and the ocean. What I didn't count on was losing my pelt and being landlocked.

Although, I hadn't lost it.

It was stolen from me.

I could feel it, thrumming with life, but it was locked away and sitting inside a vault of steel, and there was no way to get it. I wasn't strong enough to break it out. Not yet.

Selkies were mythical creatures, part seal, part human, not quite accepted on the sand but fawned over in the water.

My memory was starting to become cloudy, and I struggled to put into words what the kingdom looked like. It felt like the feeling of a spring breeze, mild, warm but entirely difficult to describe into words that made sense unless one knew that feeling against their skin. There was a level of serenity under the surface that was different to being in the loud world of the land. It was serene, and anyone in it would wonder why we could even leave—which is why a lot of my sisters didn't. They waited with bated breaths to see if I could come back, and to know that I couldn't would make a lot of them happy. They wanted the throne I was privy to because they didn't have it.

They could have had it.

The crash of waves was still ever so loud in my skull, the call of the sea itched under my skin, and I wanted nothing more than to throw myself into the deep blue sea and keep swimming until I was back in the kingdom.

I could see the tide moving further out. With a salty glass of water in my hand, I toasted to her, to the unwavering ebb and flow of her life. She rolled her tides four times a day, and was happy to show off her emotions. If the weather was gloomy, she thrashed the sand with hard-hitting waves. If the sun was shining, she was still and calm.

There was so much to take away from the ocean.

Perhaps that was why I couldn't leave her. It was the reason I was so close yet so far away.

It didn't have anything to do with the witch who held my pelt hostage—well, maybe just a little, but I didn't think I could be very far away from the ocean even if I wanted to be.

She was home for me.

Even in that loud world.

I could hear the sounds of the travellers as they walked past her, chattering like there was no tomorrow. A husband had cheated after a cancer diagnosis and expected to be taken back. I could hear each word clearly as though they were right on my balcony—a perk of my superhuman hearing that came with being a selkie.

I took a swig of the water, and it quenched a thirst I didn't realise was there.

I wondered what the human world would do if they knew just how many mythical beings walked among them and weren't just ... mythical.

Maybe that's why it was illegal to even be outside of the water. I was lucky. I kept under the radar. I didn't make any flashy friends or anything of the like. In fact, I had no friends ... unless you counted Janice.

'Miss Acionna, dinner is ready.'

Janice came with the house. She was always here, but I could have sworn she was familiar. Janice knew too much about me. I didn't talk to her much, but she could see between the lines.

'Coming,' I called out, and put my glass down on the small table that was on the balcony. I picked up the camera and checked the zoom. I could see the same spot from the balcony—only just but it would be enough for the witch to be placated with the night's image. I took a deep breath and let my finger rest on the shutter button while I waited for the buzz of the alarm to come.

Five ... four ... three ... two ...

Click.

The image was captured, and off it went into the aether. The witch had spelled the camera so that it would go directly to her. If I tampered with the magick, she would destroy my pelt. If I missed a deadline, she would destroy my pelt. If I tried to find her, she would destroy my pelt.

I wanted to rip her apart with my bare hands. I could have done it. I had the strength to, even in my human form, but I didn't know where to start to look for her.

She was lucky, though. She could see me, could see what I wanted to do to her, and she would be running for high ground and warding up the wazoo. There was no way around that. I wanted her to know that if she was going to tamper with my life, she would pay for it with her own.

I was so done with doing it, I let my mind wander as I picked up the glass and stepped back into the bedroom, shutting the sliding door behind me. I threw the camera on the bed. I didn't mean as much to me as my others. I didn't care if it cracked. She would send me another one.

I wished I knew her name.

She was just 'the witch' to me.

I wanted to change that.

I was going to start digging for more.

I need to know her name, even if it was the last thing as a true selkie I would do.

The drive over was uneventful. I parked the car and was waiting in the lobby of Ryder Hotel. There was so much to the place—ballrooms, eateries, boardrooms, bars and maybe some sort of casino. I didn't know whether that was true, though. There were whispers of an underground metaphysical cult that also held meetings there, but those urban legends were always around. Not that I could talk; I was an urban legend. And I was happy to keep it that way. I didn't want to end up on someone's hit list, or better yet, in jail just for existing. I'd never get my pelt back then.

I'd changed into a line asymmetrical top that had a tie around the waist. It was a soft blue, purposely worn to bring out the blue in my eyes and matched with a pair of denim shorts. On my feet were black wedge espadrilles. They were my favourite to wear because there was something about the way they could finish off an outfit. I ran a hand through my hair and tossed it about, the long tendrils trailing down my back. My hair was the same colour as my pelt—rich brown with light highlights. Every time I looked in the mirror, I felt my heart skip a beat and my throat tighten. I missed the feel of the ocean on my skin. The smell was never enough.

'Acionna?' I heard my name and turned on the balls of my feet to see Subira Ryder. Her effortless cream pantsuit was extraordinary; it showed her natural tan. Her blue eyes were mesmerising. Paired with her wavy brown hair, she looked just like a hotelier's wife would. Even with her blazer resting on her shoulders.

'Subira, hi, yes. How are you?'

'Mum, I thought you said you were going to wait … Oh.' Coming up behind her was the guy from the party—the son.

'I am well, thank you. You'll have to excuse my son. Devin doesn't know his manners.'

Devin Ryder.

He smirked and held out his hand to me. 'Devin Ryder. Mum thinks I don't have manners because I came back different.'

I raised an eyebrow. 'Acionna. And why would she assume that?'

'She says I came back after living in a tent or some shit.'

'Devin,' Subira hissed.

I pressed my lips together to stop the smile that threatened to give away the amusement I felt. The man I'd met at the party was just as playful with his mother as he was with me.

'Well … did you? There are awful whispers about where you were, you know. If I can make any of them come true, I'm happy to be a part of them,' I asked.

Subira tightened her hand around her binder, but I did see a hint of a smile before she straightened up. 'Devin, don't give into the gossip. That's not why we are here.'

'Oh, Mum, you are no fun. But she is right. We are here to talk business. Let me get some drinks for everyone.' Devin winked and melted away towards one of the bars. *He didn't even ask if I drink. That was ... interesting.*

Anger threatened to run riot, but there was a part of me that really loved the idea of him taking charge, even if he didn't know what I wanted to drink. I'd see what he came with.

'Subira, tell me about the event you need my services for.'

She opened the binder and started to riffle through the papers before nodding at herself. Subira came to the right page, unclipping the binder and taking the page out before she clicked it shut again. She was making a very practiced effort to make it seem like she was trying to intimidate me.

Or she was just very meticulous with her ways.

'It's a party. I'll need you for the whole night, and you are free to either roam or set up a dedicated booth. It'll be the big announcement of a project we're working on, and it's also why Devin is here. We are announcing the next location for our hotel. He is managing it, so he will be the focus for it—different from my husband, but I want images of the attendees interacting with the event.'

I nodded and opened my notebook, starting to take notes as quickly as I could to make sure I was getting everything down. It was sure to be an event that I didn't know if I could do by myself, but I didn't work with anyone, and I didn't need an assistant. Hell, I didn't even have any friends I could call on.

'Is there something happening with the room you would need photographed?' If that meant I needed a remote camera, it was going to be something I would have to take time to build and rig up so I could control it. Also, I was going to have to make sure they didn't need me at the time of the opening, or if the opening time could be pushed back.

'Yes, but Devin will be explaining that.'

As if he knew his name had just been spoken, he came back with drinks. A white wine was placed in front of his mother. He had what looked like a whisky, amber in colour, and in front of me was a concoction of some sort.

'Are you already up to my part?' He sat down next to me with a grin that said he was happy with himself.

'Yep,' Subira said.

I took a sip, and the alcohol touched my tongue just after the aftertaste of lemon did. A gin and tonic. I didn't drink often, and when I did, it took a lot for any sort of alcohol to hit. Selkies were normally immune from any sort of liquor, but I hadn't tested it since I lost my pelt. One wouldn't hurt though.

'Excellent.' Devin turned the chair that was directly in front of me and leant forward, fiddling with something on his phone, and I felt a ping on my iPad. I unlocked the screen and opened the notification. It was a full presentation. I blinked and looked at Devin.

'And what am I looking at?' I asked.

'My brief for what I want.'

'What you want?'

'Yes. This is an event where we are unveiling the next location for Ryder Hotel. It is unlike anything else we have done before, and I want to make sure it's done right. I need to know if you can do moving photography. If not, it's not the end of the world. I can find a videographer who can do that for me as well.'

I was about to say that I could do it, but Devin seemed to be in the zone and took the iPad from me so he could scroll through his brief.

'This is going to be luxe. We need to make sure there is enough coverage of the drawings, of the way the lights hit them. Mum will be there for support, but the main people on point will be my dad and me. It's the first time I'm going to be presenting something like this, and it needs to go off without a hitch. The missing piece is you. I saw the images you did for Sir Franklin, and they were of a calibre I haven't seen in a long time. If you can't do the date we're proposing, we can move it to accommodate you.'

My jaw threatened to drop on its own accord, but I pinched my thigh to think about the pain instead of the fact that they would move dates to make sure I could be the one to take all of the imagery. *Who in their right mind would do that?*

The Ryders, it seemed.

'Okay. I can do moving photography. No problem there, so no need for the extra help. I don't play well with others in my place of work. Secondly, why me? You seem so hell-bent on anything I can do, and I want to understand why.'

Subira cleared her throat. 'Matt hasn't even stayed still long enough to let me get a picture, and the ones you captured of him, the ones where he was a doting husband—nay, a loved-up husband—were all I needed to know that you were perfect. We simply can't take that away from him—or you.'

'But you barely know me.'

I knew the magnetism I had with the Undersea folk, but this was different. I hadn't ever been able to have that sort of sway with anyone. The men I'd slept with were nothing. They were just bodies. My little sisters meant more to me, and they were always in awe, but that was only because I was an older sister.

'It feels right,' Devin said, and his cloudy grey eyes held my gaze. I couldn't look away even if I wanted to. 'And that's all I know. If you're not the photographer, there will be no event. And I would hate to waste the resources and all of the time and effort I've already put into this.'

I pressed my lips together and finally tore my eyes away from him as I looked down at the brief. I flicked through it, skimming over the minor details and looking at the bigger picture. I had nothing to lose. I had no friends—no one beside Janice, who would always be there waiting for me. There was nothing standing in the way of me saying yes to the Ryders.

Nodding my head, I brought my attention back to Subira—she was safer than looking into Devin's eyes again. 'I'm in,' I said, and turned to Devin. 'Send me all of the other details.'

What have I just gotten myself into?

CHAPTER SEVEN

Devin
Phamenoth 2017
Melbourne

'Mum, this is so ridiculous. Why do I need to come with you? Dad briefed you on everything you need. You literally have to just sink the meeting.'

We walked out of the more business side of the hotel, where Dad's main office was, as well as a bullpen of other smaller offices for some of the workers. I hated working there and tried to do most of my work at home to avoid actually having to talk to people.

'Because this is your first chance to do a big reveal, and I need you to see what goes into this so you can take charge for the next one.'

'But this is the first time we've done something like this.'

'Well … technically, yes, but there is more to come. I know it.'

I shook my head and smiled. 'You're awfully optimistic, Mum. It's like you think I can actually do this.'

She turned to me and beamed. The smile took over her whole face. It was a smile that had always kept me holding on for dear life at The Camp—there was so much darkness there. Mum's smile was part of the light that kept the shadows at bay when it all got too much.

'Devin, my darling son, you will only excel at anything you put your energy into, and I can only imagine how different this world is. But you're here, and you're going to. I'll always support you.'

She'd heard the sarcasm in my voice and raised it with her supportive nature. I never understood why Lucy was always so against her. She was the best mum we could have ever asked for; she never wanted us to do anything less than our best. But Lucy just saw someone who wanted to suffocate her.

'Mum, everything is fine. I got this. It's so different from anything else I've done, but it's just a business deal. I can do those in my sleep.'

She smirked, and I raised an eyebrow. 'I wouldn't exactly call it a business deal, Devin.'

'What do you know?' I asked.

'Nothing at all.'

Mum knew more than she was saying, and that was scary—scarier than fronting a firing squad in the middle of the night.

I shook my head as my phone vibrated. I picked it up and looked at it—Jarrad. 'Mum, go ahead. I have to answer this call. I'll be there in a bit.' She nodded, and I watched her walk away before I picked up the phone.

'You have to stop calling me like this.'

'D-Man, you say that like you have a choice.'

'I do.'

Jarrad laughed. 'I love that you think that.'

I had been back nearly a whole year from The Camp, and those phone calls started three months to the day. At first, I was confused because I had changed all of my identity and hidden myself online. I didn't have social media, and my phone number was different from the one I'd had before I was taken. There was nothing to show where I was … Except that I was being trained to take over an entire empire, and Dad wanted me in press images for the hotel.

'What do you need?'

'Everyone is getting antsy. The kills are too showy.'

'You know how I work,' I uttered.

'I know that. But they are going to try to shake it up. I'm giving you the heads up before it comes because I respect you.'

Jarrad had always been a constant in the torture and the training. He had been the one I leant on the most. As much as I could bear, anyway, because I didn't want him to know too much about me.

'And if I refuse?'

'We know where Lucy lives and who she is with when she's not with you ... I don't think I need to say much more than that.'

And that was why I did what I did.

Lucy was innocent, and I wanted her to stay that way. Every hit kept the target off her back.

'One day, you won't be able to use that against me.'

There was silence for a few breaths. I heard leather shift before he spoke up again. 'D-Man, the only way that will happen is if I'm in a body bag. Or you.'

Two beeps sounded in my ear, and I took a deep breath to stop myself from throwing the phone into the floor.

Anger bubbled just under the surface, and I wanted nothing more than to hunt Jarrad down and kill him. I would be the one to do it. He knew it too. But instead, I pushed that feeling back. I swallowed it down into the back of my brain, right where all of the pain lived, and shoved my phone into the pocket of my pants, making my way over to where Mum was.

Chewing the inside of my cheek, I made my way to the lounge. I searched the room for any threats because even though I wasn't the Dreamwalking Assassin right then, I knew better than to let my guard down. It would be the perfect time for them to come at my family and me. In broad daylight, with their power, they could do anything.

I looked from left to right and then down at the floor before I looked up. Humans, by nature, never looked up. I made sure that I always did. I saw the back of Mum's head and ... *her*.

My chest tightened, and I curled my hand into a fist. Long tendrils of hair framed her face, and the rest fell over her shoulders. Acionna was even more beautiful than she had been at the party.

Fuck.

I pressed my lips together and uncurled my fingers. It was time to play the doting son. The one who had so much to lose if I didn't sink that meeting with the photographer for the party—the tightrope I had to straddle as I tried to balance both of the personas I had.

'Mum, I thought you said you were going to wait—oh.'

Oh, indeed.

Payni 2012
Somewhere in the desert

I wrenched my arm from Karrept, and he just laughed. My feet crunched in the sand beneath it, and the sun glared down as I tried to take stock of where we were.

'You are wasting your time and your energy.' The way he looked at me with that smirk ... I wanted to smack that expression off his face so badly. I took a step forward, and Karrept flicked my back with the swish of his wrist.

I have to stop trying to do that. He had offensive powers. I didn't. I got to my feet and brushed off the sand on my legs. Squinting at the sun, I looked around and tried to see what was around me. There was so much sand.

So much sand. It was so unnerving. *Why would he bring me here?*

'I am going to make a warrior out of you. I cannot kill you. Not yet. Perhaps.'

I swallowed past the lump in my throat, and I couldn't stop the shiver that ran down my spine. *What does that even mean?* I didn't want to be a warrior. I just wanted to go home. I wanted to make sure Lucy was okay.

'Where's Destiny?' I asked, and this time, I stayed right where I was. Karrept smirked harder.

'You will find her when you need her.'

'Tell me where my sister is, you bastard.'

Karrept took a step closer to me, and then another and another before he was right in front of me, his chest centimetres away.

'She is safe. You have things to do.'

'I'm not doing anything for you.'

He chuckled. 'Perhaps not now, but you will. You will beg me to give you something to do.'

'I won't.'

He didn't say anything, instead swiping his hand and revealing an opening to what looked like a school campground. There was an entrance that opened up to what looked like cabins. There was a path, and it was so ... green. The juxtaposition of the colour against the sand was glaring. *What the hell is going on?*

'This is your new home,' Karrept said.

'What is it?' I didn't have high hopes that he would tell me where I was or what I was doing there.

'It is a ... place for ... training. A ...'

'Camp?'

'Yes. A camp.'

'Why do you need me here?'

Karrept stopped moving and looked at me—or, well, looked through me. It was like he was trying to form the words he needed.

'Because you are unique. There has not been anyone like you for many years, and there will not be for many to come.'

I shook my head. 'Riddles don't help you.'

Karrept raised an eyebrow like I had said something that didn't make sense to him. The nuances of the modern language were always a problem for him. It was like he couldn't leave the past—the past that was way-too-long-ago BC.

'Come on, now. You must go in, and you will have to meet the other. You will not regret it.'

'Says you,' I said. And as I looked past the entrance and into what seemed like a mirage, I couldn't see a single soul. It made me wonder if I was about to fall into a trap—something that would plunge me to the depths of my life. Maybe that was how I was going to die. I was sixteen and had lived a sheltered life. I knew it, but that wasn't what I had in mind when we had read from those pages that were supposed to change everything. It *had* changed everything, but I hadn't realised I would be separated from Destiny and leave Lucy behind. It was the first time in sixteen years I had been away from my twin, and I could only imagine what she was feeling. It took everything in me not to search through our bond and find her, soothe her, but it would have given away that I could do so much more.

Phamenoth 2017
Dreamland

I wished that sleep was easy to come by, but honestly, I was lucky to get a few hours a night. If I got more, it was a fucking miracle.

I had thought it had been a detriment when I was at The Camp, but it wasn't. I learnt a lot about the way the campmates slept. I also learnt what scared them, and I could use it against them. But, sometimes, after my dreamwalking, I got a chance to be able to just … dream.

Closing my eyes, I felt myself slip into the dream. It was warm and always sunny. Just the way I liked it. Many would dream of the beach, but I had an aversion to sand, and I hadn't stepped foot on it since I was rescued. My dreams were no different. As I walked through trees, I could smell the dampness of the dirt and the leaves that rustled in the breeze. There were subtle movements where forest animals jumped through the trees and under the bushes.

Movement in my peripherals made me stop and turn to see if it was an animal, but there was nothing. Most of my dreams were nightmares— times to remember what they put my body through at The Camp. The scars on my body told a story, but there, in the dreamland, I was whoever I wanted to be, the scars memories of what had been.

I walked backwards and into a body.

'Shit,' I said, and spun on my heel to come face to face with the most intense seafoam eyes I had ever seen. 'I'm so sorry.'

'Watch where you're going. You could seriously injure someone. With—hi.' Her eyes widened as soon as she met my gaze. There was a faint click in my brain, and it was like a key was finding the lock that had been empty for too long. 'No ... Let me ... Uhhh.' She licked her lips and pressed them together, and I knew I was in trouble.

'What are you doing in a forest?' I asked her. I had to change the subject because all I wanted to do was take her into my arms and hold her tight.

'Shouldn't I be the one asking you?'

'Maybe, but I was here first.'

The woman shook her head. 'I don't think so. This is my place.' She took a few steps back and leant against one of the trees, looking up, and I followed her gaze. The treetops were dense, but I could see a snippet of the sky. It was rumbling with thunder, but it was clear. *Where are the clouds?*

There was a growl that broke the silence, and both of us snapped our attention over my shoulder. In the clearing stood a wolf. It was grey and white in colour, had clear, blue eyes and bared its teeth to us.

'Is that a wolf?'

I studied it further and could see that it was bigger than the average wolf and had human-looking eyes, which meant ... 'It's a werewolf.'

'Fuck,' she murmured.

My thoughts exactly. Werewolves were hard to run from. They were faster than the average wolf and didn't give up. The key here was not to antagonise it if we wanted to keep our lives intact.

'Back up slowly. Don't make any sudden movements,' I mumbled, and turned so I could see the werewolf properly.

Travis had green eyes in his human form, but they were purple in his wolf form. He was bigger. An alpha who was waiting to come into his power was always bigger, but their hierarchy was weird. I didn't even try to understand it. But Travis wouldn't hurt me. I knew he wouldn't.

'Fuck this.' The woman in question stomped in front of me, and I wrapped a hand around her wrist. 'Come at us, you stupid mutt. What are you going to do?'

'What are you doing?' I hissed and pulled her back so she was flush against my chest. She smelt like the ocean, salty and fresh. She was intoxicating.

'I'm not going to be baited into submitting. It has never been in my vocabulary.' She paused but didn't move, almost caving into me. 'Did you hear me, you stupid mutt? Come on then.'

I wanted to clap a hand over her mouth to stop any further words from spilling from her lips, but instead, I wrapped an arm protectively around her and used the momentum to spin in front of her.

'What are you doing?' she uttered.

'Saving your life.'

The wolf, infuriated by the catcalling, rushed down through the clearing. I could see it moving through the foliage to close the distance between us, the sound of its paws hitting the moist ground like wet slaps against a tree trunk. Its huffing came closer before it skidded and came to a halt in front of us.

I held her behind me and she tried to fight me. She was stronger than she looked, which made things interesting.

'What are you doing? Let me at it.'

'Shhh,' I whispered, holding out a hand to it. The werewolf growled and snapped at my fingers, but missed. I could control it; it was my dream. I could do anything I wanted, almost like I was the sandman of dreams, and in some instances, I was—except I could manipulate only that which I could control.

It snapped again, and this time, rushed at me. I let go of the woman and held out both hands, pushing power—the only kind I had in dreamland—into the wolf. It hit an invisible barrier and skidded to a stop. Instead of saying anything, I grabbed the woman's hand and made a beeline to high ground. It would hold as long as we got out of sight.

'Where are we going?'

'Away from it.'

The scene changed from the dense rainforest to the ocean kissing the sand, the wind whipping through her dress and hair.

'Wh-what was that?' she asked, and when I turned on my heel to look at her, her eyes were wide as she stared at the water.

'This is my dreamland. We can go anywhere I want.' She didn't look like she was listening because her eyes started to water. 'Are you okay?'

'I can hear it. The water. She's calling for me.' The woman took my hand and made a break for the water's edge. I let her take me with her, and we stopped short of the water kissing our toes.

'What is it?'

'I can't ...' she whispered, and tore her eyes away from the water to look at me. Unshed tears stared back at me from those turquoise colour eyes.

'What do you mean you can't?'

'I can't,' she said again.

I didn't take that for what it was and backed up into the water. It was cold, and I hissed at the temperature change, but with the way she was looking at me, I didn't care. She shook her head, but I slowly pulled her into the water. There was resistance, but that slowly melted away as she let me guide her into the sea. The woman didn't care about the temperature or complain. She just kept following my lead. When the water was at our knees, the tears flowed freely, but I didn't stop. When it was at our waists, I stopped. Her dress floated around her, and she sighed. I brought my other hand to wipe away the tears with the pads of my fingers.

'I haven't ... I ...' She couldn't find the words, but that was okay.

I pulled her flush against my body. A soft gasp left her lips, and I tipped her head up ever so slightly—she was almost as tall as I was—and kissed her. First, it was soft, exploring what I could do. When she gripped my T-shirt, I took that as a sign and cupped her head closer. There was a need that I didn't remember ever having.

She broke the kiss first and leant her forehead against mine. 'Wow.'

'Mhm,' I murmured, basking in the warmth of her body. *How long has it been since I felt like this with anyone? Even in a dream.* I needed to know if she was real.

'I don't often kiss strangers,' she whispered.

'That makes two of us. Care to give me your name?'

She smiled, and I could feel it without seeing it. 'Where is the fun in that?'

'So you're not going to tell me what your name is?'

She shook her head and slowly pulled back. 'Come find me,' she said before she ducked under the water, and I was left alone.

I knew I was alone because the dream suddenly felt so empty. Like I'd lost my key.

CHAPTER EIGHT

Acionna
Phamenoth 2017
Melbourne

I GASPED out of the dream, clawing at the sheets around me as I tried to slip back into the conscious world. The dream was more than enough to ruin any sort of a grandeur with the present. *Who was that delicious man, and why did he make me feel like I could do anything as long as he was touching me?*

I was drenched in sweat, and all I could see were his grey eyes, roiling with emotion. The way he looked at me as he guided me into the water and the way it felt on my skin … It had been 110 days since I dived under the waves, and the feeling of the water on my skin was like no other. I was so frustrated that I let myself slip out of the dream —a dream I had thought was my own, but wasn't.

'Who the hell was he?' I muttered. Swinging my legs over the edge of the bed, I slipped my tank over my head and wiggled out of my sweat-drenched shorts. On the armchair to my right was a silk robe, and I slipped it on and tied the belt around my waist. I walked to the double French doors and pulled them open, the sheer curtains billowing with the wind as I slipped outside onto the balcony. The moon was full, the tide fierce and crashing against the rocks, pulling in and out with a vengeance. The saltiness that permeated the air felt like home. It made me want to dive under the surface to see what was there. It was the quietest time—the time when humans would be terrified of what lay beyond what their eyes could see. I used to love frolicking at that time, making splashes, befriending the sharks—as long as I wasn't in my selkie skin. While it activated while I was in the water, it didn't turn me into a seal-like creature until I was deep under the surface.

It would be but half an hour until the sun came up, and the morning runners would be out in force like they always were. I wrapped my arms around my chest and rubbed my triceps. I wasn't cold. It was out of habit—a comfort I had started since being landlocked.

The witch who had my pelt was old, her magick wrapped around the camera I wished I could throw far, far away. I wasn't good at pinpointing where the magick was, but there was a taste of something cold and dark, almost sinister to it. The magick was older than anything I could put my fingers on. It predated me, and I was old.

Magick had a way of being both good and bad at the same time. The witch could do spells. She could use her magick in ways that I'd never understand because we didn't have magick like it in the world. Or at least, not that version of it.

It made me think that she was a part of something bigger—an entity or a division of people who were different.

That was scary. Scarier than I could even articulate because while I was a princess and an heir to a kingdom, I wasn't all that powerful. Whatever made the witch target me and take my pelt was unique. It felt almost personal, and I hated that I didn't know more than that.

I inhaled the salty air and let the guttural sound in my throat ride the wave to try to alleviate the rising anger of being stuck. I was taking an image of my beloved ocean day in and day out. I could see her, right from the balcony of my bedroom, and she felt foreign. I loathed that.

The witch would burn when I found her, and I would make sure she felt every inch of the flames that would lick through her home.

I won't get back to sleep now. It was near-impossible, and I couldn't dip my toes into the water because I would let the tide take me away. And without my pelt, I would drown.

A seal drowning was too comical to be real.

The ocean was too dangerous for me as a landlocked selkie. I wished for it not to be. The dream had been perfect in too many ways. The man whose eyes roiled much like the grey clouds of a storm did … I wanted to find him, thank him for the feel of the ocean on my skin again. I wanted to find more of that.

I needed to feel the ocean on my skin again, and if I had to sleep my way through the day to feel it again, I would do it.

The ocean was all that mattered to me.

Mesore 2016
Undersea

Dotting the last sentence after reading the current book Mama wanted me to look over was a relief. Studying to be the Queen of the Undersea wasn't a task for the fainthearted. There were strict lessons about the different types of kin, as well as the decisions to be made. I'd spent years learning all of it.

'Who is the ruler of the octos?' Mother asked as she sat across from me at the table.

I looked up from the book and raised an eyebrow at her. 'I thought this was supposed to be challenging?'

'Answer the question.' She clasped her fingers in front of her and tilted her head to the side. She didn't look a day over a teen, but she was aeons old. She would never tell us how old she was, but after having ten children, I supposed one wouldn't want to disclose that information.

'Sorley. He has been in power for close to 200 years and has thousands of offspring who try to take over his throne almost weekly, but he holds strong.'

'But does he?' she asked and chuckled.

Underneath the queen, there was a mother who cared. Not as much as some of the other selkie mothers, but enough. But maybe she just let me see.

'That's always up for debate. Hello, Mama.'

'Acionna, you seemed to have chewed through this lesson. Did you find it enlightening?'

The war on roanes—male counterparts to us—and why selkies were rulers over them was so perplexing.

'What made the roanes strike back at us, Mama? I'm not sure I understand why they wanted to take back power when they were always so outnumbered.'

Mother unclasped her fingers and drummed the table with her long nails. They made a clicking sound that had me watching her nails strike the table instead of looking at her face.

'They wanted to have power, and could have if they went about it differently. What do you think they could have done?'

'Roanes, in power? Never. They are too focused on war and never on what is best for the actual finfolk tribe. They just want power.'

'Acionna, answer the question.'

Many thought Mother was brash, and maybe she was, but she did everything with a purpose, and I loved it. I loved watching the way people moved out of her way or when they bowed down to her. Yes, she was tough on my siblings and myself, but she did it because we were special. Each and every one of my sisters would be a handmaiden and a guard to me when I finally took the throne.

She clicked her tongue, and I sighed. 'If they were smart about it, they would be looking at a way to make the selkies work in their favour, bring their babies seaside so they can have an army that would protect them to the end of their days. Instead, they were selfish and wanted power they couldn't get.'

Mother pushed herself up from the chair and floated a little higher, her grey hair fanning around her. It always twinkled with the catch of light; it had been black as the night sky years ago. Her grey seal tail was there by choice. She could have legs if she wanted—she had that power. We all did. 'That is one way to see it, but what is the best way to fight someone?'

'Make them fear you.'

'And why?'

'Because fear is powerful. People will follow a ruler they fear because they want to stay in their good books and make sure they are on the right side of their wrath.'

'What of a ruler who is a lover?'

'It can work. A ruler who is a lover is one who is respected and scrutinised at the same time. Everything they do is monitored and carefully adopted. A loving ruler makes their people want to follow them out of wanting to be near them.'

Mother nodded. 'How do I rule?' she asked, and I swallowed past the lump in my throat. That was a question I didn't know how to answer without her losing her temper.

'Fear. The finfolk fear your wrath.'

My mother swam so she was right at my face, and it took everything in me not to blink, startled. 'And why?'

'Because you project that.'

She didn't move, waiting for more. 'But you're a lover. While the finfolk fear you, we see the love. The kindness you show no one else. There are a select few who see that side too.'

Her thumb under my chin guided my head and gaze up to meet hers. 'And that is because you are blood and do as you're told. One misstep, and you will not be able to say the same words twice to me.'

I held her gaze when all I wanted to do was take a step back. I knew that if I did that, she would see it as a weakness. I would come up with people who would only want me for my body, not my mind, or they would just want a decision from me. I had to stand my ground. And that was what Mother demonstrated with the flex of power.

'But you let Ariel get away with murder,' I said.

She rolled her eyes and backed up. 'Ariel is a problematic child. You and I both know it.'

'She is jealous,' I murmured, and pushed myself out of my chair and hovered just out of reach. 'Every one of the selkies knows it.'

'Maybe she has too much of her father in her rather than myself. He was always so overdramatic.'

Ariel's father ... She was one of the daughters who was half human. Sometimes, it felt like she was painfully human rather than selkie. She had the same upbringing as the rest of us did—all ten of us siblings.

'Ailis and Adella think you dropped her as a pup,' I said with a smirk. Mother turned and threw a dagger at me. I plucked it out of the water and held it by its tip before I tapped the hilt against my palm.

'Only you would be the one to say that out loud. The others wouldn't dare say anything like that to me.'

'It's because they think you don't care about them.'

'And that is why they aren't heir to the throne and you are.'

'I am but a middle child, Mama. It has ruffled so many fins. Agate or Adara should have been the first pick.'

'Next, you're going to tell me that Armella or Allegra have said the same thing.'

I laughed. 'The youngest pups of the tribe would want to do nothing more than stick their noses in a book or play with dolls and never come up for air. I worry about when either of them gets to their Matchings.'

No one else got to see that side of Mother. She didn't *appear* to care for us pups, but she was always there if we needed her. And while the throne was important to her, she made her family even more so—a trait that was almost unheard of with selkies ordinarily, and perhaps that's what made her different to any other ruler in the Undersea.

Alina and Aurora floated into the room, and that was the end of the fun Mother and I would have. Her posture changed from the easy-going nature, her shoulders sharpening. Her chin turned up, and she kept her distance.

The queen was back in the room. The one who was just but also true.

'You should have seen merfolk that just came through school. It was like they thought they were the kings of the school,' Alina said.

'And you're telling me they weren't? Did you see how hot they were? I was ready to pounce.'

I shook my head and returned to the table to gather up my books and move them to my chambers. 'You both need to get to shore. It might be time to see what chasing after boys will get you.'

'Acionna, you would have appreciated them too. I know it. They had the ri—Mama, hello.' Alina cringed and stopped flicking her tail. She stood taller, tucking some of her chestnut brown hair behind her ear and crossing her palms over one another in front of her tail.

Aurora bowled right into Alina. 'What the hell, Ali? Oh. Hello, Mama.' She, too, stood up straighter. My gaze flicked from them to Mother, who pursed her lips and raised an eyebrow at me.

'Hello, girls. I was just going to check the perimeter of the castle. I take it the merfolk were on their best behaviour at school?'

They both nodded, and Mother swam out of the room without saying anything more. My two sisters looked at me like I had betrayed them.

'Acionna! You were meant to warn us if Mama was here. Now she is going to think we are chasing after the merfolk like lovesick pups or something,' Alina said as her hands came to rest on her hips—or where they would have been, if she had her human legs.

'She would be within her right mind to think so after that conversation.' I turned my back on them and swam back to my room. I could hear them shuffling behind me. They weren't going to leave me alone, and part of me wanted to be by myself. I had so many things running through my head, so many lessons, and I was so torn between the emotions that roiled between my breasts and the stoicism that came with being the sister everyone came to. Any problem, and they were in my chambers.

'What's got up your arse?' Aurora asked.

I sighed, stopped at the entrance of my chambers and turned to face them. 'You just need to be able to watch what you say. You and I both know there will be a time when I will be in Mama's shoes, Matched off with my own family. I can't keep being the middle pup.'

'But that's who you are,' Alina said.

'I know, Little Fish. But we all have to grow up sometime.'

With that, I pushed my way into my chambers and shut the door behind me. I leant up against it and realised I was going to have to come to terms with telling them what to do on a level that wasn't sisterly. And they wouldn't be ready for it.

Neither would I.

Phamenoth 2017
Melbourne

I didn't question Janice and her just being a part of the house. I couldn't. She was just there. Janice made it all okay, but she didn't have to. I knew that. And with my mother's words always ringing in my ears, I knew that it was too good to be true. Janice didn't say much, but she was always here.

'Janice …' I called out as I made my way downstairs. I'd showered and dressed. Much to my chagrin, the scent of salt on my skin was driving me insane. I wanted it to go away.

'Down here, Miss Acionna,' she called out.

The woman never went home—wherever that was—and it was part of her that made me so weirded out because there was nothing I could do to make her tell me what her true purpose was.

Or maybe she has a room in the cupboard under the stairs?

'Do you know where my diary is with all of my appointments?'

'It's downstairs on the coffee table.'

I made a beeline for the coffee table to see if it was there, and sure enough, it was. I scooped it up and padded over to the dining table. The room was open-plan, so there was a big kitchen. It was white with oak cabinets, and the statement pendants were beachy, a mixture of rattan and wood. Not something I would have picked if I had decorated the home, but it worked. There were tall windows on the other side with sheer curtains that diffused the light perfectly. I swung a leg over the bench seat of the table and sat down.

I had to prepare for the party the Ryders were going to throw, and I needed to understand the way they wanted it to be shot. Devin had sent me a floor plan, his ideas and a whole PDF of concepts.

Janice came over and brought my laptop to the table. 'Why are you always just right there? Do you have a home?' I asked.

'Yes, it's here. I have a room under the cupboard,' she said with a wink.

'Okay, that's not funny. How do you know that?'

'I have many talents. Do you want to hear about them?' Janice asked as she sat down at the table opposite me.

'Yes.' The party was on the forefront of my mind, but that didn't matter. Not when I was about to get exactly what I had just been pondering.

'There is a sense of magick in the air—one I know of that is older than you and me combined. It's laced all over the camera, and I think you know that one well. Don't you?'

I nodded.

'I'm magickal. You would have come across my type of magick in studies, Miss Acionna.'

Studies? I blinked at her. She was … She knew my mother—she was one of the Undersea. Tears filled my eyes, and I reached across to her. Janice held out her hand for me and squeezed. Her palm was cool to the touch, but there was a hum of power underneath the skin.

'You're Undersea folk,' I whispered, and she squeezed my hand harder. 'But why can't I feel exactly what you are?'

'Your pelt did more than just transform you into a seal, Miss Acionna. It allowed you to feel more of what was around you.'

'How did you know that it's missing?'

Janice let go of my hand and smiled. It was soft, comforting, like I pictured human mothers would smile at their offspring that they wanted.

'Your tears, your hesitation, the way you stare longing at the water. I can see that you're missing it, and it breaks my heart. A selkie without her pelt is like a fish without water. Slowly, you start to go insane.'

She wasn't wrong there. I could feel with every passing day that something wasn't right, like there was a switch that was waiting to be flipped. It could have been any day when my whole world would shift even more.

'I need to find it, but I don't even know where to start. I can't let this be the end of it, so I take these silly photos—the ones that kill me day after day—because I need to take a picture of the thing I can't be in the most.'

I wanted to tell Janice more. I wanted to tell her about my sister, about the man who had been a fling and was the whole reason I was stuck there, but I didn't know if I trusted her enough. *She may be here, and she may be helping me, but at what cost?*

Is she feeding information to someone? Does she have ulterior motives? Could she really just want to help me?

It was rare to find people who just wanted to help. I'd had many of those back home, but they were there because I was the heir and a sea princess, and not much else. No one did much of anything without expectation of payment or some sort of reward. Janice was different; she did what she did because she liked it, and before she knew it would be helpful. Or at least, that's how I understood it.

'Then you do what you need. And when you're ready for all the answers, I will be here, ready to give them to you.'

'But what if I want to know right now? Would you tell me?'

She clicked her tongue and smiled. It was warm—the kind of smile I had always wished my mother would give me. 'You aren't ready. But I can give you a few hints. The first is to do with music.'

My eyes widened. *She can't be?*

'The second is "handmaiden."'

Janice was a siren. And she was my mother's handmaiden.

'Janice,' I whispered. 'You ... You can't be.'

'I can not confirm nor deny at this time, but I'm sure you understand.' The riddle was more than she could say. Sirens, while typically found in deep water, were attached to selkies as a species.

'I …'

'You have some party details to look at, Miss Acionna. You have to make sure you can bring together what is needed. This is a conversation for another time.'

With a wink, Janice walked into the kitchen to start the next meal. But knowing she may very well have been a siren changed everything and nothing at the same time.

CHAPTER NINE

Devin
Phamenoth 2017
Melbourne

THE DAY WAS LONG PAST, but I was up because I knew I had a deadline. It wasn't too far away, but I needed to ramp up the efforts. I didn't notice when that became a part of my process. Or when it started. There was a time, I was sure of it, but I lost track of when it didn't all make me want to vomit. Taking the life of another was never a skill I wanted to have, but it was forced on me, my sisters' lives dangled in front of me over and over again because they knew I would have done anything for them and still would. Destiny and Lucy were the two most important people in my life. They had always been there. They'd always supported me and wanted me to be better.

Why wouldn't I do anything for them?

Why wouldn't I kill to keep them alive?

Even then, in the safety of my own home, in my childhood bedroom, I was keeping them safe. They could be reported to the special police unit and be executed without cause just because they were different from the humans. They had unique powers, and while Destiny's were now a completely different set, she was still seen as magickal because she needed the force of someone else to keep herself alive.

I rubbed my hands over my face to clear the image of them dying from my mind. It was a moment I saw over and over again in so many different ways—beheading, poisoning, gunshot to the heads, hearts carved out of their chests. Anything I could think of, I would see, though I could never see them with an arrow to the chest. It was one of the only reasons I kept up with the bow and arrow. I knew I wouldn't kill my siblings, and it kept them safe. There was only one person who used a bow and arrow as a calling card, and he was in that very room.

Was it archaic? Yeah, most definitely, but I was okay with that. I knew I could be okay with it.

In the bathroom, I looked back at my reflection—the stormy grey eyes, the brown hair, the high cheekbones and the lines of time. I wasn't old. But at twenty-two, I had already lived a whole life—or what felt like a whole life. It was funny to think back on. If we hadn't found that book, and if we hadn't read from it, my life would be vastly different. I tried to shield Lucy from that same fate. She was, through and through, my sister. Her curiosity and will to want answers was her downfall.

But that was what I loved about her the most.

I twisted the cold tap and water spilt from the faucet. I cup my hands under the stream and splash my face with water—like it would do anything to wake me up. I was about to crawl back into bed, tap Pete Housing on the shoulder and show him what his death would look like. Not where, but *how*.

As I looked in the mirror again, water dripped over my brow, down my nose and my chin. I grabbed the towel next to the basin and wiped my face. The one that stared back at me wasn't Devin, the man who was a brother and a son. It was Devin, the Dreamwalking Assassin who had a job to do.

I would get paid highly for the kill, but it would take a toll on me. All of them did.

I shut the tap off, threw the towel on the vanity and walked out of the bathroom. The light would turn off as soon as it realised there was no body heat in the room. I pulled my black T-shirt over my head and let it drop to the floor, walking to the bed. As I settled down, I took a deep breath, clearing my brain of anything else. All that mattered was the dreamland. It was chaotic inside there; if I wasn't stable and focused on who I was targeting, I could get lost in the cacophony of different dreams. The stress dreams, the sex dreams, the difficult dreams, the nightmares. It was a whole array of goodies inside the dreamland, and while I relied on the colours and emotions inside the world, it was hard to distinguish if I was unsteady.

Pete Housing wasn't hard to find. It was always easier to find a mark if I had plagued their dreams. His brand of Cu Sith was red and fiery, like he was untouchable, and that was okay because no one else could. It was why he looked over a national chain of high-end retail businesses. Pete had to be brutal, and while he wanted to make it look like he was innocent, I knew otherwise. And so would the whole world.

'Pete … Oh, Petey …' I whispered, tapping the lone arrow against the glass doors of the building. 'I know you're here. Come out, come out, wherever you are,' I said, a little louder this time.

I pressed the arrow against the glass window a little harder and dragged it across the clear surface. It left a sharp line, consistent yet jagged. As I got to the sliding doors of the showroom, they opened, and I twirled the arrow between my fingers. There were no more surfaces to drag it along. The racks and racks of clothing inside the store were disorganised, clothes out of order, some on the floor, coat hangers barely hanging on. It was a mess—like there had been a stampede of people coming into the store.

An interesting vision. When I jumped into dreams, they were always a version of a nightmare. *Is an untidy store Pete Housing's nightmare?*

'Wh-what do you want?' he stammered. I turned on my heel and tapped the arrowhead up and down against my palm as I looked him in the eye.

'Your life. You've been a bad man, haven't you, Pete? How many have you hurt?'

Tap. Tap. Tap. The soft, rhythmic sound of the arrow kept up a soft beat—something akin to the heart beating in my chest. It was steady and quiet.

'N-no, I haven't.'

I pulled the bow slung over my shoulder into my hand and pulled the arrow through the nock. I pulled the bowstring taunt and pointed the arrow behind Pete's head. I let go of the string, and the arrow sunk into the rack behind the counter full of clothes accessories. He screamed and hit the ground hard.

'Petey. Pete, I didn't take you for a coward. Where is that cu sith interior I know is there?'

It was almost as if I had flicked a switch. Pete rose to his feet, his shoulder back and head high. 'What do you mean?' he asked.

That was the man that I needed, not the scaredy-cat that he had put on as a facade.

'You know very well what I mean. How many of them said no?'

His eyes darkened, and from the human brown, they shifted into demonic red eyes that were fiery and full of hatred.

'I don't know what you mean. There was no one.'

I clicked my tongue and circled him. The clothes on the racks whispered with my movements, delicate garments fell off the rack and hit the ground with a soft thunk. The sound wasn't loud enough for many others to hear, but the silence in the room made it sound like it was loud as a firework erupting in the sky.

'Try again.'

With ease, I grabbed another arrow and slid it into place, pulling it back. This time, I sent it sailing through the air and it nicked his ear. He cried out and I grabbed another, this time, sending it through the air and nicking his hand. The skin erupted, and I could see lava through the cut.

'Stop it,' he growled.

'Make me,' I challenged.

Another bow sailed through the air and nicked his opposite shoulder. I blinked and carried myself to the back of the store, between the sale rack. I shot another arrow in Pete's direction, and it caught him in the shoulder. He roared and pulled the arrow from his shoulder, throwing it to the floor.

'You're making this too easy,' I said with a smirk.

Taunting Pete really was easy. He started moving towards me, and I could see that his human skin was starting to rip from his body as the flames started to engulf him. I grabbed another arrow, clicked it into place and pulled the bowstring back. Taking a deep breath, I rested the string against my cheek and aimed for his head. Right between the eyes.

'Enjoy your afterlife, Pete,' I said, and let go, the arrow sailing through the air and hitting him between the eyes. He dropped dead with a loud thunk.

Pete Housing would wake up sweat-drenched, knowing someone was after him and he was about to die.

I was coming for him the next day, and there would be no hiding from what was to come.

Opening my eyes, I ran a hand over my face and sat up. Time went by so quickly when I dreamwalked, but there was nothing to stop that, nothing I could change. I couldn't tell if it was weird that a small part of me took great joy in the fear that laced through Pete's eyes, knowing his death was imminent?

The Camp had changed me, and I knew it had stayed with me.

I picked up my bag and rolled my shoulders. It was the night Pete Housing was going to die. I had placed a tracker on his car—a red 2017 Toyota Corolla, go figure. He had been travelling all around the city, stopping in at various places to talk to teams or perhaps take another victim. His brand of evil was taking advantage of women who had issues with men—like he could change it for them, but there was no way he could. Instead of helping, he hindered them worse, damaging their self-image and taking them against their will.

I killed bad men and women because they didn't deserve to have the extra abilities that allowed them to do what they did. Gagliani and Housing were only two of the many, and while their names were fresh, they would fade in my memory and become distant thoughts.

Time was of the essence. While the sun started beyond the horizon, it was time to get him. Time for him to meet his maker.

The waves lapped down around me as I sat in my car overlooking the bay. Way up where the city glittered, the mountains stood proud, and there was a sense of ease in the air—like the everyday was easy. And it was, for most. But for others, it wasn't.

Being back in society, even after ten months, felt weird. The weather fluctuated like nobody's business, but that was Melbourne in a nutshell. Sometimes, I longed for the dry and unrelenting heat; it was better than the yo-yo that was cold, then hot, then windy and back to cold all over again. Clouds in the sky would usher in a storm—one that would either decimate the waterways or pull shrapnel through the air. There was no middle ground.

Pete Housing walked at the edge of the water, his feet splashing as he moved. He was alone, just like I knew he would be. *The me who first joined The Camp wouldn't dream of this.* I could hardly throw a punch because there was nothing to follow through, there was no one who could hurt me. But the me now? I had seen too many things. I had watched fellow camp mates be killed at the hands of others, and there had been many who had died by my own hands. Their names, I remembered, and their faces haunted me in the moments when I got any true sleep, but it was their life or mine. Self-preservation was another beast entirely.

I hadn't known I had it in me until I did it.

Jarrad had made sure of it. He was the one I leant on in those moments. He caught me when I needed him to, but I still kept him at arm's length. It had taken him some time to find me after I was out, but once he did, he knew how to get to me. Lucy didn't know anything, and I wanted it to stay that way because she would freak out on another level. Her attention to my life was extreme because she refused to lose me again. I didn't blame her. If the roles were reversed, I would have done the same.

I glanced at the rearview mirror to make sure there were no cars coming and reached into the passenger seat. My lucky bow—the one that killed Gagliani—was resting there. When I wrapped my fingers around the composite bow, it curved away from me so I could get extra velocity with my arrows. Resting against the side dash was the quiver full of arrows. I pulled a single one out and gripped it with the bow, checking the rearview mirror again—this time more out of habit than anything else. I opened the door and slid out of the car. Closing the door softly, I searched around again to triple-check that there was no one else.

Witnesses were a problem.

Unnecessary baggage that would need to be eliminated.

I had more arrows, but it was harder to kill people when they were closer. Guns were better for instances like that.

The lookout had a wall that came up to my waist. I held my bow and arrow down by my side and out of view. I could see Pete inching closer to the right spot. He would walk past where I was, maybe look up if he was smart—humans didn't do it, it wasn't in their nature. Metaphysical beings, on the other hand … They were accustomed to it. From my vantage point, I could see his head checking out his surroundings, moving from side to side.

'Pete, you're going to wish you didn't do the bad things you did.'

I took a step back and lifted the bow. As I clicked the arrow into place, I pulled the string back and pointed it at Pete. I took a deep breath and rested the bow against my cheek, letting my whole body loosen up. The tighter I was, the more chaotic the throw was. An arrow had the chance to soar through the air with poise and decorum if one let it, and after five years of practice, I had it down to an art. It was why no one else could beat me when I had a bow and arrow in my hand.

Pete kept walking, the daylight slowly fading away. If I left it any longer, my ability to aim and see him properly would be gone. There were no city lights to help guide my vision, and I wasn't part therianthrope, so I couldn't see better in the dark. I was a dreamwalking witch who had an uncanny ability to torment people while they slept.

It wasn't anything special.

I took another deep breath. If I waited longer, a car would come and spot me. I wasn't very well camouflaged either.

I let go of the arrow and watched it sail through the air. I had another lined up just in case it didn't hit him, but as soon as it hit Pete's chest and knocked him to the ground, I knew I had hit the mark. I watched, holding my breath, to see if he got up or if anyone rushed to see him. But there was nothing. Just the waves lapping against his body. The tide would pull him out and take him to sea.

'Clear his vision, take him from sight, remove him from life and keep him safe from prying eyes. So mote it be,' I muttered under my breath.

I didn't get a chance to do it with Gagiliani. He had spotted me, and there were too many people around, but this time, I made sure of it. I didn't want a beachgoer to find him. And if someone did, it wouldn't be a human who would stumble on him. My spell made sure of it.

There was a loophole, but I was hard-pressed to find a therianthrope or some other magickal being who would see through my rhyme.

Leaving the bow at my waist, the string resting on my forearm, I turned on my heel and searched around. No cars, no people, no witnesses, but I could hear the faint woosh of a vehicle coming. I needed to get out of there, and I needed to do it immediately.

I started towards my car when I heard the other vehicle close in—someone was speeding down the steep windy hill. I threw my bow at my car, hoping it would slide under the front of it, and pressed my lips together. It would look less suspicious if I was standing in front of my vehicle without the bow ... But the murder weapon? Not so auspicious.

I turned my back to the road and looked at the ocean again. There was a soft mist rolling through, causing a shadow over the whole bay.

Pete's body was still by the shoreline, the waves lapping up against him ever so gently. I wished for the water to take him out to sea. The quicker that happened, the better it would be.

If I was closer, I would have pushed him, but that was a surefire way to make sure I was locked away for good.

I bent down and pretended to redo the shoelace on my boots while a hand slid inside the holster that held a knife. I hated hand-to-hand contact; it wasn't a strength of mine, but if I had to, I would make sure it hurt. I could make it look like an accident if I wanted to as well. Standing up again, I kept the knife in front of me as I heard the car slow down. I gripped the hilt harder and tried to keep my body relaxed, not to give an inch. The urge to look over my shoulder was everything; I wanted to see if they were going to get out of the car or were just passing by.

It would never have happened if I was still at The Camp. There would be a team of people to make sure that didn't happen—more witches who would keep prying eyes away, but it was the real world. It was what we trained for.

I gave in to temptation and looked over my shoulder. Inside the car was a woman. She had blond hair that was up in a messy bun, and she winked at me and drove off. Like she was waiting for me to turn around. As soon her lights were out of view, I relaxed.

'Fucking hell,' I whispered.

Time to grab the bow and arrow and get the hell away from here.

Looking out at the cityscape on a day like that—where the weather was still and humid, and I could see the clouds gathering in the distance—was always a favourite of mine. There was enough sun to make the buildings sparkle if one caught them in the right way, just like a diamond that moved in the right direction. The office I stood in was mine. Dad had given it to me earlier in the week, and while I hated the idea of working anywhere other than in the shadows, there I was. I had to make the best of the moments I could. Or at least, that was what the doting son in me had to do.

I was diving deeper into the build of the new hotel, and everything was starting to fall into place, but there was more to make sure that stayed on track. One misstep could seriously fuck up all of my hard work. The moments between hits meant I was busy scribbling down notes and making appointments, showing up to meetings and picking fucking colours. I didn't want to do that, and I ran them past Lucy, but she was a writer, not an interior designer. Lili was good with colours and designs as any fashion designer would be, but she didn't help me either.

'You could have made this whole appointment over the phone,' Rhea said as she entered the room. I didn't turn around. The click of her heels was silent on the carpet, but her presence was enough to make me want to.

'Close the door behind you,' I said, and shoved a hand in the pocket of my suit pants. The shirt I had on was long-sleeved, and even in the heat, it was better than any sort of armour I could wear. I turned on the balls of my feet and leant against the desk to look at Rhea. She was in a lavender short-sleeved shirt with a leather skirt that came down to her knees. Her pink locks were off her face, trailing over her shoulders. Her blue eyes were tinged purple from her shirt, but I knew there was more … Rhea's eyes would teeter more purple if she was a werewolf, but she wasn't a wolf.

'What is so important that this needs to happen right now?' she asked, and I tilted my head with a soft smile on my lips.

'You're telling me that your heart didn't skip a beat when I called?' Cocky? You bet. I knew what I wanted, and after the last hit on Pete, all I could think about was the adrenaline that ran through my body. I had too much energy, and no matter how many times I worked out, it barely touched the itch I was desperate to scratch. The meeting I had planned had nothing to do with what we should do.

Rhea's eyes held my gaze for a little longer than necessary before they trailed down my face and down my body. I resisted the urge to ask her to keep her eyes on mine, but it was fun to watch her watch me. She chewed on her lip and backed up to lock the door. The click was louder than it should have been, but it made me smile.

There was a flick of yellow as she walked over to me—the cat shifter in her was closer to the surface than I would have liked, but it would do.

'I'm not denying it … but I'm also not going to confirm that statement either,' she murmured, not taking her eyes off me as she got closer.

'That's not going to work for me,' I said, and waited for her to come closer. It wouldn't take her long to close the distance between us. She could do it fast if she wanted to. I knew it, and she knew I knew it.

'Well, it's going to have to work for you,' she said.

Oh, sassy little thing. I smirked and licked my lips before raking my teeth over my lower lip. 'I don't think you understand. You're going to need to clarify for *me*.' My voice was a little lower as I walked around the desk and leant against the front of it, my arse resting on the edge as she stopped just short of me. Rhea tilted her head to the side and waited, like she was trying to judge what I would do next. There was a part of me that wanted to grab her hips and press her close to me, so close she wouldn't be able to squirm and could feel me through the leather of her skirt. Instead, I leant back and rested my hands on the edge of the desk, gripping ever so slightly as I did so.

'I. Don't. Need. To,' she murmured, and closed the distance between us. I grinned and looked down at her pretty blue eyes. There was a feral need in them—something I was sure many men would have missed. She was a cat shifter, and that meant there were probably too many out there who weren't even the slightest bit intimidated by her. But there would be many more that would be. Therianthropes were dangerous and could infect people very easily if they weren't careful.

'Oh, really, now?'

'Mhm.' She snaked her arms between the spaces of mine and tilted her head up. Her lips crashed against mine fervently, and it took everything in me not to moan. My hands left the desk and cupped her face, pressing her even closer.

Rhea melted into my body, and I knew she was going to end up bent over my desk. *What a way to christen an office.* She pulled back, and I watched that yellow glint in her eyes shine through. There was no hiding it now.

'You're not scared,' Rhea whispered as she blinked slowly. Her irises turned from human to cat-like slits.

'You're not the first shifter who's kissed me, Rhea.'

'How did you…?'

'I'm good. I've been away for long enough to call it out. What's your flavour?'

'Leopard.' Rhea's hands ran over my shoulders and down my chest, her purple nails undoing the first button of my shirt with care.

Care I didn't want.

I wanted the cat underneath the skin—the one that would leave scratch marks down my back. I wanted to wince as I moved while they healed.

'Not the first one I've come across.' *Or the first one I've fucked either.*

She bit down on her lip and smiled through it.

Fuck, that was sexy.

'I bet you've never had a clouded snow leopard before,' she murmured, undoing the next one.

'No.' She was going too slow.

Rhea undid another, and without missing a beat, I gripped her wrists in my hand and held them.

'If you're going to go that slow, you and I are going to have a problem. Shifter or not.' My tone was low, almost husky, but the threat was there.

'I like to play with my food.'

'I'm not food.'

Rhea could have easily ripped her hands from my grasp, but she didn't. Instead, she stared at me and waited for my next move.

'And if you think I am, this is not going to work,' I growled.

She smiled and leant her whole body into mine, grinding her hips against me. I bit back the moan that threatened to leave my lips. It felt good. My cock throbbed through my pants, and I had to steel myself.

'Oh, but we're just getting started.' She crushed her lips into mine, and I let her hold me there for a moment before I let go of her hands. This time, her fingers ripped my shirt open, buttons flew and she broke the kiss to chuckle. I licked my lips and pulled at her shirt, untucking it from her skirt before tugging it up her body and over her head. I threw it to the floor and grabbed her boobs and squeezed hard. She gasped, the sound music in my ears, and I slid a hand to the clasp of her bra and unhooked it with my fingers. It freed her breasts from their cage, and I yanked her bra away from her body. Glorious round breasts stared back at me.

'Mmm … gorgeous,' I whispered, kissing a line down her throat, sucking ever so slightly. There was no leaving any marks above the neck.

That sort of shit could be traced back, and I didn't want those sort of questions.

'Not too bad yourself, Mr Ryder,' she whispered, and that did something to me.

I brought myself back up to her level and, with a wicked grin, gripped her hips and twisted her body, shoving her against the table-top. She gasped, and in one whole movement, I undid my belt and pants, springing my cock free. I bent Rhea over the table and gripped her hair in my hand, tugging her head back.

'What do you want?' I whispered in her ear and pressed my lips against her skin. I felt her swallow hard.

'You.'

With her body pinned between mine and the desk, there wasn't a lot she could do to move.

'Stretch your hands out,' I commanded.

She did as I asked, and my free hand trailed down her naked skin before slipping underneath her skirt. My fingers danced across the dainty piece of lace that hid her clit from me, and I traced circles around the softest parts of her. I could easily rip the lace aside and slam my cock into her, but I wanted to make sure she was ready for me.

Rhea pressed herself into my hand—or at least, she tried—and I chuckled. 'Eager little kitty, you are,' I murmured, and she practically purred as my fingers slipped under the lace and rubbed circles over her clit. Slowly at first, up and down, trying to find the spot she needed. When I found it, she arched into me and moaned.

Good girl.

'Can you reach into the box to your left? There's a condom in there. Grab it for me.'

Did it matter that she was a therianthrope? No. It was harder for them to carry human babies. Did it still make me cautious?

Fuck yeah.

I didn't need a little me running around the place. She held the condom square between her two fingers. I let go of her hair and took it, ripping the wrapper with my teeth while my other hand slipped into her, tentatively at first, but I thrust my fingers into her hard, her body buckling against mine as she cried out.

'Shh ... There's a building full of people,' I whispered, and took my fingers from inside her.

'What the fuck ...?' Her protests were silenced as she heard the crinkling of the wrapper. I slipped the condom over my hard cock and lined myself up against her slit. I rubbed myself to get her wetness over me before I thrust into her, hard.

I knocked the wind out of Rhea, and before she could come back, I thrust my hips into her harder again, the anticipation of release driving me faster. It was like the adrenaline from the hit and having a sexy woman bent over the desk was the perfect combo.

'Dev—in,' Rhea moaned.

I held her hips, digging my nails into her dips, and thrusted harder again. Shapeshifters didn't break; they were stronger than humans in every way. I pounded at her, hoping to find her cervix, and when she arched back into me, I knew that I had. But she wouldn't get there with my cock inside her. She needed the friction of her clit being slammed.

I pulled out, and she growled. It was a full-leopard growl, and I couldn't help but laugh. 'Such a deep noise for such an intimate moment.'

And without any other words, I flipped her so I could see her face as I slammed my cock back into her. Rhea's eyes widened before her legs wrapped around my waist, coaxing me closer—like there was even a chance to get closer—and my hips started to move, thrusting into her hole like nothing else mattered. And in that moment, nothing else did. I wanted to fill the void that was left after taking a life, and what better way than the act that could make life?

Rhea pulled me in close, her nails raking down my back, and I hissed, the only real sound I gave her. I crushed my lips against hers again, this time not holding back, my hips driving my cock into her harder and faster. Her tongue filled my mouth, and it took everything in me not to bite down—that would put a dampener on the festivities.

The edge teetered so close, and I shoved myself into her faster, not changing the momentum as I felt her muscles clamp around my cock.

'Come, Rhea, I can feel it. Come now,' I murmured into her mouth as I groaned, unable to hold back how good she felt around me. Pulsing, breathing, coaxing me closer.

She cried out into my mouth, and I swallowed up the climax as her whole body shuddered around me. It ripped the control and my climax from me too. I ripped my mouth away from hers and muffled my cries into her shoulder.

As the last wave of ecstasy shattered my whole decorum, I fell against Rhea, matching her heavy breathing with my own.

'Well … that certainly was worth the late appointment, Mr Ryder,' Rhea said when I could finally see straight again.

I chuckled. 'Please, call me Devin. Mr Ryder is totally for Dad.'

'Your dad wouldn't fuck me, so he stays as Matt.'

And like thaaaat, everything was back to normal. No, Rhea wasn't Dad's type. She wasn't a childhood friend and was way too young for him, but it was enough to make me pull out of her. I pulled the condom off, grabbing a few tissues from the desk to wrap it up in.

I dumped it in the bin and pulled my pants up, careful not to snag anything.

'I guess that's a plus then. Thanks for the chat. Did you want to see the progress before you leave?'

Rhea raised an eyebrow at me. She shimmied her skirt down and picked up her bra from the edge of the desk, slipping it on. I sat down in the chair and pulled up the file for the hotel.

It was a meeting, after all. Just because there was sex before didn't mean anything.

CHAPTER TEN

Acionna
Phamenoth 2017
Melbourne

THE PARTY WAS in four days, and I was at Ryder Hotel taking images of what the building looked like. The location was nestled in the heart of the city, the Yarra River boarding one side and the botanic gardens boarding the other. It was always so surreal to see that a building was smack-bang in the middle of running water and such an open piece of land, but it made sense. Sort of.

I appreciated the water, even if it was stagnant, only ever so slightly moving, dirty and there were no waves. It was water nonetheless. I ached to feel something other than the splash of water across my back from the shower.

I sighed and took a snap of the river. It was right across from the main train station as well as the business district. Mr Ryder was smart to build there before it was snapped up by another corporation. It would have been prime real estate all those years ago.

'I need to make my way inside,' I murmured to myself. The unrelenting heat of the day, so late in the season, was almost so normal in the city—a fact that I was steadily learning after dropping in and out of the city for many years. I never thought I would be stuck there for a period longer than I wanted to be.

I turned on my heel and dodged the people walking past, potentially going to the hotel or back to work. It was the middle of the day, after all.

I opened the door to the hotel and was instantly greeted with a flush of cold air. I sighed in relief. It was much nicer inside than it was outside.

Bringing the camera up to my face, I snapped an image of the main lobby. There were summer decorations, hints of spices associated with the summery days turning into autumn. They would get shorter, darker and colder. I didn't like the cooler months, but I hoped to be Undersea by then. The small hints of decorations also said more about what sort of people were behind the hotel; they were closely tied to the sabbaths and selkies. I'd had to learn about the magick that came with witches. Mother's training always had to do with a bit of everything in the world, not just the Undersea. Could I pick a witch from a human? No. Most hid it really well, but there were telltale signs, and in a world where being different could get one killed, it was easier to blend in.

The front desk was made of marble, and there were streaks of black, white and grey. It was rather traditional for the hotel, but it was the first one that opened way back when. As if my eyes had been looking for it, there was a plaque on the wall, right next to a wall of photos. I got closer and found that there was Devin Ryder, but the date said 1989, and that would have made Devin … older. I leant in closer, saw that Matthew Ryder's name was under the picture and breathed a sigh. That was a relief. Then again, it wasn't like I could talk. I was thousands of years old …

'It's so mind-blowing that Dad was that young. Or that he looks like Devin.' A voice from behind me pulled me out of my thoughts, and I turned around to see a woman with brown hair swept back from her face and a fringe that came up to her eyebrows with some tendrils of hair that framed her face. Her stormy grey eyes were curious and held a hint of laughter in them. She had similar features to Devin, and even after taking her picture when she was glammed up, the woman was gorgeous in the shorts and muscle tank she was wearing.

'I kind of had to do a double-take,' I said with a smile. 'I'm Acionna.'

She returned my smile and held out her hand. 'I'm Lucy. It's nice to formally meet you.'

I took the hand offered and shook it. Her grip was firm but also comforting. She was so used to shaking hands in a world where it was expected. 'Yeah, Dev told me you were going to be taking photos at the event. Do you need anything now?'

Having Lucy around would make it easier to get around the hotel and not have to disturb anyone—and potentially give me a chance to get an insight into the inner workings of the Ryder family.

'Maybe a bit of a tour guide. I need to take some preliminary photos to see the space properly and understand the angles and the lighting. Do you know any of those details?'

Lucy grinned at me before she shook her head. 'Nope, but I have a phone, and I can call up my brother at a moment's notice.'

I smiled, her grin infectious. 'That does sound really enticing.' I paused and took in the lobby. 'Okay, I'm sold.'

'Perfect. The lobby is going to be like the big reveal. This much, I know. Dev was talking about having some photos of the past on either side and a red carpet, except it's not going to be red, which I think is weird, but he's working with it.'

I took a step back and brought my camera up to my eye, snapping the lobby again. It was big, and I was interested to see what Devin's plan looked like. *I should have done this when he was here so he could have shown me the whole plan.* I liked to do my reconnaissance by myself because it meant I would be able to feel the way the space breathed and the way the light hit certain parts of the room.

I should have done it alone, but Lucy's offer was too good to refuse. And it meant that I would also be home faster. I had to take the night's photo in four hours.

'After the lobby, where to?'

Lucy turned away from me, her brown hair swishing as she did so. I was around humans every day, but Lucy stuck out.

'There are two ways to get to the ballroom. One is via the lifts, which are straight this way,' she said as she started to walk towards the back of the lobby.

'I'm guessing the other option is the stairs?'

Lucy looked over her head. 'Yeah. Devin wants to put clues in both places that will activate some sort of prize in the ballroom.'

'Is it the same one Sir Franklin had his party in?' The party that would have gotten me so many jobs as a result. If I needed human money, I would be overjoyed, but I neither needed it nor wanted it. Yet, I had it.

'No, we're using the grand ballroom. It's about twice the size and more elaborate. We like to call it the Starlit Ballroom affectionately.'

'But you can't see the stars. Who came up with that name?' I chuckled.

'Dad. He has a bit of a sense of humour. Although, I kinda like it.'

I snapped an image of the elevators as Lucy pushed the button to bring the lift down to us. She seemed so at ease in the hotel, like she had grown up within the walls, and I imagined she had.

'Lucy, do you know when this hotel opened?'

She smiled softly. 'Don't I. I think it's funny that there is so much history about the hotel before I was even born. I know Dad had always wanted to do something that moved waves through the world, and he had this idea for a hotel that had not just a hotel but also restaurants, shops and a meeting place for people. I am in awe of everything he has done and achieved. He put so much blood, sweat and tears into this place. Dad worked through the whole hotel too. He wanted to get a feel for what was needed. So he did cleaning, he worked as a concierge, a wedding planner. He did it all.'

The door to the elevator opened with a ding, and inside, our reflections stared back at us in the floor-length mirror. We stepped into the elevator, and I snapped a pic as Lucy pushed the button to floor one.

'So what made him strive for more?' The rest of the elevator was dark. There was a patterned ceiling and the walls were textured. I ran my fingertips over the ridges of the wallpaper.

'He says he wanted to build an empire for us. Something we would be proud of. That we would take over.'

'We?' I raised an eyebrow.

Lucy smiled. It was soft, almost like she was worried she had said something she shouldn't. But instead, she nodded. 'Yeah, I was supposed to do it when Devin was gone. He's back, and it's his now. But part of me … The part I can't really let go of is helping him. I know what Dad wants and what he expects, and I'm just making sure Devin is doing the right thing.'

Devin … Gone? What the hell? Where could an heir to a whole empire go? I wanted to press Lucy for more information, but I knew that it would be futile. It wasn't her story to tell.

'You sound like you're the older one out of the two.' The elevator came to a stop, and Lucy shook her head.

'I wish. Dev is three minutes older than me and doesn't let me forget it. I'm learning to deal with it.'

I laughed this time. I had many younger siblings, and I knew there were a few who would have loved to be older than me, but were not.

'It sounds like he is a really nice brother.'

Lucy tilted her head as she waited for me to leave the elevator first.

'He is the best brother, and maybe this is because I live with rose-coloured glasses, but he has always been the one to look out for me. Always there when I needed him. He was the one I would go to talk about boy problems, parent problems and everything in between. He is the built-in best friend I had before I was even in this world.' She paused. 'Wow, that all sounds so cheesy. I'm sorry. If Devin knew I said that, he'd kill me. You'll have to never utter a word to him.'

I chuckled. 'I don't think there is any room for that. I'm just a photographer.'

The look Lucy gave me was weird, almost like she didn't believe me, but what else was I? I was just a photographer to Devin Ryder. He was the heir to the billion-dollar hotel chain that had been built from the ground up with his father's two hands. I would do my work, and that would be the end of it.

Anyway, I had to get my pelt back. It was more important than anything else.

The witch was going to pay for taking it.

Without another word, Lucy led the way through the hallways. On one side, there were more mirrors, and the carpet was green with yellow lines through it, almost like it was inlaid with gold. On the other side were doors with hefty handles that were meant to be pulled open by men in tails.

We stopped at the very end of the corridor. Right next to that set of doors was the stairwell that led downstairs—and probably upstairs too.

'This is where people who will take the stairs will come up. And the ballroom is just here.' She pointed to the doors I had already been eyeing off. The handles were gold and intricate, like they hid a story of how they mounted to the door, how they were picked and brought down.

'The ballroom.'

'Mhm.'

Lucy pulled the doors open. They swung towards her, and she motioned for me to go through. I did so without a second thought.

'Wow,' I whispered as I stepped into the ballroom. I looked up and saw the towering ceiling filled with little lights that I was sure glittered at night. The walls had panelling that gave them that old feel. You know, the one you would see in Victorian-aged films? The carpet was the same as it was in the hallway, but there was a huge wooden dance floor in the centre of the room.

I pulled my camera up to my eye and snapped the ceiling, the dance floor, the walls, the carpet. As I stepped onto the dance floor, I could see directly out of the tall windows. The skyline of the city would shimmer at night. And suddenly, I could understand why it was the grandest of ballrooms in the hotel.

'I get it,' I murmured.

'I bet you do,' Lucy replied. 'Is there anything else you need? Feel free to spend as much time as you need. I'll just be across the way in the offices. Let me know if you need anything.'

I turned to face her and smiled. It would have taken me so long to figure out on my own, and Lucy had cut down the time I needed. I was indebted.

'This is more than I could need. I'll take some more pictures and be out of the way. Thank you so much.'

She beamed back at me. 'I can't wait to see the magick you pull out at the party. It's going to be great.'

Lucy had a lot of faith in me for someone who had only just properly met me and only seen a snippet of my work. Maybe she was too kind, or maybe she just believed in me.

Either way, I was going to make sure the Ryders were not disappointed with the images and the service.

Athyr 2016
Melbourne

Breaking the surface of the water, I knew the beach. It was oh, so familiar, and it was always warm during those months—my favourite kind of weather, if I was honest. The sand was just like any other, except for that one beach in Greece. That one was different. Probably one of my favourites.

I swam until my feet touched the sand and I felt my skin start to shed, my feet starting to form toes, my webbed flippers becoming hands and my snout shifting away. My brown hair trailed down my back, and I ran my fingers through it to get it out of my eyes. As I walked up to the sandbar, the water dropped to my waist, the wind rustled the fine hair in place of the skin I'd had, and in my hand, a small scrap of pelt appeared—it tied me to my roots and was the only deterring factor of being mistaken as anything other than human.

Stepping off the sandbar, the water rose to my chest again before it started to descend as I got closer to the shore. As soon as I was in my human skin, the world below the surface disappeared, and being able to communicate with my sisters or my mother was null and void. It was weird to have my head be so quiet.

As I walked onto the sand, I saw mothers hiding children's eyes and the lustful look of every single man on the beach. I smiled because any one of them would do anything I wanted, and they would be rewarded with sex. I sauntered past them all to the rocks where I knew I had a bag. It had clothes stuffed inside it, but I knew it wouldn't matter.

'There are a lot of people who would take advantage of your condition,' a man said to me, and I stopped my trek to my bag and looked over my shoulder. He was covered in tattoos, had short hair and a crooked smile, his skin sun-kissed and his eyes a hazel-green.

'Oh, yeah? And are you one of them?' I asked before I moved again. I could see the bag in sight and closed the distance between myself and it. I could hear Tattoo Man following me. I was sure he wasn't going to stop until he got a touch or something. I dropped to my knees and unzipped the bag. I swapped the pelt in my hand, which was a small square now, for a turquoise bikini. I slipped on the bottoms. Sand flicked up, and I was careful to make sure there wasn't anything to get in the way. The top was a bra-style, and I hooked it up and turned to the Tattoo Man, who had an odd smile on his face.

'One of who?' I asked now that I looked at him properly. He seemed familiar, so familiar, and I couldn't place where from or how I knew that.

'One of the mystery girls who come and go as they please?'

I raised an eyebrow at him. 'You mean a normal woman? You know, those people who seem to do what they want and go where they want without the need of a man?'

He licked his lips and rubbed the tip of his nose like he was embarrassed, but there was more to him. Almost like, under the bravado, there was an addiction that lingered. Selkies were not supposed to be addictive. It was why we had sex with multiple men. Too many times with one of them could leave them yearning, and I wasn't about to deal with that.

'I ... Uh?'

'Listen, I'll help you out here. I'm not the woman you're looking for. Go back to your friends while you can, and I'll forget that you were ogling me while I was naked, yeah?'

I picked up a pair of shorts from the bag and slid them over my legs before doing them up and looking back at the tattooed man. It was like he was just too stunned to move or was waiting for more. I would have to talk to the girls back home to see that we moved on from this beach, or find out who was taking it to heart when it came to the men who hung around.

'No, that's not what I mean. I'm sorry. This isn't the normal time I'm around, or that I've seen one of you. But you're ...'

'Look, buddy, I don't know what you're about to say, but for the both of us, let's leave it there. You need to make sure you're home before it gets too dark or you miss your curfew. I've got places to be.'

I turned on the balls of my feet and walked away. *What the hell was with that guy?* It was something that had never happened to me since I'd been going to that beach. Since I was there in Melbourne. I knew something was off, but what was it?

The urge to look over my shoulder was there, but I kept going forward. I could see the stairs to the street right there. I never wanted to leave the beach, but there was a feeling, deep in my gut, that told me I needed to get out or it would be the last thing I did. I gave in and looked behind me. The tattooed man was gone, and my shoulders dropped as I breathed a sigh before I hit something solid.

'Ooph.' It took everything in me to centre myself, but there was a hand on my elbow, steadying me. I looked up at the person who had caught me. Blue eyes as deep as the ocean stared down at me, I pressed my lips together because my first thought was to pull him close and kiss him stupid.

'Are you okay?' he asked me.

I nodded. My voice would betray me, but I couldn't be a mute. 'Yes … I'm sorry. I just had some guy staring at me, and I just wanted to get out of here.'

'Sometimes, boys have stupid ways of showing affection.'

I took a step back because I was still in his space, but he hadn't moved either. 'It's a bit like that,' I said, smiling as I pushed some hair behind my ear. I didn't have a place there, or at least nothing permanent. I was just there to finish the job I had signed up to do and go back home.

'Are you hungry?' he asked.

I tilted my head and frowned. *What is he playing at?*

'Why? I barely know who you are.'

He chuckled—a sound that was warming and comforting, if a chuckle could be. 'Oh, I'm Ben. I like to hang out at the beach, wait for the waves and read girly romance books in my spare time.'

I shook my head. 'I knew it. The girly romance books get them all the time.' I was careful about giving him my name; it was unique, and not many forgot about it once they heard it.

'What?'

'The men. They want to see what happens inside the minds of women, so they think that reading them is the easiest way to get there.'

'I didn't catch your name.'

'I didn't give it,' I said, and stepped around him to make sure I could get past him easily.

He wrapped his fingers around my wrist and pulled me flush against his body. Some would call it unwanted attention, but my body instantly reacted, and I gasped as soon as I felt his body against mine. It was much warmer than mine.

'Well, that is a shame.'

'I think you might be barking up the wrong tree here, Ben,' I murmured, and he grinned, all that boyish charm that I leant into.

'I don't think I've had that one.' He leant down, and his lips hovered over mine. It would have been so easy to close the distance, but it was much too easy for him to get there. I didn't know him—not that that had ever stopped me before. I could entice a man with little effort, but there was something about Ben that made me want to challenge him. No, not want—*need* to challenge him. I wanted to see how far he would go to be able to get me. *Would he get me?* That would be a situation that would be so very different.

'Perhaps there's always the start for it.'

I pulled myself out of his arms and walked away. This time, I looked over my shoulder and saw him staring at me with his jaw agape.

I didn't think he'd ever had a woman walk away from him, and I loved how that felt.

Phamenoth 2017
Melbourne

I'd ditched the camera I had taken photos of the hotel with and swapped it for the spelled camera the witch wanted her photos on. I wondered what her real name was … and if I really wanted to find out. It would give me a sense of power over her, but it wouldn't change anything about where I was or how I could get my pelt back. That was a long game, and the longer I went without my pelt, the more I could feel the sanity I had slowly slipping away.

A hundred days had come and gone since I'd had my pelt. Then 105 days. I was closing in on 150 days since I had felt the salt in my hair, the water in my lungs and the warmth that came with knowing I was home. 121 days, ten minutes and thirty-five seconds to be exact.

The ocean kissed the sand ever so softly, leaving a trail of foam behind, and my body ached for more than those light touches. After being inside the hotel—that was noisy after Lucy left me—I needed the salty air and the coarse sand in my toes. What I didn't need was the people still lingering at the beach. It was an unseasonably warm day. There were many beachgoers who loved to bask in the last rays of the day, but I wanted to be alone with my thoughts and with the ocean.

There wasn't much that could destroy the camera, the witch had made sure of that. As I sat down at the edge of the shore, I didn't care if the camera got wet. It would still work the same. I glanced down at my watch; there were only moments before I needed to take the image, but all I wanted was to forget it all and lose myself to the waves.

Devin had sent through a list of items he wanted shots of. *I wonder if Lucy mentioned she'd bumped into me and shown me around.* Maybe that was what had prompted him to send the email.

> Hi Acionna,
>
> Attached is a list of shots that I 100% need from you. The rest of what you do between them is all up to you, but it's imperative that you can get all of them. There will be a wristband for you to make sure no one hassles you, but also to make sure that you're able to enjoy the festivities as well. Please wear attire that matches anything close to forest green. If you don't have anything, I have a friend who is great at designing, and I can pull from her personal collection.
>
> I look forward to seeing you in two days.
>
> Regards,
>
> Devin Ryder

The attachment had detailed images of what he needed, the angles he wanted and who was high up on the priority to be shot. People like his mother and father, his sisters and their boyfriends and A-listers in that upper Melbourne royalty circle. Names I was fairly familiar with. But what stuck out was that he was willing to help me find a dress. A friend of his could supply me with one. I had plenty to choose from, but I wondered who the friend was.

My watch beeped, and I stood up and brought the camera to my eye. I snapped the sunset without thinking about it. I took another shot and noticed some debris bobbing in the water.

I brought the camera down and squinted, trying to make out what it was. It didn't look like it was a log, or even some sort of animal. There was ... *Is that a person?*

I gasped and took a step back to drop the camera to the sand, wiggling out of my jean skirt and throwing my tank over my head. I couldn't just ... I might have drowned, but the person could have been in trouble. I swallowed hard. Surely, I could get to them and bring them to shore.

'There's someone in the water. Call 000,' I called out and took the leap. It was then or never, and I just had to hope the sandbar held up to its name. I didn't know how to swim without my pelt; I just had to hope that I could float.

There was a flurry of movement behind me, but I didn't wait to see what it was and dashed into the water. As soon as the water hit mid-calf, my mind began to race. *It's too late, you're going to drown. You don't know what you're doing. Go back to safety.*

But it was too late. I couldn't go back to safety. I knew I couldn't, and that was the hardest part.

The body seemed close, and they weren't moving, which made my belly twist in knots. It was too late for them, and I was risking my life for nothing, but no one deserved to be bobbing around the sea alone. They floated into the sandbank because the tide was coming in and not out.

I waded through the water, careful to watch where I was stepping. If there was a single dip, I would have drowned. My heart raced faster in my chest, and I could hear the thumping drown out the splashing of the water. I pushed the water out of my way as my legs carried me closer to the body, and I held my breath. I reached a hand out and tripped over my own feet, my eyes wide as I tried to catch my fall, but found myself scrambling to keep my footing. I was tumbling, and the ocean wouldn't catch me. I knew she was wild, but to know that she wouldn't be forgiving to someone who loved her more than her whole life was something else entirely. My chest ached as I tried to keep myself on my feet and not just plow into the body. As close as I was then, I could see that there was no helping whoever it was. There was an arrow sticking out of his body, and that was what had killed him.

Strong arms wrapped around my waist and brought me back to my feet. 'Careful there,' the voice said, and I looked around. The man was handsome. He had dark hair, deeply sun-kissed skin and a sleeve of tattoos around one of his arms.

'I must have lost my footing,' I said.

He was human.

Everything in my body screamed at me. It was built into me that humans were just there to procreate. My body *wanted* him, but I held it back. It wasn't the time nor the place to flirt myself into his bed.

'Lucky I was here then.'

I smiled. 'Very lucky.'

'What were you chasing, anyway?' he asked.

I gawked. *Can he not see the body that is right next to him? What is he talking about?*

'There's a body there.' I pointed just in front of both of us. He looked, but his eyes were blank as he narrowed them.

'I don't see anything.'

Oh, shit. Oh, shit. The body was spelled so humans wouldn't see it. Whoever had done it had magick, and they knew how to hide a body. The human was not going to understand anything, and I looked like a crazy woman.

'Ummm ... I could have sworn I saw someone bobbing around for help.'

'I would bet.' The man let go of me and started to inch back. *Great, now I look really crazy. I shouldn't have changed my story so fast.*

The normal human police would have done nothing because they wouldn't be able to see the body. The special metaphysical branch would have known what to do with it, but they would also not have been able to tell a soul. If I called, they would have been able to trace me back to my phone and potentially point the finger and lock me up. I would miss a day, and I would be landlocked here forever.

'I'm okay. Sorry. I could have sworn someone was drowning and was in trouble. I guess it was just me.'

I turned to smile at him and realised the nameless man was going to bob around until someone metaphysical found him, and that could have taken days. But it would also have been enough time for him to float in and then right back out to sea, where a shark would have gotten him and devoured him before anyone else would find him.

Who the hell would kill a man, executioner-style, with a bow and arrow?

I let the human lead me out of the water, but I looked over my shoulder as the body bobbed with the gentle waves that took it deeper to shore.

CHAPTER ELEVEN

Devin
Phamenoth 2017
Melbourne

I SLOUCHED INTO THE CHAIR. Dad was out, and I knew I had at least ten minutes before he was back. I rubbed my eyes. The night before was rough. The dream girl was there again. She was so familiar, yet I couldn't see her face, which was beyond frustrating. Everyone else, I could see clear as day, but that woman? There is no way in hell.

Which could have meant that I was supposed to meet her in the flesh or I already had, and there was more I had to learn before I got so close to her. I wanted to know more about her, but I had to wait.

It was … Whew. I didn't think my body had ever felt so intense before. The way she made my skin tingle. *Mmm.* I pressed my lips together just thinking about her. I wanted more. So much more.

The meeting could have been over in a matter of seconds, but I was there because I had to be and because Dad had asked me to be there. I wasn't doing any speaking that I knew about, but I was going to have to do something about the way he was looking at me, like he was trying to get me to do more. I didn't have the mental load to do that. Not with all of the other things I had to do.

I feel like Dad was trying to keep me busy so I didn't leave again—probably the worst thing he could possibly do, but it was okay. He made sure I had jobs to do so he could keep an eye on me.

My phone buzzed, and it took everything in me not to check it. It wouldn't be important. Everyone there was important, and they would be the ones who would contact me.

I looked over my shoulder at the door. It was about twenty steps, give or take, and I would be out of there. I would be in the safe zone of my own space and not there. Not that I had much of my own space, living at home with Mum and Dad.

'Devin, did you speak to Clara about the colouring for the hotel?'

Clara … *Who the fuck is Clara?* There were too many people involved with that project. 'Are you sure it was Clara who had the colouring?'

Trying to remember everyone was the hardest part about the job.

'I'm sure it was. But I could be mistaken.' Always trying to make sure that everyone was in the loop.

'Yeah, I'm not too sure about Clara. But I did speak to the person in charge, and we're waiting for the samples to come through. They should be here any day now.'

My phone vibrated in my pocket. I tried to wait it out, but it kept going.

'Whose phone is that?' Dad asked, and everyone scrambled to look at theirs, fearing they would be singled out.

I reached into my pocket and pulled out my phone. Jarrad was spamming me with messages about a hit.

Fuck.

Without saying anything, I turned on my heel and walked out of the room.

'Devin?' Dad asked. Because saying any more would have made him look weak.

I didn't turn around. Instead, I started walking faster. As soon as I was out of the boardroom, it took everything in me not to sprint out of the office.

As soon as I was in the elevator, I loosened my tie and undid the top button. I called Jarrad.

'I am inches away from setting up a hit on you,' he said as a greeting.

'What is so important?'

'No "hello, Jarrad, I'm sorry I missed your gazillion texts?"'

'Jar, I don't have time for this. What is it?'

'The hit we sent you needs to be actioned ASAP. It's a special case.'

'You said that about the last one, and you promised me there would be more warning.'

'Special cases don't get very much warning.'

'You know I hate this shit. I need time to get through the process.'

Jarrad chuckled. 'You know you are one of the best soldiers we have—and one of the ones who has the worst systems in place. We need you to do the hit fast, and you're not using a bow. Check your email. All of the details are there. The next time I call you, pick up on the first go.'

I heard the sound of the trash icon on a computer and closed my eyes. He had done it for flair, but I knew he wouldn't hesitate to make a hit out on me, and if it wasn't me, he would go for Lucy or Destiny.

He hung up, and I sighed, resting my head against the back of the elevator as I waited to get down to the basement. As soon as it stopped, the chime felt like a drill in my skull, and the doors opened. I pulled the tie out from my shirt as I made a beeline towards the car. The 2017 Ford Mustang was black—that was no surprise as I loved the colour. I clicked the key and the door opened. I slid into the driver's seat and slammed my palm against the wheel before I put the key in the ignition and switched it on. While I put the car in reverse and sped out of the car park, I needed to look at the documents, but I couldn't. Not until I was out of the firing line of the company. Dad would already have been about to kill me. I'd heard it in the way he said my name when I left the boardroom.

I gunned it as soon as I was clear of the pedestrians and pulled over down one of the side streets. I didn't know why, but my breathing was laboured, almost like I was stressed. That was exactly what they had trained us to do.

'Fuck,' I swore. I couldn't believe I walked out of that meeting. The power The Camp still had on me was fucked. *I thought I had gotten past this.* I was the perfect soldier. I did everything they wanted me to, but they still pushed.

I didn't like that I still asked how high when they asked me to jump.

I opened the email and saw a familiar face and name. She was one of my mother's best friends.

Terra Hardy. Forty-four.

The crimes were listed—

Extortion. Murder. Child Slavery.

Harpy.

Motherfucking Harpy.

I dialled Jarrad. He picked up on the ring.

'D-Man?'

'Are you meeting me there?'

'I thought you'd never ask. See you in an hour.'

In one hour, I was about to kill Subira's friend. My mother would be devastated.

I pulled up to the South Yarra suburb. No one would have been stupid enough to pull up in front of the house. Not that they could—there were armed guards, cameras and a pretty high fence that they would need to scale. It was pretty hardcore. I wasn't great at climbing any kind of wall.

I got out of the car and walked around the boot of the car. Pushing the button, it popped open, and inside was a duffle bag with clothes to change into. I stripped off the navy suit jacket and undid the cuffs of the shirt and the buttons, pushing the shirt off my shoulders and wrapping it into a ball before I shoved it in the boot. I grabbed a black T-shirt and a black pair of cargos from the duffle bag.

I slid the shirt over my head and my chest. It fit snug, just the way I liked it. Just as I undid my belt and kicked off my loafers, I heard a chuckle.

'You always were a bit of a showman, D-Man.'

Glancing over my shoulder, I shook my head. 'No, you just liked to think you had the ability to spy when you shouldn't.' I slipped my suit pants over my hips and lifted a foot to pull them free. I dropped them in the boot with the balled-up shirt and suit jacket, switching them for cargos and steel-capped boots. I sat down and pulled my leg up to tie the laces.

'What's so special about this one?' I asked.

'Gagliani was too showy. The bosses need something a little less theatrical.'

'That's bullshit,' I swore. It was like they were unhappy I had killed off someone so easily.

'That's what they tell me. I'm here to make sure you finish the job using this.' In his left hand, he had a brown leather briefcase. It matched the outfit he was wearing. He looked the part with the corporate outfit.

I took the briefcase from him once I had laced up the other shoe, laying it in the boot as I unclipped it and lifted the lid. I shut it immediately at the weapon inside.

'A gun? Are you fucking serious? You know how I feel about them.'

There was something too ugly about a gun. They were cold, calculated, easy. There was no joy in taking a life if it was easy.

Sixteen-year-old me would have felt sick looking at it, but after all the training at The Camp and the death on my hands, this was minute.

'Sorry, D-Man, this is what they said you needed to do. I don't make the rules, I just dish them out.'

Whoever was the top needed to grow a fucking clue.

'Shit,' I muttered under my breath. I opened the briefcase again and got the gun out. It was a Cyclone bolt-action rifle I whistled. It had everything I needed with it. Ammo which were 7.85x51mm NATO, a laser pointer and a scope. It was the perfect gun to kill.

'Isn't she a beauty?' I looked over my shoulder, and Jarrad had a shit-eating grin on his face. Like it was the best thing that could ever happen to him.

'She does okay,' I said. Pulling it out of the case, I shoved parts into one another, slapped the scope on and clipped the strap around it. I slung the gun over my shoulder and looked at Jarrad. 'So why was it necessary for you to come?'

'You know the vic.'

'Obviously. Anyone with two eyes would know she is someone close to my mother.'

'Exactly, so I'm the insurance. If you don't make the shot, I finish the job, then you.'

The words cut like a knife, and I felt a cold shiver run up my spine. 'What? Why is there a sudden target on my back? I've done everything you have ever asked. I've done every fucking hit.'

And as soon as the words were out of my mouth, I realised what was happening. The Camp was testing me. They needed to see where my loyalty sat. Whether it was with them or with my family.

How much have they been watching, and what have they seen?

'I can see that you've figured it out.'

'And they sent you because they knew if they sent anyone else, I'd kill them,' I said without any emotion. I wiped my face clean of anything that could give much away, and Jarrad nodded.

I didn't say anything, and instead checked my watch. It lit up: 3.36 p.m. We were doing the fucking hit in broad daylight.

'So no getting out of this. It has to be done now?'

'Yup. If you stall, I get to kill you,' he said gleefully.

'Don't look so happy.'

'D-Man, I fucking hate this more than you do, but this is what happens. Everyone who is back with their family for too long has the same task.'

I shook my head and slammed the boot closed. I shut the doors and clicked the lock button on the keys, shoving them into my pocket.

The sun was hidden behind clouds, and it was dark and dreary—a typical Melbourne autumn day.

The kind of day I used to love.

Terra's house was a block down, and I knew the tree that over hung her front yard would give me enough coverage to be able to make sure she wouldn't know I was coming.

Jarrad and I skulked through the street. A lot of the suburb had narrow streets that were almost always empty, with lots of townhouses built so closely together. All it would take would be for someone to look out their window and spot us as we made our way to Terra's.

'Broad daylight is fucking dangerous,' I muttered under my breath. 'I bet none of the others had to do it in broad daylight.'

'You'd be right there.'

I didn't say anything because it would be better for me to stay silent. As I stopped in front of the oak tree, I slung the gun to my back and climbed up the trunk. Not only was it a ridiculous hit, but it was also tricky. My car was distinctive—Ford Mustang. It was my everyday car, a present from Dad, who wanted to make sure I stuck around. Like I cared about the materiality of things anyway. The Toyota Klugar would have been more adapted for me—it blended in more, but I couldn't take that one to the office.

Thinking about the car took my mind off possibly getting made in the tree. Jarrad was right behind me. I found the thickest branch and straddled it. There was so much cover, I breathed a sigh—but only just. I had to make sure I didn't move, and I was grateful that it was a dense tree. I took a deep breath and sighed before I used my bodyweight to lean forward and hug the trunk. I swung the sniper from my back and flicked the stand out from the sides, resting the butt of the gun against my shoulder and looking through the peephole. I could see Terra pacing around in her kitchen. She was prepping some sort of food and talking to someone on the phone. I saw her mouth move and could see the AirPods in her ears. I looked to my right, and didn't see Jarrad.

Fuck.

After a ruffle from higher up and farther to the right, I could see him positioning himself. The problem I was having was that no matter what happened, they would be looking in our direction.

'You're going to need to make a move from there or to the left. What do you want?'

I looked in his direction before I shook my head. 'I need you to be on my left. Far left so that when I shoot, you shoot with me, and it confuses the guards.'

'I'm already in the tree and in position.'

I smirked. 'If you want this to be a success, you're going to need to listen. I'm on point because this is my mark.'

'I hate the rules.'

I snickered softly. The guy on point—the one making the hit—was the one who got to call the shots.

I had some control back. I dropped my shoulders and rolled my neck from side to side to crack out the tension. I looked through the scope again and tracked Terra's movements. I wondered who she was on the phone to, who was about to be traumatised.

'This tree isn't as fucking comfortable as yours.'

'If you want comfortable, you are definitely in the wrong job.'

'Someone has to keep you on your toes. Don't dawdle too much. We need this to be fast and clean. Tell me when.'

I went silent. It took everything in me to not turn on the laser sight so I could make it more dramatic, but it would be seen and traced back to where I was. The Camp was all about making it look like it was in and out. Nothing too flash.

And that was why I was getting punished like that; my stint was too public. Even in a sea of everything, it was too much.

I sighed and cocked the gun.

I'm sorry, I whispered in my head. 'Now,' I said as I pulled the trigger.

The bullet catapulted out of the gun with a small punch, the silencer doing its job, and broke through the glass door before sinking into Terra's head. She dropped to the ground. I pulled the gun back and pushed in the rest before I swung it on my back. Everything happened too quickly. Guards—men in black shirts and black pants—pulled out their concealed weapons and pointed them into the direction the bullet had come.

Jarrad and I both fired at the same time so it would confuse them. I slowly pushed myself back on my branch. I needed to get back to the trunk to be able to slide down it ever so slowly. The gun would stay on my back, and we would slink back into the alley. I watched to see where the cameras were because any sort of movement could set them off, but I knew I was out of sight. As soon as I hit the trunk of the tree, I carefully tucked my head down and scaled down. There were no words between Jarrad and me. As protocol demanded, radio silence was mandatory after a hit to ensure that if there was more than one person involved, everyone could get out without being made.

I stepped back into the alleyway and jogged to the corner. Jarrad gave me a jacket—black, of course—that I threw on over the gun to hide it. I adjusted the collar and hoped that we got away without anyone seeing us.

I'd be fucked if anyone did.

Devin Ryder, heir to the Ryder fortune, caught in the death of Terra Hardy—one of his mother's best friends.

Jarrad disappeared with a small pop sound. It was always so jolting to hear, knowing that he travelled where he needed to without much of an issue. His ability to teleport always made it seem like it came out of nowhere, but it was why he was the main man in charge. He could be anywhere in the world without even trying. He didn't need to get on a plane to get to the next person or the next hit. Jarrad just had to single in on an aura, and bam, he was there. As soon as he was gone, I sighed and popped the boot. I pulled the jacket off and unhooked the sniper from my back, disarming and dismantling it, not caring that it went back into the briefcase. I picked up my phone and cringed as the screen lit up.

Ten missed calls.

Two voicemails.

All from Dad.

'Fuck,' I murmured, and slammed the boot shut. I slid into the driver's seat and rested my phone in its place, starting the car and steeling myself for what the first message would say.

Devin Noah Ryder, what the fuck do you think you're doing? How dare you leave that meeting like that. You have embarrassed me and the company. I order you to come back, right this instant. If you don't, there will be dire consequences. This is so unlike you. I thought that after everything, you would make sure you were always here. You promised you weren't going anywhere—I'm on the phone, Lydia—Oh ... Oh, okay.

He hung up, and a rock settled in my stomach. I'd never heard that tone from him before. It was a mixture of disgust and fear, like he was worried I was going to pick up everything and leave again. Like it had been a choice the first time around. I hated Karrept for what he did; for the way he took Destiny and me. Even more so for leaving me at The Camp and turning me into what I became.

I was trained to kill people, and there was no remorse in the scars of the memories I had as a result.

Did I take pleasure in it? Sometimes. Was it something I wanted to take pleasure in? No, but it was either adapt or end up spat out—or dead.

And I needed to stay alive for Destiny, for Lucy. I didn't have a choice, and that was what killed me the most.

I guided the car into a free pocket of traffic and played the next message.

That was unprofessional of me. Devin, I'm sorry. Could you call me back as soon as you can? I would love to get to the bottom of what happened and what caused you to leave like that. Thanks, Dad.

What the actual fuck? That was a different message altogether. It was like there was a flick of the switch, and he had remembered who he was.

I pushed Hunter's number instead of Dad's because I didn't think I could handle that conversation right then.

'Dev, what's up?' He sounded like he was preoccupied.

'Have I caught you at a bad time?' I asked.

'Nah, just a long day at work. I'm just about to clock off after the overtime I didn't know I needed to do. Are you okay?'

I nodded and remembered he couldn't see me. 'Yeah, I'm just avoiding calling Dad back. Have you heard anything?'

'You mean how you stormed out of a business meeting and didn't return any of his calls?'

My stomach sank. 'He called you?'

'Mhm. After Lucy did because he called her first to see if you had gone to help her out or something. What's going on?'

'What did you say to him?'

I wanted to avoid telling Hunter anything that would put him in danger. He was a witch, and I knew that if anyone from The Camp knew, they would put him on their hit list. And that was not a conversation I wanted to have.

'I said that you needed to do something urgently for me. What am I covering for, Dev?'

I slowed the car down at a red light. 'I had a thing to do, and I needed to get it done right then.' It was as much as I could give him.

'Dev,' he warned. I heard him pick something up that had keys that jingled. It was a familiar sound—he always had too many keys on a chain—but it was comforting.

'Hunt, don't ask me. I can't give you what you need.'

'I just want to help you. You know that, right? I can help you. I'd rather know what I'm covering for so I'm not in the dark and can make sure that you're 100% clear.'

It would be so easy to tell him, but would he believe me? Would he be able to see me in the same light that he does now? Would it change our friendship?

'I know. I just … I can't. Thanks for covering for me. I'll make it up to you.'

'You better. Are you going to call him back?'

I didn't want to.

'Yeah. But I might do it later.'

Mum's name flashed through my screen, and that ... was unexpected. 'Hunt, I have to go. Mum is calling me.'

'Say hi to Subira for me.' I could hear the smirk in his voice without needing to see it.

I hung up without saying anything and answered the call.

'Hi, Mum.'

'Oh, Devin. You're okay. Thank goodness.'

'Like I wouldn't be?'

'You haven't called your dad back yet.'

'I was about to.'

I waited for what was to come next, but nothing came. Mum was silent, and I clicked my tongue as the light turned green and I drove on.

'Mum?' I called out.

She sobbed, and I went cold. *Who hurt her?*

'Mum. Are you okay? What do you need?'

She hiccupped, and I put my foot on the pedal harder—if I got a speeding fine, so be it, but I was going to make sure I could get to her.

'It's Terra.'

Oh, fuck. 'What about Terra?' I tried to keep my voice even and not give away anything that could be taken out of context.

'She's dead.'

'What? What happened?'

'I don't know. We were on the phone.' *Oh, fuck ... Fuck!* 'And all of a sudden, she went silent. I yelled out her name, and I couldn't get a response until Javier picked up the phone and told me she was dead. I don't understand. She was right there. We were making plans for tomorrow night, and now she's dead. Who would do something like that?'

Me. I would.

I had to.

'I don't know, Mum. Do you have any idea what happened?'

'No. Javier didn't tell me anything except that she was dead. I didn't think she was dying. She couldn't have been. Terra was healthy. She would have told me if anything was different.'

Would she? I wanted to ask. She was a harpy, and part of me wanted to know if Mum knew, but that would make her an accessory to it all.

'We'll figure it out. I'm on my way home. Is Dad home?' I really hoped he wouldn't be, but it would be about the time that he would be back. Unless there was paperwork that I'd caused.

'He'll be home in about ten minutes. Please make up with him. Whatever you did isn't worth it. We need to be a family right now.'

Be a family. That was what she used to say to me when I was misbehaving as a kid. It was like she knew how to hit that nerve that only she knew how to hit.

'No promises.'

'Dev.' Mum's guilt through her tone was enough to make me want to turn around and keep driving in the opposite direction of home.

How did one explain to their dad that they had to go, and they couldn't give him an explanation without putting their whole family in danger?

'I'll try,' I said. 'I'll see you soon. I'm about fifteen minutes away.'

'See you soon.' I hung up with her and sighed.

I wondered how I was going to spin having to leave because Hunter needed me. how to make it believable. Because I didn't even believe it myself. And that was part of the problem.

CHAPTER TWELVE

Acionna
Parmuthi 2017
Melbourne

'Acionna, do you know where you're standing first?'

Devin's voice pulled me away from my daydream as I stared out the window at the city skyline.

'Yeah, I'm starting by the door and taking snaps as people come into the room.'

I'd set up a professional photo booth to the right of the ballroom as patrons walked in. There was an usher who would direct the masses if they wanted to take their own pictures. I was standing on the left to get the photos of them as they walked in to give them something to start with. Each shot would show up on a board behind me, and they would be able to manipulate the image if they wanted to, or they could just print it out. It was a free portrait for them to take away, the Ryder Hotel logo in the bottom corner.

'Okay, perfect. Let me know if you need anything else,' Devin said, and held my gaze for a little longer than necessary. But I couldn't turn away from him. Something had shifted, and Devin was there, but he was also preoccupied. He finally broke eye contact and turned on his heel. I looked at Lucy, who smiled back at me. I held my camera up to my eye and pointed it in her direction. She tilted her head to the side and held up her glass. Lucy was solo for the moment, but looked stunning in her deep green floor-length gown that was off-the-shoulder and glittered in all the right places with a gorgeous leg split. I snapped her picture and pulled it back from my eye to look at the viewfinder. She looked ethereal, and I motioned for her to come over and take a look.

'Oh, wow! That is … Acionna, you really do have an eye,' Lucy marvelled.

'I try,' I murmured.

'Yeah, trying, my arse. You are so skilled.'

I opened my mouth to deflect, and it was like she knew what I was about to say.

'Just say thank you, Acionna,' Lucy said with a smile.

'I … Thank you.'

'Good. Wait, let me get a pic with Devin. Hey, Dev! We need a picture.'

He turned around to look at his sister. Devin squinted for a moment and then nodded. He was nervous, and far from the cocky man I had met at the initial meeting. I knew Devin had a lot riding on that night, but there was something else under his skin that was bugging him.

'Luce, I have …'

'Dev, this is your night, can you take a chill pill and take a photo with your sister? You have one of Melbourne's most talented photographers here. You've paid her, and she is going to get a nice picture of us.'

Devin gaped at her, and he opened his mouth to say something, but Lucy raised an eyebrow at him, and he shut his mouth. I was in awe of her. She had a relationship with him like I had with my younger sisters. They would bicker the same way, and I would be the voice of reason. I understood that while Devin was gone, it would have been so hard on her. I missed my sisters dearly, especially Aurora and Alina; they would be lost without me, or at least without my sound advice.

'Okay, okay. Let's do this.' He snaked an arm around Lucy's waist. She was shorter than Devin, even in her heels. She leant into him and wrapped an arm around him as well. I brought the camera up to my eye—I preferred to shoot that way than look at the display because I could make sure it was all lined up correctly before I took the image. I didn't want to guess if I'd cut out anything. They looked like twins through my eyes, their brown hair very similar in shade and their grey eyes playing off one another—where Lucy's were stormy, Devin's were calm, like he wanted to make sure no one could penetrate the hardened exterior. I clicked the shutter and took the pictures of two of Melbourne's most famous siblings, then took another and another rapidly. When I pulled back and looked at them, I smiled. They were both smiling easily at the camera, except in the last one. It must have been something unsaid, but they both looked at each other and smiled—the kind of smiles that held secrets only siblings would be able to decode. It was sweet.

'These are great. Did you want to have a look?' I asked, waving the camera at them. Lucy nodded and came over. I waited and watched Devin hesitate.

I brought back the first image as Lucy leant over to see the small screen.

She gasped. 'Holy cow, they look *so* good. Dev … what are you doing?'

I hadn't taken my eyes off him, but Devin couldn't seem to bring himself any closer, his eyes locked on mine. It was the second time that he was just staring. *Do I have something on my face?*

'I … Not sure. I trust that you think they look good.'

'Dev, you need to see the shot. Don't be in such a sour mood. You're going to ace the presentation, and the investors are going to be blown away. I don't know why you're worrying so much.'

Devin raised an eyebrow and walked over to us, not saying anything as he did so. He came up behind me and pressed his body against mine. I bit the inside of my cheek to stop any reaction because as he did so, a shot of electricity ran up my spine. Almost like there was magick in his touch. And there probably was, but this wasn't the time, nor the place to explore it. I looked over my shoulder at him, and his eyes were still on mine, perhaps a little wider. *Did he feel that spark between us?*

'Actually, that is a really good picture. Mum is going to love that.'

'Am I?' another voice filled the room. Subira Ryder took up space in the most stunning taupe gown. It had a V-neckline that was goddess-like, it cinched in at the waist and there was beading all down the main skirt that swished with every moment, a sheath of chiffon trailing around it.

'Mum, you …Wow,' Devin said, and stepped away from me. My body mourned the loss of his warmth, but he made way for Subira to take a look at the image on-screen.

'You flatter me. Oh … that is beautiful. You'll have to snap a picture of Devin and Lucy with Destiny when she arrives later, won't you, Acionna?'

'Absolutely, Mrs Ryder.'

'Subira, please,' she followed up, and I smiled. I wasn't going to change my ways just because she had corrected me, but I would let her think that I would.

'Okay, I can't keep standing here. Everyone is about to start turning up. Everyone in their places. Let's get this going.'

Devin walked away, and I forced myself to take my place and look over my shoulder to stare at him because he was just a man. I didn't understand why I found him so attractive. Well, I did. The selkie in me wanted him. He would be the perfect partner, but sleeping with the man who had hired me to make him look good would be bad … so very bad.

Right?

Tybi 2016
Undersea

The water was heaven. It was warm evermore. Even in the coldest part of the kingdom, it was still warm and welcoming. Allegra came over to me and smiled.

'Acionna, have you seen the list of men that Mama has made for you? Some of them are gorgeous. She's waiting for you to come and choose the one you want, or she will start just randomly promising you to people. I'm not sure that's something that you will actually like all that much.'

Allegra was right. My older sister may have been flaky and weird at times, but she was always right, and that was what was so frightening about it all.

'I'm coming, I'm coming. Have you seen Adella? She said she wanted me to braid her hair before the Matchings.'

Allegra shook her head. That wasn't anything new. Adella was the sister who was always somewhere else, but she was always prompt whenever she got a chance to be primped and spoilt. That's why she was the baby of the family, and why everyone indulged her. It was easier to do so than to hear her tantrum.

I guessed I had to go without Adella. she would probably be there behind me to beg me at some point, but it was weird for her not to be there. I would have to ask her later. I wouldn't have dared ask her in front of Mother because she would scold both of us in front of potential Matches. I didn't want to have to get an earful in front of the man who would be my husband in name. Mother wasn't the most maternal of parents ... All of us were replaceable.

Except me. I was heir. I wasn't the oldest either. Mother just picked somewhere in the middle. Or at least, that's what I told myself. I always thought that our oldest sister, Agate, would be the one to inherit everything, but it seemed like our mother had other plans. I was grateful, even if it meant I was thrown into the spotlight.

'Come on, come onnnnn.' It was Adella, back from wherever she had been.

'Your hair, Little Fish. You were meant to come over, and I was meant to fix it for you, remember?'

'Oh, yeah! I got caught up.' She bounced and pulled me over to the meeting place.

'With a boy? You always get caught up, Della. Why did you ask me to do it?'

'I've got nothing to say to your first question. I do know that I wanted you to help me look pretty, but I know I don't need it now. I've got a Match, but I'm too young. But that's okay, he will wait. He said he would.'

I laughed. The girl's mind was up in the shallows. Adella always had some fantasy that she was all the way wrapped in. This time, it was a boy who would wait until she was ready to be Matched. They would be waiting a long time.

'Of course he will, Little Fish. Come on, let's go.' I wrapped an arm around her shoulders, and she bounced with excitement. I remembered being that young and excited about everything, but there was a point where one had to grow up and really learn to be responsible. I wondered what it would be like if I could forget it all. Just be one of the lucky ones who didn't have to learn about hierarchies, or why Matchings were so important. Mother would never let me throw it all to the waves. There were rules—a code to stick by—and because I was heir, I had to make sure I was the example for my other sisters.

Everyone else was allowed to be carefree and excited about the world. I wasn't. I had to follow the code. I did it because I had to. There was no other choice. The rules Mama enforced would be the same ones I would enforce when she was done ruling, but I could change them ... She would hate them. It was in my best interests to listen and learn as much as I could. Even if I didn't agree with it. Mama had been Matched to my father, and I was the only child who was his. Sometimes, it worked out like that.

Mother wanted me to have a head start, so I was meeting my potential Match before I left for my next stint Abovesea.

Matchings were tiresome. My name would be thrown into the water, and I would be Matched with a man. He would get some time to plead his case, rationing why he would be a great Match for me, and I would have to weigh up everything he said. Except that it would be no easy feat. The man I Matched with would be king. He would need to match my energy to a T. There would be no room for error. A spark would be there, and I would know if there was anything further. If there was nothing, all I had to do was give Mother the nod, and another man would be placed in front of me. It would keep happening until I either found one I could tolerate or one I needed to have in my life. Male Selkies were rare—there were only a handful of them, and most of them would die for a chance to be Matched with a female.

The female had all of the power, and it would always stay that way. I doubted I would find a man I loved. In fact, I knew I wouldn't. None of the male selkies interested me much. I had an inkling that my Matched man would be Abovesea. I couldn't explain why I felt like that, but I had a feeling that I would fall madly in love with a human, and that would be the end of it.

But I wouldn't be able to keep him. I would be a queen. I couldn't be landlocked and tied down. The ocean would forever be my first real partner. I didn't want that to change, but I wanted to know what love felt like, even if it was just for a little while.

When we finally came to the Matching Hall, Adella smiled and went off to sit in her chair. I could see my nine other sisters sitting there too. The older ones had all been Matched and were still in their courting time, trying and testing. They'd all found someone, and I was happy for them. But I still knew I wouldn't find my person.

Ariel was sour-faced. I knew there was a man in the Matching she wanted. I just hoped that he wasn't the one who Matched with me.

'And for the Matching cohort for the first time, my daughter and heir, Acionna.'

I took a deep breath and walked to where my mother was. She had a hand outstretched to me, and I took it with a smile. I looked out at the crowd that had gathered. Because I was Mother's heir, it was bigger than usual. Everyone wanted to see the man who could be their future king.

'Eain, you are first.' As he took a bow, I curtsied, and we took our seats at the table.

No one would be able to hear what we were saying. They would be watching our body language, seeing our lips move, not knowing if we were getting along or not. When we sat down at the table, no one was allowed to break the current surrounding it. It was sacred and a time-honoured tradition, utterly private.

No one made fun of traditions.

'Hi,' I said with a smile as Eain sat down at the table.

'Hi. You look beautiful, Acionna.'

I smiled at him. 'Thank you. You don't scrub up too badly.'

'I suppose you want to hear what I have to offer you?'

I shook my head. 'How about I just get to know you? That would be the proper thing to do. Otherwise, I'll be hearing the same thing from everyone.'

'Well, you don't need anyone else. I'm the one for you.'

I raised an eyebrow at him, impressed. 'Oh, do I now? Do tell me why you're the only one I need.'

'Because I will take care of you. It doesn't matter if you never love me or if you want to take time to be on land for a while. I will always be here, waiting for you. I've loved you for as long as I can remember. I watched you grow, and willed and willed for us to be Matched. I had to push my way to the front because I didn't want to take the chance that you would want someone else and not me. I don't think I could have handled that. So trust me when I say you don't need anyone else.'

I blinked at his statement. He wanted to be the one. I was far more selective than that, but he wanted it to be him. Eain wanted me to choose him so he could be the future king.

'I don't even care about the king part. That's not why I'm here. You being heir is honestly a perk, but I've always seen you for you, and that's all I need. Say something, Acionna.'

I licked my lips and leant into him. 'Does anyone tell you that you're a little intense? Perhaps a little *too* intense?'

'Some people, but I never really listen much. I don't like listening to what others have to say.'

'Oh, you're one of those?'

'One of who?' he asked, and raised his eyebrows at me.

'One of those who pretend like they don't care, but they really do.

It takes a lot of caring to not care what others have to say about you. And you know that's going to be something you might have to learn to do if you are to be my king. Because I care about our people. I care about all of them, and I have to. They will be mine to rule, so I need a man who is willing to care right next to me. Maybe I should try for the next one.' I went to turn around, but Eain covered my hands with his, and it forced me to look into his eyes. They were roiling with emotions, most of which I couldn't grasp. It was forceful and surreal.

'What?'

'I will care. I'll care so much that you'll have to wonder who cares more, me or you, and it might well be me. Pick me, Acionna. Trust me when I say I will wait for you, no matter what. You'll never want for anything, and while I could be unfaithful to you, I will never love another. I will always be here when you need me, and at a single call, I will come running in your time of need.'

'Do you understand what you're saying, Eain? I mean, seriously? You are willing to be basically whatever I need you to be to keep you as my Match. How long have you wanted this?'

He pressed his lips together, and I held my breath. *How could I have missed this?* I had known Eain a long time, just like I knew all of the male selkies, but I didn't know them well enough to care too much. I was always looking after my sisters or making sure that something else was being prepared right. I never took any time for me or any time to look at the men who were interested in me. I had no time for them. But it looked like someone had had the time for me.

'Since that day in the sea ground. You wore a pretty pink shell in your hair. That's when I knew you were going to be the one for me.'

'I was five, Eain.' That was a very long time ago.

'I know. I just knew you would be mine or that I would be yours. There was no one else.'

I looked behind me—not at my mother because I didn't think I could do that to Eain. I looked at my sisters. They were all leaning in, excitedly waiting for a reaction ... All of them except Ariel. Eain was the man she wanted, and he wanted me. I couldn't. I didn't know how to make that okay.

'My sister loves you, you know.'

'I know. But I tried to love her. I wanted to make her happy, but I couldn't stop my feelings for you. I told her before too.' He paused, and with a finger, gently guided my face away from my sister's view so that all I could see was him. His turquoise-coloured eyes shone with adoration like I had hung the moon on a clear sky. 'I need you in my life, Acionna. I pushed to the front because without you, I can't breathe. I feel like there's not enough space around me when I don't see you, and I want to make you happy. I want to make sure you never doubt that you're wanted. That you can do what you need. I want to let you spread your fins. Please let me be the roane who does that.'

I hesitated. To confirm the Matching, all I had to do was kiss him. Kiss him like I meant it, and that would be the end of the Matching ceremony. Behind him were more suitors ... At least ten of them. To end the Matching would mean that we would begin our courtship. *Shit.*

I leant into him and cupped his face.

'Eain, you know there will be no going back,' I whispered as our noses touched.

'I know.'

I closed my eyes and pressed my lips against his. I couldn't hear it, but I knew that Ariel was up on her feet, screaming at me as I kissed him. I put everything into the kiss that he wanted. A mate, a love, someone to mirror and complement him. When I pulled away, I opened my eyes, and he smiled, his eyes full of dreams and love.

'Thank you. I won't let you down. I promise.'

'I know you won't, but you might want to stay out of Ariel's way for a while. She's uber pissed at me right now, and probably you.'

'I told her I was choosing you before this. She's had her time to accept it.'

He didn't know my sister very well. When Ariel wanted something or someone, she went after it, and there was nothing else that came close. If Ariel didn't get what she wanted, everyone knew about it.

CHAPTER THIRTEEN

Devin
Parmuthi 2017
Melbourne

THE PARTY HAD STARTED. I was trying hard to focus on what was going on, but after trying to console Mum and tell her it would be all right, that Terra's killer would be found, my mind wasn't there. I wanted to be done with the killing. Most of the hits didn't bother me. In fact, hardly any of them did. Once upon a time, they had, but not anymore. Not after years of doing it. All that had changed was that Terra had been a friend of Mum's, and her reaction to losing her friend was … It was hard to comprehend.

I had done that. I'd hurt my mother by killing one of her closest friends. She may have been a harpy and doing bad things in society, but at the end of the day, she was my mother's best friend.

Ugh.

My heart wasn't there, but it had to be. I had to command a whole room and unveil a new concept for Ryder Hotel. It was the start of my legacy—a legacy I shouldn't have had.

'Acionna, do you know where you're standing first?' I asked her.

She looked amazing. Her hair was down in soft waves, and she was wearing a forest green jumpsuit that hugged her in all the right places. It was wrapped around one of her shoulders in a tie so her perfectly sun-kissed skin was on show.

'Yeah, I'm starting by the door and taking snaps as people come into the room.'

I nodded and took everything in. 'Okay, perfect. Let me know if you need anything else.' My eyes caught hers, and I started to drown in her aqua blue irises. *What is it about her that is so familiar? Or is it just the magnetism of her aura?*

I broke eye contact and turned around to look out of the window. The view would be the highlight, if nothing else. The night was riding on my ability to present the new Ryder Hotel concept and what was to come. What I would make of it.

My head wasn't in it, though. After Terra and Pete, I felt rattled, like the assignments were too close to home. Terra, especially. *What did Jarrad gain in going after someone who was my mother's friend?*

Camp Devin would be unmoved. I knew it, but watching my mother at home, trying to put together the pieces of why someone would want to kill her best friend was tough. It was even tougher knowing she was on the phone as I had pulled the trigger.

'Hey, Dev! We need a picture.' Lucy's voice pulled me out of my daze, and I turned to face her. She was by Acionna, looking over her shoulder. She moved over to me, and I indulged her in what she wanted. If that was what she needed, I would let her have it. It was the least I could do.

Sometimes, I wondered what life would have been like for her if I hadn't been taken and had been there the whole time. Would she have been the person she was? Or would she have been more reliant? I'd never know. Maybe that was my problem. I was too easily slipping into guilt about leaving her—something I had no control over after Karrept kidnapped Destiny and me. The things I'd done before I was rescued ... I wasn't proud of them. It was a survival instinct, and it kept me alive. I'd thought I was done, but Jarrad and the rest of the army didn't want me to be. I was stuck in it. As long as I kept killing people, my family would be safe.

They had promised.

I watched Luce go over to Acionna and look over her shoulder at the image on her camera. My eyes moved from my sister to her, and she caught my gaze. I didn't break away. I couldn't. I didn't want to. She looked gorgeous in the jumpsuit—no doubt one of Liliana's designs. It had to be.

Lucy's words grazed over me. *What am I doing?* I felt like a fraud. *I shouldn't be doing this.* I would have been better off lurking in the shadows with my bow and arrow instead of being in a room full of people who waited on my every word.

The words out of my mouth were autonomous, and I broke my gaze away from Acionna and walked towards her and Lucy.

I leant over Acionna, the warmth of her skin shooting a jolt of electricity through me. I resisted the urge to show that it affected me, even though I wanted to.

The pictures looked amazing. She'd managed to capture Lucy in her element. She was totally the right photographer for the night. Mum had been right.

It was as if she knew I was thinking about her as Mum walked into the ballroom. I smiled at her. Behind the perfectly set makeup was so much pain. My stomach dropped, knowing I was the cause of that pain. I couldn't do anything to make it better, no matter how much I wished I had the ability to go back and change the hit.

Mum leant up and kissed my cheek. I resisted the urge to wrap my arms around her and hold her close. It was a hard feat, but I squeezed her arm. I wished I could run away and not return, but I had been taken against my will, and I vowed I'd never leave again unless I had to.

'Okay, I can't keep standing here. Everyone is about to start turning up. Everyone in their places. Let's get this going.' I tore myself away from my family and Acionna and forced myself to step to the side.

The room would fill up with investors, people who were a part of Ryder Hotel and those that wanted a slice of what Devin Ryder would do. There were also media outlets coming along. Rhea had mentioned that it would be good press to have them there. And I needed all of the good press I could get when it came to the new direction the hotel had to go in.

'The place looks amazing,' a familiar voice said. I turned to see Rhea staring at me, her eyes ablaze with heat—or at least, they had been. The flash of emotion was gone in an instant, and I was sure she had purposely shown me to remind me of what we did. The sex was great, but it wouldn't happen again. It shouldn't have happened the first time, but the adrenaline and need had taken over. That wasn't the best for my self-control, and I was damn good with my self-control.

'Yeah, it does. But that shouldn't surprise you. You helped with the bulk of it,' I replied.

'I know, but it's always different seeing it in the flesh, you know?' Rhea replied. 'Is there anything you need for tonight?'

A stiff drink.

I rubbed the back of my neck and shook my head. 'I think I have it all. I've got my speech and the prompts. Just waiting for everyone to turn up.'

What if there aren't enough people showing up? What if some of the investors chicken out and don't help? What will happen to the new era of Ryder Hotel?

'You are thinking too hard again,' Rhea said.

'Shhhh. I don't like that you're doing that freaky shifter thing … again.'

She chuckled. 'I think it's more that I was just being observative. You are thinking too hard, and your face becomes too serious when you do so.'

'My face doesn't become too serious …' I caught my reflection in a mirror and saw myself frowning, so I softened my face. My grey eyes were too hard, and I could see the back of the room from the huge mirror that covered one of the walls. People had started to spill in. Before long, the room would be full, and it would be time to go on.

'It does, doesn't it?' Rhea responded with a smirk.

Shut up, I thought, but it would be too childish to say out loud—to Rhea, of all people. I raised an eyebrow and ran my tongue over the back of my teeth.

'This is so important,' I said softly.

'I know. But you're going to be okay. Here are your speech notes, and the slides will be cued. I've got the click, so I'll be able to get you to the right slide as you need.'

'Are you my assistant now?'

She beamed. 'I'm multitasking. Plus, your dad said you needed me more than he needed you.'

'Yeah, yeah.' I took the notes from Rhea and slapped them against my palm out of nervousness. Or just the act of making it seem like I was nervous. I couldn't tell the difference anymore.

Rhea chuckled. 'Okay, you're going to need to socialise with people before you do your speech. You should do that.'

Like I wanted to do that. She was right, though. Once I did my speech, I would have to make small talk with investors, and I hated small talk. 'I guess that's my cue to skip out on you,' I said with a wink, walking away from Rhea.

The patrons slowly filling up the room were dressed in varying tones of green, beige and brown. I hadn't thought that anyone would take it seriously. In fact, Dad didn't even think they would, but it seemed like the socialites wanted to fit in more than they wanted to stand out. I was about to walk over to Destiny and Josh, who had just arrived, when the scent of smelling salts took me out of the lush room I was in and into a memory.

Payni 2012
Somewhere in the desert

It's hard to breathe.

The heat was thick, and every breath felt like it was going nowhere.

I couldn't remember how long I'd been trapped in there—or where *there* even was—but my thoughts kept flittering to Destiny and Lucy. I felt my twin sister through our bond, and she was panicking, her actions are erratic and jolty. It had been over twenty-four hours since Lucy had seen us. *God, or is it more than forty-eight? Or has it been a week already?* Maybe it was all a bad dream, and I was going to wake up and be back home in my own bed.

Lucy didn't like being left alone with Mum, no matter how many times I told her she had nothing to worry about. There was something about Lucy's attention that I could feel. She kept trying to call me back, and I kept trying to will myself to sleep so I could slip into her dreams. But she wasn't dreaming, and I didn't have the strength to tell her. Whatever was in the walls was preventing me from regaining my strength and hold of who I was.

There was no food, no water, and I kept knocking on the walls.

From time to time, I heard laughter coming from the wings, but other than that, it was silent. A pin could drop, and I still wouldn't hear it. I was stubborn—that much was true—and it kept me strong. But just how much could I endure? Like many others, I was afraid to die. I was only sixteen. Sixteen was too young to die. I hadn't had a proper girlfriend, and I wanted to get married someday. I wanted to tell Dad that I didn't want to take over the company right away. I wanted more life moments, and I wanted to watch my sisters get married and have kids. I wanted so much from life. I couldn't be left as a shell of a person.

What if they want to kill me, or use me as bait to get to Lucy? My stomach knotted, and I scrambled onto my feet. If they weren't going to come to me, I would make them. I curled my hand into a fish and banged on the walls, the door, any surface I could. 'Let me out! Let me out of here, you motherfucker. Come and face me like a man,' I shouted.

Which was so ironic because I wanted nothing more than to curl up in a ball in the corner and rock myself to sleep to beg Lucy, Destiny, Hunter—anyone I could get hold of—to come and find me.

The lock unclicked, the sound so loud, and the door opened. Light filtered into the box. I covered my eyes from the onslaught. They'd gotten so used to the dark.

'What is it, little man? You're not going to get anywhere. You think you're so strong. You're nothing.' The voice was rough, deeper than the last one I had heard. I pulled my arm away from my eyes and saw the dingy, blood-stained walls and the dirty floor. The room was devoid of anything.

The man, whose face I couldn't make out, had arms that looked as big as my head. He shuffled through the door, and I scrambled back to get out of reach. Instinct always told one to step back from something that was threatening. Fear was natural. Fear was smart. Did it help me then? Not really. But I felt better being a few steps away from the big goon, and that gave me some confidence.

'Where am I? Who are you?' I said, and made myself stop in place. I could hold my ground and face the bear of a man. It was hard to think of anything but his sheer size, but I focused on Destiny and Lucy. Their thoughts alone could get me through it.

'You'll get to know me soon enough. Have we broken you? You don't look broken yet. He said you have some sort of power. You're a witch, yeah?'

I kept my mouth shut and didn't take my eyes off him.

'I asked you a question, boy.' Before I knew it, he had taken up space in front me. I held my breath. I could smell liquor all over his breath. 'Answer me.'

A fist to the stomach had the air rush out of my lungs. 'Y-yes.'

He grinned a shit-eating smile, smug at the thought that he had a way to make me talk. 'I've always wanted to collect a witch. I think we'll be able to make a fine example out of you.'

His eyes were dark, but they lit up. I watched the cogs turn in his brain. My body was weak from the confinement and the lack of nourishment. *What does he mean, a fine example out of me? What does that ...?*

'Why?'

He punched me again and followed it up with a crack to my jaw. 'I didn't say you could ask any questions. Don't make me tell you again. Do you understand?'

My heart drummed in my ears. I could barely hear anything, but my silence wasn't warranted, and he punched me in the stomach again. Stars flew through my vision, and I could taste blood. I'd bitten my tongue. 'Yes.'

'Yes what?' he asked, gripping my shoulders. He lifted me up and shoved my back against the wall, my feet dangling off the ground, and I tried to find my breath again.

'Yes, I understand.'

He nodded and made a pleased sound. 'Good boy. Now we can bring you out of here. There's only so much solitary one can handle.'

I wanted to ask about Destiny. Had they seen her? Did they know what Karrept did with her? Rocking up at The Camp without her was weird. Being asked my name was weird. And then getting locked up … I could handle a lot, but if I could avoid another crack to my face, I'd take it. I liked my nose, and I didn't want to end up with a broken one that healed crooked because I knew they would just leave it as it was. I swallowed the words on the tip of my tongue and made an effort to take a look around. There were rows and rows of tables, most of which were full of men and women, and all of them had their gaze squarely planted on me. I wasn't a shy person, but suddenly, all of the attention made me want to run. *Can I do it?* The bear of a man held me tight, and I clamped my mouth shut.

The whole room looked weird, like it was some camp lunch hall or something. It reminded me of my first year at school camp. But instead of it being a welcoming space, it was the opposite. Cold, sterile and no one wanted to get to know me.

'New guy here thinks he can talk back. What do we say, team?'

'Get the whip. Get the whip,' they chanted. My brain tried to shield me from it all, but there was no getting around it. They were talking about corporal punishment. Whipping people had stopped years before my birth. Before my parents' and grandparents' births. *Why the fuck is it allowed here?*

Dread filled my body, and I had to make a practiced effort to breathe because the thought of someone whipping me was … too much to bear. The scars it would leave would be enough of a reminder every time.

'Naw, you guys, I think he can wait for the whip. Anyone want to adopt him? He's young, and a witch. We know how rare those are.'

Everyone stood to attention—every single one of them—and turned to face me. My eyes must have been so wide because everyone laughed. It was a collective chuckle that I tried to block out. It felt like, in the next moment, they would pick up their knives and start throwing them at me as if I were a pincushion. *Fuck.*

'Oh, come on. Someone has to want him in his team. He looks like a good fit. We can't leave him alone here. He needs a home.'

I would rather be left alone—even taken back home. But instead, I was there. Karrept had dropped me off like I was nothing, ignoring my pleas and leaving in a poof of sand.

Someone pushed through the throng of people. His hard green eyes were like steel, but he looked at me like he was ready to make me a soldier.

'I've got him. He'll be one of mine.' He held out his hand, and the big guy holding me clasped his wrist in a salute of honour.

'I knew it would be you, Jar. You're only the best. I think this one will love joining your ranks. You'll need to break him in, of course, but he needs it.'

The man whacked me across the back of my head with a hard object, and I fell to my knees. Shadows were spinning in my vision, and I heaved. There was nothing in my stomach, but the pain that radiated through my skull was enough to make me happy I hadn't eaten.

'You're a moron, Jace. You just gave him a concussion.'

'Oops.' There was no remorse in that Jace guy's voice, and I felt arms wrap around my waist, lifting me to my feet.

'Take him to the G-Wing. We need to watch for that concussion the idjit just gave him.'

'What did you call me?' Jace asked.

'Not the time for your macho dick contest, Jace. I have to make sure my soldier is not going to die on me. You're dismissed.'

There was a growl before I blacked out. *Just perfect.*

Parmuthi 2017

'Dev?' Destiny's hand on my forearm took me out of the memory, and I stared at her with wide eyes. It was the first time that I'd had a memory kick me in the gut in a public space. Most of them were just there, but this time … *What the fuck?*

She held my gaze, and Josh crowded in to make sure no one else could see my face—probably the media and Acionna. No one needed to take a snap of me like that.

'Sorry. I'm here. Memory attack,' I muttered.

'What? In broad daylight? What the *fuck*?' Destiny whispered. The anger lacing her profanity was almost cute.

'I don't know. It's never been this bad before.' The only time it had even come close at The Camp was when Nadia and Gidget had been in the room. I had made sure I was never alone with that much pain or those memories again.

Josh handed me a glass. I inspected the contents and found scotch. *What a saviour.*

'Thanks, man.' I took a sip and used it to cleanse my palate. *What the fuck indeed.*

'There's someone here. Someone who has the ability to use some sort of mind coercion,' I said softly. I surveyed the room and brought the glass to my lips again. As I looked over it, I tried to find Gidget's familiar face—the one I had memorised in more ways than one. But instead of seeing long tendrils of black hair, the petite body I would always remember and the piercing hazel eyes, I saw a sea of people who were milling about, chatting to one another. And no one was pinpointed on me. But then again, if I was in a room with a hit, I wouldn't be looking at them. I wouldn't have to. That was part of the problem.

'Are you … What is going on?'

'Dest, I can't get away from anything. You know that this is so hard to do right now.'

'Wait … you're still'—she looked around as if saying the words would do anything—'killing people?'

I took her hand and noticed she was warmer than usual. *Will she stop trying to kill herself in the process now? Is that why she is here? To prove a point? Or is she finally starting to listen?*

'Yes.'

'Devin,' she hissed. 'Why?'

'Because they've threatened to throw Lucy to the wolves. And you of all people know how hard we worked to give our baby sister a normal life. One where she doesn't need to worry about who she is or getting caught. She needed us then, and if I have to do this to keep her alive, I will.'

Destiny tried to interject, and I shook my head. 'They've also threatened you, Mum and Dad.'

'But they're not …'

She didn't finish, but both of us knew our parents weren't plain Jane humans and that they kept what they truly are a secret from us. Like they were protecting us from something bigger than us. We wouldn't be who we were if they were simply human.

'It doesn't matter. I didn't expect to have someone shove memories on me just before a big speech, so you'll need to excuse me. Thanks again for the drink, Josh.'

My sister's husband was something else. He was neither human nor shifter, but there was something else to him. I just hadn't figured it out yet. He wasn't safe, either, which was a problem for my sister, who was undead and needed a necromancer.

I made a beeline for the doors and passed Acionna on my way through. Her fingers brushed against mine. Whether intentional or not, the simple touch put me at ease, and I breathed a little easier. I needed to make sure Lucy didn't catch me because if she did, she would ask questions I didn't think I wanted to answer.

As I stepped into the lobby, I made a beeline to the bathrooms. I threw back the rest of the scotch and checked each of the cubicles while I pulled out my phone. I keyed in Jarrad's number without a second thought. That shit wasn't saved because I'd had to scrub his number from my phone multiple times over.

'D-man. What can I do for you?'

'Pull Gidget or whoever the fuck you have here out. You promised you would leave me alone if I did what you asked. I am *doing* it.'

I ran a hand through my hair as I locked eyes with my reflection in the mirror. There was a haunted look that I hadn't seen in a while. Reliving memories was not on my bingo card for the day.

'What are you talking about?'

'Don't play coy with me, Jar. I just relieved a memory, and I have a full fucking room of people to pretend in front of. Why the fuck would you do that?'

Leather creaked in the background, and I inhaled deeply, trying to sort out the rapidly beating heart in my chest. It just needed to calm the fuck down. The real issue was that someone was closer to the people I loved than I'd realised.

'Look, if it was Gidget, you'd know. It's not. It's a formality. Just ...'

'A formality. Jarrad, I did what you asked. In fact, more than you asked. And you are punishing me like this. Why? Who has their jocks in a knot? Because I will come for them.'

Jarrad chuckled. 'Jocks in a knot ... That's a good one. Just get through this and it'll be okay.'

It wouldn't be. Right then, I knew there was nothing I said or did that would change it. He would make sure there were always people around. While I had been a favourite at The Camp, being in the real world ... Karrept was out to get me. I knew it. He was pissed that I had gotten out, even if it wasn't me who had done it. He was still pissed, and it had been a year since I'd left.

'Yeah, we'll see. Thanks for nothing.'

I hung up the phone and resisted the urge to throw it at the mirror. Shoving it into my pocket, I composed myself. I had a whole-arse speech to talk about, and as soon as I left that bathroom, I'd have to put the Devin Ryder facade back on—the one that was the hotelier's son and heir, not the Dreamwalking Assassin.

With that firmly in mind, I left the bathroom. In the short time, everyone had filled their seats. I caught eyes with Destiny—she was seated next to Lucy—and nodded. Everything would be okay. There was no other option.

I stood to the side. Dad was standing behind the dais. 'Welcome to Ryder Hotel, and welcome to a very important night. It's a night where many of you, previous investors and incoming, are going to be challenged by what's to come. And for once, I'm stepping away from the helm and handing this project over to my son, Devin. Dev?' he said, looking in my direction. Claps surrounded me, and I resisted the urge to swallow past the lump in my throat.

Any sign of weakness was a death sentence in front of investors, much like The Camp had been. I worked hard not to show any weakness. A speech would be a drop in the ocean with all of the killing I'd done.

I got to the dais, and Dad squeezed my shoulder. 'Good luck,' he murmured, and I smiled at him before I turned to face the room.

Many of the faces that stared back at me were unfamiliar. They all looked so foreign, but that was to be expected with people who wanted to donate more money to us.

'Hi, everyone. For those who haven't seen me in a while, I'm Devin. No, I wasn't dead, but that's a story for another time.' A collective chuckle came from the room, and I smirked, putting on all the charm I could.

'As Dad said, welcome to Ryder Hotel … Or at least, as you know it. Under every chair tonight is a word that describes the evolution of what Ryder Hotel will look like under me. If you can reach under your seats and grab that word. I'll give you some time.' Material rustled as each person in the room reached under their chair to pull away a card.

'What does the word say?' I asked the whole room. 'Collectively, let's say it. On three. One … two … three.'

'Metamorphosis,' the whole room chanted.

'Exactly. Like a caterpillar doing its thing, going about its life before it's time to cocoon and wait out the changes to come, Ryder Hotel is much the same. While it was in its caterpillar stage, it was taking its time, waiting and watching what was to come. Building its empire, bit by bit.' I looked down at my notes and smiled. Rhea had put a little smiley face on it as a reminder to smile. 'I'm looking to change it up. We've used the same materials, the same look through each of our hotels, but the locations are not the same. So why should the hotel match our aesthetics and not that of the space around it?'

I grabbed the microphone off the stand and left the notes. I knew the speech by heart, so I could wing it if I forgot something.

'I want to look at the materiality and texture of different stones. Let's look to the future and bring in neutrals, softer stones that look just as amazing. Change up the standard colours of marble, work with different artists and play with everything. The Ryder Hotel you know will still be here, but it'll appear changed, altered. It'll rise like a phoenix from the dead—just like I did.'

There was a collective gasp around the room. Everyone had been thinking about it before it came out of my mouth, and I wasn't about to sweep it under the rug.

'Any guesses on where the newest addition to Ryder Hotel will be?'

Every pair of eyes was trained on me, and it took everything in me not to run away from it. I smiled, and instead took a step aside. 'Maybe it'll be another in Melbourne? Or perhaps Adelaide? Maybe even Sydney, hmm?'

No one took the bait, and that was fine. I didn't expect them to.

'It's probably Queensland. You're waiting for a few more on the east coast, for sure. And it would make more sense to have the first one open over there. The materials would fit in so well, and after saying that we would look at the materials of the surroundings, maybe some of you could entice Matthew to let me open one there.' The room chuckled, and I turned my back to look at the slides. The hotel would be closer than they thought, and I was excited.

'What if I told you we were refurbishing the very one you're all inside?' A collective gasp flitted through the room, and I knew it was not what was expected. I turned on my heel and waited for the slide to click through. 'Or if I told you that we are opening up on the east coast and refurbing this one at the same time?'

Was I insane? Yes. Absolutely insane. But Dad had come up with the idea of doing both; a mini refurb to test what it would look like here, and opening the one in Queensland. 'That's right. We're doing both. If you will dig deep and help be a part of history, this is your chance to have a part of Ryder Hotel in your back pocket.'

Applause broke out, and people were on their feet. I smiled and nodded as Dad came up beside me, clapping with the rest.

'You did so great, Dev. Welcome to the fold.'

Those words should not have eased anything in my chest, but they did. I hadn't realised that I was still fishing for my father's approval after everything I had been through.

CHAPTER FOURTEEN

Acionna
Mechir 2016
Undersea

SINCE OUR MATCHING, Eain and I had been scarcely apart. I didn't love him. I told him I didn't think I would, but he was okay with that. He was giving me the time to grow and explore new things. I was leaving for the surface in a matter of hours, and he was okay with it. Eain knew I wouldn't be back for some time—a normal outing for who I was. It was encouraged to go Abovesea to take some time with humans. Really, it just meant that we were expected to copulate with humans, get pregnant and bring the babies back. I was perplexed that there was that connection between us, but also that he was okay with the level of non-touching between us. Eain wasn't someone who wanted to keep me locked up and out of reach of what really mattered: the throne. It was at the top of my mind as Mother became more and more invested in our lives. I could see her already picking out the drapes that hang in our wing of the castle—a weird concept to even think of because I was used to my own space.

I moved through the corridors of the castle, taking in what would be ours when a voice pulled me out of my thoughts.

'You bitch!' I was tackled to the floor, and someone clawed at my face. Instinctively, I put my hands up to stop the onslaught of nails.

'Ariel!' Allegra pried our sister off me, and I scrambled back and clumsily got to my feet.

'What the hell, Air? What's gotten into you?'

'He was mine, and you picked him! Mine! We were meant to be.'

Eain had assured me that it was over, that Ariel knew about it, and rightly so.

I shook my head at her. 'He said he was ready to give you up, but you didn't want to give him up. Give it up. He's going to be my husband, and you need to find another Matching.'

'But I *love* him.'

I shook my head at her. 'Love has nothing to do with it. It never has. It's why Mama picked me to be her heir and not you. You're too hot-headed, too ruled by your emotions to think about anyone but yourself.' Ariel wouldn't be able to rule with a clear mind if she had it up in the corals.

'And you're not? You're a walking emotion, and now you're just placated by the man who was meant to be mine. Why can't you get your own? You had a whole pick of many more Matchings, and you had to pick the one who was mine. You're a bitch. I hate you, and I hope that one day, you understand what it's like to have this much hate for someone.'

I could have corrected her and told that Eain had picked me first, but she wouldn't listen to reasoning. And by the way her chest huffed and puffed, Ariel was dead set on what she thought was hers. And that was that.

'Air. I love you. You're my sister, you can't hate me. I won't let you. There will be someone else who is meant to be Matched with you. I know you will love him, and he will love you back. You just have to let it happen. Wait for it to happen. I know it'll be soon for you.'

'I curse the day you were born, Acionna. If you were never born, it would be me with him and me as the heir. Mother would care about me more than she does you.'

I gasped. *How has it come to this?* Ariel was my sister, older by a few years, and she was acting like the baby of the family. The fact that she hated me enough to curse me … I felt something inside me snap, and I knew that my own sister would never be happy for me. She wouldn't want to be at my wedding or to watch me have children and someday take over the throne. Ariel was …

'I'm going to tell Mother about you, about how much of a thief you are, and she'll kick you out. She'll make sure that you never come back, and she'll disown you. Why would she want you?' Ariel asked.

I blinked and tried to find the words to reply to her. She was out of line. More than out of line—she was in a different ocean system altogether. 'Take a deep breath and calm down. Tomorrow will be another day, and this will look a little different. I promise you, Air. You're hurting, and I get it.'

Allegra let go of Ariel, and she swam off in the other direction. I watched her leave and turned to Allegra. 'Did I do the wrong thing, Alle?'

She shook her head. 'No, she's being a drama queen. You are allowed to pick whoever you like for your Matching. It was *your* Matching, not hers. Ariel wants what you have, and she is trying to be a bitch about it all. Don't take it to heart. We all know how much of a hot-head Ariel has always been. She was like that from the womb.'

I hoped that Ale wasn't lying because I didn't think I would have been able to survive if my sisters turned on me.

'That scene was uncalled for,' I murmured, and looked around at the peeping eyes that stared back at me. 'Let's go somewhere else, where there are less eyes.'

'Yeah.' Allegra took my hand and we made our way back to our living quarters. They were just to the left of the space Ariel caused a scene in. Mother would hear about it, no doubt, before I could tell her what had happened, and she would chew my ear off about how it wasn't very regal to fight with siblings in the light of everyone else.

'Alle, Eain swore that he broke up with Ariel and that he had told her. I can't change what Mother has decreed or that Ariel is older than me.'

Allega sighed. 'Ariel has always been a troublesome little fish. Her jealousy has stemmed from anyone younger than her. She was so used to being the baby of the family, and anyone after her was dimming her light.'

'Alle … There are four of us after her.'

'I know.'

Allegra was my older sibling, and probably the one who had the most experience with life. She also had a child of her own and a husband who was devoted to her but still allowed her the freedom she deserved.

'Eain is a fine man. I watched him strong arm his way to the front. Ariel didn't see that, but he made a winning case, didn't he? You're pretty level-headed, and I know your decision was definitely about the throne and not love. I can tell that much, and it would have been amazing for you to have gotten a love Matching, but you'll make it work. Ignore Ariel. It'll blow over, and she'll be back to her annoying self in no time.'

If only it was that easy. I knew Ariel wouldn't let me forget it, and she would make sure that life was not easy in the slightest.

Pachons 2017
Melbourne

Devin had called to meet up and go over the images. I had been working on editing them between jobs and the monotony of taking the same picture over and over again. As the season changed, the sky did, too, taking the tide with it. Each image was different, the waves lapping inwards one day and then further out another.

I checked my phone for the time. It was 1:26 in the afternoon. Devin would be there in four minutes. *Why am I suddenly nervous?* Janice was somewhere else in the house, or she could have stepped out, for all I knew. Either way, I was going to be alone with him. *What was I thinking?*

I swiped my fingers over the trackpad. The images from the party night were so good. The photo booth alone was so successful with the number of images I'd gone through already, but the ones I had taken of Devin doing his speech and all those after looked so good.

A knock on the door pulled me from the computer, and I stared at it for half a second. He was early. *Why did I decide that this was okay? Who am I?*

The butterflies in my stomach—a feeling that was actually foreign—seemed to flap a little harder. I took a steadying breath and walked to the door.

'He's just a guy,' I whispered to myself.

I opened the door, and Devin stood there with flowers in one hand and a bag in the other. He was wearing a light grey T-shirt and black jeans with a black cap.

'Hi. Sorry, I brought food. I didn't know if you'd eaten, but I haven't, so I thought sushi was a good choice. Oh, and these are for you, as a thanks,' he said when he held out the flowers. There was a mixture of green, purple and blue florals and foliage.

'Hey. Oh, wow. I hadn't, actually, but you didn't have to …' I said.

We stared at each other for half a second like we were waiting for the other to say something more, and that's when I realised. 'Shit, come in. Sorry, I'm not used to having people come over.'

At all. I had made no friends, and that was the way that I liked it. But Devin was there. It was all business. I stepped out of the way and motioned for him to come inside. He smiled at me and walked through the doorway. The door opened up into a corridor that led into the main living area.

'Just follow the corridor down,' I said, and he nodded. I stepped back into the house and closed the door, resisting the urge to lean against it and stare at him as he walked away. *Who is this person?* I didn't get attached to men. In fact, it was built into my genes, but there was something about Devin Ryder that made me catch my breath and want to be around him more than usual. Men were naturally attractive. As a Selkie, there was an instant bond there, but that was because we came to shore to sleep with and potentially have children with them.

I walked after him and let him take a moment to look around, as was human nature.

'Sorry if the place is a bit of a mess. I've been non-stop editing to get these images to you as fast as possible.' I'd been working double-time to get them to him. For a job this big, it normally took me two to three months to get the images back. To get them finished within a month was the biggest feat I'd ever managed to pull off. I put the flowers on the island bench with the intention of putting them in water later. It was the first time a man had gotten me flowers Abovesea before … It was nice.

'Look, it's way tidier than my room, and that is saying something,' he said with a chuckle.

'Take a seat.' I pointed at the dining table where I was currently set up. 'Can I get you anything before we dive in?'

He shook his head and started to unpack the food from the bag. 'Nah. If you want plates, we can do that, but otherwise, we can just use the containers?'

'I'm not too fussed. Dishes can go into the dishwasher,' I said with a smirk. He smiled and took the lids off the sushi boxes. There was a gentleness to the way he did it. Devin methodically took out the chopsticks and opened the packets before cracking them so they were separate. I grabbed a couple of cans of drink from the fridge and walked back over to the table. Placing them down, I realised I didn't know what else to say to Devin. I hadn't spent any time with him since the event, and the one time before that had just been pure banter.

'The images turned out really nice. I'm excited about them,' I said as a starting point. It was like that was easier to broach than whatever was happening there. 'I'm excited to see them. You will have done an amazing job. But I also want to apologise for the way I barked orders on the night. It was a pretty stressful event, and I didn't mean to cause any offence.'

'I ...'

He shook his head and held up a hand that had chopsticks already poised in them. 'I know I was a bit of a nightmare. Lucy reminded me that I needed to make sure I apologised to everyone. I don't make a habit of doing shit like that. I had some things happen earlier that had really riled me up, and I took it out on the people who were helping and trying to make it successful. I shouldn't have done that. Can you forgive me?'

I leant in and picked up a set of chopsticks. 'Look, that was a pretty hard night ...' I stared off. His eyes widened, and I chuckled. 'No, it's okay. There is no need. I've been in worse situations, so it's totally okay. I appreciate the business and getting the chance to take pictures. It's something I love doing, so thank you.'

Devin's shoulders dropped, and his posture relaxed. He had been gearing up for a fight, which was so very interesting, but I wasn't going to do that. Not to a man who had made me not have to worry too much about work for a while—he'd paid my fee and then some.

'I appreciate it. Now, let's eat before we dive into the images you're so excited to show me because ... Well, it won't get cold, but it won't actually ... Oh, god. What if you're allergic to sushi? I didn't even think. I just figured it was something that was easy. What have I done?'

'Who are you?' I asked, and he looked at me with wide eyes.

'Devin Noah Ryder. And you are?' he asked, and held out his hand.

'Acionna—uhhh, Kirby.' I took his hand and said the first name I could think of as a last name. Selkies didn't do human conventions, but if I had to keep up the facade, I could do that.

'Nice to meet you.'

'You were giving me so much lip the first day I met you, and now, you're offering me your hand,' I said, and held out. Devin's hand was warm yet calloused, like he had spent a lot of time using his hands. I noticed there were some scars on the back of his hand, but I didn't say anything.

'Absolutely. It was like a test to see what I'm challenging.' He squeezed my hand and held my gaze. There was something in those cloudy grey eyes that made me want to lean.

'That would be challenging the cliché, wouldn't it?' I said, and he grinned and let go of my hand. Devin picked up some sushi—it was salmon—and popped it into his mouth.

'And to answer your question, I love sushi. It's one of my favourite foods.' Well, the part on top of it. The rice, not so much. The carbs that came with it would be hard to digest, but that was okay. It was temporary.

'Oh, good,' he said around his food.

I laughed and grabbed some of the sashimi first—it was tuna—and popped it into my mouth.

'You did that without any flavouring … What?'

'Can't handle raw fish without something on it?' I asked, raising an eyebrow.

'I definitely can.' And to prove a point, Devin picked up a piece of salmon and plonked it into his mouth. He chewed and made it look easy, but I watched the ways his eyes wouldn't meet mine and chuckled.

'Okay, strong man, you don't have to look like someone has tortured you.'

Devin swallowed the fish and covered his mouth like he was being demure, but there was a glint of laughter in his eyes, and I bit my cheek to stop myself from saying anything.

'Look, I know it's good, but it definitely needs flavour …'

'That's your opinion.'

I poked at the tuna with chopsticks and picked it up with ease.

'I know this could have been done at the hotel, but I wanted to apologise if I was rude. Actually, I know I was rude. I was barking orders like it was nobody's business, and that isn't me. That's something my dad always did.'

I held up a hand, the chopsticks roughly held between my fingers, and shook it to make my point. 'You don't have anything to apologise for. I was a worker. You're entitled to boss me around.'

'No … You don't understand—' he started, but I wasn't finished.

'You're new at this, and you're going to need to get a backbone when it comes to being in charge. I don't mean to come across like I know it all, but you're going to need to make hard decisions and boss people around. It comes with being a leader.'

Or the king of an empire. Mother used to tell me the same thing, and while she wanted me to sit on the throne and rule, I didn't know if I even wanted to do it anymore. Not after being in the human world. Or maybe the challenge of being there would help. I didn't know.

'You say that like you know where I'm coming from.' Devin frowned at his food before he looked up at me. 'Do you have some secret identity that is more than the most sought-after photographer in Melbourne?'

'If you hang around long enough, you might find out,' I said, meeting his gaze. A shiver ran down my spine and settled somewhere low. The way he was looking at me had me wanting to understand why he was really there. *Is it to see the images, or is it something more?*

I broke eye contact, and my gaze snagged at the flowers I had left on the counter behind him. *I should put those in some water.* I got up off the chair, keenly aware of the way I felt Devin's eyes on me. I didn't need to do it then, but I wanted to do them to avoid the situation of what could come out of my mouth. Or what could come out of his.

'You're so confusing,' he said.

'You are too,' I replied, and stretched up to reach the cupboard. I was on my tiptoes and pulled a vase off the top shelf. I turned around and found Devin right there. I gasped.

'There is something about you. I can't figure it out, but since I first saw you at Sir Franklin's, all I can think about is how to see you again.' He pinned me against the counter, his arms on either side of me. The vase was between us, but right then, it could slip from my fingers, and I wouldn't care.

'What are you doing, Devin?' I murmured, and he shook his head.

'I don't know.' And with that, he lifted a hand to turn his hat backwards. My knees felt weak, and he took the vase from my hand and put it on the counter. With the same hand, he cupped my cheek. 'This may be too forward, but I'm going to kiss you now,' Devin said breathily, and leant in. I could have pushed him away, but the butterflies that had been there when he knocked on the door were back, so, instead, I closed my eyes. His lips pressed against mine ever so softly before he deepened the kiss. I kissed him back, hands going to his waist to bring him in closer than he already was.

I'd been kissed plenty of times before, but this one ... It was different. It was like something was finally sinking into place, and we were right where we were meant to be.

The ferocity of the kiss picked up for a moment before Devin pulled back slowly, letting our lips naturally part.

'Wow,' I whispered, and opened my eyes slowly. I was staring into stormy grey clouds that were ready to hail. They swirled with so much emotion, and I couldn't understand what it was—it was almost like he had done something he shouldn't have.

'I haven't felt anything like that in years,' Devin murmured. 'Sorry if it was too forward.'

I shook my head. 'Don't apologise for showing emotions or acting on them.' Everything in my body was screaming for me to jump him, take him back up to my room and have my way with him. The innate reaction that was the norm wanted me to do it, and I wanted to so badly, but Devin wasn't there for me to sleep with him. He was there to look at photographs from the party. That was what he was there for ...

'It's a new thing ... The emotions, that is.' He didn't move and still had me pinned against the bench.

'We should look at the pictures, maybe while we finish lunch.'

'Good idea.' Devin pushed himself away from the bench, and my body mourned the loss of his heat and closeness. She was a traitor. I pressed my lips together and nodded to myself more than anything. The flowers could wait. I needed to take Devin through the photos sooner rather than later, before we did anything we would be proud of.

CHAPTER FIFTEEN

Devin
Payni 2012
Somewhere in the desert

I FLITTED in and out of consciousness, and honestly, it was the best fucking sleep I'd ever gotten. Normally, my sleep was a state of dream-riddled consciousness that wouldn't let me have any real rest. It was bullshit most of the time, but occasionally, it actually helped. Dreams could re-energise me, but that brought a whole different level of trouble too. Even at sixteen, it was still trouble.

Groaning, I tried to sit up, but the room started to spin. I shut my eyes instantly and lay back down, covering my eyes with my forearm to stop the spinning and feel my arm tug. My eyes shot open, and I forgot about the spinning room, seeing that I was hooked up to a drip. 'What the fuck?' I murmured. There was a girl next to me checking some stats.

'You're awake. Look at that. Let me get Jar.'

I reached out and gripped her wrist. 'Where am I? Who are you?'

She smiled, and it was probably the first hint of friendliness I'd seen yet. 'Oh, he's going to like you. He likes those who ask questions.

I'm Layla. You'll find out more soon. Hang in there, and try not to close your eyes. I'll get Jar.'

She was gone before I could call her back. I wanted to demand to be let go, to tell her, but she literally blinked out of the room, clipboard and all. It was like some X-Men shit. I blinked at the space where she had been. *What the fuck? Am I siting with people who are happily powerful?* The world wasn't cut out for metaphysical beings, and if the plain-janes knew I could jump into dreams, I'd be facing the gallows without a trial. I wanted to tell Hunter. He would be able to find out where I was or if the place even existed. It was what he was good at.

Fuck, could I get in touch with him? He could help me. He was always— No, he was angry at Luce. He wasn't going to come after me when he had shut down everything to make sure there was no bleed off from her. It was hard to get used to calling him again when sometimes I could think him over to my house or slip into his dreams. Daydreams too—those were fun to play around with, but he was completely closed to me. Probably for the better.

Jar walked in. He had on a cap, a T-shirt, cargos and heavy, shit-kicking boots. They were probably steel-capped. He sat down in the chair opposite me and leant in.

'Oh, good, you're awake. I'm sorry about Jace. He lets his authority get to his head sometimes. I was hoping to save you the humiliation, but he got there before me. What's your name? Layla said you spoke, but no one knows your name, and no one can get into that thick noggin of yours to find out. You have a nice strong wall going there. Most don't.'

I baulked at him. He was actually nice and talked to me like a human being. But there was an instant sense of distrust. I narrowed my eyes and looked around the room. It was a typical hospital setup. There was the bed I was in, a table that would have wheels, a few chairs and things beeping. It was cold, sterile, utilitarian. A shiver ran down my spine, and I pulled the scratchy blanket higher up my chest. I realised I was practically naked. *Oh, fuck.*

'Why does it matter?'

'I'd prefer names over numbers. Let's try another. What's your flavour of ability, magick, whatever you call it?'

No one I had ever known or read about had the ability to walk through dreams like I could. It was an anomaly even in my family. I didn't think I wanted to tell them that, though. I looked Jar in the face and kept my expression as blank as I could. I was only marginally good at playing poker.

'Walls. I can put up psychic walls.'

'Lie,' Layla said without looking up from her clipboard.

Can she smell a lie? I didn't like that there was someone around with that ability. Or at least, she had some sort of shifter in her. They were the ones who could smell a lie.

'Dude, we are all very honest here, but we need to know what you are so we can start to train you right. So people like Jace don't take advantage of you.'

'I can't tell you.' The words were out of my mouth before I even stopped myself, and I waited for the hit—the one I knew was coming. I shut my eyes tight and waited, but when nothing came, I opened them one at a time. Green eyes started back at me.

'You'll tell us. Eventually, you'll have to.' He stood up and leant in. 'You're in a community now. We take care of everyone, but if you can't share, we'll have to let you go. And I can tell you this now, leaving The Camp is going to be harder because you're either with us, against us or in a body bag. I don't want to lose my first recruit to stupidity.'

He held out his hand, and I took it like I had just confirmed that I would be there. Jar pulled me up, and the room spun for a moment before it levelled out. I gripped the blanket with my other hand. I wasn't normally a modest person, but I didn't want a stranger to see me completely naked.

'Get dressed. You've got some food to eat before training. You'll be happy for some real food, believe me.' He squeezed my hand and dropped some clothes on the bed. Layla unhooked the drip from my arm, making sure there were no sticky electrodes left on my bare skin.

He smiled and left the room, and I took in the clothes. They were all black, and the boots looked heavy. I picked them up, and the weight of them was enough to make me rethink it. *Steel-capped for sure.* But also, I was sixteen. I needed food, and if I had to put on those boots and clothes to get fed, I was going to do it. I wouldn't be there for that long. In no time, I'd leave and be back with Lucy and Destiny. I was going to hold onto that hope. I swung my legs out of bed and slipped the black T-shirt over my head, careful to not move my head too much. There were some boxer briefs tucked in there, and part of me was glad—free-balling it with random strangers was not my idea of fun. I finished getting dressed and laced up the boots. I couldn't see my reflection—there was no mirror—but I could see Layla in the corner of my eye. She smiled at me, and I turned to face her, but wished I hadn't. Her sepia-coloured eyes swept down my body and took in the way the clothes hung off my body before she looked me in the eye. Hers were filled with hunger, and I swallowed past the lump in my throat. I groaned, and my body reacted to that heat. Being a sixteen-year-old in that situation didn't work in my favour.

'Fuck,' I whispered under my breath just as the door opened. Jar was standing there.

'She got you too? Layla has a way with men,' he said as he held the door open for me. 'Don't let her actually get her hooks into you. She won't let go.'

I looked down at my boots, and he stopped me and made me face him, his fingers under my chin to guide my head up so that I met his eyes. 'I haven't earned you averting your gaze, not yet. Layla is a jokester. She uses it to her advantage, but that won't be the last time you see her.'

Jar guided me away from the hospital room and down a corridor that was as cold and sterile as the hospitals back home. We turned a few corners—left, right, right, straight, I lost count—my head throbbing from the movement, but we stopped in front of double doors at the end of one corridor. I assumed it led to the dining area, but what I found was open air and the smell of the sea. But before I could bask in it, everything went black again.

Payni 2012

I groaned as I came to. I went to lift a hand to rub the back of my head, but I couldn't move them. They were tied to the chair I was sitting on. The strong scent of smelling salts was in my nose, spicy and unpleasant.

'What the fuck?' I muttered.

'Oh, he's coming to. Jar, come see,' a voice said.

My head felt thick, like it was full of cotton, but it was throbbing. *How hard did he hit me?*

'What's your name?' the guy asked me. He got down to my level and rested his arms on his knees. My vision focused and I could see Jar staring back at me. He had green eyes, brown hair and stubble that said he was at least three days behind on his shaving routine, but there was something in the way his eyes searched mine.

'Why do you want to know?'

Normally, I would have told him, but after being hit in the back of the head and being tied to a chair, I thought I had enough to make sure I could keep my name.

'It doesn't work like that.' He tilted his head to the right—or was it my left? 'I could get your name out of you against your will, but I feel like that's a little too extreme. I could try and call Karrept back, but I don't know if that will work either. So I'm going to ask you again. What is your name?'

He pressed his hands together, leant his chin against his fingers and waited.

'Am I supposed to be scared?' I asked.

'Perhaps. But I'm hoping I can plead to the better side of your mouth, you know? Save you some pain.'

I raised an eyebrow. 'Pain? What for? I don't even belong here.'

Jar clicked his tongue and smiled. There was something sinister in the way he did that. He didn't say anything else and stood up.

'Nadia, I think it's time for you to do what you're good at,' Jarrad said, and he didn't even look back at me as he said it. But a woman with skin as dark as chocolate with dark eyes, stepped in front of me. Her hair was tightly packed in braids. I supposed it was easier to manage. I didn't know for sure, though.

She looked right at me and began to sway. I swayed with her. Her smile was different, soft, —welcoming, even.

A sharp twinge started in the base of my spine, but I continued to sway with her until the twinge turned into something more. I bit the inside of my cheek as the twinge turned into what felt like someone stabbing a knife into my back. I couldn't breathe, and the more I stared at her, the more I wanted to cry out. But I held back.

What the hell is going on? Why are they doing this? Why am I even here?

Stars exploded through my vision, and I couldn't see Nadia anymore. I couldn't see anything but the pain that suddenly wracked every inch of my body. It was stabbing, searing-hot pain that was relentless. It didn't stop.

I couldn't stop the scream that was ripped from my throat with the next breath.

And then it all stopped.

I pushed my body into the chair, and my head hung as I tried to form the words and catch my breath. I had never experienced pain like that—ever.

'That's but a taste of what is to come. All you have to do is give me your name, dude, and it'll stop. We don't normally hurt recruits on the first night, but I can make an exception. Well, you can see that I have.' Jarrad paused. 'What's in a name?'

Did he just fucking quote Shakespeare at me?

Breathing hard, I lifted my head—it felt so heavy—to find his gaze. 'What do you need a name for? Give me a number and be done with it.'

He chuckled. 'It doesn't work like that. I need your name, or you're going to stay here until we get it. It's early—something like 3.00 a.m. I can stay here all night. I've had enough sleep, but you haven't. And the more pain and strain we put on your body, the more it'll take out of you. How's that bump on the back of your head?'

When he mentioned it, pain flooded through my brain, and I squeezed my eyes tight. The stars were back, but this time, all I could see was red. There was no other vision. The bile rose in my throat as I felt the hurt move deeper. The pain was sharper than it had been before, and my whole head throbbed. *Thump. Thump. Thump.* I couldn't stop it from rising and spilling out of my mouth, but I narrowly missed my lap as I vomited from the agony.

'Oh, vomit. Nadia, pull back a little.'

'Are you sure?'

'Mmm …'

The pain stopped, and I wished I could wash my mouth or wipe it with the back of my hand. But my hands were tied, and I didn't think they would be in the giving mood for that water.

'Just give us your name. You don't even need to give us your full name.'

My last name was well-known. I knew that. Dad's hotels were in every major city. His brand sponsored a lot of athletes and sporting figures. Jarrad could trace me back to anything if he had that. But my first name … It was common. It was a unisex name, so it wouldn't give him anything. But my pride was more in the way, and I knew it.

I licked my lips and looked Jar in the face now that Nadia's pain had stopped.

'Devin. It's Devin,' I uttered.

'See, that wasn't so hard, was it? Untie D-Man here and get him to bed. It's going to be a big day tomorrow.' Jar turned on his heel and walked out of the room. I watched as Nadia raised an eyebrow and followed suit. I was left with two juiceheads who untied me as quickly as they could.

'Nadia never pushed us to vomit. We told Jar our names after the first push.'

That said a lot about them and not me because I hated that I had caved. That they had my name. But I wasn't about to throw up any more of my empty stomach for them.

Mesore 2012

I gasped as I was awakened brutally. Cold water splashed my whole body, and I tugged at the binds that held me against the chair. The room came into focus, the walls dirty and covered in steel, the floor cold, hard concrete that had seen better days, and the single hanging light bulb above my head illuminating the entire room so it looked dirtier than it was.

'What the fuck?' I swore, pulling my attention away from the room to Jarrad, who just grinned at me. I was back in the same fucking room where they had pulled my name from me. Probably coming to in the same way as well.

At least there was no sign of vomit on the floor.

'You were having a little bit of a cat nap there, and that wasn't going to do it. Why do you think that is?'

I stared at him like he had grown an extra head. *Is he blind?* They were sleep-depriving the already sleep-deprived dreamwalker—a fact they didn't know about. Yet.

'Do you really want me to state the obvious? Because I can if you really want me to.'

Jarrad wasn't stupid. He knew I would just backchat him until I got my way. But I wasn't going to get out of it. I didn't even know how they had gotten me there. The last thing I remembered was eating dinner and going to bed.

They'd drugged the food. I wanted to rip them limb for limb, but I wasn't a werewolf, and I didn't have preternatural strength. I didn't have any fancy skills except being able to haunt them in their dreams and make them mad. That was my special thing.

'You drugged me. The food was drugged. You said it was safe!'

'I said a lot of things, but that doesn't always mean you should listen to me. Do you know what you're doing here? Right here?'

I shook my head because I didn't know, and I didn't want to know. But I knew Jarrad was going to tell me. He would make sure I knew.

'You're going to tell me what makes you so special because, so far, all of our tests have come up with "human". Just plain old human, but you wouldn't be at The Camp for no reason. We don't do plain vanilla humans. It's against The Code.'

I bit the inside of my cheek—maybe the only smart thing I could do right then—to stop myself from telling him to shove whatever it was up his arse.

'It doesn't matter. If your test doesn't show anything, I don't think you're doing the right tests.' Smart-arse comments never got me anywhere either.

I could see as he picked up a small electrode and twirled it between his fingers. 'I don't want to have to do this,' he said, and I tried to swallow past the lump in my throat. Having electricity run through my body was going to hurt, and I *was* human, after all. But why did I let it get to me? Why did I not just tell them?

Maybe it was a pride thing, and all I wanted to do was get out of that hellhole. But I couldn't. At least, not in any way I had just seen. I didn't want to give them any other reason to keep me. I was useless to them. Dreamwalkers were a myth, and I wanted to keep it that way.

'Devin, you've got the right look we need in The Camp. It would be a shame to get rid of you, to make you useless to me and to The Code. Karrept would never take someone so useless.'

A shiver ran down my spine as the mention of his name. *Karrept.* He was the motherfucking mummy who put me there. Karrept took us as payment for disturbing his slumber earlier than he wanted, and it was a price I was still paying—one that had led me to that very chair. The one that made sure the connection between me and my twin sister, Lucy, was severed. I didn't want her to see it.

But what was more was that he took Destiny, my older sister. She was a pain in the arse, but she didn't deserve whatever was happening to her.

'That got something out of you,' Jarrad muttered, and moved in closer. I pulled at the chair and the restraints to see if there was something that was loose. There wasn't.

I wouldn't be there if there was something that was loose. They knew it. I wasn't overly muscular, but I had some strength behind me.

Jarrad peeled off the backing of the electrode and settled the sticky part of it on my temple.

Fuck.

He picked up another and placed it on the other side, and I yanked at the restraints again.

'I can see the fear in your eyes, Devin. It should be there.' Jarrad grabbed another electrode and stuck it on my chest. 'All of this can stop any time. Just tell me what I need to know, and you'll be able to get out of this. I won't have to do this. Is that so hard?'

I wanted to tell him that it wasn't, but what would they do to me if they found out I could dreamwalk? Would there be some or trial? Would I be punished to death?

Too many questions were left unanswered, and I didn't want to know what would happen to me when it was all said and done. That was the scary part. Where would my body go? Would my family know I was dead, or would they just be going on forever without knowing what had happened?

'This can all end if you just tell me what makes you so special. That's all I want to know.'

'Bite me,' I said. I couldn't help it.

'I warned you,' Jarrad said, and attached the thread to the end of the electrode pad. He repeated the step two more times until they were all in place. With my skin wet from the water he had dumped on me, I knew that it was going to end badly.

'Why would you care?'

'Who says I do?'

I stared at him, trying to see if there was anything behind the cool exterior he was giving me, but all I could see were his dead green eyes staring back at me. I swallowed past the lump in my throat and tried to think of more to say, but I didn't have anything. My life was on the line, and I didn't have a single thing to say.

I'd rather die than tell him what my abilities were. As far as I knew, he could put me on death's row anyway.

'Come on now,' another voice said in a sing-song tune. 'You can't let a gorgeous face like that get ruined. What are you doing, Jar?'

'Is, you think every man here is gorgeous,' Jarrad said.

The voice was familiar, and I didn't look up, focusing my attention on the ground. And with Jarrad distracted, I carefully tried to pull at the bindings. *Maybe if I pull at them slowly instead of yanking, they'll loosen up.*

'You're not wrong, Jar, but this one is different,' Is muttered.

Is—short for Isolde—had a skill set I had only heard whispers about, nothing more. *Why is she here? What is she going to do to me?*

'Different how?' Jarrad turned to face her, and I tore my eyes away from the floor. I looked past him and saw her. She was wearing leather pants and a loose button-down shirt that had one side tucked in. Her hair was black, her skin was darker than a standard tan and she looked out of place in the room. But I couldn't take my eyes off her.

She was beautiful.

'You're going to need him. Isn't that right, Devin? You can stop trying to undo the binds. You're good and proper held in.' Isolde looked around Jarrad and straight at me. I swallowed past the hard lump in my throat and stopped trying to pull on the bindings.

Why I did that, I had no idea. My brain said to keep going, but my body just stopped.

'Is, go a little easy on the ability there,' Jarrad said.

Powers? Does she ... Can she manipulate the way others act? Surely not. Abilities like that would be so illegal.

'What did you just do?' I asked.

She just smiled. 'I could tell you, or you could tell me what's so special about you. You don't want J-Man over here to shock it out of you. It would hurt too much.'

I clamped my mouth shut and pressed my teeth down on my tongue hard enough to taste blood. The action made me think clearer. I could hear the enticement in her voice; it was like she was a siren, drawing attention from me.

'Devin, I don't want to see you dead. Just tell me what your abilities are. What can you bring to the table?' I felt that push back, and I wanted to clamp down on my tongue more. But I was scared that if I did that, I was going to tear it in two.

'D ...' I stalled because I wanted to see if I could resist, but as she stared at me, my head started to throb. *What is she doing to me?*

'Yes?' she asked, and Jarrad moved out of the way for her. She knelt down between my legs and reached up to grasp my head between her hands so I had nowhere else to look but her face. 'What are your abilities, Devin?' she asked again.

I got lost in her eyes; they were green.

'A dreamwalker.'

'Motherfucker,' Jarrad swore, and Isolde smiled and got to her feet.

'There is your answer as to why Karrept wanted him. He's perfect for the soldier you'll want.' She turned on her foot and strutted out of the room.

The door slammed shut, and I looked from it to Jarrad. 'She's so out of your league, buddy. But she's helpful. I guess I'll unhook you now.'

The electrodes would have been better than the verbal rape that had just happened to me. I felt dirty. I wouldn't get the luxury of a shower. That would be way too kind.

CHAPTER SIXTEEN

Acionna
Pachons 2017
Dreamland

WAVES CRASHED AGAINST THE SURF. The soft rumble of water rolling over itself before it kissed the sand was the only sound in the world that could make me more at ease and altogether anxious in the same breath. It had been too long since I'd properly felt the water on my skin, and the tingling salt in the air made my heart beat faster in my chest. My gaze snagged on the rippled sand under the surface, the water clear and inviting. I wanted to dive right in.

Could I?

Would I drown?

Is this space the same as the real world?

I knew it was different to the real world. Everything felt a little lighter, almost like anything could happen.

Like I wouldn't get hurt.

It wasn't a feeling I could put into words, but it was a feeling almost like a warm, secure hug. And it felt good. So very good.

'Fancy meeting you here,' a voice said, and I looked over my shoulder and saw the man from the last dreamland … Or that's who I thought it was anyway. There was a familiarity to him, the way those stormy grey eyes looked back at me with mischief and his crooked smile. My heart leapt into my throat, and I realised why he looked so familiar.

He had just been in my dining room not a week before.

'Devin?' I whispered.

'You know me?' he asked. And he turned to face me, his back to the sea, and really looked at me. His eyes left mine and trailed over my face before stopping on my lips.

'Acionna,' he breathed, and that's when it all sank into place. That dreamland was mine—it was ours—but there was more to it. More than I realised because it was impossible to have that experience without magick, and that meant that Devin was a witch. He was doing something illegal, and if the powers that be found out about it, they would kill him. They would throw him in jail … or he might wash up on a beach.

'But how?' I asked this time.

He looked past my shoulder, and I turned to see what he was staring at. There was nothing that could be seen, just rocks and a wall. He was stalling.

'I … This isn't a conversation we should be having in a dreamland. I feel like it needs to be in the flesh.'

'What, so we can have more awkward sushi dates where you suddenly kiss me and then we forget it happened, so we can stare at the photos I took of your party?'

He laughed, the sound like music to my ears because his laughter was contagious. I smiled in spite of it all. 'Look, I panicked.'

'Yeah, if that's what you want to call it.' After the kiss in my kitchen, we'd had to get down to business and sort through the images he wanted to keep and which he wanted to enlarge. It was the hardest few hours of my life because all I could think about was jumping his bones.

'You have to be some sort of special creature to be able to be so lucid in these dreams,' Devin finally said. Instead of saying anything, I stood on my toes and held his face in my hand. I leant in and pressed my lips against his, kissing him slowly at first before deepening the intensity.

Devin wrapped his arms around my body and crushed me against his torso. The warmth of his body was comforting—maybe just as much as the water. He broke the kiss and leant his forehead against mine.

'Why the water?' he whispered against my face.

'Why not?' I asked.

Really, I wanted to hide the ache of being so close to it and not being in it. 'I miss the way the water feels,' I finally admitted.

'But you live right across from it,' he replied.

'I know.' I untangled myself from him and walked right up to the water's edge, not knowing if he would follow me, though there was definitely a hope that he would.

'Did you know that there is a whole Undersea of animals that are just beyond the surface? A whole civilisation the human world hardly knows about, and if they did, it would blow their minds?'

'I've read about many of the creatures.'

I laughed. 'Read. That's cute. You've only read what they want you to find, and that barely scratches the surface.'

'And you know this firsthand?' Devin asked, his shoulder touching mine.

'Yup,' I said, and left it at that. If he wanted to push for more, he could.

I pulled back from his warmth and walked towards the water. I could shed clothing like I could my skin, but I wondered if I should do something like that in the comfort of a dream. Or whatever it was. Would it be the same? Would it feel the same? Could I breathe underwater like I always had? I wanted to.

'Why you?' he asked, following me closer to the water's edge. I dipped a toe in the water. It was the perfect temperature: not too cold, not too warm. Although, to humans, it would feel chilly.

'You tell me. I thought these were just normal dreams. You are the one who has roped me in.'

He chuckled. 'I've never had anyone who wasn't a family member or someone I was purposely looking to …' He trailed off, my gaze finding his. Or trying to. His eyes were lost, looking at the sand. *What doesn't he want to say?*

'What would you be looking to do?' I asked, and while I still looked at him, I stepped into the water, walking until it was halfway up my calves.

'It's not something that concerns you.' He looked up and snagged my attention.

'That's a lie.' I motioned for him to follow me, and he did so, his legs cutting through the water like it was nothing. And maybe to him, it wasn't. After all, he was the one in charge of that world. Whatever it was.

'How can you tell?' he asked.

'Devin,' I said, and he reached out for me. I let him take my hand, and he pulled me close. 'You are good at lying, but maybe you're not so good at doing it here.'

His fingers danced along the small of my back, and I pressed my lips together to stop myself from giving anything away.

'Maybe that's true.'

'Why are you speaking in riddles here?' I asked.

He took a deep breath and one of his hands cupped my face, his thumb brushing over my cheek. 'Because I don't know how to act around you. You make me nervous, and I've never had this sort of visceral reaction to anyone before. Or at least … not to anyone human. And that scares me.'

'Why?' I asked, my body melting into his. My fingers toyed with the edge of his T-shirt. I wanted to see what he looked like without it, the power in his arms. The way he held me was like I weighed nothing, and I wanted more of it. So much more.

'Because I … Can you keep a secret?' he whispered.

'I'm good at keeping those,' I replied.

Devin was silent for a moment, and I was about to say something when he spoke up. 'I hunt things that shouldn't be allowed to live in the human world in some aspect. I've never fully trusted anyone not fully human before.'

Like you.

The unspoken words hung in the air and licked my lips. What would he do when he found out what I was? Better yet, what did he do with those he hunted? Was he connected to that poor man who had been murdered?

'Well, I promise I don't bite.'

'What are you?' he asked.

'Only time will tell,' I murmured and kissed him. I'd had enough of his talking. Enough of his fishing. Devin kissed me back, slipped a hand under my shirt and trailed his nails over the small of my back. I could have ripped the shirt off his body, but I held back and let him explore my mouth with his tongue, let his hands roam anywhere they wanted while the water rocked us ever so slightly. In that world, nothing mattered but him and the water.

Devin broke the kiss to pull my shirt over my head, flicking it out of the way. I let my eyes follow it briefly before he guided my chin back so I could look at him. 'Eyes on me, love.'

My body tightened at those words, and I smirked.

'Love?' I challenged.

'I could have said "princess."'

'You would have been closer to the truth there.' *Or hit the head on the nail.*

He chuckled and guided my hands to his shirt. I lifted it and threw it out of reach. The water would take it far away, and that was okay with me. It could keep it for all I cared. I ran my hands over his shoulders, down his chiselled pecks and over the ridges of his stomach. He had power, strength and looked like a god. I needed all of the help I could get to keep myself there, to stay away from him in the real world.

Yeah, right. Like that's going to happen after this.

'Wow,' I murmured.

'You're pretty wow yourself,' he said, and kissed me again. Devin's fingers made fast work of my bra, and his hands cupped my breasts, his fingers calloused and rough. I didn't mind in the slightest.

I tugged at his pants and undid them, pulling them down without any care. Devin did the same and crashed his lips against mine, like he was searching for a heat he couldn't seem to get enough of. As he did, his fingers rubbed against my clit, and I melted into his body, letting him do as he pleased, my core tightened down low. I scraped my nails down his back, and he groaned into my mouth before slipping a finger inside me. I broke the kiss and gasped at the way it fit.

'Dev—in,' I whispered as his fingers moved, slowly at first before he built up the momentum. But I was ripped from the ocean's grip with a sound—one that was foreign but so familiar at the same time.

Pachons 2017
Melbourne

A shrill vibration ripped me from the dream, and I scrambled into a sitting position. The noise was coming from my bedside table, and I groaned as I snatched up my phone.

'What?' I asked without looking at the name on the screen.

'I'm sorry, I'm looking for Acionna Kirby?'

I rubbed the sleep from my eyes and tried not to sigh too loudly.

'My apologies. This is her.'

'Oh, amazing. I'm hoping I can book you for a job,' the voice said.

I blinked and pulled the phone away from my ear to look at the time. It was 11.00 a.m. *How the fuck did I sleep in?*

'If you send me an email, I can organise it.'

'Don't you need more information?' she asked.

'I'm wondering how you got my number. It's not listed on my website, and there is a strict protocol with how to get a quote. You also haven't told me who you are. So, for me, as a safety thing, getting you to send me an email is the easiest way I can verify all of your details.'

It was weird to have someone call me up out of the blue. Yes, there were times when it happened, but more often than not, I spoke to people via email first. Someone must have already used me and given my number out. Or there was a serious security breach somewhere in all of my details, and I had to close that gap because there was a leak.

'My apologies. My name is Greta. And I got your details from Sir Franklin. He said you were the best of the best, and I'm looking for a photographer for my daughter's birthday.'

I was quiet for a moment. I really needed to talk to Sir Franklin. It wasn't on, and it wasn't the way I did business. There were protocols, including a form on my website. I trawled through the forms to make sure I was safe and I didn't have to worry about anything bad happening.

'Okay, that's all good. Shoot me your details via email, and I'll give you my rates and get the details I need from you.'

'Thanks. Sorry for the rude awakening.'

I resisted the urge to groan and smiled, not that she could see that. 'Not a problem. I'll talk to you soon.'

I ended the call and groaned. *What a wake up.* I slid down in bed and dug my head into my pillow.

I didn't know what love was like, but all I could think about was Devin. That was who was in the dream, and after the kiss ... *God, that kiss. It was ... perfect.* I didn't expect to feel things, mushy feelings, and I couldn't stop thinking about him. It wasn't the first dream I'd had with him, but it was the first one that was ... explicit. My body was primed and ready. I chewed on my lower lip before I fanned my hand over my breast, down my stomach and between my legs, I was wet—so wet.

The tip of my pointer finger stroked my clit, softly at first, testing the waters as I kept my breathing even. It was hard to think that, somewhere, that man could exist and wasn't already there in my bed. With me.

The way his lips caressed my body, finding spots that were unmarked by anyone else had the muscles in my lower stomach tightening with something fierce. A second finger joined the first, and I threw my head back into the pillow and headboard as pleasure wracked through my centre. Finding my own pleasure was fast. I knew my own body and its triggers. My fingers quickened, and I brought myself over the edge, muffling my cries into my arm because I could hear Janice puttering around.

Breathing hard, I ran my free hand through my hair; it was messy and sweat-slicked. I was going to have to do something about that. A shower would help.

I grabbed my phone and texted Devin.

Are you free to hang out?

I typed out and held my hand over the arrow to send the message. It could have been a totally weird thing for him to do, and all I could really think about was having him between my legs. But that was also part of my nature as a selkie. Sex was like breathing. It was second nature to me.

But do I just want that from Devin? Can I really do this Abovesea thing and be okay with it? He wasn't a prince with a tail, but he would look damn good in a set of tails, dressed to the nines.

I pushed send and waited for the response. It came instantly.

Yep. Pick you up in an hour?

I had an hour to get ready before he was there. *Shit.*

CHAPTER SEVENTEEN

Devin
Pachons 2017
Melbourne

'Fuck.' I rubbed a hand over my face as I was jolted out of the dream at such a pivotal moment.

Acionna.

It was there all along.

The girl in the forest, and even before that. She had plagued the dreams between work and all of it. I didn't know what came over me, but I had to have her. All I could think about was her—every part of her. I swiped a finger over my bottom lip and groaned. After the kiss, we looked at the photos from the event. They were all amazing. Acionna managed to capture everything I needed and then some. It was like we could dance without talking, and I had only ever experienced a synchronicity like that with one other person—and we'd happened to share a womb. Did I believe in fate?

No.

Humans made their own fate and the decisions that came along with it. I had made decisions based on self-preservation. If I didn't kill, I would be killed. If I didn't kill, my family would be killed. I made that decision daily, but there was something unspoken between Acionna and me, and the way I felt about her. I didn't even think I could put it into words. I had watched the way Lucy and Hunter moved around each other, and the bond the two of them had. They'd always had it, from the moment they met, but it took them a little bit of time to get them on the same page as the universe. Now, they were inseparable.

I didn't think I would find someone who would be my version of that. Maybe I had, but it was a weird situation. Acionna wasn't human. I knew that much. But what was she? I couldn't put my finger on it. She tasted like the ocean, but there was no way that anything from the ocean would be walking on two legs on land.

Mermaids had tails, fish needed gills and there were a few mythical beings, but there was no way they could be even real.

Although, it wouldn't be the first time I was proven wrong.

A knock on the door pulled me out of my thoughts, and I instinctively grabbed a pillow and put it over my lap.

'Dev?' Lucy's voice through the door was hesitant, almost like she didn't know whether she should even be knocking on the door.

'Yeah?' I looked at my phone, and the time was just going on shy of 11.30 a.m.

'Hey,' she said as she opened the door. Lucy was wearing a pair of leggings and a tank. She must have come back from the gym or was on her way there.

'Hi,' I said. She walked into the room hesitantly, like she was worried I would be broken.

'Look, I know you're probably going to think that I'm being insufferable and always asking if you're okay, but I'm worried about you. I …' She looked down at her feet as though she was waiting for me to interject, but Lucy didn't need that. She needed to get whatever it was off her chest. 'I am … It feels weird to ask things of you, knowing that it's only been almost a year since you were … at that place.'

I sat forward and leant my elbows on my pillow. *Is Lucy about to ask me about where I went? Why I have so many scars, or even about the rescue itself?* We hadn't talked about it, and before The Camp, there was nothing we didn't talk about. I knew all of her secrets, helping her with the ones she wanted to keep from Hunter even if it killed me to hold her while she cried, saving her when she needed it. Lucy was truly the polar opposite of me, but she was my sister, and I kept her safe. Even then. It was all I knew.

'Lucy-Bell, just ask. Don't pussy foot around it,' I said abruptly.

'The old Devin wouldn't do that,' she said quietly.

'The old Devin died a long time ago, Luce.'

'I ...' She stopped, her mouth open ever so slightly. 'You're an arse sometimes. Whatever the fuck you have going on, you need to stop or spill because I barely know this version, and I want to. I miss my brother. I miss my best friend. He ...' She trailed off, and I waited for her to finish. 'He wouldn't hide things from me. Not like this.'

'He also wasn't beat, whipped, trained and more sleep-deprived than he had ever been. Luce, are you sure you want to know about this? I need you to understand that once I say this, I can't take it back. I can't uninvolve you. It's a clusterfuck of what I have done and what is going to come. You have to be sure. And if you're not, if there is even the smallest inkling of doubt, you're not ready and I'll wait. You know I'll wait.' The last words were soft, like the brother she wanted, and I could do that. I could be the brother she wanted at that moment.

Lucy pressed her palms against her eyes and sighed like she was trying to sort out her own demons.

'I don't know ... I don't know if I want to know, but I do. I want to understand what happened and why you are the way you are. You're more agile than before. You sneak off randomly. Dad gets worried and mad in the same breath when he can't find you. I don't know if I'm helping or hindering when he asks me where you are, and I try to cover for you. How am I supposed to cover you without the full story?'

My phone buzzed, and I picked up. A text from Acionna.

Are you free to hang out?

What a loaded question. I would have much preferred hanging out with her than having that conversation with my sister. I looked at Lucy, and her eyes narrowed.

'Who was it?' she asked.

'Acionna.'

Her face instantly lit up with a small grin, and if she had been at The Camp, that action would have been beaten out of her. It was too much emotion.

'I want to know, Dev, but I don't know if I want to know right this instant.' *Because you want to go and see Acionna.* The sentence wasn't said aloud, but her face said it loud and clear, and I was sure that if I peeked through the twin bond, it would tell me that without it needing to be said out loud.

'When you're ready to hear all of the truth, I'll tell you, but you have to be ready for it. It's Ugly, Luce, with a capital U. I'm not going to sugarcoat that.'

And you might want Hunter close, I thought.

'Dev, I miss you,' she murmured.

'I'm right here. Your room is just down the hall,' I said.

'Not what I mean.'

'I know. But you're different from the sixteen-year-old I remember, so we've both changed.'

Yep. Pick you up in an hour?

I texted back and put my phone down.

'Yeah, I guess you're right. I want to take the hurt out of your eyes,' she said.

'You'll be trying for a while, Luce.'

Try years. I couldn't run from the demons The Camp had created because they had made me one.

Thoth 2012

Somewhere in the desert

My legs burnt, starting to die on me, but that wasn't the real problem. The real problem was that I could feel what I ate for lunch in the back of my throat. I hunched over and vomited. My stomach heaved all of the food that was supposed to keep me fuelled up and going. *Fuck.*

'D-Man. One too many burgers for you.' Jarrad clapped a hand on my back, and I heaved harder. I wasn't afraid of vomit, but I grew up with a sister who used to scream and sob any time someone puked because she was a sympathetic vomiter. I hated seeing her so distressed, so if I needed to be sick, it was always when she wasn't around.

Jarrad laughed, and when I felt like my stomach was done, he handed me some water. 'Swirl it first to rinse, then drink.'

I nodded, my throat too raw to even think about words. I did as I was told. I swirled and then spit before taking a drink.

'Bet you didn't think that was going to happen,' he said.

I stood up straight and strained to control my breathing. 'No … I have never … vomited … from … that … before.'

Jarrad chuckled. 'Hang in there, D-Man. You'll be able to get through it. I promise it gets easier.'

'It gets easier?' I was confused. There was no way in hell it could get easier.

'Yeah. You vomit less and get more movement in you. I promise.' He grinned and handed me a towel. I used it to wipe my mouth and my face. The smell of vomit laced through my nose, and I had to breathe through my mouth so I didn't gag.

'Anyway, back to it. You still have to finish fifty sit-ups, twenty push-ups and your sprints,' Jarrad said.

My jaw dropped. Surely … he wasn't being serious. 'You're—'

'For your own health, I wouldn't finish that. You won't like the punishment. It's the only warning you're getting.'

I stared at him for half a second and realised he was serious. *Fuck.*

It had been weeks—or what felt like weeks—since I stepped onto

The Camp's grounds. All that I'd done was eat, train, sleep, rinse and repeat.

Life was pretty monotonous.

There was no way to get out, so I stopped trying to figure out how to get to Destiny or contact Lucy. I still wanted to find them, but the training kept me occupied. At the end of the days, I passed out and was watched like a hawk. Everyone kept a close eye on me, like they were waiting for me to break.

I wanted to.

But I was stubborn.

They wouldn't see me break, see my tears. They didn't deserve them. Jarrad pushed harder and harder each day that went by. There was a difference in his eyes, almost like I was a soft spot for him, and I had heard the whispers from the others. Jarrad hadn't taken any sort of interest in anyone but me. No one else got that sort of personal training.

I dropped to the ground, my arms shaking as I started my set of push-ups.

One, two, three, four, five. It was easy—it was the next fifteen that were a struggle.

Every day was the same routine, and every day it was harder. That day, there was ten kilos worth of weight around my wrists and ankles. My body had changed. I was stronger, but then again, all I did in those days was eat, sleep, train, and repeat. I'd lost count of what day it was, and while I thought about my sisters, I couldn't get to either of them. I'd broken all ties to Lucy and let her think I was dead. I couldn't break her heart, knowing I couldn't go home.

I finished my last push-up. My arms felt like jelly, and I shifted to do my sit-ups when Jarrad whistled. Everyone stopped what they were doing. As I tried to gather myself, I looked up and saw Gerry standing over the light, blocking me from seeing past him. In his hands were swords—two of them—and I rolled over as he slammed one down.

It sliced the ground right where my head had been. I kip flipped to my feet and wobbled as I stood, my body sore and lethargic from vomiting and exercise.

It was not a battle I was going to win on that factor alone, but I didn't have a weapon.

Fuck.

Gerry threw a sword at me, and I fumbled as I caught it. That gave him enough time to slice a gash in my arm. I cried out and gripped the sword in my uninjured hand. It was also my non-dominant hand.

Double fuck.

'Sometimes, things don't go your way, and you have to improvise. You need to have two hands—two working hands that mirror each because you never know when you'll need to switch or when you'll need to find out what someone needs. D-Man, Gee has temporarily taken out your dominant hand. What do you do?'

I would have run because my left hand was useless to me.

'What are your instincts telling you?' Jarrad pushed as I refused to take my eyes off Gerry. He was going to kill me one day. His eyes were ablaze with fury.

'Run,' I spoke up, and everyone zeroed in on me. It was like I had said something that offended them.

'Then run,' Jarrad said. He walked around the circle with his arms crossed over his chest. 'If your instincts are telling you to run, don't be afraid to do it. But just know that if you do, you won't be able to break that instinct. That's what you're really here to do. We need to break the contact between the part of you that wants to hide. Instinct will keep you alive, but it won't help you make the choices you should be making.'

Jarrad looked past me and found Gerry. In the peripherals, I could see him contemplating what to do next.

'You need to think everything through, but it needs to be a practiced effort, D-Man. You need to be in charge. You can't let it rule you, or you'll get hurt.'

Gerry came at me, both of his hands wrapped around the hilt of his sword. I brought my sword up to block up the next attack. With pain radiating through my right, the sword wobbled, and I tried to use it to push back against Gerry. He was too fast, and the adrenaline that pumped through my veins didn't do anything for me. My arm wasn't strong enough to retaliate against him. Gerry knocked the sword from my hand before he swept my legs out from under me. The tip of the blade balanced between my eyes, and instead of looking at the weapon, I stared at Gerry.

'Good. Keep him in your sight. The instant you look at the sword, he's got you. Pull back. Gerry.' He switched the sword to his non-dominant hand and held out a hand for me.

'Let's get that arm looked at,' Gerry said.

I stared at the hand he held out. The switch had flipped in his brain, and there was no fury left. Or at least, that's what it looked like. I took his hand and let him help me to my feet. Blood pooled down my arm, and I held it close to my body, while my other arm supported it. I tried to stop the blood, but it looked like I might need stitches.

Great. Another scar to add to the growing collection.

The walk to the infirmary was silent. It wasn't far, but the silence between us was enough to make it feel like it stretched on for all eternity. The building was the same beige that every other structure was. The only difference? The red cross on the sign that was to the left of the door. There were stairs, but the wood slatted building didn't stand out.

'Devin, another one? You need to stop coming into my house like this,' Luna said as she patted one of the beds.

'Thanks for the escort, Gerry,' I said.

He raised an eyebrow and left the building without saying anything.

'I take it Jarrad told him to escort you over?' Luna asked.

'Yep. Think you can stitch this up fast? I need to get out of here before something else happens.' I didn't want to end up on my back there again.

'You always flatter me so much, Devin.'

'You know I try,' I said with a grin. Luna peeled my hand away from the gash, and it started to bleed again. She clicked her tongue and grabbed some gauze, pressing it against my arm.

Jarrad walked into the building, his green eyes honing in on me, and I huffed in frustration and from the ache that throbbed hard in my arm.

'You did good,' Jarrad noted. A compliment from him was more than anyone could ask for.

'But I let him hurt me,' I said

'Sometimes, you need to get hurt to learn a lesson. That's a completely different lesson in itself.'

'He wants to kill me,' I replied.

'I know. You have to kill him first if you want to survive.'

I swallowed past the lump in my throat. *Can I do that?* I was going to find out.

CHAPTER EIGHTEEN

Acionna
Pachons 2017
Melbourne

I PACED BACK and forth in the living room. Devin said he'd be an hour, and we were getting onto that now. *Is he coming? Was he just saying that? Did I interrupt anything?* My brain was firing on all cylinders like it was trying to figure out exactly what was happening outside of it. I ... I didn't know how to react to that feeling. It felt like I was a youngin again, exploring what it was like to be a woman for the first time. I wiped my hands on my jeans, but besides them, I only had a T-shirt that was close to the colour of my eyes but not quite there. My hair was down, and it was a mess. Honestly? I couldn't think about anything else but Devin.

The dreams and the kiss were all I could think about. I wasn't human, but they had me feeling all of those human emotions.

The doorbell chimed, and I jumped at the sound—one that should have been familiar, but the likelihood of another person coming to my house was small. Real small. Just Janice and me.

And now Devin.

My heart pounded in my chest as I walked to the door. *What am I going to say? What is he going to say?*

As I took a steadying breath, I opened the door, and Devin looked back at me. His eyes were wide for a second before he wiped the surprise from his eyes.

'Hi,' I said.

'Hi,' he replied.

We both stood there and stared at each other, not sure what to say.

'I knew you looked familiar,' he said after what felt like a full five minutes. 'When I saw you at Franklin's party.'

'I didn't pick up on it,' I said.

'Dreams are funny like that.'

'What are you?' I asked.

'Human. You?'

'Not,' I replied.

Devin hesitated at the door as I moved out of the way, and he wrapped an arm around my waist and pressed me against the door. Before I could react, he crushed his lips against mine. My arms snaked around his neck and I kissed him back, matching his feverish pace. His hand slid down my back and cupped my arse before using the momentum to hike me up. I wrapped my legs around his waist. With his foot, he slammed the door shut before he carried me down the hallway.

Our tongues met in a clash of fury as I clawed at his shirt. I yanked it up his back and broke the kiss momentarily to pull it over his head. I threw his shirt to the floor.

'Bedroom. Where?' he asked, breathing hard.

'Upstairs,' I replied as I tried to catch my breath.

His eyes were impossibly dark, like the clouds before thunder rumbled through the sky. 'You want this, yes?' he asked.

'Fuck yes,' I whispered, and tightened my legs around his waist. His hands slipped under my shirt and he pulled it up my chest. I helped pull it over my head and let it fall to the floor before his mouth crashed into mine again. He walked us through the living room and stopped halfway up the stairs, pressing me against the wall.

'You're sure?' he asked as he pulled away, his heated gaze making things inside me clench as I nodded. 'I need to hear it, Ash.'

Ash. No one had ever called me anything but Acionna. Ever. And part of me sang with delight, my body ablaze with need and want.

'I'm sure,' I said as I reached between us to undo his pants. He pressed me against the wall harder and clicked his tongue.

'Not on the stairs,' Devin growled.

Who is this man? He was rough yet soft. Charismatic yet clumsy. Sexy yet demure.

All I could do was nod before he pulled us away from the wall and finished the walk up the stairs. I pointed to the right, and he followed the direction. He paused at the threshold of the door and kissed me again, his mouth begging for more. My whole body felt alight, like his touch scorched my skin, and I wanted for nobody else. His lips traced a wet line down my throat. I inhaled sharply as his lips hit my rapidly beating pulse. My muscles clenched again, and I moaned.

'I want you,' he growled and unfurled my legs from around his waist, yanking down my pants, taking my underwear with them as soon as my feet hit the ground. The motion was fast—almost shifter fast. He was human, but there was something more to him. I smiled and pushed him into the room, walking him back to the bed. Without any words, he undid his pants and pulled a wrapper from his pocket. Protection was a must for most humans, but I didn't care for it. I was nowhere near fertile, and there was a dull ache in the depth of my chest like a piece of me was missing.

'Show me,' I said.

Devin grinned, and with the same speed, his pants were gone, the wrapper crinkled and he pulled me in close.

'You're going to regret those words,' he murmured into my ear, his lips skimming over the skin just below as he walked us back to the bed. The backs of my knees hit the mattress and I sat down, pushing my body back on my elbows, I pressed my lips together and took him in. From the scars on his chest to the ridges across his stomach, the V that was so lickable to his hard cock. Devin smirked and leant over me, his legs between mine.

'Oh, really?' I taunted.

Can he really make me regret my words? I hoped so. His hand slid over my stomach and between my legs, two fingers rubbing my clit in slow circles. I bit my lip and arched my hips up into his hand.

'Really,' he whispered, his voice husky with lust.

That sound was music to my ears, almost like the waves crashing against the surf just across the road.

My breathing quickened, and Devin slipped a finger inside me, testing the waters while his mouth feasted on my breast. I didn't know where I ended and he began. Every part of me breathed him in and took in every part of him.

I moaned and dug my head back into the bed like it would help bring me closer to him. My hand gripped his shoulder as his fingers inched me closer to the edge of reason. He kissed a wet line down my body, and it made me open my eyes and groan.

Instead of letting him go down any further, I used my strength and pulled him up against my body and kissed him hard. He chuckled against my lips and kissed me back.

'Enough.' *Teasing, driving me crazy, fucking edging me closer without getting me there.* The words were on the tip of my tongue that was now warring with his. I made space for him between my legs and slid a hand between our bodies to guide him inside me, but Devin grabbed my hand and stopped me.

He broke the kiss and clicked his tongue.

'Oh, Ash,' he murmured. 'You are not the one in charge here.' He held my gaze and raised my hand above my head, guiding himself inside me. Devin never took his eyes off me, and I held my breath as he pushed his whole length inside me. I wanted to close my eyes and bask in the way he fit, but I didn't dare take my eyes off him.

'Dev,' I moaned.

'I love hearing my name from your lips like that. I wonder if I can make you scream it.' Devin licked his lips and pressed them together. 'Lift the other hand, Ash,' he instructed. And without a second thought, I listened.

I had never listened to a man when he was inside me. I always had the power.

Right then, I had none.

And I was utterly okay with that.

He thrust his hips deeper into me before pulling out and driving harder into me.

'Fuck,' I cried out.

What is he doing to me?

Without my hands, I wrapped my legs around him and held him in place. Or at least, I tried. From that position, I could rub back against him, my hips not only meeting his thrusts but also hitting that spot on my clit as well.

His incredibly slow pace made my muscles clench around his cock, trying to draw him deeper. I'd had many lovers, but none of them felt like him—like he was fixing all of the fractured pieces of my soul.

All of them but one. But that was a thought for another time.

He thrust harder and faster inside me, my hips meeting every thrust with need.

'De—Devin,' I moaned, the pressure building in my lower belly. 'I need my hands.' I wanted to run them down his back, to feel every ridge, scar and muscle.

'If I let go, my control is shot,' he uttered. And right then, I didn't care. I could take back my hands—I had that power—but the way he looked at me like he needed it more than I did had me pausing.

'Kiss me,' I demanded. And he did. His lips crashed into mine as he thrusted into me harder with every brush of lips, and I moaned as he inched me closer to the edge.

The pressure built up in my belly, and I ripped my mouth away from Devin's as I screamed his name and came crashing over the proverbial cliff.

He kept moving inside me and let go of my hands, clenching the sheets either side of my head. I scraped my nails down the sides of his body, and that action alone had him shuddering above me.

'Fuck, Ash,' he cried out before he came to a stop.

Our syncopated breathing was the only thing louder than the waves crashing outside my window.

He dropped his head and buried it into the crook of my neck before he laughed. 'That was not what I had in mind when I answered your text.'

'Funny about that. That was all I had in mind.'

'Liar.' He chuckled, and brushed his lips against my jawline before he got off me and lay on his back next to me. 'So, what flavour of not-human are you? You taste like the ocean.'

I shook my head. 'I don't kiss and tell on the first fuck.' I looked at him with a playful smile on my face.

Part of me wanted to grab hold of the sheets and hide my body from him—that kind of vulnerability was not anything I had ever experienced. I'd almost always had sex with a man, smiled and left his life forever. No one had lingered.

Devin was going to linger.

The ocean seemed to settle, and the waves lapped at the sand, the water refreshing against my bare feet, not only grounding me but cooling me internally too. An hour before that, Devin had been in my bed, and part of me was in disbelief that he was still there. I had my camera slung over my shoulder, and he walked beside me. I couldn't help the grin, and every couple of steps, I looked to make sure he was there with me. It was moments before the timer would go off, and while Devin had been in the shower, I silenced it so it would look natural. But on the inside, the turmoil my body felt ... I could have missed it, and my pelt would have been gone just because I had thought that sex was more important than a photo.

Don't get me wrong, it was fantastic sex, but was it so good I should lose my pelt over it?

'What?' Devin asked as I looked around, and he slipped his fingers through mine and pulled me to his side.

'Like, how are you even real? What man wants to stick around after what we just did?' I said, and let myself melt into him. *Who is this person?* Everyone else was held at arm's length, yet that man ... He wasn't. Devin had plagued my dreams for months. He had a mouth that could drive me insane, both with words and the way he trailed it over my skin. He had eyes I could get lost in. And I didn't know how to react.

He chuckled and wrapped his arms around me. I rested my head on his chest and listened to his heartbeat—*bombom-bombom-bombom*. It was steady, unlike anything I had ever heard of. Roanes' heartbeats were so different. They beat to the feeling of the ocean, like an invisible sound that no one but the Undersea folk could hear.

'Your standards are too low,' he replied.

Or maybe I was just used to leaving them and not having to talk about anything. 'I have to see you again,' Devin whispered, and pressed his lips against my forehead. I pulled back ever so slightly to look him in the eyes. They were clear and focused on me, the intensity in there was not something I was even familiar with when it came to human men. Most of the time, they just wanted the sex and were done with it, but there was more to his gaze. Like he wanted to know about me—no, *needed* to know more about me.

'Are they?' I murmured, and he pressed his lips against mine, kissing me with care. The feeling travelled right down my spine and pooled in my belly. I could have pushed him to the ground and taken him right there and then, but there was a vibration in my back pocket. The timer went off, and I pulled back, turned to face the sea and brought the camera right up to my eye and took a breath. I centred it on the horizon, the sun almost blinding me, but I tapped the shutter and clicked the image. It would go off to the witch almost instantly.

'You are obsessed with taking pictures of everyone and everything without asking.'

I laughed and brought the camera down. He stepped to the side so we were both looking out to the horizon. I held the camera at my shoulder, taking in the setting sun.

'The ocean never needs permission. Not from me. I have free reign with her.'

'You speak like it's a person.'

'It is,' I said, and looked at him. He was staring back at me. 'It's a living being. There is so much under the surface, none of which anyone on land can comprehend.'

He tilted his head at me. 'You say things like you know that, like there is more to you than being here.'

'There is. Am I ready to tell you? No. But in time, you will see it. If you want to,' I said. I wanted to tell him I was a selkie, but then I'd have to have explained how that happened. And without my pelt, I couldn't show him. He wouldn't get it.

Maybe he would, but more than likely, he wouldn't. Humans had just a small grasp on the world, especially one where there were so many mythical creatures.

'I'll be ready to listen when you're ready,' he said.

And maybe he would be, but there would be some time before that happened.

'Did you hear about the man who washed up in the ocean? Actually, on this very beach. He had an arrow through him.'

He froze, and this time, it was my turn to tilt my head. *What a weird reaction.*

'What do you mean?'

I remembered that no one else had seen him … Or couldn't see him. 'There was a man … He was just bobbing in the ocean.'

'How not-human are you?' he asked me.

'What a weird question to ask,' I said, and turned to start walking again.

'It's a legit question. I hadn't heard of anyone dying in plain sight. Not like that dude, Gagliani.'

I could feel his eyes on me like he was waiting for me to admit something, but what was I going to admit?

'Acionna?!' A voice ripped my gaze from his, and in front of me stood Ariel. Her sea-green hair looked lacklustre, her normally bright blue eyes were half sunken in and her skin looked like it was ready to split in two. *Where has she been?*

'Ariel?' I gasped.

It had been 184 days since I last saw my sister, and she was there, on the same beach as me, in a state I had never seen her in—and she would never let anyone see.

'What are you doing here?' I asked to fill in the gap, her eyes wandering from me to Devin, who took a step to the left to give us more space. But Ariel would take that as an opportunity.

'Who is this piece of meat?' she asked.

'That's the first time I've been called that.'

She shrugged. 'It's the truth. That's all we see you guys as.'

'Air,' I warned.

'What, Acionna? You are telling me you don't see him as a piece of meat?' she asked, raising her voice.

I straightened my spine and took a step towards her. 'Lower your voice. You know there are rules here.'

'The rules never mattered to you,' she spat out.

'Yes. They. Do.'

Humans were not to know of our existence. It would tip the balance, and there would be those who would try to capture us, keep us as pets, wanting more than we could give. Being preternaturally strong meant that humans couldn't use their strength against us. They could keep us where they wanted to, but not much else—unless there was magick involved.

But there had been no cases of magick keeping selkies or roanes in their place.

'I should go …' Devin trailed off.

'No, stay. Acionna loves an audience. Don't you, Ash?'

I closed the distance between us and wrapped a hand around Ariel's wrist, pulling her in close. 'What is wrong with you? You either go back home or you stop this scene. We don't need humans to see this.'

'It's always your way or no way, isn't it?'

'What is wrong with you? I have only ever wanted you to be happy, to help you thrive, and your jealousy seems to take everything away from you—including the ability to love a sister.'

'Sisters don't steal.'

'Sisters don't take it out on one another. Every man is fair game unless said otherwise. And if someone chooses someone else, that is *their* problem,' I hissed.

Fury blazed in her eyes as she narrowed them and looked right through me.

'You took Eain from me.'

'No, Eain chose me. But that won't matter. I'm landlocked. What's it matter? You can have him all to yourself.'

She ripped her arm back, and her eyes widened. 'You're ... what?'

'Did I stutter?' I said.

'Truly landlocked?' she asked.

'Yes. Where do you think I've been? Just off in the human world, gallivanting? I can't go home.'

'I feel like I'm intruding here,' Devin said over my shoulder.

'Oh, you're not,' Ariel said. 'Probably makes more sense now.' She looked past me to Devin before she looked back at me. 'I'm sorry.'

'About what? Unless you had some hand in this.'

She was silent and looked to the horizon.

'Ariel?' I prompted again.

'I have to go,' Ariel said, and turned on her heel and ran back the way she came. I blinked and watched her go, every part of me screaming to follow her. But where to? My fingers covered my mouth to stop me from calling out to her.

'Sibling?' Devin asked as he came into view. I wanted to look past him to watch where she went, but I couldn't bring myself to. Unshed tears welled in my eyes, and his hands cupped my face.

'I ... Older sister. But that was weird. How much did you hear?' I remembered that I had just said I was landlocked.

'Enough,' he whispered. 'But that doesn't matter. Are you okay?'

'Far from it,' I said. And I needed to know where my other sisters were. *Why did Ariel look the way she did, and who was she looking for?* I could see she was searching for someone … or something.

'Come on. Let's go back to your house, and we can talk about it. Or not talk about it. It's completely up to you.' He wrapped an arm around my shoulders, and I let him guide me away from the surf and back to the house. There was so much I could say, but where would I start?

And how much of it would I get out without sounding crazy.

CHAPTER NINETEEN

Devin
Pachons 2017
Melbourne

Physical files were hard to hide. It always was a risk having them at home, but I knew that Lucy and Mum would be occupied for a while yet. I pulled the current file out from under a pillow. Jarrad sent it to me because he wanted some sort of flair, just to remind me that they were in charge. It was rare for them to send me two marks at once, but they had. Fiona Locklier—a witch and an eighteen-year-old body jumper who liked to steal bodies and leave them in other countries with the police after them. It wasn't the normal hit I would go after. I liked to stick to people who really did bad things, but the whole concept of body jumping caught my attention when the file was delivered.

Guy Hanson.

He was fresh out of high school and about to start uni.

The kid was studying to be a doctor and came from a good family. There was no sign of abuse in his file. He literally had it all. Guy liked to go out and body hop into girls, older women, older men. But he seemed to stay away from guys his own age. Strange, but not uncommon for people to steer clear of what they were most terrified of.

I held his picture in my hand and lay back. The key to getting the dreamwalking correctly was to be comfortable. I touched the picture with my pointer finger and focused on Guy's face. He was handsome, in a rugged way, but I wondered what had happened in his past to make him do his body jumping thing. Most other times, I didn't care, but he was younger than me … Not by much, but enough to make me very curious.

Or maybe he didn't understand what he was doing, and needed to do it for his own sanity.

That, I could understand—I'd been there when I first started dreamwalking.

I took a deep breath. 'I protect myself with light, with joy and with all that's good in the world. I protect my soul from being anchored in the dreamland, and I thank the goddess for allowing me to have this gift.' Sometimes, the words helped with the drawback, and sometimes, it was just my way of protecting myself while I was in the dreamland. I didn't know if Guy would try to jump into me while I was dreaming. I didn't know the extent of his abilities, and neither did The Camp.

I didn't want to take that chance.

With my finger still on Guy, I closed my eyes and pictured him in my mind. My body softened and melted into the mattress as I let sleep take it. I knew I would be in and out with no time gone.

The darkness surrounded me, and when I opened my eyes in my subconscious, it was all I could see until a rush of pictures moved all around me. There were lights, colours, sounds, smells, and all of it was blur. It was like waiting for a train at a station and watching an express train drive straight past in a blur of movement. The first time it happened to me, the movement used to drag me out of the in-between dreamland. Even though I was meant to be there. Loud actions and noises used to be hard to hold onto.

I took a deep breath and looked at the different colours—the strings that led to people's dreams. The one I wanted would lead me right into Guy's subconscious, and that was always a scary thing when it came to people's internal beings. I could fall into a dream in the middle of a really good moment, but it could also be a nightmare, and I would be stuck there until it played out or I got the hell out of there. While I manipulated dreams, I could lead them wherever I wanted. I didn't always want to—not with the people I loved anyway. There were always people sleeping. It was late, but it was also early. Dreamland didn't differentiate. It just was.

Dreams were what I was good at—well, besides killing people, but that was a practiced action. And a reaction to the life I had to live. Dreams had come naturally to me ever since I was a child. I'd always been able to surf dreams. I learnt about sex through dreams and death, heartbreak and love and so much more. It was hard to remember a time when I didn't have such a hard grip on dreams.

I didn't sleep much.

Dreamwalking was never restorative, and I operated on little to no sleep. It was like I was slowly being driven insane, but I knew that as long as I was able to do what I did, I would never get a full night's sleep. I would run on next to nothing until I died, and whether that was then, or maybe the next day, or even in fifty years, I would still be the same. Could I give up dreaming and the ability to manipulate them?

I tried.

It didn't work.

I pulled on the string in front of me. It shimmied with energy and light, begging for me to touch it like it craved my presence. I never wanted to dreamwalk for fun—it took too much out of me—but I needed to find a calling card that was unique, so I pushed myself to torment those like I had been tormented into killing people. If I had to do it, I wanted to do it my way.

Others used weapons, and they did it well. I chose my bow and arrow because it meant I could be further enough away, and it gave me an edge. At The Camp, I had practised while everyone else was asleep because it wasn't as loud as a gun and wouldn't wake anyone up. If I wasn't sleeping, I had to find something else to do with my energy.

Dreamwalking was dangerous to me. If anyone was to sneak up on me, they could kill me. I would be stuck in dreamland, so I made sure I could get in and out without too much effort. Locked doors also helped. I found that if I drove people to the point of insanity, when they were within an inch of losing their minds, they would want to take their own lives. So I didn't feel as bad when I killed them. It never mattered when or how they had those thoughts, or even why—they would see that death was the best way out.

It would be the only way to make their lives easier.

I was numb to what it used to feel like. I almost looked forward to being able to torment people in their dreams. At The Camp, the dreams were vivid, and I could slip into the dreamlands of others there. It was easier because I could just picture their faces and be there. Some would scream in the middle of the night with night terrors. The Camp made murder an everyday thing, something that would come up at the dinner table and be as casual as asking about one's day. The things that happened … The near-murders in the middle of the night. Abilities inside The Camp meant that emotions, fears and realities were warped, subconscious sanity was suspended and the irrational fear of someone trying to murder you in the middle of the night were a reality. Many had, and Jarrad had always made sure that I survived. He was always there to make sure our door was well protected.

I was stuck with men whose abilities to manipulate one's fear was enough to drive them to suicide.

Maybe we were just the scarier abilities that were silent killers.

Jarrad had told me that once he found out what my ability was. That I would be the keeper of everyone's secrets because dreams told more than words ever did. And I was. I knew more about the men and women in The Camp than anyone else.

Even Jarrad.

I was dangerous, and no one else around me realised it because I hid it well. I let them think I could function without the need to dreamwalk, but the truth was that I needed to do it for my own sanity as much as I needed it for a calling card.

My body hummed as I stopped in front of Guy's dream thread. It was yellow, sunny and full of joy. I could feel it. It was happy.

It wasn't going to be for long.

I touched the edge of the dream and watched as it darkened the landscape. A window opened up, and I stepped inside, careful not to snag a boot on the edge.

'Wh-what's going on?' Guy asked.

He couldn't see me. Not yet. I could come and go as I liked, and I wanted to see how much I could play with him before I tipped him over the edge.

How many times would I have to enter his dreams to get him to the point of being completely paranoid and on edge?

I felt the licks of excitement thrum through my veins. It was like my blood vibrated. I couldn't remember when the thrill of being in someone else's dream and being able to manipulate started to excite me. Somewhere between my kills, I supposed, it started to be something I looked forward to.

The part of the process I loved the most.

'What is happening?' he echoed again, and this time, I sat on the floor, crossed my legs under me and shut my eyes

I focused on a lion—big, with a mane that demanded attention and paws as big as my head. Guy jumped and screamed as the lion roared from behind him. I opened my eyes, forcing myself to be visible to him. He saw me, and his face went pale.

'You know, it's not very nice to scream at a lion. They're known to attack people quivering in fear.'

Guy seemed to wake up to that and squared his shoulders. He knew which ability he had, and he reached out to me almost like he wanted to see if he could jump into my body. I stepped back with a smile on my face. I controlled this space; he could try and jump into me. And maybe he would succeed, but I would fight to make sure he didn't touch me.

As I stepped back, the lion bolted in front of me, baring his teeth, and Guy jumped back.

'I wouldn't try that. He's not in a very good mood right now. Do you know why I'm here?'

Guy wouldn't know me. He wouldn't even remember when he woke up. But in six hours, he would feel like he was missing something or that something was off. He would remember the lion. The dream would stay with Guy long after he forgot it, and then I'd be back tomorrow, and the next night, and the night after that until I came for him.

'What the fuck?' he asked, and I grinned at him.

'I bet that's what your hosts say when you jump bodies, don't they?'

I watched as Guy's body stiffened, his eyes widening and his mouth dropping open. I felt it as he pulled on his consciousness to pull him out of the dream, but I slammed a hand to the wall to keep him there. I locked the door shut on his mind, tilted my head and waved a finger.

'I wouldn't do that. You could get stuck in here indefinitely, and that would be no fun for me. How are you supposed to run if you're stuck in your mind? I like the chase more than anything.'

'You're fucking crazy,' he said, stepping back. I came side by side with the lion and rubbed my fingers through his mane. He chuffed at me, nudging my hand, and I ran it over his snout before he bared his teeth. I would die for him if someone hurt him, but he would kill them with a single swipe of his paw before they tried.

'"Crazy" isn't what I would call myself, really. I'd say eclectic, and probably the only way you'll be able to wake up. If I let you. Or you'll find out how hard it really is to be trapped in your own mind. I went there once. It wasn't so nice. Everything was pretty murky. And repetitive. Always repetitive.'

'What do you want?' His voice wavered, and I smiled. *Ahh, sweet, magickal words.*

'If I told you that, I'd have to kill you, and you're not ready yet.'

'Wh-hat? I'm only eighteen. Too young to die.'

One.

Bargaining.

The first step when it came to one's life ending. He wanted to stall. His eyes darted from side to side as he made a step backwards before he drilled his gaze on me.

He blinked, and I blinked with him. I made myself indivisible and invaded his personal space. I reappeared in front of his face and he screamed, tripped over a branch and scrambled backwards. It was like it all happened in slow motion for him, but it was fast.

'You're not too young to die. You're not in control here. I can feel you trying to pull away. It's not going to change anything. Did you think you would get away with it?' I paused and was careful not to touch him as I crouched down to his level. 'What about that poor girl who was stoned to death because you decided it would be fun to sleep around? Did you think about that once when you were in her body? Riding those men, fucking them like it was a sport?'

His eyes widened further, like they were big and as round as saucers. 'I-I didn't do anything.'

'Don't lie to me,' I snapped at him. I clicked my fingers, lightning ripping through the sky, and thunder crashing. He jumped at the noises.

'I'm not lying,' he said again. I clicked my fingers again. This time, lightning cracked and hit the ground next to where Guy was. He scrambled to his feet and stared at the earth as it ripped in two.

'I know you're lying. The more you do so, the harder this is going to get.'

He looked from the ground to me, and his eyes shone with tears. Tears used to make me weak—they used to be the one thing that stopped me—but I'd learnt a hard lesson when I was nearly killed because of them.

Never again did tears from a mark worry me.

It was the whole reason I'd learnt how to switch off and bury my emotions. I didn't want to get hurt and I refused to let it happen ever again.

'I didn't mean it. I just didn't have the strength and the control. I never meant for any of them to get hurt.'

Two.

Reasoning.

Like telling me the reasons would help him.

'You wouldn't be lying to me again, would you, Guy?' I asked, and he seemed panicked.

Liar.

'Who are you?' he asked, and I smiled at him.

'Your Dreamwalking Assassin nightmare. I'm going to come for you and make you sorry for everything you've ever done.' Guy turned to run, and with a flick of my wrist, vines reached up and wrapped around his limbs, holding him in place. I circled around him, and the lion stood next to me, huffing as I looked him in the eye.

'I'm going to make sure that you're sorry.' I got into his personal space and forced him to look at me and nothing else. 'I'm going to make you wish you'd taken your own life before I'm finished you. You'll live in fear of when my arrow will strike your heart.'

Guy was shivering now. I could feel it, and the fear in his eyes was enough to satisfy me. I walked away without looking back at him. As I hit the window, I clicked my finger and let him out of his prison.

Slowly, I woke up out of the dream. My body slid into its consciousness, and I looked up at the ceiling. Dancing stars glittered back at me—the only way I could sleep, or not sleep.

I scrubbed my hand over my face and sat up. 'Fuck.' My heart raced with excitement, and all I could think about was Acionna. After the past few days, I couldn't keep doing that.

I was tired of my double life.

I wanted to fall in love without the fear that she was going to end up on my kill list.

Because Acionna wasn't human. I knew she was some sort of ocean creature. I wanted to keep her a secret, and that was going to get harder.

Choiak 2012

A shrill alarm sliced through the air. My body jolted out of what little sleep I'd had, and I swallowed hard. That alarm felt like the kind one set before getting up for work or school. It made me think about those times I should have just stayed in bed. And that felt like one of them.

It was the dead of night.

What the fuck?

I rubbed my eyes and sat up in my bunk.

'D-Man,' Jarrad whispered.

My eyes glanced at the clock. It was 3.37 a.m. I groaned and lay back down.

'Not happening,' I said.

'You don't have a choice. Get dressed,' Jarrad said, and threw some clothes at me. They hit me in the gut. I shook off the sleep and rolled out of the bunk. The clothes were dark—probably black—but in the slivers of moonlight I could hardly tell. There was a pair of cargo pants and a T-shirt. My fingers pressed along the collar; the T-shirt had a hood. That was new.

'Boots?' I asked.

'Steel caps,' Jarrad replied.

They were heavy, and even after weeks of training with them, they never got easier. More worn in, yes, but still not easier.

The weather was still hot as fuck, but that didn't change a thing. He wouldn't care that it was hot, only that I was there. Following orders.

Jarrad was outside the dorm, leaning against the other side of it with his hand folded over his chest. His dark hair shone in the moonlight, but that was all that could be seen.

'What's going on?'

Too many questions ran through my head, and I knew they would hate it. We didn't ask questions at The Camp. We just did. The scars on my back were enough proof that asking questions was too much.

'Misson for you.'

'Just me?'

That was odd too.

'Mhm. This way,' Jarrad said, and pushed off the wall. He turned on his heel and shifted to the right. Jarrad began walking, and there was no other choice but to follow him. I followed him because if I didn't, the consequences would be harder to deal with. Our footsteps echoed through that section of The Camp. All of the dorms had slated wooden exteriors. The lighting was minimal—flickering fluros that gave everything a sickly tinge no matter where one looked. The ground was cobblestoned, and there were rows and rows of dorms. I likened it closer to the dorm rooms and the configuration of the campsite I had stayed at in high school on our first-year camp.

Jarrad paused at the armoury shed and looked over his shoulder. 'Grab your bow and arrow, D-Man.'

I paused and raised an eyebrow. 'Jarrad, I don't know if I like this. It's the middle of the night.' I'd been at The Camp for months at that point. I lost track of the days, and the way that made me feel ... Destiny was slowly fading in the background. I could feel her every day, but it was a practiced effort to keep her out of my head so I could train without worrying. A few moments here and there, I got a flash of emotions that made me want to punch a wall. It was at those moments that I trained harder, pushed my body further. I didn't want to feel those feelings, but knowing she was hurting somewhere was too much to bear in quiet moments.

'It's the only way. Come on. We have to get this done before sunrise.' Jarrad was colder than I had ever seen him, and hiding every inch of who he was. He had on clothes that mimicked mine—black cargos, black T-shirt, black boots. In the moonlight, I could have sworn I saw a flash of purple, but that would—*No, it was the trick of light.*

I entered the armoury, grabbed the quiver full of arrows and slung it over my head so the strap sat across my body. The smell of freshly conditioned leather was comforting—it reminded me of Mum's couches when she was on a cleaning blitz. I hesitated for a moment and picked up my bow. I was there against my will, but I was going to do what they said to keep my family safe. I'd seen the images and the surveillance they had. They could get to anyone, and while The Camp had a code, I didn't trust them.

Everyone told me not to trust them. Even the guys who slept in my dorm didn't trust me either. Either of them could easily kill us in our sleep, and the only thing that stopped them was knowing the reaming they would get for killing someone we shouldn't.

'We don't have all night, D-Man,' Jarrad called out.

I hugged the bow to my chest with one arm and grabbed the wrist protection, slipping my hand through it and strapping it in place. I walked out of the armoury. Jarrad nodded, and I followed him without a word. He led us to the entrance of The Camp. I blinked and my jaw dropped. *Could this be my chance to run?* Jarrad chuckled.

'Don't get any ideas, Dev. You're going on a mission, and we're waiting for—that.' A black van pulled up right in front of us, and the small delight of joy that had shot through my body at the prospect of leaving left, replaced by a heavy set of dread in the pit of my stomach. The back door opened, and Jarrad nudged me to get in. I didn't have much of a choice, so I stepped into the back of the van. Inside were two guys I had never seen before. They tilted their heads at me and went back to the screens they had installed in the back. On the screens was surveillance of The Camp, but also a house—one that didn't look familiar but was quiet. It was in a residential street with bushes as hedges and looked like it needed a white picket fence to make it complete, but surely we weren't that close to civilisation.

'Jar ... what is this?' I asked finally as the car was moving and everyone was strapped in.

He handed me a file, and I took it from him. Jarrad watched me for a moment before I tore my eyes away from his and stared at the manila folder in my hand. I opened it, and inside was a picture of a smiling woman. She had bright red hair, dark lipstick, green eyes and freckles. She was gorgeous by many standards, but that didn't matter. I had seen what gorgeous women could do, and I wasn't going to make that same mistake twice.

'This is your mission.'

I flicked past the picture and found her details. Lisa Davidson, twenty-five, Mechanical engineer, Naga … My eyes widened. 'Naga?' I asked.

Jarrad nodded. 'Keep reading.'

My eyes scanned the rest of the document. She was grooming young boys. *What the actual fuck?*

'Ahhh, you saw it. This is what you're going to do. You're going to kill her.'

'Excuse me? What?' The file dropped from my fingers and hit the floor. I stared at Jarrad like he had grown another head. 'You want me to *what?*'

'No time like the present. This is what we're training you to do. To be.'

'Get fucked. No. *No!* I'm not taking another person's life.'

'You don't have a choice, Devin. You have to.'

The car came to a sudden stop, and I jolted in my seat. *Are they just going to throw me out of the car and let me find my way out?* I could have done it. I would have found my way back to Lucy if I had to.

'No. I do have a choice. I'm a human being.'

'You are a soldier, and you need to do this part. Everyone else has had to do it, and you will too. And the next one, and the one after that, and all those after that.'

'You're training us to be assassins,' I said. The car idled, almost like it was waiting to hear what Jarrad was going to say next.

'Yes. And you don't have a choice. You were hand-picked by Karrept. That's your legacy. The others did something to be here. You were just picked.'

That fucking book. I wanted to burn it, make sure it never saw another sign of daylight ever again.

'I can't take another person's life,' I said finally.

'You can. You will. And you have to.'

With those words, the car started moving again, and I shook my head. *I guess I am doing this.*

The ride felt like it went on for hours, but it was probably more like an hour. It would make the time just before five in the morning, and it would be light soon. The car came to a rolling stop, and Jarrad unclicked his seatbelt and stood up. I took that as the sign and did the same. I gripped my bow tight, not believing I was about to end someone's life.

What did I think I was practicing for? Self-defence? To get out of The Camp? Everyone was in top physical condition. If they were still there, what hope did I have?

'You okay?' Jarrad asked as he looked over his shoulder, a hand at the door, ready to open it.

Bile rose in my throat, and I swallowed hard. 'Not really.' *Fuck no.* I was terrified, and he was asking me if I was okay? He knew I wasn't. There was no way he was that oblivious.

He smiled and opened the door. There was not a hint of anything … No crickets, no cicadas. Like there was dead air. Or there was something really dangerous living there.

Lisa Davidson.

Yeah, she was pretty dangerous. Nagas were half human, half snake, and were normally a thing of fairy tales. Or myths. *What the hell have I stumbled on?* I knew the world was full of metaphysical beings, but this was next-level.

There would only be a handful of Nagas still alive.

'Dev, keep your head down. Put your hood up and follow me,' Jarrad said.

I wondered how many of those he had to do. How many green-faced men and women were in the same position I was.

My body screamed at me to run, to just get out of sight. But if I did that, I left Destiny alone. She was relying on me.

Jarrad ran along the footpath like knew where he was going, I followed and tried to watch for anything that could trip me. I looked from side to side to see if there was anyone awake, but all the houses were quiet, dark.

It seemed odd that there was no animal movement around. *Could nagas scare off native animals? Are they that powerful?*

I hadn't prepared mentally for that.

Jarrad stopped abruptly, and I balled into him. 'Fuck. Dev,' he hissed.

'Sorry.' I rubbed the back of my neck with my hand and tried to step back, but Jarrad gripped my shoulder and pointed to the right. I could see movement in the house—the one that had been on the screen in the van.

That was Lisa Davidson's house. *Shit.*

'Now set up. I've got a scope,' Jarrad said, and let go of me.

Set up? How the fuck am I supposed to do that? I pulled an arrow from my quiver and sank it into the notch on the bow. My hand shook for half a second, but I took a deep breath. It didn't matter that my insides were shivering in fear. I couldn't let them see it externally. I took the scope from Jarrad and hooked it up to the bow. It would sit just at eye level. I rested my eye against it and could see Lisa. She was moving around her house, her hair in a messy bun. Lisa moved like she was slinking around, and as my eye trailed down from her face, I saw it—the huge snake body. It started at her hips, green, luminescent scales hugging where her legs should have been. I swallowed hard and wanted to say something, but Jarrad squeezed my leg. Whatever was said, she would most definitely hear.

I inhaled sharply, and with that breath, clicked the arrow in place on the string. Then, I pulled it back to my face. My thumb rested against my cheek, and I watched Lisa sashay through the window. She was doing something I couldn't see from her body. I wondered if, when she was in her full human form, she was as tall. Or maybe she was shorter. I'd never be able to test that theory.

Aim for the parts that will do the most damage.

Words I kept repeating to try to separate myself from what I was about to do. I was going to take her life, and she wouldn't have any idea of who I was. Or why.

Just that she needed to die.

I took another breath and let go of the arrow. It was what I had been training for. It was what I had spent the late nights honing that bow and my reflexes to do.

It sailed through the air and cracked the window. I watched as it sliced through her head, and she dropped to the ground.

A headshot was the fastest kill possible.

I didn't miss.

From the scope, I saw a man on the table. He looked young, but he was in shock.

'Let's go,' Jarrad said.

Without arguing, I followed. We ran back the way we came … or at least, that was what I thought. I was just going through the motions.

We kept running, and I felt the bile rise. I couldn't hold it back anymore. I stopped cold and bent over, vomiting up whatever was in my stomach. *I just took a life.*

'D-Man, now is not the time to chuck your guts.'

I could hardly hear him, but the vomit burnt my throat, and I couldn't stop it even if I wanted to. I coughed and spluttered until the vomit stopped. I wiped my mouth with the back of my hand.

'Here.' Jarrad handed me some water. *Where the fuck did that come from?*

'Thanks.'

'Let's go.' He pulled me away from the curb, and we hightailed it to the van. As soon as we were inside and the door was closed, we took off. It didn't speed away. It did nothing out of character. Just started up and went on its merry way.

'Congrats, Dev. You've done your first kill.'

I was breathing hard and took a swig of the water. The feeling that sank in my stomach told me there was more to come, and I'd have to get past that feeling.

CHAPTER TWENTY

Acionna
Pachons 2017
Melbourne

Ariel being around was weird, but what was even stranger was that she looked so lethargic and pale. That wasn't normal. I wondered where she was and if something had happened to her. Being cut off from my family meant that unless they were on land and had access to modern technology, there was no way to get in contact with me.

I had mourned that fact over the past 184 days, and there was a part of me that wanted to try and get back to them, risk the chance of drowning so I could be with them again. But would they actually see the value in it? Ariel was so angry. I had seen her mad before. It seemed like my decision to Match with Eain had set her off. But this was different. Like she had seen me and realised that my very presence insulted her.

I was so torn between going back to the beach to find her and calling Devin to explain. I didn't want to talk after the encounter, and he had accepted that and let it go.

I walked onto the balcony. It was mid-morning, and now that the cooler change had settled in, the days were getting shorter, darkness settling in a little sooner than expected. It made me wonder how humans did it every day. The Undersea had days, but they were different. There was no night and day under the surface. We didn't conform the same way.

As I leant against the balcony banister, a wave of dizziness hit me, and I gripped the rail hard. I pressed my fingers against my temple in an attempt to push that dizziness away, but instead, it seemed to make it worse.

'What is going on?' I murmured to myself. I stepped back from the edge. What I thought was graceful was more like a stumble. The last thing I saw was the calm shimmer of the ocean before everything went black.

As I came to, I heard voices arguing above me. One of them was definitely Janice, and the other was a man. I shot up in bed and instantly groaned before shooting back down again.

'Ash,' the voice said, and it was full of worry. No man had ever had that tone with me. For a second, I tried to place it before I let my eyes linger on the room. Devin's frowning face stared back at me.

'Devin? What are you doing here?' I asked.

His face softened, and he sat down on the bed, right next to me. 'I was coming over to give you a gift. I was downstairs when we heard a huge thump and came running up.'

'What happened?' I looked at Janice, and she was more worried than Devin was. But there was also a hint of fear in her eyes. It had never been there before. It looked so odd on her face. I tore my eyes away from her and looked at Devin.

'You tell us. We found you unconscious on the floor on the balcony. You might have hit your head. Janice and I were arguing about getting you a doctor.'

'No! No doctor,' I said quickly.

Devin clicked his tongue and sighed. 'That's what Janice was saying, and that's what I'm afraid of. The not-human part of you must really be something no doctor can see because I have never seen two women so strongly oppose medical treatment before.'

'It's complicated.'

'I bet. I have a sister who is on her way to being a medical practitioner, and she is a witch. I can ask her to give you a once-over. She's not a practicing doctor, but it would make me feel better.'

I shook my head, and that rattled my whole jaw. *Ouch.* 'I'm good. It's okay. I must have forgotten to eat or something.'

But the realisation that it could be more than that had terror digging into my stomach. Ariel had been pale, and she was the only hint of home that I'd had access to in all of the months being landlocked. Whatever happened to me was related to seeing her. Or at least, that was all I could think of.

'Look, I'm okay with letting most things go. I have been around enough women to know that when they don't want to say anything, they won't say anything. But I'm here, and whatever you need, I'm here for it,' Devin said. His hands were in his lap, but he was itching to touch me. I took his hand and interlaced my fingers between his. He relaxed and squeezed my hand. 'I don't know how to do this thing … I've only been around women who have some sort of relation to me, or they've been around so long they're practically another sister. This worrying about someone is new to me,' he admitted.

'I didn't mean to make you worry.'

'Miss Acionna, I'll bring up the gift Mr Devin brought for you,' Janice said in the background as she walked out of the room.

'You brought me a gift?'

'Yeah, you seemed a little lonely. Mum had so many of these lying around, so I thought I'd bring you one.'

My eyes widened. 'Like, it's something alive? Devin … I don't think I can keep it alive. I can barely keep myself alive.' And that wasn't far from the truth. I was sitting around living a half life without my pelt.

'These are easy, trust me.' He grinned and leant down to kiss me.

His lips touched mine, and for a moment, I forgot about anything else in the world. All that there was, was Devin, and he smelt like what I pictured heaven would be like—a little bit of citrus and whisky.

He pulled back, and his smile softened. 'Can you not worry me like that again? You weren't responding, and it scared the shit out of us. Me.' He pressed his lips together and smoothed my hair out of my face.

'I'll remember that for next time. I thought you'd be sick of seeing me.' My voice was a little raspy, like I was worried I would say something wrong.

He shook his head and tilted my head up as I had unconsciously looked down. 'Could never be sick of you.'

A small meow broke the silence, and I blinked at Devin before looking past him. Janice was holding a small carrier with a kitten inside it. It was a grey colour, and around its neck was a sea green bow.

'Devin ... What is this?'

'A small gift. Mum sometimes breeds her cats, and this is one of the last litters this cat is going to have. When I saw this one, I thought of you. She's got green eyes that may change, but she's playful, feisty and really loves a good belly rub. I thought you would want something that would give you unconditional love. And she also gives me more of a reason to come and see you. Not that I need a reason.'

I motioned for Devin to help me up, and he gently assisted me into a sitting position. My head throbbed, and I steeled myself against the wave of nausea that came with the movement.

'Are you okay, Ash?' he asked.

I nodded. *Why is this happening? I've had months of nothing, where I felt normal, and now this?* After he left, I was going to have to sit down with Janice. We were going to need to figure out what was going on.

'I'm okay,' I replied.

Janice handed the carrier to Devin, and he took care with placing it down. He unzipped the door, reached in and grabbed the kitten. He cooed at her, the most endearing thing I had ever seen him do, and pulled her out ever so gently. He rubbed the spot behind her ears, and she leant into his touch. *Oh, she likes him just as much as I do.* Devin handed the kitten to me, and I took her. I stared at her little body and couldn't find the words. She was utterly perfect.

'Dev,' I whispered, afraid my voice would spook her. 'She's so soft and cute.'

'I know. I hope you can name her something fun. Is there anything you need?' he asked earnestly.

Who is this wonderful man? He had a smart mouth on him, but underneath it all, Devin was soft, and all I wanted to do was curl up into him and forget about the world.

'Stay a while with me. Janice, can you bring some food up?' I asked, and she nodded before disappearing.

'Janice is always here, isn't she?'

'Mhm. She's more like a friend than the help though.' That was because she was tied so closely to home, but I didn't know how to explain that to him.

'I like that. At home, there's help. You hardly see them because Mum keeps them in line. It's weird knowing that my clothes just randomly turn up clean and ironed ... Like, what?'

I chuckled. 'I wouldn't let Janice near my clothes. She tried once. I changed that quick smart.'

He smiled. 'What is your secret, Ash? I'll tell you mine if you tell me yours.'

I shook my head and cuddled the kitten closer. 'Not yet.'

I was scared he was going to run, and I liked him too much for that.

CHAPTER TWENTY-ONE

Devin
Tybi 2010
Egypt

There wasn't much I ever wanted. Dad made sure that we always had everything … as long as we worked for it. From the time I could walk, Dad always made sure that I did chores, had small feats of input into the hotel business, and always made sure that Mum was looked after. He taught me from an early age that women were to be respected, and that there was no other way about it.

Mum always got flowers on Mother's Day as well as her birthday. Lucy and Destiny were always treated like they were queens. They got a single stemmed rose for Valentine's Day. I never understood it when I was a little boy, but as I got older, Dad explained that women were powerful beings. They would carry our children and shoulder a lot of the burden so we could do what was needed. They deserved to be treated like they hung the moon, and we were just there to help them.

I believed him.

I lived to see Lucy smile when she was down and made sure Destiny was always cared for.

'Dad, I'm going to tell you this, and know that you don't need to do anything. I don't know if Lucy will ever say anything, but I need to tell someone,' I said as I walked into his office.

We were in Egypt. The room had our paintings on the wall—a guise for the vaults hidden behind them—and there was a huge mahogany desk in the centre of the space. Bookshelves flanked the wall behind him, all full of architecture books and stories from our childhood. I got a flash of Antony leaning over Lucy on the desk, and my blood boiled. Lucy was sleeping in her room, and I was still shaking with anger.

'What is it, Dev?'

He shut his laptop and gave me his full attention. I closed the door behind me to make sure Mum or Destiny wouldn't hear. Or goddess forbid, Lucy.

'Lucy was hurt.'

Those three words forced Dad up from his desk. I shook my head and held my hands up. 'She's okay now.'

'Devin,' he said, his voice laced with rage. It vibrated off him in waves, and I had never seen him so angry before. I didn't want to think what would happen if I hadn't been around.

'Antony Pazalogous tried to force himself on her.'

'The magickal kid who was around earlier?' Dad ripped his glasses off his nose and rubbed his fingers against his eyes like he was trying to rub the image from his mind.

'Yes. I stopped him, and I may have very nearly hurt him more than I would have.' I would have killed him if I knew how. It was left unsaid because that was how I protected my sisters.

'Where is he now?'

'I had a driver take him to the hospital,' I said, and looked away. I glanced down at my hands. My knuckles were bruised and aching, but I'd do it again.

'And the driver?'

'Paid off.'

'Dev ... you're fourteen,' Dad said.

'I know, but you had money lying around, and Lucy was crying out. You were at the hotel in an important meeting.'

Dad clicked his tongue, and instead of saying anything else, closed the distance between us and pulled me into his chest. He hugged me tight, and I let myself melt against his chest. That was Dad. He was the strongest person I knew. He was always there when I needed him. No matter what happened, he was there.

'I just saw red. He was hurting Luce, and I acted accordingly. No one hurts Lucy.'

'I know,' he said as he rubbed my back. I couldn't see his face, but I wondered if he felt the same way I did. I had never seen Dad angry or lose his cool in any sort of way. He was cool and calm. Lucy joked that we got our hot-headedness from Mum because Dad was so cool.

'I'm sorry if I did the wrong thing.'

'Devin, protecting the women in the family and the women in your life is never something to be sorry about. It is about how we keep our family safe and loved. Do you want to talk about it?'

He was genuine, and I didn't know if I wanted to talk about what happened or that I had basically bloodied a man up. I wasn't violent, but seeing a man force himself on my baby sister just made me lose it. It was like a switch was flicked, and that was all I could think about.

'Am I a bad person, Dad?'

He pulled me back and held me at an arm's length away, his fingers pressing into my shoulders so he could see my eyes. 'Never think that you're a bad person. There are urges we shouldn't act on, but when someone is hurt or hurting someone we love, it's not an option. You did everything you could in the moment, and I will never say otherwise.' His eyes roamed down to my hands, and he clicked his tongue. 'Let's go and get these iced and fixed up before your mother realises what happened, hmm?'

'Dad, did you want to know what happened?' I asked.

'No. Because I'm afraid the laws here about murder are far stricter than back home, and I can't risk that.'

Shit. He was right.

Pachons 2017
Melbourne

The kitten had been a hit, but it was so worrying to see Acionna passed out on the balcony. I hadn't been able to wipe that memory from my mind—almost like when Travis filled me in on the details of what had happened while I was at The Camp. Lucy and her suicide attempt … It had nearly killed me, hearing that, but it was worse hearing it from Travis' point of view because he still remembered the blood. He could smell it.

Being kidnapped had never been on my bingo list. I'd tried so hard to get out, but it was impossible. Lucy and Hunter had done something I was able to do, and it still amazed me. The strength and poise that Lucy would have had to have to get through the fear of not knowing if I was dead or alive …

Acionna looked so clammy and pale, so different from her sun-kissed skin and vibrant eyes. She looked like that girl on the beach—her sister. They looked so similar, and not just in facial features—their skin seemed to have the same sickly twinge to it too.

I grabbed my phone and texted her, my fingers a flurry of movement over the letters.

I'm almost done here. I'll be back with chocolate … and food.

Janice had mentioned that Acionna was strictly a pescatarian. That was an easy feat to gather up, but I was annoyed that my meeting had to happen right at three. Just in time for the school rush. Traffic would be a nightmare once it was done, moving right into peak hour. I hated driving in peak hour traffic.

Make sure it's sea salt. And can you grab some toys and treats for the kitten?

The kitten had taken over her whole personality, and it was cute.

'Can we get this meeting started?' I called out as I walked into the boardroom. Inside the room, there was a long table. It was walnut in colour, or was it mahogany?

Seated at the table was Dad. He was at the head of the table. To his right was Mum. Surprisingly, she sat in on some meetings. Lucy would kick herself if she knew they were doing things without her, but she was also probably happy to not be involved. The best thing that happened to her was me coming back and her relinquishing the heir business over to me.

'We're waiting on—ahhh, Fred, you're here,' Dad said. I looked at the door, and Fred, the lawyer, came striding in. I could tell he wasn't human; there was a sickly scent of death that covered him. He was undead. Not the vampire flavour, but a zombie. Like Destiny, but different.

'Hello, everyone. Apologies for the lateness. Traffic is honestly a bitch, and if it's not traffic, it's parking.'

Dad chuckled. 'I appreciate you coming in on such short notice.'

'Dad, what are we doing?' I asked, suddenly realising the meeting would only consist of Mum, Dad, Fred and me. It was serious shit.

Fred shut the door behind him and laid his briefcase out on the table with care. He clicked it open and lifted the lid. Fred shuffled around and took some papers out of the briefcase, and dropped them on the table. They hit the wood with a soft *thwack*.

'We can now,' Dad said. He motioned to a seat, but I didn't think I wanted to sit down.

'You going to sit, Dev?' Mum asked. I glanced at the seat she motioned to sit down in.

'Why am I here?' The good soldier in me didn't normally ask questions, but I wanted to know why I was there and not Lucy or Destiny. It would mean that it would have something to do with the company, but I didn't want to do anything without them. I refused to.

'We're updating all of the wills and contracts for you. When the time comes to take over, we aren't going to risk something out of the norm happening,' Dad said.

'Matt.' Mum rested a hand on Dad's arm.

The immature boy in my head wanted to mimic Mum, but instead, I looked at Dad and didn't say anything.

'It's time to have you start the takeover, Dev. We need to get this out of the way so the legal proceedings can happen, and we need to make sure it's all in order.'

'So why are we doing this with Lucy and Destiny? I don't want to make any decisions without them. We've spoken about this before, and I want to make sure that promise is kept up.'

I refused to sit. I used my height as an advantage. It took everything in me not to cross my arms over my chest in defiance. I was a good soldier, but I was also still a son to a father who pushed the boundaries.

'This doesn't need them. It's not a decision they need to make. We're literally here to go through the contract and have you sign your name. I'm sure Lucy and Destiny would be bored out of their brains during something they didn't need to be here for.'

'Lucy, yes,' I muttered.

Dad beamed at me. 'Lucy, definitely. Come on, Dev, sit down. We're here to make it all run smoothly. You can then leave and continue with what you need to do. It won't take too much out of your day.'

He had a point, and the longer the meeting went on, the longer it would take to get back to Acionna.

Which seemed to be all I wanted to do lately.

I sighed and pulled out the chair to the right of Mum and sat down. Fred nodded and shuffled through the papers to hand out a copy to everyone.

'In these documents are legal agreements between Matthew and Subira Ryder and Devin Ryder. Are we okay to record this meeting for future references?' he asked.

'Yes,' Dad answered without hesitation, and he looked at me.

'Yes from me too.'

'Also yes,' Mum chimed in.

An uneasy feeling settled in my chest. *Why does this need to be recorded? Is there going to be someone who needs this later?*

I wished that I could understand what Dad wanted to do with it and why it was so important that it needed to be done right then and not in years to come.

I was just starting to take an interest in the business, but that didn't mean I wanted to be the head honcho right then and there. Dad had so many years left on him.

'Perfect. Okay, so you'll see as we run through this contract that there are a lot of nuances. And Devin, if you have any objections, speak up now because we can change anything you need changed in there. And nothing is too small to change.'

I nodded. 'Can I take a few moments to look over the documents before there is any discussion on them?'

'Absolutely. Do you need to do that in another room?'

'No, here is fine. Give me a bit.' I skimmed the document. A lot of it was the same old stuff. I would be named the heir of the company, and everything would transfer out of Dad's name into mine. Lucy and Destiny would be free to help however they wanted to. But the kicker of it all?

Mum was to stay on the board—lead from the inside so there was order in a time that would be chaos. She would make sure no one was being guilty of trying to undercut it all and take away the company she and Dad had worked on so lovingly.

'Okay, so this says that I'm named the heir. Is it only me?'

'Yes.'

'The same rules apply here?' I asked, and I held Dad's gaze.

'Yes.'

'How does this change what is currently happening?'

'It doesn't. Everything is the same until something happens to me, whether that is something medical that leaves me bedridden or in the untimely event of my death.'

I nodded and flipped the page over to read more about the terms and conditions of what I was signing. I picked up a pen and clicked it three times really fast. I could kill a metaphysical being with no remorse, and that didn't terrify me, but signing my name across a contract where I inherited a billion-dollar company that I had basically grown up learning how to run scared the absolute shit out of me.

Because a world without Dad in it would be weird, and it was not one I would be ready to face.

'And this only takes place if something happens to you?'

'Mhm, not that anything will. It's a fail-safe. I don't want to leave the business in a critical position.'

'Okay, I have one condition before I sign this.'

'Name it.'

'I get the right to keep my office and not move into yours.'

'That's easy.'

'And a right to change the name.'

'No. Absolutely not. It's been Ryder Hotel for as long as it's been standing, and that's not going to change any time soon,' Dad countered.

Did I really think that that would fly? Absolutely not, but I needed to make sure he was serious.

'Okay,' I said, and signed my name on the first dotted line. Then, I flipped the page and did the same on the second page, and the third.

'Devin, congratulations. Ryder Hotel will be all yours in the event that your father is unable to make a sound decision,' Fred said.

Great. I was going to have a whole company to myself, and I had to make sure I could run it and not just kill people for a living.

'Thanks, I guess?' I said, placing the pen on the table and standing. 'Thanks for this. I have to go and meet a friend.' Because Acionna wouldn't wait longer than necessary, and I wouldn't let her wait longer.

CHAPTER TWENTY-TWO

Acionna
Pachons 2017
Melbourne

The edge of the cliff was smoother than I would have imagined. I didn't know how I'd gotten myself out there. I felt dizzy, but I couldn't let that pain stop me. I had to get the night's picture. I couldn't risk losing the very thing I needed the most. The most time I had ever spent away from my pelt before was a day, and it had now been six months. I thought it would get easier, and on some levels, it did, but the need to be with the sea was all I could hear. And after fainting earlier—something I had never done before—it was louder than it had ever been. I wanted to make it all go away, but if I did that, I would be just ... gone.

The wind whipped up around me, tossing my long hair into my eyes. I had my camera slung on my shoulder. Taking a small step forward, the weakness that settled in my legs threatened to take away everything I had. *I could plunge over the edge and maybe survive.*

My pelt called to me, and each day, the call got quieter. Muffled, like it was losing steam. There were no records of what happened after losing one's pelt for long periods. Nothing in the archives mentioned what happened. Ever.

Could this be a fever? A pelt fever?

Perhaps it was a result of what happened when one was away from their pelt for too long. That would mean that Ariel would be in the same … *Holy shit.*

She is landlocked too.

'Fuck,' I whispered under my breath.

The soft rumble of thunder brewed in the sky, and I looked up. I hoped the storm would hold out for me to get my picture and try to figure out how to fix that weird feeling.

'Acionna, what are you doing out here?' I jumped at the sound of Devin's voice and looked over my shoulder at him.

'You scared me. Didn't anyone tell you it's not nice to sneak up on anyone?'

The fact that Devin could do that when I had preternaturally reflexes and senses meant that the situation was way worse than I had initially thought.

'I thought I was being pretty loud, actually,' he said, and snaked an arm around my waist. Part of me wanted to melt into him, but there wasn't much time left. I had to get a good shot or I would lose it.

I squirmed out of his embrace, a flash of hurt clouding his eyes before it was gone just as quickly as it appeared. My gut twisted at that very motion, but I had to get the picture, and I was afraid that by melting into his embrace, I would miss it.

'I have to take a picture. The storm is getting in the way.'

'Then let's go back to yours and take it from there.'

I shook my head. 'You don't understand. I can't. I have to take it here.'

'Ash, it's getting choppy,' he said, and looked past me and out at the ocean. I wanted to follow his gaze, but I looked at my watch. It was so close to the time, and normally, I was set up. 'And you're not well. You shouldn't be out here.'

I wanted to be mad at him for saying that, but he was right. I shouldn't have been out there. But there was no one else who could do it. Nothing would stop me from keeping my pelt safe.

'It's okay. I can do this. I just have to get down there.' I pointed to the left of us, and he followed my finger.

'Ash, that's dangerous.'

'I'm going to climb down.'

Devin gripped my bicep and shook his head. 'No. I don't care if you're not human, but you're going to hurt yourself.'

'Devin, let me go. I have to get the picture or she's going to destroy it.'

'Destroy what?' Devin asked, and he held me tighter. 'Acionna, it's too dangerous.'

'My livelihood, my skin, my pelt. She's holding it for ransom.'

'Pelt? Acionna, are you a selkie?' he asked.

I nodded and wrenched my arm out of his grip and ran back down the spine of the rocks. If I made it, I would be able to get the shot, and it would be okay. But if I didn't do it then, I wouldn't get the chance.

'Ash! Wait,' Devin called out behind me, but I didn't let that stop me. I held my camera close to my chest and ran onto the sand. There was a loud crack of lighting before another huge rumble of thunder rolled over us. It made me jump, but I needed to get the picture. I was breathing hard as I got to the spot, brought the camera to my eye and snapped quickly, but the water came rushing in, right up to my knees, and it made me stumble. The alarm went off on my watch, and I took another snap, capturing a bolt of lightning in the shot.

'Acionna!' Devin called out. I turned to see where he was. He was running up to me, but a huge wave knocked me over, and the camera flew from my grasp. It hit the water, and I screamed.

If I had lost that camera, my pelt would have been as good as gone too. That camera was the whole reason I could do it. If I lost it, there was no going back.

'Devin, I need that camera. Don't let it float away.' I frantically shifted in the water and tried to see where it was going or where it landed.

'I can't see it,' he said.

An invisible hand gripped my heart and squeezed. I doubled over at the pain. If I lost the camera, life wouldn't be worth living.

'Ash!' Devin's supportive weight pulled me against his body, my breathing suddenly ragged. 'It's going to be okay,' he murmured.

Will it be? Could I live there without my pelt? Knowing I would never be able to go back home or feel the water on my skin in a way that I had always known?

'Oh, fuck.' Devin let me go and dived under the water. I watched him go, and part of me wanted to die. If I dived under and stayed at the bottom of the ocean, would it take me away and take me out of my miserable half life?

Devin broke through the surface, and he had something in his hand. My eyes were so unfocused, and refused to find him.

'I got it,' he said, and took my hands and put the camera in them. The hand gripped around my heart eased up, and I hugged the device to my chest.

'Thank you,' I whispered.

My teeth chattered, and Devin picked me up in his arms and carried me out of the water. He cradled me against his chest. I didn't see any of the world, but I knew I was safe and sound in his arms. I barely felt the way the rain battered us.

In the bathroom, he looked at me like I was fragile. I hated that look, and I didn't know how to change it.

'Don't look at me like that.'

'You're a selkie, Ash—without your pelt. You were muttering that someone has it. Who has it? And what does a photo have to do with this?'

In the heat of the moment, I had said too much. Back in the Undersea, I'd never have said so much. It was why Mother had picked me to be her heir; I was good at keeping secrets and working around anything that happened.

'I … I made a mistake, and I've been cursed to take a photo a day at the same time or my pelt will get destroyed. I … I can't let it get destroyed, or I'm never going home. I might be weak forever.'

'Wait, what? You're telling me that your fainting episode earlier today is linked to your pelt?'

I pressed my lips together. 'It could be. I didn't think that it was, but it's possible. I feel like death warming up, and I have never felt like this before. I have only ever been away from my skin for max twenty-four hours. It's been longer than that.'

'What?' Devin stared at me like I had grown an extra head.

'Did I stutter?' I asked and instantly regretted it. 'Sorry, that was mean. I'm a little touchy.' He grabbed a few towels from the cupboard to the left of the bath. How Devin knew they were in there was beyond me, but I didn't say anything. He sat down on the floor with me, his legs open so I could slot myself inside them. I let him pull my top over my head—it was drenched. We were both soaking wet. He wrapped a towel around my shoulders and rubbed his hands up and down them.

'I'm just finding it hard to believe that this whole time, you haven't tried to find whoever has it.'

'I've tried. She covers her tracks and uses magick to make sure nothing can be traced back to her. Her gifts, the camera, everything. I'm terrified of what she'll do to my pelt. Wait … you're okay with me being a selkie?'

He smiled, and something inside me melted. 'Ash, if I wasn't, I would have left you at the beach. I'm okay with it.'

'How do you know about what I am? We're a myth.'

'You're obviously not a myth because you're right in front of me, but I … There's more to my dreamwalking. I can't go into details about it because it'll put you in the firing line, but I know a lot about metaphysical beings.'

'Metaphysical beings. That seems like you know more than you're talking about because not everyone uses metaphysical beings as a blanket term.'

'Fuck,' he muttered. 'When I can tell you, I will. I promise. But right now, I can't. Can you accept that?' he asked.

Can I?

Is this something else I can do? Like, he was there. Devin had brought me a cat. He came back after a meeting and found the camera. I decided I could accept anything he wanted from me.

'I guess so.'

'How long have you been away from your pelt?' he asked me, the towel in his hands gently wringing the water from my hair.

'It's been over six months, closer to seven now.'

'What the fuck? Acionna! That's beyond dangerous. Who is the witch that has it?'

'I don't know, but I need to find her. I can't keep doing this.'

'And you're not going to. I'm going to help you. We're going to find her.'

I closed my eyes and breathed the biggest sigh in six months. 'You don't have to do that.'

'I'm not asking.' He dropped the towel and guided my chin up. 'I'm sorry you've had to do it by yourself for so long.' He kissed me, and I let him. It was soft at first, like he was just tasting me for the first time, and then it was more demanding, almost hungry. My hands bunched his wet shirt up and started to slide it up his torso. My fingers snagged on scars—linear ones that went different ways, almost like he had been hurt.

I pulled back from the kiss and stared at him. 'You have scars all over your back.' My hands went a little higher, and he tried to squirm away from my touch. 'No,' I whispered. 'It's okay. I promise.'

Braver than I thought I was, I lifted his shirt up higher and let the towel fall off my shoulders. His chest was littered with scars. 'Turn around,' I murmured.

The last time we'd had sex, it was in a flurry of need and want. I hadn't had any time to explore his body like I wanted to. 'A-Acionna,' he stammered.

'Please,' I asked, and held his gaze. Devin nodded and pushed himself back, turning so I could see his back.

I gasped at the raised scars on his back.

'What happened?'

'I was whipped for not following orders.'

'Orders?'

'I … Acionna, if I tell you this, you can't say a word to anyone. And I mean *anyone*.'

'Devin, who am I going to tell?'

'Lucy,' he said.

Almost like he was expecting me to be friends with his sister. I liked Lucy—a lot—but we weren't at that level yet.

'I won't.'

'Promise.'

'I swear,' I said, and traced my fingertips over some of the scars. He shivered at the touch.

'I didn't follow orders, and the trainers whipped me.'

'Like, you were in the army?' I asked.

Devin shook his head and looked into the mirror. I met his gaze in it. There was so much sadness in those eyes, and I wanted to take it all away.

'Not quite.'

'What does that mean?'

He inhaled sharply, his shoulders moving with the motion. 'I was trained to kill people.'

I swallowed past the lump in my throat and pressed my lips tightly together. 'What kind of people?' I finally asked.

'Mythical beings. Therianthropes, witches, paranormals.'

'So you kill people like me.'

'And me,' he said.

'I'm sorry. There were all of these whispers about you and how you went missing for years, but I didn't pay attention to it. I didn't have much of a need to listen to it, but maybe I should have.'

I traced another scar with my fingertips, and Devin shivered. 'If you're going to tease me like that, you're going to need to do something about it.'

'You're trying to change the subject.'

'You're trying to make me talk about a time in my life that I'm still very firmly in, and would prefer not to be.'

'Humans are weird creatures. You know that, right?'

'Something tells me selkies are equally as weird,' he said, and I couldn't help but chuckle. I kept my gaze on Devin as the palm of my hands grazed up his back and over his shoulders, down his now naked torso.

'What are you doing?" he asked, his voice full of heat, and I resisted the urge to bite down on my lip because the lust in those words did more to me than I could admit.

'Getting to the bottom of it all. Why were you tortured?' I asked while one hand toyed with the scar across his chest. My other hand made its way down over his chiselled stomach and to his pants. I undid them and slid my hand inside his pants. With that heated gaze, I couldn't help myself. I wrapped my fingers around his cock, and suddenly, everything else fell away.

'Ash,' he hissed. I loved hearing my name come from his mouth, especially when he said it like that. 'You can't ask me that now.'

'I can and did,' I murmured, my lips brushing over the shell of his ear. My hands worked slowly to bring his cock to a standstill. My favourite.

CHAPTER TWENTY-THREE

Devin
Pachons 2017
Melbourne

'You're not good enough, D-Man. You're too cocky. This will help you remember where your place is,' Jar said as he buried a knife in my chest. He dragged the blade down, and I bit the inside of my cheek to stop the scream that threatened to leave my throat. Blood dripped down my chest, and I couldn't make a sound. A sound would betray how much it hurt, but it didn't just hurt—it fucking killed. But I couldn't give him the satisfaction. He didn't deserve that.

There was more hurt than I admitted to anyone, or any that I actually let myself feel. Jarrad was both a mentor and a foe.

'Dev?' Acionna asked again.

I didn't want to go back there. I looked at her. She could see that my attention waned, but her hand picked up speed. I cried out and had to take her wrist away. She shifted her weight so I could see her in the flesh and not through the mirror.

'Dev, talk to me.'

'Tortured. I was tortured for not being good enough, for not having enough, for being lazy. That one was because I failed to kill my first body. I hesitated.'

Acionna's eyes widened, and she took my face in her hands, her thumbs rubbing the side of my temples like she was trying to soothe me any way she could.

'Fuck,' she whispered, her fatigue lost in the despair of my ridiculousness. The pain The Camp had inflicted on me was one I kept buried. I learnt to hide all of my feelings so no one could hurt me—physically, mentally or emotionally—but the scars that littered my back and chest also dived way deeper. They changed my soul, the way I felt about myself, who I loved and why I loved.

The real reason The Camp stayed away from my family was because they knew I would destroy them. There would be no Camp left to bring in more recruits, and Karrept's fucking army would be dead.

'They're too much,' I said, and my eyes filled with water because the pain of going back there was too much.

'Forget it all. Forget it all and stay with me. You're always safe with me,' Acionna whispered before she kissed me.

It was like a match was ignited, and I pulled her closer, kissing her deeper, harder. If I could make the pain go away, I would. *Am I ever going to be safe? Right now?* I could count the people who made me feel safe on one hand, and Acionna was one of them.

She pulled me in closer, and I let her because I wanted to chase the bad memories away. And if the moments in between that were too hard to deal with, and the ones that made me want to run away from her weren't good enough, I didn't deserve to be there with her.

Her hips moved, and I groaned into her mouth. She pulled back, and we were both breathing hard. 'This is okay, right?' Acionna asked for permission, and my brain couldn't see anything else.

I nodded. 'God, yes, I need you,' I breathed, and she took that for what it was.

She made short work of her pants, and before I knew it, I was buried deep inside her warmth. I groaned at how complete I felt at that very moment. No other woman had felt that way, and I didn't want to know another.

I let her control the tempo, and we locked eyes as she did most of the heavy lifting, my hands helping her. But she knew what she was doing with those hips. I groaned. Part of me wanted to hide that reaction, but I couldn't stop it. I couldn't tear my eyes away from Acionna, and she made sure I wouldn't forget her.

Her body was perfect, and with every thrust, I tried to keep myself in check, but with her controlled movements, I couldn't. Her hips thrusted into mine, and I used her momentum to spin us so I was on top. Her back hit the bath mat, and I pumped my hips into hers. Harder, faster, hotter. All I could feel was her, all I wanted to feel was her. Acionna's body moulded to mine, and she wrapped her legs around my hips, egging me on to go deeper inside her still.

I had sacrificed so much of myself to survive and to keep surviving, but she had unravelled it all in the span of a few months. Who the fuck could say they could do that?

I drove my hips into her faster and harder, unable to stop. She cried out, her whole body shivering around me, but I wasn't not there yet. I kept going. Her fingers dug into my hip to slow the momentum, but I wanted her to be writhing under me with another wave of pleasure. I took her hands and held them above her head, and as Acionna cried out, my name on her lips, she whimpered her pleas. With the scream, I let go.

I let go of the hurt and the pain that came with so much.

I collapsed on her and let go. Tears spilt from my eyes and my whole body shook, but she held me tight. The last time I had cried was the last time I was whipped hard enough for it to almost break my back. I never made the same mistake again.

'You're always safe with me,' she whispered, and I let go. I didn't bother to hide the sobs.

Oh, god, what has she done to me?

I couldn't get Acionna out of my head. The sex was mind-blowing, and I had never felt that sort of connection with anyone. It made doing my job harder because I wanted to spend all of my time just with her. I could hardly eat or sleep—not that I did a lot of that without thinking about *her*—but there I was. In the middle of a field, waiting for my next victim. She knew I was coming. Fiona Lockier was a socialite who had an inclination for booze, drugs and voodoo. She loved to dance naked in the fields, just like she was right then. I was perplexed at how someone could do that, or even want to. I liked nudity, but it was better in the comforts of one's home. All those bugs that were out and about ... Not in the least bit fine to have bites in places where bites shouldn't happen.

'I invoke thee, oh, horned one. Fill me with your being. Give me your seed. Make me one.'

She was doing some weird-arse hip shake thing. I had seen a lot, but there were things that didn't make sense, and that was definitely one of them. It was just too fucking cold to even be doing that. The time spent in the middle of nowhere for so long had broken my internal temp, and the switch from summer to autumn was steep.

I pulled the quiver back, ready with my aim to end her life, and was about to let go when she spoke up again.

'I know you're out there. I can feel you. Show yourself.' I froze.

No one had called me out like that. No one had seen me or felt me. It was like Gagliani all over again, with him locking eyes with me. *What is going on?*

Have I slipped up?

I wasn't sure what I was meant to do. I knew there was a tactical magick team in place, and all I had to do was put the word out, but they were a *last* resort. I was trained to deal with it on my own. I closed my eyes and took a deep breath, doing the only thing I knew how to do: magick. I reached deep inside me and weaved the spell of nothingness in front of me. Fiona could still feel me, but she wouldn't be able to see where I was or what was going on. I opened my eyes and pointed the arrow at her chest. It would go straight through, and her death would be immediate.

I was that good.

'Make it unseen. Let them see only what they need to see,' I whispered, and let go of the arrow. It flew through the air towards Fiona. It hit with a loud *thunk*, and the impact threw her to the ground just as the horned god came out of the ground. He looked around and roared, the sound so inhuman, it made my bones rattle.

'Oh, fuck,' I whispered. It was time to run, not even try to hide the evidence—just go. It would have to be the team that was there as backup's clean-up job.

I slung the bow around my chest and strapped my quiver tightly to my body. I legged it out of there as fast as I could. I had no defensive magick, and if I had to fight him, it would be hand-to-hand. I knew I would lose. I was good, but I wasn't *that* good. I paused and pulled the bow out again.

'Why the hell not?' I muttered to myself and pulled an arrow out of the quiver. I sank it into place and pulled it back. I let go of the string and watched the arrow as it sank into the hardened outer skin. The horned god looked up and smirked.

'Double fuck.'

I turned on my heel and pushed off, my bow in one hand as I pushed my body out of the woods and towards my car. I pulled the keys from my pocket and unlocked it. As soon as I got within reaching distance, I opened the door, slid in and clicked the button to start the vehicle. I revved it, slipped it into drive and ripped out of there. Taking a relieving breath, I looked in the rearview mirror. The horned thing was closer than I'd thought.

Fuck, fuck, fuck.

I dialled Jar's number, but it went straight to voicemail. *What the fuck?* He always picked up. *What the hell? Plan B.* I scrolled and pushed Greg's name. He picked up instantly.

'Yeah?'

'There is a horned thing chasing me in Madders Field. Do something about it.'

'What do you mean?'

'I mean the target was conjuring something as I killed her. It came out of the ground, and now I have a fucking horned thing after me. Greg, do something about this.'

'Magickal tactical team is in place.'

'Not fast enough. Have them spring into attack *now*. Oh, fuck.' I looked in the mirror and watched it spring towards me. I slammed on the brakes, and it jumped clear of the car. It turned to face me, and I tried not to cringe. 'Okay, it's staring right at me. Greg …'

I put the car in reverse and pushed it back. Hunter could do it with his eyes shut, and part of me wished I could have had him as an ally. His stupid talent for being good at driving cars didn't help him when he'd changed career paths. I hadn't quite mastered that. I looked over my shoulder and tried to avoid crashing into a tree.

'Affirmative. D-Man needs the magickal tactical team.'

'Greg!' I cried out again.

There was more field coming up, and as I broke through the tree line into the open field, I could see the outline of the horned god. He moved so fast. *What the fuck is taking so long?*

'Yeah, I'm getting there.'

The horned god growled and puffed at me like a bull. I wasn't sure that the thing was all that safe.

'Greg! I'm running out of field,' I cried out.

'Got him.'

A net shot down and encased the horned thing. I slammed the brakes and yanked the wheel to the left, doing a donut in the grass. It was going to be a hard one to cover up. I screamed out of there, leaving them to deal with it.

The hit was fucked. *Who the hell has a horned bull thing run at them? What is with my luck lately?* Although, the missions The Camp were sending me on were like they were rigged somehow. Pete's didn't even count because Acionna had mentioned him. I'd brushed it off, but the fact that all of my last targets had some weird inclination to look me in the eye, get found or know I was there … I pulled my car into the driveway. It was late but not too late. I was covered in sweat, and I leant against the seat and opened my phone to see I had a message. Dad's name flashed, and I had a moment to panic before I pushed the button to listen to my voicemails.

'Dev, can you meet me at the office when you get in? I'll be here late. Thanks.'

Dad's voice sounded weary on the phone. I'd heard him angry. I'd heard him apologetic. But weary? That was a new one. I contemplated a shower. There was dust everywhere, and I could feel the sweat dripping off me. The other option was going into the office looking like I did—black cargos, black shirt, sweat and dust everywhere. I would have to answer a lot of questions, and I wasn't not ready to do that.

Quick shower it was.

I stripped out of my clothes as soon as I shut the door in my room and padded into my bathroom. I started the shower—as hot as I could stand—and thought about everything that had just happened. *What are the chances of finding a woman like Acionna—a selkie, nonetheless—and getting chased by a horned god?* I jumped under the blazing stream of water, and dust and sand hit the tiled floor before going down the drain. If Dad hadn't been waiting, I would have stayed in longer, but the man hated to be left waiting, so I was in and out before I could actually relax. I turned the shower off and grabbed a towel to dry off. I hadn't even given the mirror time to fog up. With the towel left in the bathroom, I found a clean pair of jeans and a white T-shirt and shoved them on. I grabbed my phone, keys, wallet and was out the door.

In the car, which needed a wash, I could only think about what Dad would want to talk to me about. After I signed the contract, he'd been extra diligent to make sure I was okay. But this felt off. *Is there something wrong with the next hotel? Is he doubting that I can do it?*

I pulled into the office building and saw his office light still on. The lobby was lit up as normal, but just his office was bright compared to the others. I slowed down and pulled into the parking area. A valet came up, and I shook him off.

'I won't be long. Can you just leave the car where it is?' I asked.

'Oh, Mr Ryder, I sure can,' he said as he recognised me.

'It's just Devin. But thank you'—I glanced at his badge—'Henry.'

He nodded and smiled.

I walked into the building and was struck by the simplicity and the changing decor. Autumnal tones were shifted into the space, hints of orange and muted greens. It always was such an odd liminal time before jumping into the dead of winter, when everything was cold.

I veered to the lifts that would take me to the offices and saw a familiar face on post.

'Hey, Jordan, how's it going?'

The security guard smiled at me. 'Devin, old boy. You always make me feel like I'm ten years younger than I am.'

'You're only as old as you feel. Is Bossman up in his office?'

'Yup, hasn't come down. I'll buzz you up.'

After hours, we had a security guard, just in case. There had been times when people had tried to get up, and there were secret plans the public couldn't get to. It was also to make sure no one got hurt when they were working late.

Dad was serious about protection. It was always his number one rule when it came to anyone working alone.

'Great.' I sent him a salute and punched the elevator button, waiting for it to come down. The night may have been weird, but this wasn't out of the ordinary. While I waited for the lift to come down, I pulled out my phone and texted Acionna.

You and me. Tonight. I'm bringing champagne.
You'll not believe what happened to me.

She replied instantly with a smiley face and the words:

I'll be waiting. I have new lingerie. 😉

I smiled to myself, already looking forward to what she'd look like. She was hot in a pair of jeans and a tee, and now, to see her in lingerie … *Fuck me.* I don't think I'd survive the night.

I stepped into the elevator and pushed Dad's floor. It moved fast, and before I knew it, I was there. The doors opened, and there was an eerie silence.

Something's not right.

From the elevator, I could see his door. It was slightly ajar, and light spilt out and into the hallway. I shoved my phone in my back pocket and wished I'd brought a weapon. It was stupid to leave the house without one. Or not to even leave one in my car.

Fuck.

'Dad?' I called out.

I blocked out anything else and switched modes, crouching down, ready for whatever was about to happen. The silence in the building was unsettling. It was like there was a skeleton about to jump out at me.

Or someone who shouldn't be there.

I hugged the wall and pushed the door open. As I gingerly stepped into the office, there was paper strewn everywhere, broken glass and frames littered the ground. There was shit everywhere, and my heart dropped into my stomach. I stopped to listen to the silence.

'Dad?' I called out again.

More silence.

I walked deeper into his immediate office, and that's when I saw it —his shoe, sticking out from behind his desk. The position was too weird for him to be taking a nap.

'Daddy?' I called out. I hadn't used that word since I was kid, and I held my breath as I looked past the desk to find Dad slumped on the ground, a bullet between his eyes.

Bile rose in my throat as soon as I saw it.

'Motherfucker,' I swore as I skidded down to his level. I knew he was gone. No one could come back from a bullet between the eyes.

'Dad? Dad ... are you ... Oh, god.' Blood was all over me, and I stared down at his lifeless body, his dark grey eyes hazy with death.

I closed his eyes and stood up, looking at the window to search for a bullet hole. There wasn't one. Grief tried to take me, but I closed my eyes and took a deep, steadying breath. When I opened them again, I had pushed back all of the pain and looked at the facts. *I can do this.*

There was a small precognition thing we were taught. It took years to master, and there were people at The Camp who had excelled at it way better than I ever had. But in dire times of need, I could do it.

This was that time.

I closed my eyes again, and with my mind's eye, I stepped around my dad's body and looked at the world as it was. The man who killed him was not someone Dad knew. How he got up there was a mystery. And Jordan hadn't done his job right. I didn't recognise the man—at least, not immediately—and I watched as he entered the room. He took in nothing and everything at the same time. One bullet was shot as a warning, into the board in front of him, and Dad stood up and held up his hands. As soon as Dad got to his feet, the second bullet was put between his eyes, and he died instantly.

As soon as I saw that, I dropped to my knees and the breath left my lungs. I started sobbing.

Who do I call? What do I do? Where is security? How did they let this happen?

Why the fuck was I out on a hit and not here with Dad? I should have been here. It's all my fault. I scrambled over to him and held him again, and this time, the filter between grief and productivity smashed.

I was going to murder whoever took him from me. I wasn't finished with him. He had so much to teach me, so much to tell me how and what to do. It was a direct hit against me. It had to be. They told me my family was safe if I kept working for them. If I kept going, then it would be okay. That this wouldn't happen.

The Camp *lied.*

I wiped my nose on the back of my hand. Blood covered the front of it, and my gaze snagged on the hole in the bulletin board. I got to my feet and dragged myself towards the bulletin board. In the middle was a bullet. I grabbed a pair of scissors from Dad's desk, careful to avoid looking at his body, and pulled the bullet out.

As soon as I did, I saw it, and my stomach knotted. The Eye of Horus was stamped on the small shard. I knew who did it.

I held the bullet in my hand, blood still all over them, and pulled my phone from my pocket. I scrolled to my recent call history and pushed Jarrad's number.

'D-Man. What's up?'

'You better have enough magickal protection to save you from me because I'm coming for you.'

'What?' He seemed surprised, but I'd seen him lie to someone's face and not give anything away.

'You heard me.' I clicked off the phone and walked over to Dad's phone. I punched in 000.

'Hello, what's your name and the state you're calling from?'

'Hello, my name's Devin Ryder, I'm from Melbourne, Victoria. My father, Mathew Ryder, has been killed in his office.'

'Wh-what?'

I sniffed, unable to stop the tears coming now—partially because I knew that call was being recorded, and if I sounded too cold and detached, they'd assume I did it.

'He's dead. I came to talk to him, and he was here, dead. Someone shot him. I tried to wake him up, but he wouldn't wake. I don't know what to do.'

I could hear tapping on the other side of the phone.

'Where are you?'

'In his office, in the CBD.'

'Do you know exactly where you are?'

I did, but they didn't need to know that. 'His office.'

'Okay, we're sending people over, and your security is being notified. Are you okay? Are you in any state?'

I look down at the bullet in my hand. I could see it was covered in blood. 'There's blood everywhere. I touched him to see if he was alive. I'm bloody.'

'Okay. Devin, it's all okay. I'll get someone there. Are you hurt?'

'Hurt?' I repeated. *Why would I be hurt if I found him? What a stupid question.* I took the bullet from the scissors and dropped them on the table under some ruffled paper.

'Yes, hurt anywhere?'

'No, I found him, that's all. I found him on the floor.'

'Okay, someone is coming right now.'

'Thank you. I'm going to hang up now.'

'Okay, Devin, thank you for staying on the line.'

I hung up just as Jordan came up. He looked at me and then looked at the blood.

'Devin? Are you okay? What happened?'

'He's dead,' I said, and pointed to Dad. Jordan's eyes took a second to focus before they looked back at me. His fingers started to shake.

'Did you see anyone?'

He shakes his head. 'No one came in before you. I swear.'

I pocketed the bullet and realised I had to hide the hole. I walked over to the board, bloody fingers and all, and looked at what's on there. I could see a note—one dated for that day.

'He was taking notes.' I pulled the pin off it and pressed it just over it, showing Jordan.

Jarrad was a dead man walking.

'Notes?' He blinked, and I could see that colour drain from his face. I rushed over and caught him before he hit the ground. 'He's dead, and I didn't stop them. I didn't help him. I don't … What?'

Before I could reply, the ambos were there. They looked at me and Jordan, and one came over to me and checked me over.

'I'm not hurt, just bloody from touching my dad. Jordan here is having a panic attack, I think.'

'Are you okay?' she asked.

'Shocked, angry, but okay. I have to call my family. Is he going to be okay?' I nodded at Jordan. My emotions were removed—a tactic I learnt to save myself from the shock of taking another person's life.

She nodded. 'I'll help him. Contact your family.'

I wanted to do it before there was a policeman at Mum's door. That would break her more than hearing it from me.

The first person I called was Destiny. She picked up the phone.

'What's wrong?' She already knew something was wrong.

'Dad's been murdered. I need you to get to Mum. Now. I'm calling her last, but someone has to be there to catch her.'

'What about Luce?' she asked, and I could hear her grabbing keys. Josh would be up and moving already.

'Calling Hunter to make sure he's with her, and then calling her.'

'Is it … organised?' She knew it could have been a possibility, and I loved her for already getting there without me needing to tell her.

'Yes.'

'Do you know who it is?'

'Yes.'

'You're going to get the bastard, right?'

'You know it. Make sure Josh drives, Dest. I don't want you on the roads, okay?' In other words, I knew she would break the instant she was off the phone. Her husband would be there to help her through it.

'Already on it. Trust me. I'll see you soon.'

'Yep.'

I hung up and stared at the ambos checking for signs of life. They had a duty of care, and even though he was dead, they had to do it.

I pressed the tip of my phone against me and took a steadying breath. That was the easiest call I had to make.

Next, I phoned Hunter.

'Yo, dude, what's up?'

'Are you with Luce?'

'Yup. Why?' I heard the chair squeak, and I knew he was in his room.

'Catch her when I tell her what's happened.'

'Devin, what happened?' he asked.

'Please, Hunt?'

'Okay.' I heard him call out to Lucy before he handed the phone to her.

'What's up, Dev?'

'I need you to be calm, okay?'

'Why wouldn't I be calm?'

'Something has happened to Dad, Luce.'

'What do you mean? I spoke to him, like, an hour ago. He was on his way home.'

'He's still at the office, and I'm here too. But Luce, he's been murdered. He's dead, Luce.'

'What?' Something crashed, and I heard Hunter try to soothe her as she shrieked.

He picked up the phone. 'What the fuck was that, man?'

'Dad's dead. He's been murdered. Can you look after her?'

'Fuck. Yeah. I'm sorry.'

'Me too. Just watch out for her. Sharp objects and the like need to stay away from her. If you have to, find a way to placate her.'

'I will. I've got this. Just look after yourself. Have you told your mum?'

'No, Destiny should be there now, so I'm calling now.'

'Good luck.'

I hung up, and the police rocked up. They looked at me and then took in the blood. I looked down and realised my white shirt was fucked, and the jeans.

Shit.

'Who are you?' one of the policemen asked. *I guess I'm not as well-known as I thought.*

'Devin Ryder. That's my dad,' I said, pointing at the body bag. The office was about to become a crime scene.

'You found him?' His face softened, and I was forced to show some emotion. It was hard to flick on and off, but I could do that on command in those days. I nodded in response to him and took a step back in case he wanted to touch me. People were too touchy when you lost someone.

'I'm sorry for your loss, but are you able to answer some questions?'

'I … Can I please call my mother first? I need to make sure she hears it from me.'

He looked like he was about to say no. 'Please. She's not going to take the news very well, and my older sister should be at the house with her now.' I couldn't take much longer because Mum would get suspicious about Destiny being there.

'Okay, son. Make your call.'

'Thank you, sir.'

Manners got one everywhere, I knew that much. I dialled Mum's number and stepped away from the chatter. I could feel the blood caked on my fingers, and I wanted to vomit. I could do blood, just as long as it didn't dry on me. The memory of having it caked on my skin after kills was too close.

'Devin, why is your sister here?'

Damn. I took too long, and now she's suspicious. I looked at the police officer, who was staring at me, and swore under my breath.

'Mum, are you sitting down?'

'Yes. Now tell me what's wrong.'

'Dad's dead.'

'What?' I could have sworn I heard her stop breathing.

'Mum, breathe, please. Is Destiny there?'

'He's ... Why is he dead? What happened to him? Devin, how could this happen?'

'Someone killed him. I'm sorry, Mum, but that's all I know. I just needed you to hear it from me. The police have to talk to me now, so I have to go. I'll call you when I know more.'

I hung up before she could argue and dialled Acionna's number.

She picked up and said hello.

'I need you at the office. Dad's dead. I don't have time to talk. Just come.'

'I'll be there as soon as I can.'

I believed her.

CHAPTER TWENTY-FOUR

Acionna
Pachons 2017
Melbourne

As soon as I hung up, I changed into a pair of black jeans and a green T-shirt. Devin's dad was dead, and nothing was going to come between me and getting there in record time. I got to my car, and Janice held a bag for me.

'Mr Devin's clothes from the other day are in there, plus a jacket. I overheard.'

'Janice, you are a saviour.'

'I try. Get there safely.'

Her being from the Undersea came in so handy right then. I didn't need to ask; she just did it.

I swerved through traffic, and it was a miracle I didn't get pulled over. By the way Devin had sounded, I knew he needed me.

I got there in twenty minutes—the fastest I'd ever gotten to the city before—and pulled the car over as close to the hotel as I could. There were people milling around. I grabbed the bag and elbowed my way to the front of the line.

I was stopped by a policewoman in full blues. She had a vest on, her hat and I could see the gun at her hip. She was one of many, and they all looked the same.

'Miss, you can't come through here. It's a crime scene.'

'My boyfriend is up there. He called me.'

'I'm sorry. Someone else tried that, and they were a reporter.'

'I can call him.'

'That's not really okay. Miss, stand back.' Without taking my eyes off her, I called Devin. He picked up. 'Dev, I'm outside, and they won't let me up. Can you talk to them?'

I handed the phone to the policewoman, and she stood up straighter. Her eyes narrowed on me. I didn't know what he was saying, but it was enough for her to let me through. She gave me back my phone, and I knew Devin had hung up. I slipped the phone into my back pocket and made a run for the office.

The elevator wait felt like an age, and as soon as it dinged, I jumped in and frantically pushed the button to go up. The eerie elevator music was out of place. When the doors opened, I made my move. As soon as I was out, I caught the attention of a policeman.

'Hey, you're not allowed in here,' he said to me. I looked him up and down before I gave him a withering look.

'Where is Devin?' He looked at me like I'd grown an extra head. 'Don't make me ask again, or I'm just going to start guessing.' He blinked again, and instead of waiting for an answer, I moved to the right and passed him. Someone groped me, and I pulled myself free.

'Not fucking on.' Because I knew that hitting a police officer would be the worst thing I could do, I let it go.

For now.

I pushed my way through the throng of people and saw him. Devin was talking to an officer. He had an arm wrapped around his waist, a finger curled on the tip of his lip and he was covered in blood. My stomach dropped. *Is he hurt? Did I get here too late?* It was like he sensed me in the room because his eyes found mine. I could see them glaze over. He was barely holding it together, and we both stared at each other for half a second. I was afraid that if I went up to him, he was going to break and not stop.

He couldn't afford that right then.

But it didn't stop him. He held up a hand and shifted between the policemen. Closing the distance between us, he pulled me into a hug that almost crushed me raw. I whimpered, and he didn't let go.

'Ash, he's dead. I don't know what to do.' He was a mess. Not like the bathroom floor. Worse.

'I'm here. It's okay. Let's get through this slowly, okay?' He nodded, and together, we walked back to the police officer.

'I'm sorry, officer …'

'Detective,' he corrected

'Detective. Where were we?'

'Who are you?' he asked me.

'I'm his girlfriend. He called me for support. I'm here to do that.'

'You're not allowed to be here,' he said, and Devin gripped my hand tighter, almost crushing the circulation in my hand.

'She stays. Please, can you finish asking your questions? Or I'm not going to talk.'

The detective stared at me like he wanted to say more, but he held his tongue.

'So, you came to find him after the voicemail he left. You get up here, say hello to Jordan and come up. That's when you see the office in disarray.'

'Yes.' Devin's tone was monotonous, and I knew he was pulling back out of his body. *Shit.*

I would, too, if my dad had been murdered.

'And then you see his shoes and find him propped up. What do you do then?'

He stared at the detective. I could only imagine what number that run-through would be. 'He wasn't propped up, he was on the floor. But I dropped to my knees and shook him, trying to get him to wake up. But nothing happened. While I did that, I pulled his head into my lap to try to make him wake up, but there was blood everywhere. It's everywhere. Can't you see it?' he growled.

The hand that wasn't being squeezed to death reached up and rubbed his arm. 'Dev, they're just trying to help. Come on.' My voice was soft, almost like I was talking to a child.

'Sorry. After that, I called 000, and then everyone came up.' He looked tired. I held onto him so he could get through it.

'Okay, thank you, Mr Ryder.'

'Devin. Call me Devin. My dad is Mr Ryder.'

'Devin. If we have any more questions, we'll get in touch. You should probably go home and get changed. Have a shower.'

He nodded, and I took him away from the room, his body slowly starting to shake. *If I can get him to my car, things will work.* But then I remembered I'd had to park on the street.

'Dev, where's your car?'

In the garage is where I hope it is. Please tell me that's where it is, I will him.

'The valet had it.'

'Fuck.' I can't believe that this is going to be what's going to grace the front page of the paper in the morning. *Shit, fuck, crap.*

'We need a bathroom, Dev. We have to get this blood off you before we go out. Or at least, off your hands and arms. White really wasn't the right colour to wear.'

He looked down and saw the blood again.

'I had a hit tonight, and a shower. I didn't think about my clothes, just that I needed to come over. I have to change. I can't go out with this blood on me, Ash.'

'Let's try to see what we can do, and then we can go home. We'll make sure that everything is okay. Do you have a change of clothes in your office?'

'Yes. I do. Nothing casual, though.'

If it had a collar, we could work with that.

Devin let me lead him into the bathroom. I didn't pay much attention to which one it was, but I grabbed a wad of paper towel and wet it before I brought it to his face. He had some blood splatters on his face, and I started with those—they were the easiest. I wiped at his forearms and then his hands. *Who knew how much blood could get into places it shouldn't?*

The silence was deafening, and after a bit of a go, his arms were clean and ready. I looked at his face, and he took mine in his hands and kissed me hard. His tongue thrusted into my mouth, and I was forced to open up or risk him taking my lips off. I gripped his shirt, which was dry with blood, but it was enough to anchor me back to what had happened. He didn't pull away, but I gently pried him back.

'Come on. We have to get home before anything happens.'

It was funny, how in moments when things were the worst, we leant into sex to make us feel.

'Acionna,' he whispered, and my heart shattered. It wasn't like the bathroom floor. This was different. He was raw in a way that even I couldn't understand.

I had a mother. She was tough on me. I even had a father who was around. I didn't know what I would do in the instant that either of them was dead. Selkies stepped down from power by choice, never because they died.

'Dev, let's just get you home. Then, we'll deal with everything, okay?' If I could get him home, everything would be okay. We just had to get through the throng of people. I looked him over and I knew there was not a spot I'd missed, so I flushed the paper towels to hide anything that could be used as evidence and took his hand.

I remembered I had the bag with me. I dropped his hand and leant back on the vanity bench. I unzipped it and pulled out the T-shirt he had been wearing the other day.

'Look, let's do this.' I held it out and draped it over my forearm before I pulled his shirt up over his body. I took in the scars once again, but didn't say a word.

'You don't have to do that,' he said.

'I do. You're about to be papped with the number of people out there.'

'What the fuck? Are you kidding me?'

I shook my head, and Devin took the shirt from me and shoved it over his head. I put the bloodied shirt in the backpack and let him lead the way.

'Key?' I asked him. He gave me the key, and we walked out of the bathroom and down to the lobby. 'Can you do this?'

As soon as the elevator door opened, he looked at me and shook his head.

'Not really, but I don't have a choice,' he said.

I watched as he put up his facade to keep the people from seeing what was really happening.

There were flashes of light and questions thrown every which way, but I gripped Devin's hand and got to his car. It was hard to miss. I unlocked it and slid in just as he did. I lock the doors to make sure no one could wrench them open to get an unsolicited picture. The heavily tinted windows may not have been legal, but no one batted an eye. Devin closed his eyes, and I started the car. One of his hands covered mine as I shifted the gear into drive, and we left the office.

The police could question him at his home if they had more to ask.

Devin directed me to his house on the outskirts of the city. I turned down a quiet street lined with trees that towered over each of the homes.

'Just the house there, with the green gates.' He pressed a button on his clicker, and the gated doors opened. The house was grand. It had a driveway that stretched on for ages and a fountain in the middle. There were stairs that led up to the main door. *What the heck?*

It was so luscious and green, even in the middle of autumn. I pulled the car up right next to the stairs, and as soon as I cut the engine, I saw Lucy tear down the stairs and straight into Devin's arms. He held her tightly while she sobbed, his bottom lip quivering at the motion. I got out of the car to move towards them when I saw Hunter come down the stairs, his eyes puffy, and I could tell he was barely keeping it together too.

'Hi, Hunter,' I said

'Acionna, hi. Dev called you. Good. I was going to see how bad he was first. Is he bad?' He frowned like he wanted to say something more. *How much does Hunter know about Devin's life now?* 'Do you want to get him upstairs?'

Hunter was a lot more level-headed than I would have thought he would have been. After all, he'd just lost someone who was a father figure in his life. But I didn't know a lot about him. Not yet. For all I knew, he could be in the same boat as me. We were outsiders who looked in.

'Yeah. I need to get him in the shower. He's gone a little shocky, and I need to clean the rest of the blood off him, but I can wait. How's Mrs Ryder?'

'Medicated and in bed. Destiny is lying next to her, and Josh is watching Destiny. It's a bit of a mess.'

At least someone was going to be sleeping. 'What about Luce?'

'I'm trying to keep her busy. Magick is out of the question, but I'm going to try to get her to do some writing, or even reading, maybe chuck on a movie or TV show. I just need to distract her. But she's ... The only reason she is up here is because she was so desperate to see Devin.'

'Sometimes, a girl just needs her older brother, you know?' I smiled and squeezed his arm. Hunter looked down at my hand and then back at my face. He wasn't coping either.

'That's about right. Good luck with Dev,' he said.

'Thanks, you too.'

Hunter pried Lucy away from Devin, who had kept really stoic through it all. I guided him up the front stairs and into the massive foyer. I had half a mind to try and take it all in, but it wasn't about me being interested in their home. I had to get Devin into the shower.

'Dev, which way?'

'Up the stairs and to the left.' I let him guide me up because he needed to do it for himself. 'I should see Mum,' he said.

'Let's get you in the shower first. Wash off the blood before you see her, you know?'

Because I didn't think Subira would be all too happy with her son coming to her covered in her husband's blood.

'Oh. Yeah. You're right.' Devin turned right, and we walked towards a door that was shut. He opened it, and we were inside his room. There was a king-size bed in the centre of the room with dark bedsides, masculine lamps—black with a black shade—a walk-in robe, TV mounted to the wall and some weird whisky corner. There were two leather chairs and some little table thing. He hadn't seemed like the kind of guy who needed so much stuff.

'He's dead. Like, actually dead. He's not coming back. I'm not ready for it. He's meant to be around still. I want him to see me marry you eventually, because you will marry me, and I know that it's not over. He's just ... He's gone,' Devin rambled.

I pushed his door closed as soon as we were inside, my eyes wandered off towards the bathroom, I could see his dirty clothes littered over the floor. I turned to Devin, and he had already pulled his shirt over his head. It dropped to the ground, and his gaze changed. Without any words, Devin reached out for me. He looked like he wanted to eat me up.

'Dev, shower first,' I murmured, and stepped back. *If we can get the shower, it will be easier for everyone.*

'Shower,' he mumbled. 'Are you going to join me?'

'Maybe. Help me with your pants, Dev.' His eyes held so much hurt in them. Devin looked at me before he looked down and undid his pants. Basic motor functions were a go. He undid his pants and pushed them down, along with his boxers. I lost my jacket and directed him in the direction of the shower.

'Can you turn on the shower?' I asked him. He looked at me again and nodded, leaving my side to go and do it. I waited half a second until I heard the water. I slipped out of my clothes and wished I'd changed out of the lingerie I had on. It would have been easier, but it would have to do.

I walked into the bathroom, and he'd sat himself on the floor.

Shit. I had taken too long.

I crouched down next to him. 'Dev, come on. In you get.' And I used whatever strength I had left to pull him to his feet.

Devin's eyes had glassed over, and he searched my face before his gaze roamed down my body. 'I like them,' he murmured before he followed my direction. I checked the water and added some cold to it before I put Devin in the shower. He started shivering almost instantly. I could have taken the lingerie off, but something in me made me stop. I didn't care if I got the set wet. It would dry. I tipped his head back and let the water fall over his hair. He was taller than me by a few inches or so, but that didn't matter. His arm snaked around my waist, and he held onto me as I made sure there was no blood in his hair. Or at least, from what I could see. The tiles were darker than I would have liked, but that was what we were working with. I couldn't be sure, but I had to hope he was blood-free. I ran my hands over his face, scrubbing out bits I might have missed before my hands moved to his neck, then his chest, where the brunt of the blood was. Next, I moved down his legs and helped him with that.

His body reacted to my touch, growing harder, and before I knew it, he had me pressed between the wall and his body.

'Dev,' I whispered.

'Acionna, I need you. Help me feel.' His voice cracked, and I shook my head.

'Not like this. Come on, we have to stay on task here. Your mum needs you just as much.'

I hoped mention of her would bring his head back into the right place, and it seemed like it did.

Devin kissed me hard, and it took every bit of self-preservation I had to break it off. The kiss was epic. It made my body instantly tighten, and I knew that if I pushed, I would be ready to go. But I had to made sure he was okay, and fucking me wouldn't help.

'He's gone,' Devin cried, and instead of pulling away, I held him close. His sobs filled the bathroom. The shower would have muffled it on the outside, but there we were again. In tears.

And there was nowhere else I'd rather have been.

CHAPTER TWENTY-FIVE

Devin
Pachons 2017
Melbourne

My reflection stared at me with distaste and sadness. He was wearing black slacks, a white shirt, black tie and a black suit jacket. His hair was messily slicked back, but his eyes were hollow, deeper. I felt so empty. In my pocket, the bullet burnt a hole in my pants. Jarrad had been keeping low, but tried to call me daily.

I wasn't picking up his calls.

I didn't have to.

I was done with The Camp.

Done with the whole concept of Karrept's Army—that was what it was called once we 'graduated' from The Camp.

I couldn't get away from the fucker.

Jarrad's calls were a punch to the gut every time I saw his name flash up. It was like he had some sort of actual remorse for what he did.

I didn't care what he wanted or what he had to say. He killed my father, and he was going to pay. But not that day.

That day, I was Devin Ryder, and I was burying my father. Acionna walked into the room, and my eyes flicked to her silhouette. She was in a black pencil skirt and loose-fitting blouse. Acionna had black pumps and black stockings on, her hair pulled back, showing off her chiselled cheekbones and her eyes sparkled. She looked hot, and my body reacted to her.

It always did.

After the past two weeks, I knew I would marry that girl.

In her hands was a black piece of ribbon and a pin. I frowned.

'What is that?'

'Ribbon. I need your right arm, babe. You're going to wear it.' She'd taken to calling me 'babe' over the past few days—something I'm sure wasn't her idea, but probably a way to get me going again.

I was hyperfixated on the fact that Jarrad—a man who was a mentor but also what I would have called a friend, who had broken my spirit, my mind and my soul and then put it all back together—was responsible for killing my father. It was harder to comprehend than I expected. There were times I wanted to tell Ash who it was, but I couldn't. She'd been so patient and caring, and I wondered if she would see me differently if she knew.

'What's this for?'

'You're a pall-bearer, and you need to have one of these. Josh has one too. Your two uncles, and Hunter too. Your dad's best friend is also wearing one.'

I held out my arm, and she wrapped it around my bicep before pinning it together. 'So this means I'm going to carry the coffin.'

She nodded. 'That's what the woman said. Are you okay?'

'No. But when is a good day to bury your father?'

'Never. But I'll be right there, no matter what happens. Just find me and I'll step in.'

I chuckled and shook my head. I could see that she was smiling. 'You can't carry the coffin for me. You're a weakling.'

'But I'm a selkie. I have preternatural strength. I just look like a weakling girl. That was so rude.' She scoffed, but there was a hint of laughter in her voice.

'I know.' I pulled Acionna in closer and inhaled deeply, holding her tight against my body. She smelt like the ocean, salty but fresh, and having her close placated me from doing anything stupid. 'I ...' I wanted to tell her that I loved her, but it was too soon. Far too soon. But it didn't stop the way I felt. 'I don't know what I would have done without you, Ash. I want to make sure that you know that.'

'Dev, there's nowhere else I'd rather be.' She clung to me, and while she shared being with me and back at her house, I knew it was all taking a toll on her. Her skin was a little less sun-kissed than it was the day before.

My gaze snagged on the folders on my desk. They were advisors, people who would help me, but none of them were right.

None of them had the right attitude I needed, and honestly, Jarrad had consumed all of my thoughts. I waited to see if a hit would turn up, to see if it would happen before the funeral, but I was sure even an assassin was afforded a chance to mourn their dead.

'I don't want to have to take over the company,' I started, and it was like there was someone else in the room with us. It was the same conversation we'd had between moments of lucidness.

'Dev ...' she started, and sat on the bed. 'We've spoken about this. You already signed the contract.'

'But I thought I had *time*. I wanted to learn more from him.'

Acionna looked at me almost like she was looking through the bravado and half-truths. 'You're going to have to step up, you know? Wearing suits and going to meetings.'

My stomach dropped. I turned away from her, looking at myself in the mirror again and adjusting my tie.

I was not fit for human consumption.

'Ash, I'm a trained killer. What hope do I have in a boardroom with suits and negotiations?'

Dad was meant to keep going until he couldn't, and by then, I could have taken over. I would have been ready to do it. He was still young, for god's sake. Rage filled my entire body, and I felt it bubble up inside me. Without a second thought, I punched the mirror.

It cracked, and Acionna gasped. 'Devin!' She was on her feet before

I could register, pulling out the chunk of glass embedded in my skin. The pain that should have vibrated through my hand wasn't there.

I was numb.

Acionna left for a second, and I watched my reflection through the fractured pieces of the mirror. My eyes were hard, harder than I remembered, and it felt like the moment that I got out. Really got out.

Blood dripped from my fist. I covered it with my other hand.

'Don't get it on your shirt,' Acionna called from the bathroom. I held my fist further away from my body as the bleeding only got worse.

'What's gotten into you?' Acionna said as she pressed the towel to my knuckles.

I wished I could tell her.

Someone knocked on the door. 'Come in,' I said automatically as I watched Hunter walk in. My stomach plunged. *Where's Lucy? Lucy can't see this.* I sighed when I realised he was alone.

'You punched the mirror? Dude, that's seven years of bad luck.' He came over and stood next to me, looking at the brokenness of the mirror.

'I don't think my bad luck can get any worse, Hunt.' He wrapped an arm around my shoulders, and it took everything in me not to just crumble. I'd never been someone who did that, but that day was a different story.

I was responsible for the loss of a man who was not only a rock for me, but was also the head of the family. He was the one who was level-headed. I was the reason he was dead.

Dad was someone I looked up to and someone I wanted to imitate as a child. He was loving, calm and always patient with us. He loved us more than words could express, and even though his stoic exterior was always just that, he was a father who taught us how to fix a skinned knee, or what to do in the event that there was no chocolate in the house with three women. But most of all, he taught me the skills I needed to grow up.

I had close to five years of our relationship stolen from me because I was kidnapped and trained to be this ... thing, but it wasn't enough. I wanted those years back so badly. I needed the time back.

'You never know,' Hunter said.

'There. You're going to have to deal with the discomfort and hope that you're not carrying the coffin with your right hand,' Acionna said. 'Probably not as good as what Kali could do, but it'll do in a pinch.' Her hands were dainty and delicate, and as she let go of my hand, Hunter took it and waved his hand over it. He took a little bit of pain away. Not that I told him. I smiled thankfully at him. It was the least I could do.

'What did you do?'

He smiled. 'You have your surprises, I have mine. I just gave the healing a little nudge because you need to be at the top of your game. Today is going to be hard.'

I sighed. 'You mean the last two weeks weren't hard enough?'

'That's a moot point.' Hunter laughed. 'Also swiped this.' He pulled a bottle of cognac from behind his back.

'You know, I could say something about it being far too early in the day for this,' Acionna started, 'but who the fuck cares?'

I loved her more right then. I smiled at Acionna and kissed her cheek as Hunter uncapped the bottle and handed it to me. I took a long slug out of it. The liquid burnt down my throat and numbed some of what I knew was to come. I handed the bottle to Acionna, and she took a dainty sip before it was back with Hunter.

'To your dad. He was one hell of a man.' He tipped the bottle in the air and took another swig at it.

'To Dad.'

Processing the death of someone else? Easy. But processing the murder of my father? That was not something I had been ready to deal with. I still wasn't. The past two weeks had been pandemonium as I tried to figure out how I was supposed to behave and how I was meant to take those things on.

How do I remember to be sad?

What does it feel like to be there as a brother and a son?

I stared at Acionna and Hunter, and was completely removed from what was going on. It was like I was looking down at my body from above. They were both putting on brave faces for me, but I knew they wondered why I was withdrawn. Acionna knew. Hunter, not so much.

'I'm a killer-for-hire,' I blurted out, and Acionna looked at me, her eyes wide.

'That makes a lot of sense,' Hunter said, swigging another mouthful of cognac and handing the bottle to me.

The liquid courage was not going to help me right then. Nothing would. It was all my fault.

'I kill beings, Hunt, and I like it. I can't stop. I haven't stopped since I got back.' He looked at me—really looked at me—and I wasn't sure if I'd want to be friends with me either at that point. 'This is like punishment. I must be slipping, and they killed Dad to make it happen. I have to take over now. I won't be able to do both. I'm barely doing both now.'

I was broken time and time again. What was different about then?

'You can't blame yourself. Do you hear me? You need to stop.' Acionna had been saying that over and over again, and it still hadn't sunk in.

Jarrad killing my dad made it personal. It made it serious. He was calling me out, and I had to answer.

'Stop thinking,' Hunter said. I looked at him, surprised at the words out of his mouth.

'What?'

'You're thinking it's your fault. But it's really not. Life happens. *Things* happen, but your dad ... He knew things. I think he knew about this.'

I looked at Hunter, and before I knew it, my hand was out and I was about to punch him, but my fist stopped at an invisible wall. Acionna gasped, and most would have taken a step back, but not her. She held true to her words. That terrified me more than anything else.

'Dev, what's hitting me really going to do? I mean, besides ruin my face before we are in front of so many paps. What do you think I'm going to do? You're better trained, yes, but you forget that I *know* you.

And I know the way you work, even if you've been gone a long time. You're my best friend. I know you.'

I stared at him like he'd grown another head. *Who is he? Why is he doing this to me? Why can't he just be ... Not who he is? Is that too much to ask?*

'I'm so fucking broken.' I sat down on the bed and cradled my head in my hands. 'All I itch to do is kill someone else. My dad gets killed, and all I want to do is go and find someone to kill. How does that work?'

There was another knock on the door, and without looking up, I knew it was Lucy. I felt her. 'I can't look at her,' I whispered to Acionna.

Almost like she could fix it.

The door opened, and Acionna crossed the distance to get to her.

'Hey, Lucy. I don't know if this is—'

'Hi. There isn't ever going to be a good time,' she said, cutting her off.

I felt movement around me, and I knew Hunter had left my side. Lucy's heels clicked as she walked over to me, and I wanted her to not be there, but she was. She sat down next to me and wrapped an arm around me, her hand resting on my lower back. I looked up at her. I expected her to want to run, but instead, she held my gaze.

'You're not alone, Dev. Not anymore.' The understanding in her eyes was like Acionna's. She knew that there was something I wasn't telling her, but she would wait.

'Luce ...' I choked out, and she wrapped her arms around my neck. She used to hang off me like a monkey, and this was close, but we were both much bigger, so I let her hold me. She'd always leant on me, but now it was my turn to lean on her. She and Hunter had rescued me—an impossible feat for the girl who was my sister. She was stronger than she gave herself credit for. I buried my nose in the crook of her neck and took in her scent. Lucy had always smelt the same, familiar and kind, loving and innocent. No matter what happened, she'd always be my sister, but it wasn't enough for me.

She'd always been in my corner.

I wanted her to be happy, to have a life that was full of love, happiness and joy. She needed to get away from me. Hunter too. I was toxic. I pulled back, the thought sobering enough to ruin the moment for me, but Lucy looked back at me, her eyes rimmed red from crying. But she was who she always was.

My little sister, who would always be there.

If I asked her to jump, she'd ask how high.

If I wanted her to help me hide a body, she would be there with a shovel.

Luce was my ride or die because we were tied in so many ways that no one would ever begin to understand. The twin thing was real, and we had that connection.

I was so tired of hiding so much from her.

I wanted her to know it all, but it wasn't the day. She wouldn't be able to handle it.

'You're going to be fine. You know why?' Lucy was so confident, so sure that everything would work out.

'Why?' I choked out.

'Because you have us. All of us. We're going to be here to help you, to support you, to make sure that when you fall, we'll pick you back up.'

She didn't need to say all of those words. There would be a time when Lucy had to pick, but for a second, I let her tell me that it is true. That it was all that mattered.

'Thank you,' I whispered, and held out my hand for the cognac. Hunter shoved it into my hand, and I took a deep swig. I held it out to her, and she mimicked me.

'To Daddy,' she whispered, tears filling her eyes.

'To Dad, and the hardest fucking day of our lives. We need to get Mum and Dest.'

I stood up and hugged Luce tightly. Something in her relaxed.

We were about to be slaughtered by the media.

'Don't forget your big sunnies,' Lucy muttered.

'You're the pro at funerals. I saw the pictures from ours.'

'Oh, god. Too soon to joke about that, Dev.'

Never too soon.

Athyr 2015
Somewhere in the desert

My hands were above my head, a sword pressed between palms. If I moved a muscle, I got whipped. If I thought of moving, I got whipped. The whole point was to stay very still, to keep going and not move. It was a training demonstration—something to show the rest of them that they couldn't get away from anything. Jarrad kept checking in. He walked up to me and started a conversation like he was expecting me to break, but I was stubborn, and I was going to send a message that I wouldn't be fucked with. I had been there for thirty hours straight. My arms started to really sting, and my back was a bloody mess. My body couldn't take much more. I thought I had another hour, or so I hoped.

I didn't care if they thought I was weak. I was done. I was sooo done. I had felt Destiny the other day. She was hurt, and I wanted to kill someone. That day, I nearly killed Enric. He was in the wrong place at the wrong time, and I couldn't help myself. It was why I was standing there. Did I mention that I was on a stool? They nearly made me squat for the entire time, but Jarrad talked them out of that idea—that would have been absolute pain.

'D-Man, I think you're nearly done. Do you understand what you did?'

Why did he ask the same question again? I couldn't answer it without getting whipped because it moved a muscle or hundred.

'I'm going to take the silence as a yes. Good. Lower your arms slowly.' I looked at him and didn't even blink. 'It's okay. Your time is over. I promise.' I did as he said and expected the whip on my back. Instead, the relief I felt was immediate. The sword dropped from my hands, and Jarrad caught me as I fell forward. He was supporting my weight, and I let him drag me away from the square and to the medical room.

'You did great, D-Man. I think the most someone has lasted is twelve hours. You have some real skill there.'

'Twelve hours?' I choked out as he handed me some water. I took a sip before spitting it out. *That's not water.* 'Fuck.'

'Vodka. You're going to need it for what's to come. I'm sorry.' He was sincere, which was fucking weird, but whatever.

The sting that came after that was intense and immediate. 'Motherfucking fucker,' I cried out. The pain was instant, and I dropped the vodka and gripped the bed. The bottle hit the ground and smashed into a million pieces, but I was too far gone to care. More alcohol was splashed on my back, and I screamed, this time unable to stop myself. I didn't like screaming. It gave them the satisfaction and normally invited more torture, but fucking hell. Bile rose up my throat, and I was going to vomit.

'Nearly done.' I heard through the throbbing of my pain. Something touched me, and I gripped the edge of the bed tighter.

'Okay, done.'

I exhaled, trying to catch my breath at the sudden throbbing pain that made my body hum. *Shit.*

'Bucket,' I stammered.

'You are a strong motherfucker. We sure as hell didn't expect that,' Jarrad said as he lowered himself to my eye level. I couldn't form the words because I was going to vomit all over him, but he stared right back at me. 'You won't be able to lie on your back when you sleep for at least a week. Maybe more, depending on how deep some of the lashes are. You'll also be excused from training.' Jarrad raised an eyebrow, then chuckled. 'I think you did this on purpose so you didn't have to do any training, D-Man.'

'If only,' I choked out. My brain didn't care about anything anymore. I just wanted the pain to stop. I needed it to stop. 'I need that bucket ... now.'

Pain burnt through my entire back. It was like thousands of cuts were being doused with nail polish remover or lemon. A bucket was thrust in front of my face, and I vomited. That was not a regularity either. Even when they pushed our bodies to their limits, I didn't vomit—except that first and only time at the beginning of training.

The heaving made my back ache and pulled on the damaged muscles. When I was done, I wiped my mouth on the back of my hand and threw my head back. The sudden movement made me want to vomit all over again, but if I looked at the bucket, it would happen.

'And vomit. Wow. Okay, we'll give you something for the pain, buddy. Rose will look after you until you can be moved to your quarters. Next time, just cave. It's easier than having to go through this.'

I didn't say anything. I couldn't trust the words that would come out of my mouth. I let Rose and another nurse help make me more comfortable. One of them took the bucket away. I was grateful for that.

My mind was running. Normally, it would be ways to get my way out of a situation, but right then, all I wanted was for the pain to stop.

'Here.' I looked, and Rose held a little capsule and some water. Or at least, what looked like water. I looked at it hesitantly. I'd heard about them drugging people and switching shit around, but right then, my common sense lost out.

I wanted the pain to stop.

'It's just a painkiller and some water. I swear to you on that.' An oath meant it was true—no one messed around with oaths. Not in a world where one's word could be used against them.

I leant up. The agony in my back came back in full force, and I grabbed the painkiller. I shoved it into my mouth and downed the water before collapsing back onto the bed. I wasn't sure if there were any gashes that needed stitches, but I could only hope that if they did, they'd fix that. *I hope.*

The painkiller was fast-working, and I felt myself slipping out of consciousness and into the nice blackness. It was a welcoming feeling.

CHAPTER TWENTY-SIX

Acionna
Pachons 2017
Melbourne

The funeral was brutal.

Subira had wailed like a banshee, and it made me think twice. *Could she be one?* But Lucy and Devin had reassured me she wasn't. She could have been though. Or even closely related to one. The blood-curdling scream stayed with me when I closed my eyes, and it terrified me. Subira had lost her soulmate, and she mourned for him, for herself, for her soul and for her children.

That kind of love was enchanting, but it was also terrifying.

Devin was lounging on a huge picnic blanket, dressed in a hoodie and jeans, but no shoes. 'How can you *not* be cold?' he asked. Devin rubbed his hands together to try to build up some warmth.

'This isn't cold.' I scoffed. 'When it's cold, you won't see me.' I grinned at him and heard the warning buzz on my watch. I set up the camera, the tripod dug into the sand, and at the right angle. Devin lifted himself and wrapped his arms around my waist. I had a leg crossed and one straight out in front of me. He waited for me to be done before saying anything, and when I pulled the camera away from my eye, he sighed.

'Every single day at the same time. You know, this means I can never whisk you away.' He brushed his lips against the shell of my ear, and it was my turn to sigh.

'I know,' I said, turning in his arms to look him in the eyes.

'How do you stand it?' Devin asked. His eyes were so grey that day —almost too grey, if that was possible.

'I don't, but I love my pelt. I need it, and if she destroys it, I'm going to lose a part of me I won't be able to get back. And it's been a part of me my whole life.' That was the simple answer. I wasn't sure if I was ready to just give it all up. I wanted to, some days, but not then.

'How long has it been? Have you been tempted to just walk away from it?' He brushed a strand of hair out of my face, and I smiled at him.

'I'm older than I look, Dev, but it's been a while. There have been so many times I've wanted to just say fuck it and give up. Because this is a half life. I can't explain it, but there is so much more out there than this. I've had a moment where I nearly missed the time, and the pain ...' I shuddered at the memory of the agony that had radiated through my body. It was like a thousand shards of glass were scratching against my skin. 'It was excruciating. The warning alone has kept me going every day.'

Devin tightened his arms around me.

'How old are you?' He was quiet for a moment and leant a little closer. 'What's out there?'

Am I ready to answer these questions? I had no one close to me but Janice, and she had guessed a lot of the details. Knowing she was from the Undersea had made it so much easier, but she was ... different. My whole life, I knew I'd be in a position where I would be at the top, all alone, so I had distanced myself as much as I could. But I wanted to lean on someone.

I needed to lean on someone.

My watch vibrated, and I clicked the shutter and snapped the picture. The waves rolled in as the sun set. I wouldn't belong until I couldn't see the ocean as the daylight shifted.

I was there because someone had betrayed me. My pelt wasn't gone by chance. Someone I knew had given it to the witch. Who? A mystery, and when I found out, I would make sure they paid for it.

'I'm way older than you. Perhaps, I have a millennium on you,' I teased. 'The witch who has my pelt ... She put a curse on me. I have to take the picture at the same time of the same thing because it's torture. I can see the ocean, but I can't *be* with the sea. I can't be with the ocean because I need my pelt.'

Devin kissed my nose and untangled himself from me, taking my hand and leading me down the shoreline. 'What does she get out of it?'

'A debt well paid, I suppose. Someone sold my pelt to her. I don't know who it was, but they made sure it was all I could do.' The words made my chest tight.

'Do you think it could have been your sister?' he asked, and I looked over my shoulder at him.

'What do you mean?'

I hadn't thought about that, but it would track. She was always so angry with me, and after Eain ... I ... I didn't think about that.

'Well, she was pretty angry the other night on the beach, and that screamed like she was mad at you,' he said.

'Ariel is always pretty mad at me. She's mad I Matched with the guy she wanted.'

Devin tensed, and I shifted my bodyweight so I could turn to see his face.

'What?'

It was then or never. 'I'm a princess back home. Destined to be queen. And there's a ceremony called a Matching. Essentially, we pick the roane ...' I trailed off in case I needed to explain that.

'I know what a roane is,' Devin said softly.

'Oh, good. Well, yeah, we pick a roane we will be with to procreate. The one she wanted—it wasn't anywhere near her Matching—wanted me to pick him. He put forward a strong case, so I did, but I don't think it was that.'

'Could there have been any other instances? When was the last time you saw your pelt? How did it happen?' The questions came fluttering from Devin.

'There could have been. I … The last time I saw it was the last time I came to shore. You know that selkies, by nature, aren't monogamous, right?'

He pressed his lips together before he nodded. 'I'm well aware. I know that your kind comes to shore to sleep with men, and essentially have more selkies.'

'Okay, good.' I didn't know why I needed to make sure he understood that.

'The last time I came to shore, I met a guy. He was cute, but it was the last time I saw him—and my pelt.'

'Do you know if he knew anyone else? Maybe your sister had a thing for him too?'

'Surely, she wouldn't be malicious enough to sell my pelt to the witch.'

'It's a possibility, isn't it?'

He was right. It was. Ariel was definitely the kind of woman who would do that, but what would she have to gain from it?

Does she want my place?

'I need to go back to the princess bit. You're royalty?' Devin asked and shifted his weight. He got to his feet and held out a hand for me. I took it and let him help me to my feet.

'Mhm, I was in training to be the queen.'

'That's pretty cool. I'm dating a princess.'

'Oh, we're dating, are we?' I teased.

'Duh. Why do you think I keep sticking around?'

'Mmm … You've just lost a parent, and it's a pity thing,' I said, and squeezed his hand.

'You know how to say the most romantic stuff to me, Ash.' He brought my hand to his lips and pressed a soft kiss against it. He was laughing without sound. I liked seeing him happy.

It warmed a part of me. I didn't have that sort of connection with anyone else.

'If it was Ariel, I'm not sure what I'm going to do. I have never been betrayed by someone I care for. Someone who is blood.'

'Those are the betrayals that hurt the most,' Devin said as he looked out into the distance.

I let go of his hand and unscrewed the camera from the tripod. He took that as the sign to pick up the picnic blanket, and he shook it out and folded it up haphazardly, shoving it under his arm.

'I'm living a half life, Dev. I can't do this anymore, and I think the tiredness I feel is from the lack of touch I have had with my pelt. I need it soon, or I'm going to get sicker. I have to get it back.'

Devin pulled me into his arms and held me close.

'I can't lose you, but I will accept you coming back to me.'

I buried my nose into the crook of his neck and inhaled his scent. He reminded me of the forest where we met in my dream—fresh and earthy at the same time.

'You won't. I'll keep coming back to you, Dev, but I need the salt on my skin. I need the water in my lungs. I need it all. You can't lose me if I'm never lost.'

The ocean was my first love. She would always come first, but Devin was definitely making his way in there.

'You're like me, half in and half out,' he murmured.

Devin got me. He really did, and it was weird because I knew he felt exactly the same.

'Yes.'

'Me too. When I'm without you and killing, I'm living a half life. You light it up for me. I told you I would help you, but you have to know that sometimes, I don't want to. I want to be selfish, but I'll help you today, tomorrow, next year. Whenever. We'll find your pelt, and you'll be able to swim away. But if you don't come back, I'm going to hijack a mermaid and come after you. You hear me?'

'I hear you, my sailor.' I laughed, pulled him in close and kissed him hard.

I didn't want it to end. Ever.

After the night before, I sat on the floor with my legs crossed under me. On the coffee table was a map of Melbourne as I tried to find places that could be used as a witch hang out. It was a big city, and in a place where everyone had something to hide, it would take weeks, if not months to find her.

I didn't think I had that much time left.

A knock on the door pulled me out of my thoughts. I nearly called to Janice, but she would be upstairs, and calling her down to answer the door would be mean.

I got myself up off the floor and closed the distance between the living room and the front door. When I opened it, I saw Devin on the other side with a huge, boyish grin on his face.

'Hey, Ash, I brought some help,' he said before kissing me lightly on the lips. I looked behind him. Lucy and Hunter were there—and Kali. I'd met her at the funeral, but she looked like a completely different person out of typical funeral clothes.

'What are you …?'

'Doing here?' Lucy answered.

I nodded like an idiot.

'Dev said you need help finding a witch. You've got three of the best witches in town right within the family, so we figured we'd come and help.'

It took everything in me to not let my jaw drop because, out of anything to expect, that was not it.

'Devin?' I asked as soon as they were all inside. But he was still leaning against the door. 'What are you doing?'

'Do you really think I'm going to let you not get what you want? I want to take you away. I want to be able to whisk you away on a moment's notice so we can have sex in some luxurious place or in the back of the limo on the way to the country. I want to help you. This is me helping you.' He took my face in his hands, and I was forced to look at him and only him. 'I wanted to try and do it myself, but I'm no good with magick. Lucy is. Hunter's better …'

'Hey, I heard that!' Lucy said from inside.

'Kali is freaking awesome. They're my family. I wanted a witch. I didn't tell them why, but they all wanted to help.'

I held my breath because no one had ever done something like that, nor did I expect anyone to help me. I came from a place where everyone was out for themselves, but Devin ... He wasn't. He was going to be a fine CEO of a company after the man who'd been in charge ran it so well.

'Breath, love. I can't have you dying before we get your pelt back.'

I inhaled sharply and tried to keep myself from tearing up. 'You're something else, you know that? I didn't expect that, and you do all of this, all of it for me, and you know that in the end, I'm going to take off. But you know ... You know that ...'

'You're going to come back to me. Ash, I'm all in this. All in. Are you?'

I nodded. Without a question or a doubt. 'I'm all in. Every little bit of me is in. What do I need to do?'

'We need you down here, and we need the camera too. If it's enchanted, we can find out how and fix that,' Kali said. She started to pull things out of a bag while Hunter pushed furniture out of the way. I hadn't even noticed that Kali had a bag when she came in.

'Miss Acionna, I must ask them to stop. They're ruining the living room. It's unacceptable.'

I chuckled at Janice. 'Janice, it's okay. They'll put it all back, right, guys?' I looked at them, and Lucy turned to Devin.

'Okay, I guess I'm putting it back, but yes. Janice, it will all be back in place. I promise.'

Janice blinked. 'Oh, hello, Mr Devin.'

He beamed at her, and I watched as her cheeks changed colour. My boyfriend was flirting with my maid. 'Hey, you, stop that. Pay attention, Janice. Can you get some drinks and the like for us?'

'Of course, Miss Acionna. Will soda be okay?'

'Soda is fine. There should be some cookies too. For later.' I looked at Lucy, and she looked back at me with surprise and confusion.

'For after, right? I don't know if it works the same now, but I'm thinking you'll need something to boost your energy up, and I have an abundance of cookies.'

'Yeah, wow. Thank you.'

I smiled at her. Devin wrapped an arm around my shoulders, and we walked into the living room. He pressed a soft kiss into my hair. Could the project of helping me be masking his own pain? Or helping him try to figure out what to do with the pain? I looked at him. *What if he can't feel pain? What if he is just trying to fill in the void that is there?*

I wrapped my arms around his waist and hugged him tightly. 'Acionna?' he murmured, surprised at the sudden touch. I held him tight and sighed into his skin.

'I just needed to do that. I have some things to ask you later,' I said, and kissed him softly on the lips.

'I'm all yours later. All of me.'

That made me smile like a crazy person, and I knew I looked like one. It was hard not to be happy though. Especially when he was who he was. *God.*

'All right, Acionna, are you ready?' I looked past Devin to Hunter, who was gesturing at a circle that wasn't completely closed.

'I'm as ready as I'm ever going to be,' I said, untangling myself from Devin and walking over to them. 'What do you need me to do?' I asked.

In the middle of the circle was a little altar with four points—water, fire, earth and air. Each element had a different item attributed to it.

'Your camera, and then you in the circle,' Hunter said, and held out his hand for me.

I grabbed the camera off the hallway console that was in the opposite direction of the living room and cradled it with care. Lucy grabbed it from me, and I took Hunter's outstretched hand.

He was Devin's best friend, and I knew that whatever was going to happen, I was in safe hands. He would make sure of it.

'You're right,' Hunter murmured, and I looked at him in surprise. He laughed and tapped his temple. 'I can hear some things when they pertain to me.'

'That's freaky. You know that, right?' He rubbed my shoulders and laughed again.

'Yup, but you get used to it.'

'I should have probably warned you about that before we came,' Devin said in an amused tone.

'You should have warned me full stop,' I pointed out.

'But where would the fun in that be?' He grinned at me when I looked over my shoulder at him.

'Okay. So what we're going to do is I'm going to close the circle now. Devin won't be allowed in.' He was interrupted by a little meow. 'Oh, hello there. You're pretty and familiar. Is she ...?'

'One of Mum's? Yeah,' Devin said.

'How did you pull that off?' Hunter asked as he picked up the kitten and rubbed the spot behind her ears.

'Mum doesn't know.' Devin grinned.

'Dev ... when did she disappear?' Hunter asked.

'Almost a full three weeks ago,' I answered for him. They were talking about me like I wasn't in the room.

'So sneaky. When Subira figures it out, she will be a little lost for words.'

'Maybe,' Devin said. 'But I'm sure if I told her it was for Acionna, she'd be okay with that.'

Would she be? Life was a little harder in those days, and Subira would want all of the comfort she could get. Devin took the kitten from Hunter and stepped out of the way.

'So, as I was saying, we'll be closing the circle and wrapping it in energy. The kitten won't be too much of an issue, but anyone else who steps on the line will ultimately hurt someone, so that's why everyone needs to steer clear. Next, we'll invoke the elements and the spirit just to help us, and then we'll hopefully try and find the witch who has you under her curse. I'm not sure if we can break it from here, but we can try. But I personally don't want to try that as of yet. It might be too much at the moment. But if it does come to that, we've got you. You don't have to worry about anything. Kali?'

I appreciated that he went to the effort to tell me what was happening with the magick and spell.

'Do you come into this circle with perfect love and perfect trust?' she asked me. Her voice didn't waver, and I knew that it was game time.

'I do,' I said.

'Welcome, and blessed be. Let's get this going. Luce?'

'Got it! Elements are ready. Let's go.'

'Hail from the watchtower of the north, we invoke thee, fill our space.'

'Hail from the watchtower of the south, we invoke thee, fill our space.'

'Hail from the watchtower of the east, we invoke thee, fill our space.'

They looked at me, and I knew I had to be part of it too.

'Hail from the watchtower of the west, we invoke thee, fill our space.'

'We welcome the goddess and god into our circle. Help guide us and protect us from those who seek to harm us.'

I felt warmth spread through my chest and my body as the circle was cast. I looked around. I could see the bliss on Lucy, Hunter and Kali's faces. They were at their happiest in the middle of the circle, and I was in awe. Witches weren't a thing in the Undersea, but magick was a universal power we all knew about.

I was happiest under the sea, crashing through the waves and frolicking with the people I cared for.

'Okay, let's have a look at this. Maybe we shouldn't touch the camera first,' Lucy spoke up, but her fingers went towards the camera, and my eyes widened. If it dropped, it would end everything. I almost lunged for it, but Hunter grabbed me in the nick of time.

'It's okay. We're not going to actually hurt it. We just want to study it, see the spell that's on it.'

'I just ... It's a camera. I'm attached to all of those. You know?' His eyes were soft, and I knew he understood. With that look, I felt so seen.

I could see the way he and Lucy fit together. They were yin and yang. Dark and light. Night and Day. *Wow.* I shivered, and Hunter looked at me, at the smile on my face.

'You just realised that, huh? Wait to see what happens with you and Devin,' he whispered, and I looked at him, surprised. *What does that mean? What the actual hell?* I swallowed hard and looked over my shoulder at Devin. He was leaning forward with a hand resting on his chin like he was trying to decode what had just happened.

'Okay, let's do this.' Lucy grabbed the pepper and sprinkled it over the camera. I watched it hit a forcefield, and she laughed. 'This is child's play.'

'Luce, that's the sort of thing you did four years ago,' Kali pointed out, and dipped a crystal pendulum into a liquid. 'You can't talk.'

'That was then. This is now. Gimme the sage.'

I felt like I was intruding on something. *Why am I here? Why do I need to be here? Couldn't they have done it themselves?* The urge to look back at Devin and ask him to help me get the camera away from them was far more intense than I'd expected.

My heart rate quickened, and I dug my nails into my palms as I watched Hunter step closer to the camera. He held out his hand, and I hesitated again, this time because I wanted to feel the anxiety. But he didn't waver—he waited. I took his hand, and instantly felt some of it drain away. *What flavour of witch is he?* He let go of my hands, and I shoved them into my pockets. It kept me from digging my nails into my palms.

'Relax. We've got you, Acionna. You're not going to be here for much longer.'

I watched as the pendulum swung, and Kali muttered words under her breath. Hunter let go of my hand and covered her hand with the same one that was just touching mine. Together, with closed eyes, they focused and pointed their energy.

'Ash, can you take my hand?' Hunter asked and held out his other hand. I hesitated, and Lucy looked up at me like she was amazed I was second-guessing them. I felt like a coward at that moment.

'Yes,' I said, even though my insides were shaking.

I'm a bloody selkie. Magick should not be an issue for me. I inhaled sharply and took Hunter's hand. I felt a spark fling through my body. I jumped without meaning to, looking at Hunter. He just smiled and reassured me.

How can a man like that be so patient?

'Got it,' Kali cried out.

'Can I let go now?' I asked Hunter. He shook his head.

'Is that the ranges?' he asked.

Kali looked down at the map and frowned. 'I think so.'

'Why would a witch be hiding in the ranges?'

'Why not? It's perfect. There's enough cover that no one will find it, and you can keep a lookout without needing to. Plus, the chances of randoms just showing up is really small.'

Lucy and Kali looked at Devin like he'd grown another head, and Hunter and I glanced at each other before we took in the map. We knew why Devin knew that and they didn't, but that wasn't our secret to tell. Hunter let go of my hand, and I stared at the map on the coffee table and sighed.

'That makes sense,' Hunter murmured. 'Okay. What's the plan now?'

I turned around. Devin stared back at me, his eyes staring through me, and that's when I knew he'd already decided that he was going to kill her.

'We come up with a plan and go in,' I said, but I saw Devin's subtle shake of his head. I was going to save him from himself, and this is my chance.

'Okay. We might need a bit more of an army. We can call in the wolves,' Lucy said.

'I have a few more witches I know of,' Hunter said.

'I don't think we'll need the wolves,' I said. Lucy looked at me.

'Trust me, we really might need them.'

I would let her think we called the shots if it was easier for her, but we didn't. I knew that.

CHAPTER TWENTY-SEVEN

Devin
Thoth 2015
Somewhere in the desert

My back ached with every hint of movement, but the scabs were healing. It was a slow process, but I'd been benched. It meant that there were more drills, more work to be done and I was out of the field. Jarrad made sure I was occupied, sparring with me. I wasn't sure if it was because he felt guilty or he actually wanted to, but after a heavy session, the scabs cracked, and he ended up having to dab the blood from the leaking wounds.

Should I have been doing that?

Absolutely not.

But I couldn't lie in bed all day while they healed slowly. There were healers who could speed up the process, but I wanted as little intervention as I could get.

The walk from the dorms to the weapons shed wasn't long, but that day, it felt like it was a hundred miles away. Maybe I was just overtired. I still trained as much as I could with the wounds, but it took a lot more out of me as a result of the healing.

I pushed too much, but I didn't want to give them the satisfaction of showing just how hurt I was because they would take advantage. I didn't have time for the repercussions that came with that.

I dropped to my knees as a sharp pain cut across my stomach. My hand dropped to the place, and I expected it to come away with blood, but there was nothing. Not even a hint. I lifted my shirt to see if there was any mark, and as I swiped across my abdomen, there was nothing.

No physical pain, but it was there. I had felt it.

My eyes widened as I searched through the connections in my brain. Lucy was there—barely—but when I searched for Destiny, she wasn't. My chest tightened. The only way for her not to be there was if she were dead. The bond between us was gone, and there was a hollow hole where she used to be.

I'd failed and lost a sister.

I didn't know where she was—they wouldn't tell me—and suddenly, she was gone.

'D-Man, what happened? What is it?' Jarrad came into view and wrapped an arm around my shoulders before he carefully pulled me to my feet.

There were no words. She was just gone. *Destiny can't be dead ...* It was the only answer for her presence not being there in our connections. Karrept wouldn't have killed her. I was sure of it. In between it all, I visited Destiny's dreams just to check in on her, but the last few had been reoccurring dreams of Karrept hurting her. It had started innocently, but it had gotten worse. I tried to get more, but she said she was so tired and couldn't keep fighting back any longer.

Jarrad didn't say anything as he walked me to the side of the building where no one would see me fall apart. My body shook at the trauma of what could have happened. Tears threatened to leave my lids, but I held them back and focused on the pain of my back. If I focused on that, I wouldn't cry in front of Jarrad. He was a support then, and no one else had been since I had gotten there. They saw me as a threat, or they left me alone—honestly, that was my own fault, but I preferred it that way anyway.

'D-Man, what is it?'

I shook my head, the words refusing to leave my lips. It was like they were stuck in my throat, forming a lump that didn't budge. *How do I tell someone I hardly know, who is half of the reason my body aches day in and day out, that I can't feel my sister? How fucking weird is that?* I knew that if I hadn't grown up with that feeling, I would find it weird as shit.

'Spill it, Devin. What is it?'

'My sister,' I choked out, finding the words. 'Something happened to her.'

'Who is she? Your sister. Where is she?'

What if I just left and went to find her? Can I just leave? Will they try to find me?

My thoughts were a mess, coming out in a jumble like I could really leave that place. My chest tightened even further. I loved my sisters more than anyone could ever understand. I missed Lucy so much, and if something were to have happened to her, I would have lost my shit. I couldn't lose my twin—that would be like I lost a limb that would never grow back. But Destiny ... She was my older sister. Destiny had always been there, my partner in crime, but she had changed. Karrept had changed her. He had broken her slowly. She didn't say much, but the way she looked and the illusions in our dreams ... I would kill him for it with the skills his camp gave me. I would find a way to put him back in the book, and as long as he stayed, I would make sure that book was destroyed. The only person who could read it was Lucy. She was in Melbourne, safe from everything that was happening, and far, far away.

'Karrept has her. She's ...'

'Dead,' Jarrad finished for me, and I nodded. I gripped his arm for support and dug my nails in. He showed no notice that it hurt.

'I have to get to her. I *need* to get to her,' I said, and this time, I tried to make a move, but Jarrad held me against the wall and shook his head.

'No can do, D-Man. Karrept wouldn't let you anywhere near him.'

'He *killed* my sister. He has to pay.'

As soon as the words were out of my mouth, I felt something—a spark of life. I gasped. It wasn't possible for her to be alive again. *What the hell happened?*

'He did what he always does, didn't he?'

I swallowed hard and looked at him. 'What do you mean?'

Jarrad was tight-lipped. He let go of me, his fingers resting on his lips before speaking. 'He breaks his toys and animates them again.'

'Animates them?' I asked, pushing away from the wall, finally able to stand on my own two feet again.

He nodded. 'With power. Necromancy.'

'That exists?' I'd read books on necromancers, but they always made them sound like they were just a myth, a story put out there to make sure people believed something.

'Of course. They're not vampires.'

'Can I get to her? I need to …'

'Not going to happen, man. Most of the animated girls don't live long—they need a constant source of energy, and Karrept loses interest pretty fast when they're broken.'

'I have to get to her,' I repeated. It wasn't even a question anymore. I had to get to Destiny.

He shook his head. 'You can try, but you won't get very far. Trust me.'

'It's happened to others?' I asked, and he just shrugged.

Fuck.

Phaophi 2015
Somewhere in the desert

'Dodge it,' Harlow said as he threw a spear at me. I dropped to the ground, my hands supporting my weight. I pressed my whole body flat. The wounds had healed, and I wasn't used to the power that was laced through my body. I was stronger than ever, toned like never before and I knew more things than I should have. I could snap a person's vertebrae in six places, and they could still walk away and not be dead. I could decapitate a person without blinking. But my weapon of choice, everyone knew, was a bow and arrow. The first time I used it, I was shit, but I trained harder every day to become the best. I could make it swing around corners. No one could get that, but I understood the bow. The guys got into the habit of making sure I didn't have access to a bow and arrow to defend myself because they knew they had no chance. A skill I had honed was used as a detriment if I didn't have the tools.

They thought it would be harder for me. It wasn't. I was smart, and trained harder as a result. I rolled onto my back and kip-flipped to my feet, blocking the kick that came my way from Harlow. I punched and kicked out until I heard the air leave his lungs. *Good.* He was winded, and with that, I kept moving through the maze of men and obstacles. The prize at the end of the course was what made it worth it.

And I wanted it more.

I was nothing short of competitive when it came to those weird tests that were put in place.

'D-Man, heads up,' the voice chattered. A chortled chorus of words drowned out almost all of the noise, but those three words got through. I stopped in time to see a knife coming at me. I watched it cut through the air as it came flying towards me. I held my hands up and watched. I blocked out all of the chatter—they were telling me to duck, but I was on par with the knife. I snapped my hands together in the nick of time and caught the blade just before it would have sliced my head in two. The motion was fast, and I didn't think about it, but as I caught my breath, I held the knife steady as a hushed silence settled over everyone.

'Fucking hell, you *did* it,' Harlow exclaimed.

The training session stopped, and cheers echoed through The Camp. I slowly brought my hands down, and everyone rushed over to me. Even Jarrad seemed happy to see it. Everyone was recounting how I did it and smiled, but my mind was onto the next thing I could master. What was left.

'Come on, guys, give D-Man some air. It's all he's got to do.'

Everyone parted for Jarrad, and I flipped the blade in my hand and threw it at him.

His reflexes were infinitely better than mine, faster and more precise, and he missed it. Whatever paranormal flavour he was, he just wasn't having it.

'Not on your game, Jar?' I challenged.

He laughed. 'I'm always on my game, D-Man. What's the last thing you used?'

'Sticks,' I said, and someone got two sticks and threw one at me. I caught it in a two-hand grip and looked up at Jarrad. He was grinning back at me.

'You know, this could be really bad for you, considering you're coming off a win,' Jarrad said as he moved back, his footing careful, the staff twirling in his hands.

I shrugged. 'Who cares. I thought it wasn't about points, Jar.'

'It's not, but I'd hate for you to look bad after you looked so good.' He laughed, and I waited.

Jarrad always waited too—he watched and waited for one to first move and then swooped in for the win. Jarrad made more mistakes when he was the one who made the first move. I doubted anyone else noticed that. They all rushed in for the action, thinking it would get them points. It wouldn't. Everyone there was an opponent. No one was safe enough to trust. It was drilled into us not to trust, but some of the others did. And they always got hurt.

I wasn't about to get hurt. I'd spent too much time getting hurt. I had the scars to prove it.

'What's the matter? Are you too chicken?' I piped up, and twirled the staff in my hand. It whizzed around in the air, and Jarrad laughed. He lunged, but didn't bring his staff up, waiting for the right moment. His eyes skittered from my face, the staff and my feet.

I had all the time in the world to wait for him to attack, but did he?

He swung the staff out at me, and I brought up mine and deflected the hit. The sound of wood hitting each other was all that was heard. Everyone gasped, the tension in the air almost too much to handle.

It positively electrified the place. *Beautiful.*

Jarrad swung out again, this time down low, and I stopped him with the staff and pushed him back. He grinned at me.

'You know, that silent treatment is not going to get you anywhere. You think you have it all figured out, don't you?'

I smiled at him. 'Silent treatment will get me everywhere. What won't get me anywhere is you chattering,' I grunted, and pushed Jarrad back further before I jabbed either side of him to keep him on his toes. He deflected easily, a grin on his face. I was patient. I could sweep his legs out from under him and be done with him. Unless he got to me first. I was hoping he wouldn't though.

'Most of the others take this chance to psych me out. To get me talking and really work out my weak spots, but you're smart. You already know that talking won't do a thing to me. Isn't that right?'

I didn't answer him, instead pulling back and holding my staff in a defensive position. 'Are you going to talk my ear off?' I finally asked, knowing he wanted to take that time to try and get in a cheap hit. But I deflected it, and the surprise on his face showed me what I needed to see. It was gone as quick as it was there, but I swept Jarrad's legs out from under him, and he fell hard. Before he could react, I was on him, the staff pointed at his Adam's apple. 'I told you talking was a waste of time.'

Jarrad was breathing hard. I had knocked the wind from his lungs, and I could see him trying to figure out what to say. For a moment, no one spoke. No one even moved while they waited to see what happened. Life wasn't meant to work out the way I wanted, so in that moment, every single pair of eyes saw that I was a threat.

Good. Maybe they will back off.

I stepped back and lowered the staff to my side. I held out a hand to Jarrad, and he took it without hesitation. I helped him to his feet, and he brushed himself off. Jarrad clapped a hand on my shoulder and grinned.

'You're good. You've been watching more than I realised. But just remember, if I wanted to kill you, I would. You may have gotten me good this time, but just know that if I have to do what is necessary, I will. If I'm pushed to finish what is problematic, I'll do it so no else has to suffer.'

Point for me. Everyone around me looked at me like I was foreign.

Maybe a little more fear would be good.

Pachons 2017
Melbourne

The hotel was quiet. Since the murder, Dad's office had been closed up tight. No one even peeked inside. I stared at the door and the police tape that was still there. They had given us the okay to remove it, and I had taken a few extra days.

Well, I'd thrown myself into helping Acionna. She had to get her pelt back, and with the location—well, the broad location—of the witch, I wanted to make sure we could make the camera situation work for us. That spell was a little trickier, as we had to make sure we could link another device to it.

Hunter and Lucy were working on it, but it was a little more detailed than I wanted it to be.

I could have had Acionna come, but it was something I had to do for myself.

I swallowed hard and ripped the police tape off the door, pulling down on the handle and pushing it open. The office smelt musty, like death had settled in. The carpet would have to be completely replaced, and everything scrubbed down with a heavy-duty industrial cleaner.

Better yet, I could just set it on fire and it would cleanse it all.

Start afresh.

'Fuck,' I whispered, and shut the door behind me. The light turned on by itself, and I was blinded by it for a moment. I hated the lighting in those offices, and it was going to be the first thing I changed. No one needed that much fucking light to sign contracts and run an empire.

As my eyes adjusted, I looked around the room. Everything was still in the same place. Nothing had been moved. The police had taken away the shit they needed, but everything else was there.

I walked over to the pinboard and grabbed the note Dad had written that night. It hid the bullet hole—the one made by the bullet in my pocket. I hadn't seen what was written on the note, but it was Dad's perfect handwriting.

D, you know what you have to do. Don't be upset. I saw this coming, and what happens next ... You'll get your satisfactory result.

Grief did funny things to people. Maybe that was why I hadn't seen it initially, but shit. Dad was a witch, and so was Mum. It was the only way we had all ended up with some ability to use magick in some way, but I'd never asked what it was. From the note, it seemed like it had something to do with precognition, and that was terrifying. He had seen his death—lived it twice.

I was furious at Jarrad for it. He had put that image in my father's mind, and now, it was the last thing he had seen.

Jarrad had always been right there whenever we needed him. It was a hard pill to swallow, knowing that he could get anywhere in the blink of an eye.

My phone vibrated in my pocket, and without looking at it, I answered it.

'Yeah?'

'So you are alive.'

I stopped cold and nearly dropped the phone.

'Jarrad,' I said coldly.

'Good to hear from you, D-Man.'

'It's Devin,' I said. 'You lost all rights to call me that the moment you pulled the trigger on my father, and you know it.'

'Remember what I told you all those years ago?'

I was silent. There was so much shit he had said. It was hard to pinpoint exactly what he wanted me to say.

'I'll remind you. If I'm the one who had to do the kill, it's because you've pissed off the wrong people. It's an attention grab.'

'I'm going to find you, Jarrad, and I'm going to make sure you don't see the light of day ever again. I hope you understand that.'

'I do, Dev, and I look forward to it. You're one of the only men at The Camp who could test me like you did and get away with it.'

'I'd sleep with one eye open.'

I hung up the call, and it took everything in me not to throw my phone. It would be the third phone that week, and I couldn't put Rhea through that again. She was going to have a heart attack.

CHAPTER TWENTY-EIGHT

Acionna
Pachons 2017
Melbourne

'ARE you sure this is something we should be doing?' I asked as Devin handed me a shirt. He had come back from the office in a foul mood, and I didn't ask about it. I wanted to, but in that instant, I felt it was better to actually just wait for him to say what he wanted. But the sex had been damn near earth-shattering—I was still seeing stars.

If I had to wait all night, I would.

'Yup. Luce and Hunt said they wanted to go out, and we waited until after your picture. So you don't have much of a choice when it comes to excuses.'

'I wouldn't make an excuse.'

'Yeah, you would. Plus, Luce wants to get to know you more.'

'Or she wants to scope out how much she might have to hurt me if I hurt you.'

Devin beamed at me as I pulled my black shirt on. It was sheer with gold patches through it. I did the buttons up and tucked it into a pair of skinny-legged jeans that clung to all of my curves. Not that I had much. I was a selkie, and that meant that I had a pretty thin frame.

'Smoking hot,' Devin said, and pulled me into his body. He pinned my hips against his and licked his lips. 'Are you sure we can't just go again over there?' He nodded towards the bed, and I laughed.

'I just asked if going out was something that we should do, and you said yes, and now, you're asking for rounds two and three?'

He beamed at me. 'What can I say? I'm an opportunist, but you look so hot in that shirt. And knowing what is under it ... Mmmm.'

I shook my head and laughed as I untangled myself from his warmth. It would be so easy to just stay there and have more sex. I was contradicting myself, but what we should be doing and what we wanted to be doing were two very different things.

'Flatterer. Come on, we need to get a move on,' I said, and grabbed my ankle boots. They were black with a strip of faux snakeskin down the side of them. After being in Melbourne for so long, I was picking up the black on black-on-black trend that hit the instant the weather started to get cold.

'Hey, you're pretty all right,' Devin said with a soft smile. He kissed my cheek and took my free hand and let me out of the room—a safer bet than staying in there.

I put my boots on, and Devin opened the door. We were at my place because it was closer to the restaurant that Lucy and Hunter picked.

It was going to be interesting to see if their seafood was as fresh as they had promised it would be.

We left the house, and the trip there was shorter than I realised. Devin parked the car after ten minutes of driving. It was almost smack-bang out the front of the restaurant, and as I opened the door, he closed it again.

'Dev ... what are you doing?' I asked.

'Ladies shouldn't open their own doors,' he said, and opened the door. He held out a hand for me, and I took it. I couldn't help the giggle that left my lips. Devin smiled, and it reached his eyes for the first time all day. Part of me melted at the very action.

'You're a gentleman too?'

'You know it,' he said. I shook my head as Devin closed the door. He clicked a button and locked the car.

'It's definitely just Lucy and Hunter, yeah?' I asked.

He nodded. 'Just us. I think they had some things they wanted to ask you.'

'Oh, god, are you telling me I'm about to get interrogated by your sister and best friend?'

'Nah, they'll be cool, but maybe just keep it clean.'

I swatted at his shoulder. 'Dev! What am I going to do? Try to jump you in front of them?'

'I wouldn't say no,' he said, and his voice lowered as it filled with heat.

'Down, boy,' I murmured just as we walked into the restaurant and spotted Hunter and Lucy at a table. They waved, and we made a beeline for them.

'Hey, Acionna. It's good to see you again,' Lucy said, and stood up to wrap her arms around me. I wasn't expecting that, and stared at Devin over her shoulder. He just shrugged.

Devin could have warned me about what she was going to do. But he didn't.

'It's good to see you again, Lucy. How are you? How's the book coming along?'

She was a writer. Devin had made that blatantly obvious many times over because he didn't want her to feel like she was a failure or that she had to make things for other people.

'It's a slow process, but Hunter is a huge help. He takes on most of the domestic duties so I can write in my own room.'

Lucy pulled back. 'That sounds like you're a very lucky girl. Hello, Hunter.'

'Hi, Acionna. How are you going?' he asked. I wanted to give him the right answer, but how did I say that I missed the water on my skin and being able to frolic among my people? I was stuck there.

'I'm doing okay. A little more tired today.'

By the way my health had declined, I could see the ability to function was slowly fading away, but I made a practiced effort to make sure I could still do what was needed.

'We're going to help with that. We wanted to talk about a plan for the … snitch that we found. While we have a roundabout position. It's not quite concrete, which has never happened before. Kali is most offended about that.'

'I'm sorry, Devin said this was just a plain dinner. You'll have to forgive me for not being straightforward. '

'Of course he did. Would you have come otherwise?' Hunter asked.

And risk you getting found out if people figured out what we were talking about?

'Maybe not. But won't you get in trouble?' I asked.

'We're just talking, not showing anything and not selling anything, so that is the loophole. You obviously know what we mean by "snitch?"' I nodded. Everyone knew that.

'Okay, so we have her location, and granted, it's not her exact location. But we need to know if you're all in on this?'

'Yes,' I said without hesitation. 'You don't understand, but I want her dead. I will call the people who need to do it if I have to, but I will make sure that she understands she messed with the wrong woman. I won't hesitate.'

'Absolutely. We have to break through the field she has around the location,' Lucy said, and she lowered her voice. 'Her magickal wards are intense. We've already tried to tap at them, and they are pinging like crazy. It's like if we were meant to find a location of where someone lived and it was rerouted through so many different towers. It's basically that.'

I looked around the restaurant. There were a lot of humans who were just casually eating their food or drinking their drinks, but there was a huge selection who were not. I could feel the preternatural beings in the room, and there were a lot of them. It was dangerous to talk about magick outside like we were. And the fact that Lucy, Hunter and Devin all did so with ease was even more terrifying.

'Should we be talking about this here?' I asked, and shifted my attention back to the group.

Hunter smiled. 'We're all good. There are a lot of magickal wards around us. If you want to say anything that you don't think could be said in public, you'll find that no one will be able to hear it.'

'Did you spell the restaurant?'

Lucy shook her head. 'Nah, just us. It's easier to affect a smaller group than a whole cohort. But we wanted to make sure we were safe. And it's too hard to do this at home without it looking suspicious to Mum. She's been through enough.'

That made sense. 'Do we have a timeline?' I asked.

'Do you?' Hunter asked.

'Now?'

He chuckled. 'We need a little more time than that, but we are working as fast as we can. The intricate details of the wards she has up make it harder to pinpoint, but I promise you, we are working on it. The next issue is the camera. We think we've got it figured out, but it's going to be a bit of trial and error.'

'What?' My heart thumped faster in my chest at those last three words. *Trial and error?* They wanted to play with my pelt's future to get it right? 'Absolutely not. I'm not taking any chances. This is my whole life on the line,' I said.

'They're aware of that, Ash,' Devin said, and he wrapped an arm around my waist. The touch was grounded, but I felt like the room just rose in degrees.

Did it suddenly get hotter in here?

'Are they? Because that camera is attached to whether or not my life stays the same or changes. If I lose it, I can't go back. Ever.'

'We know,' Lucy said. And she held my gaze. It was like she wanted to reassure me without saying so many words. 'We're taking so much care with it, and we're treating the camera like we are the wards. It's a meticulous, weaving system that is just taking a bit of time to get through. We have to make sure it doesn't trigger anything that will endanger you or ruin the camera.'

'I just don't want to live a half life with a part of me missing,' I said quietly, and Devin squeezed my shoulder. I leant into the touch and let him comfort me.

'I know. But you have my word, I won't let that happen,' Lucy said. 'I know what it feels like to live without a part of you that has just disappeared.' She said that as she looked at Devin. I knew there was more to that statement, but it wasn't my place to ask.

'Do you need anything from me?' I asked.

'Just some of your hair,' Lucy said.

'And maybe your blood,' Hunter chimed in.

'Blood?' I asked.

'Yeah, just to make sure that this will work. I promise we won't misuse it.'

I nodded. 'I guess we're doing this.'

'We are doing this,' Devin said softly.

'Okay. Let's look at the food then?'

'Let's do it.'

Hunter held the camera in his hands, and I shifted from side to side. I wanted to take it from him and hold it tight. *Do I really trust them to do this right?* It was nearly time to take my photos, and I didn't know if I trusted it to work. We were all on the balcony connected to my bedroom.

'Are we sure this will work?' I asked.

'Yeah. If it doesn't, we will make sure it works tomorrow, and if that doesn't work, we'll try again. We're not going to leave you hanging,' Hunter said.

I breathed a small sigh, but I wanted to run. I wanted to go down to the water and make sure I got the picture, but I was putting my faith in Hunter. I looked over my shoulder at Devin, who was lingering in the bedroom. He smiled but kept his distance. I wondered what was going through his mind. *Is he as apprehensive about this as I am?*

I finished setting up the tripod and held my hand out to Hunter. He put the camera in my hand, and the weight of it was comforting. I put it on the tripod and clicked it in place. I shook the camera and the tripod to make sure it was secure.

I had attached a good lens that allowed me to really zoom into my spot, and it would look the same—or as close to the same as it had to be. Each day was slightly different. I just needed to take a photo of the beach.

'I need your phone.'

I gave my phone to Hunter after I unlocked it, and he pushed some prompts and then waited for something to load.

'How do you know how to do all of this? Better yet, how did you program it?' I asked Hunter.

'It's all pretty simple, really. I just attached a timer to it that allowed it to be synced to a phone. We had to play with some of the warding to make sure the technology didn't hurt the spell around it. It's going to be a good test to get it going, but if we have to run down to the beach and snap the image, we will, and we'll go back to the drawing board. But I'm hoping it works. Lili's dad had the equipment after we went digging. Something about needing surveillance.'

'That family,' I said with a laugh.

Her family was well-connected, and I had a feeling they were connected to The Mob—or *were* The Mob.

I rubbed my hands over my arms, and Hunter smiled at me. Devin and he had gone downstairs for a moment, so it was just the two of us.

'You know that he's going to try and do it himself,' Hunter said as he lowered his voice.

'I know, and I want to try to get him to stop before it's too late. Do you know how much I don't want his hand to be covered with her blood? It's not good enough for him, and I think he deserves better. Better than the life he's living.' I shoved my hands into the back pockets of my jeans and stared out at the ocean. 'How can someone like him have so much pain and not show it to anyone else?'

'He has it,' Hunter said. 'He just doesn't know how to express it. His life has been up and down in the last few years. I can't tell you everything. Only he can. I know that he will, but it's been rough.'

'I can tell, but that's what terrifies me. I just want to make it better and make him not have to think about it, but then this happens, and something like his dad. God, my heart aches for him. How do you survive losing your dad?'

'I can't tell you, but all we can do is be there for them. And you're doing a great job. Devin has done so much more than he would have since you've come into his life. I promise you that it's worth it. Devin is opening up to you. I can see it. I've never seen it happen before, and I've spent a long time with him. You have to just trust me. You're good for him.'

I sighed. 'What did you mean before? About what's to come. What does that even mean?'

He grins. 'Ah, I can't tell you. If I did, I'd have to kill you, and then I'd be in the same position as Devin. And I really don't want to have to explain to him that I killed his girl. But it's for the best. You guys are great together, especially you. He needs someone who will push him when he really needs it, and you do. You push back when he does, and you don't stop. Most in your position would have stopped before he was ready to give up, and that's what's bad. He would be alone. You're not going to give him the chance, are you?'

I shook my head. 'No. Not really.'

'Good. That's exactly what he needs. Promise me something because I know Devin would never, in a million years, ask you this himself. Can you watch out for him before he breaks? He's going to, and I know I can't do a thing about it. I'm just his best friend, but you're the girl he loves. He's going to listen to you over me any day.'

'Hunter ...' I started.

'No, it's the truth. Shit happened to him when he was gone. He's an assassin now, and can kill coldly and move on. I can't do that. I can't even begin to understand how that can work for him, but I'm going to try because I love him, and I know you love him too. Devin needs us, Acionna, but he needs you more. Please don't let him go without you.'

I didn't know what to say. It felt like we were standing on the balcony for ages before Devin came back

'Hey, love, you're still there?' Devin asked with a jacket in his hands. He stepped onto the balcony and draped it across my shoulders.

'Hey! Yeah, Hunter was explaining the whole set up. He should go into IT or something. He's wasting his talents as a fiery.'

Hunter laughed. 'Acionna is only saying that because she's your girlfriend. She's funny, though.'

'He's actually just modest. He knows he should be doing something, but he's a fire bug. Which is weird, considering his element.'

He groaned. 'Luce told you about that?'

'Yup.' Devin grinned.

I could see how easy everything came to him and them together, but it wasn't the same. I knew in the back of my mind there was something keeping me from really reaching out to them. My head was still focused on what Hunter said. It was intense. Of course, I wouldn't stop him from falling too far. But how much of that would Devin actually let me do? How much would he be willing to keep up with me and not let me see?

'You know, there's nothing wrong with being airy and being a firebug, no matter what you say,' Hunter said.

My watch vibrated, and I looked at Hunter, who gave me back my phone. 'Okay, it's time. Try it.'

I pushed the button on the phone and snapped the picture. There was a distinct click, and we waited with bated breath.

If it worked, it would mean that the past six months had been harder than anything, but I could also breathe a little easier.

Nobody said anything, waiting for the clock to tick over. The agony of not knowing if it would work made that minute seem like days.

The time clicked over, and I waited for the agony that would take over my body. I squeezed my eyes shut, and then it hit. The pain filled all of my body, and I picked up the camera, tripod and all, and ran out of the room. I bolted down the stairs and flung open the door before I made a beeline for the beach.

Even though my body screamed at me, I needed to make sure I got there. I ran across the road. Cars beeped at me, but I didn't care. I just needed to get to the sand.

As soon as my feet hit the beach, I dug the tripod into the ground and snapped the picture.

The pain stopped instantly, and I dropped to the ground, my arse in the sand as I tried to catch my breath. Devin dropped next to me with Hunter on the other side.

'It … didn't … work,' I wheezed. And this time, I let the tears fall.

I was so fucking over being tied to the beach without being able to get my pelt wet. I wanted to be able to do more than take photos, and right then, as I stared at the ocean with the camera between me and it, I wanted to give up.

'It's okay, Ash,' Devin soothed. Wrapping an arm around my shoulders, he pulled me in close, and I let him hold me.

'We'll work on it again. I'm sorry, Acionna.'

It wasn't Hunter's fault. It was too good to be true, and all I had wanted to do was believe it could happen.

CHAPTER TWENTY-NINE

Devin
Phaophi 2012
Somewhere in the desert

I WANTED to get out of there, and no matter how many times I tried, it wasn't going to bring me any closer to Lucy. Or Destiny.

It had been months. I'd lost count of how long it had actually been, but I knew that time had passed—the slashes turned to scars. But the biggest thing to change? My body was harder, faster. I had never felt so strong in my life. They threw more at me, and I could take it in my stride. I was competitive as hell, but I also didn't want to die. I did what I needed to do to make sure I was strong and could dodge whatever was handed to me.

But I still hadn't taken a life. I could calculate how to and what I needed to do, but I wasn't … I couldn't.

I knew that was why I was there; I had to become a perfect soldier. But I didn't want to take a life.

I could be more of a man who was behind the scenes, giving out the missions, or better yet, giving out the weapons. I could do that.

'All troops, please report to the stadium.'

I rolled off the bunk, slipped my feet into my boots and tied the laces.

'What's going on?' Dion asked.

'No idea. It's a weird as fuck time though,' I said. Everyone would be winding down. It was not the time to have some sort of training drill.

'I hope it's not some weird demonstration of what not to do.'

Dion laughed, and we walked out of the dorm. I didn't have friends, but if I wanted one, I'd have claimed Dion. He was a dryad, and there was a lot to learn from tree spirits. He didn't tell me how he ended up there, and I didn't tell him how I had either. And that was that. But I was curious. I wondered how many of the others had been there, dragged back by Karrept. Or not.

The walk to the stadium was short. It was already dark, so most of the lights were out. We could see the lighting from the stadium brightening the whole sky. We were joined by some of the others. I didn't know their names, but they looked familiar. Dion easily chatted with them.

As soon as we got to the stadium, we were ushered into the seats. In the centre, the ground was covered in dirt. There was a stand of weapons, swords, mallets, bow and arrows and guns, and they were all displayed on the table like we had a choice of what we picked.

We did, but most of the time, everyone went with the same weapons they favoured. The bow and arrow were mine because no one else could seem to get the balance right. But I was okay with that. If I had to use a gun, I used one as a last resort. Axes were messy, but also did the job.

'D-Man, you're up,' Jarrad called my name, and I blinked. *What the fuck?*

I shook my head.

'You don't get a choice. Come on,' he called.

Dion and the others stood up so I could get out. I shimmied across the bodies and walked down the stairs to the arena. Jarrad had come out while my mind had been occupied with the weapons.

'What is this?' I asked, and Jarrad clicked his tongue.

'Monika, you're up too.'

Up for what? It was harder to pit women against men, but it happened. I didn't like hurting women. It reminded me of my sisters, and I hated to be put in a position where I had to hurt females.

'Everyone has become too complacent,' Jarrad shouted out. 'No one is safe. No one is considered better than the other. We are training soldiers who will fight in an army. You won't understand right now, but you will as time goes on.' He paused and licked his lips. 'We are in a time and age where being different is punishable by death. All of you, if caught on the outside, would be taken to a highly guarded prison where you would get no trial, no counsel. Just a death note, a last meal and that would be it. The wait would be minimal.'

It was all information we knew. It was the world we lived in.

'Your job will be to get rid of people just like you from the world. To stop this. So, what better way than to test what that would be like?'

Jarrad turned to Monika and me.

'Grab your weapons. It's a fight to the death.'

'Wh-what?' we both stuttered.

'Don't make me repeat myself.'

Monika and I looked at each other and blinked before we sprinted to the weapons table. I was faster by pure luck and grabbed the bow, but she grabbed the arrows. *Fuck.* We locked eyes, and she reached to grab the bow. I stepped back and grabbed a sword. The bow, I wrapped around my body so she couldn't get it. There was only one, and if I had the part Monika needed to use the arrows, she'd be forced to pick something else.

She did, grabbing a sword too.

Monika swung first, and I blocked it, pushing her back with my strength. I hated that men and women were not equals when it came down to a strength-based approach. It was almost unfair, but I used the momentum to shift back further. If I could keep her off, I could make it through the fight. And maybe she would too.

Her eyes were hungry with violence. I twirled my sword like I would a bat and held it with both hands in front of me.

Monika ran at me, her blonde hair in a ponytail. All six-foot-something of her was just as tall as me, her sword raised about her. She swung hard, and I brought mine up, the clash of metal louder than I expected.

'We can stop,' I said.

'Devin, it's you or me. And I, personally, want to come out on top because I like my life too much.'

She had a point.

Her broad swimmer shoulders moved, and this time, I swung my sword up and aimed for her arm. The blade sliced her forearm, and blood spurted out. She dropped the sword and stumbled back.

'I don't want to do this,' I said. I didn't take my eyes off her.

'You don't have a choice, D-Man. This is what will happen if you face someone on the outside. They can and will kill you.'

'But we are supposed to be working as a collective,' I called back. I didn't dare take my eyes off Monika.

'No one said that. Everyone is here, and out to do it for themselves. And you should be too.'

Monika ran back to the table and grabbed a mace. It was thick and covered in spikes. She ran at me again, and I held my ground.

I had weight on her easily, and as she swung the mace with her good hand, I brought the sword up and nicked her thigh.

Monika hissed and limped back.

'Hit harder,' she growled.

'No.'

If I wanted to stab her, I would, but that wasn't fair. She deserved her life. We all deserved our lives.

'This is barbaric,' I cried out.

'Fucking yes, but it's me or you, Devin,' Monika said, and this time, I stepped back. She took three steps towards me.

It wasn't going to end well. She swung the mace up again, the momentum toppling her forward. A spike connected with my bicep, and I cried out. I pushed her back and used the sword to do so. It punctured her stomach.

The sword slid through her like it was nothing, and she dropped the mace, clutching the wound.

Blood spilt freely from it, and she dropped to her knees.

'Monika!' I cried out and rushed to her side. She retaliated with a punch to the face, and my eyes blurred as she connected with me.

'Motherfucker,' I hissed.

'Gotcha,' she said weakly.

'Devin, finish it,' Jarrad said.

'No. She's out. She can get to the medic and heal.'

'There is no turning back now. She is down, out. Finish her.'

'No!' I screamed out.

Monika's face drained of colour as the blood drained from her wound. Jarrad picked me up by my collar and dragged me to my feet.

'I said finish her, or I will finish you.'

'Do it. Kill me. At least I'll be spared anything like this again,' I said, and held Jarrad's gaze. Defiance streamed through my whole body, and I waited to see if he could do his bit. Instead, he took the sword from me, swung and decapitated Monika, her blue eyes wide and mouth ajar. Her blood sprayed over me, the metallic taste touching my lips, and I felt the bile in the back of my throat. I was going to vomit.

Jarrad was fast and turned with a blade. It was small and sharp, but he stabbed it into my chest, narrowly missing anything of importance. Pain flooded my body. It was hot, like someone had dragged oil over my skin and refused to stop.

'You will obey orders the next time they are given. Do you understand?' He dragged the knife down, and I cried out.

'Do you *understand?*'

With my right hand, I threw a hook at his ear, and he stepped back.

'Understood,' I said before I vomited from the pain.

Jarrad growled. He came at me, but Dion was there, and he put himself between Jarrad and myself, keeping him firmly behind his body. Jarrard tried to get through him, but as a dryad, he stood his ground. He tried to claw at him, but Dion didn't budge.

'Give it a rest. We have to take him to the medic.'

He stopped trying to push forward and let go of Dion, who was still firmly planted between us.

'I don't want to see him any time soon,' Jarrad growled.

I didn't trust myself to say anything. I would have preferred to bite my own arm off than face him again.

Payni 2012
Egypt

Destiny put The Book back where it deserved to be and slipped it through a cover that was nondescript—it was boring and warded with a spell that would make people walk away. We need to make sure Lucy didn't ever go back there. She couldn't.

'Are you sure this will be enough?' I asked her. Older sister knowledge and all that had come a long way for us in the past—also, the fact that she could see the future helped. Well, to an extent. Destiny couldn't see her own future. I wasn't sure how that worked.

'It should be. As long as we don't disappear or die, she'll never have any reason to come here.'

I sat down on a rock and kicked at the sand. That made sense. 'Do you think we got rid of him?'

'I think we did. We can't afford to have him floating around the place. He's a danger to everyone and everything,' Destiny called out as she walked deeper into the tomb. 'He is,' she muttered, like she tried to convince herself. I heard her scratch around, but I couldn't see her doing much of anything either. 'There, it's done. Let's go. Luce will be livid if we're not back in a couple of hours.'

'Yup. Hey, Dest, why are you always so mean to her? I mean, we've always had a great relationship, but why is it that you always seem like you hate Lucy?'

Her fiery red hair was all I could see as Destiny turned to me. 'She's going to be the one to help me so much, but until then, she needs to learn that not everyone will love her.'

'But you do love her.' I couldn't find the logic there. It was like she'd tried to push Lucy away on purpose.

'I do, but I'm also jealous that she's the baby. Before the two of you, I was the favourite. I got everything I wanted. I didn't need to share anything at all. Mum and Dad told me I was getting a baby brother or sister. They didn't tell me until later that I was getting both. And you know.' Destiny smiled, a smudge of dirt on her face as she folded out of the shadows.

'You only wanted one of us? How cruel are you? You know she only wants you to like her. She's innocent as they come, Dest.'

She sighed and clapped her hands together to dust them off. 'I know, but I can't love the both of you. I'm not wired right.'

'What do you mean?' I asked, and before I could get an answer, Samjate ran in.

'It's here,' he called out, and Destiny stopped in her tracks and looked at me, the colour draining from her face. 'The creature. It's here.'

'Fuck,' she swore under her breath and turned to Sam. 'What do we do?'

'Run. I don't know how long I can keep him busy. It's …' He choked as a hand gripped around his neck.

My eyes bulged out of their sockets, and before we could move, Sam's neck was snapped. Destiny screamed and covered her mouth.

My blood turned to ice as I stared at the creature.

'You didn't take the time to do it properly. Now, I need you both.'

Calmly, I reached over to take Destiny's hand, our power magnifying as we silently constructed a protective circle that would help keep the creature at bay. We had managed to keep him away until we thought he was done, but none of us had offensive powers. It wasn't enough. Lucy was the only one who got some. All we had was some martial arts training, and not a lot. I stopped when I got bored, which was early, and Destiny didn't have much else.

'You can't take us,' Destiny said.

I made the mistake of looking at Sam, and my heart ached. His son would never see his dad again, and I couldn't imagine living a life without mine.

'You are the ones who resurrected me, and I'm here to collect you.

I need workers. I need an assassin.' The last word tore my attention away from Sam and forced it on Karrept. He had his golden eyes locked on me. I stumbled back.

Killing people for a living? No, hell to the no. I couldn't do that. I wouldn't do that.

'No. No,' I said again. And I squeezed Destiny's hand harder. It wasn't enough to really get anything, but she squeezed back, and we fed off each other's energy. I hoped it was enough to keep us safe.

Karrept broke through the barrier we'd put up. He smiled and looked like he knew exactly what he was doing. I felt him, there, inside my head, screaming his words at the world. It was too much. I dropped to the ground, my hands over my ears, the connection with Destiny severed. But it didn't matter. Karrept was there, everywhere, and all I could think about was trying to get him out of my head. He needed to go.

'Get out!' I screamed, as he filled every one of my senses completely.

And then there was silence. I crawled out of the ball that I was in and gasped.

I wasn't in the tomb anymore. My hands shook as I got to my feet.

'Destiny?'

'Dev? Where are you? Where are we?'

I breathed a sigh with Destiny so close. But where the hell we were, I had no idea. 'I'm over here. Keep talking to me. Can you see anything?'

'No. I don't know what's going on!' she screamed, and I ran towards her, blindly tripping over roots and rocks. I fell and scraped my elbow. Pain radiated through my arm, but none of that mattered. I needed to get to Destiny.

'Dest! Talk to me. What is it?'

'Snakes. Everywhere,' she screamed again, and I pushed harder, my brain already trying to figure out how to get rid of the serpents, how to keep my sister safe.

I could see Destiny through the clearing, and I saw her covered by a fallen tree trunk. There were things that every brother was used to seeing—one of them was the fear from some kind of bug—but the look on her face was almost worse than anything I'd ever seen. I didn't know how to make it go away. I wanted to, but there was something more.

'Dest, what is it?'

'You're going to kill someone. Lots of someones,' she whispered, and I was taken aback by that. I couldn't possibly kill someone. I just ... No, it wasn't in my nature.

'You're joking. That's not going to happen. Look at me.' I cupped her face in my hands and held her gaze in an attempt to get her to calm down, to try and focus on something else. 'You're safe when you're with me. We're going to get through this.'

First thing was, we needed to know where we were. It was dark—like, night dark. Karrept had blinked us there, and we were stuck. Stuck as we tried to figure out what to do and what they were going to do to us.

Fuck.

'Devin. I don't want you to kill me.'

I gasped and pulled my sister into a hard hug. Her body shuddered with the effort to keep herself up. 'I'm not going to kill you. I love you. You're my sister. I'm going to protect you, always.'

Then, someone ripped us apart with strength that was not unlike that of Karrept's.

'That's enough of that,' the menacing voice said as they held my hands behind my back. 'It's time to go to work now. We promise it won't be nice either.'

There was a smile in their words, and I shivered, not knowing what would happen next.

CHAPTER THIRTY

Acionna
Pachons 2017
Melbourne

I STARED at the camera again. After the night before, I wasn't at all confident that something could happen. Hunter and Lucy were on my balcony again. We did the same setup—the camera was on the tripod, and the lens was in. I leant against the door frame, my lips pressed together, and my finger and thumb pressed against my mouth.

If it didn't work, I was going to just admit defeat and that was going to be it. After 194 days of the same image, I would have to accept that I wouldn't be able to go anywhere, and continue to schedule all of my work commitments after the shot was taken.

'Hunt, I think you were missing that hint of the feminine energy in the spell,' Lucy said as she clicked her tongue. She was wearing light blue denim jeans that hugged her legs—legs that looked fabulous in them—with a pair of chocolate-coloured ankle boots and a black off-the-shoulder knit. She looked stunning. They were probably on their way to date night and decided to detour.

'You're wrong. I had all of the elements. You saw it,' Hunter countered. He was wearing black denim jeans, a white T-shirt and a flannel shirt over the top.

'Something was wrong because it didn't work. We've tweaked it, and now it'll work.'

'What makes you so certain, Luce?' Hunter asked.

'Because I'm good at this sort of shit. You're better at other bits of magick.'

Hunter snorted. 'You're dreaming, babe. Like, totally over the top dreaming.'

It was amusing to watch the two of them bicker with one another. I was about to step back when Devin wrapped an arm around my waist. I leant into him and closed my eyes, letting his warmth soak in. I was wearing shorts with a tank and a knitted cardigan. It was chilly, but it didn't feel cold.

'Are they always like this?' I asked when Devin pressed his lips to my neck. It made my knees go weak, and I let him support me.

'Mhm. From the very first moment, they have always been like this. It's sickening.'

'I'd say endearing,' I said.

'We can hear you both, you know,' Lucy said.

'Well aware of that, Luce.' Devin chuckled. 'How is it going? Do you think it'll work this time?'

She was tinkering with the camera, a wand in hand—it was a twisted stick with a crystal wrapped at the end of it with copper wire. It was the strangest wand I had seen, but Lucy swore that it worked and did what we needed it to do.

'Hunter did most of the work yesterday, but there were a few things missing. I've managed to get it, but I just need one more thing. Acionna, can I grab some of your blood?' she asked. Her outreached hand was kind, and she gave me the option to say no. *But do I really have that option?*

What would happen without my blood? Would it fail to work again? I couldn't go through that again.

The night before, I had been curled up in bed after Hunter left, and Devin held me tightly. It was the most vulnerable I had ever been, and to have someone—a man, nonetheless—hold me was so strange because I'd never had that sort of breakdown before.

I couldn't go through it again.

I nodded at Lucy and untangled myself from Devin, walking towards her. I put my hand in hers, and she grabbed a pen from her back pocket. It was one of those pens that diabetics used to prick their fingers—much more sanitary than needles, and probably quicker. She pressed it to my fingerpad and clicked the trigger. I jumped from the impact on my skin, but when Lucy pulled away the pen and squeezed the skin, a small droplet of blood pooled to the surface. She took my hand and hovered it over the camera. We watched the droplet of blood hit the camera and fizzle away.

There was a huge sigh that I felt in my chest. My shoulders dropped, and I stared at the camera. Whatever spell they had done, I felt it. It changed it.

'Lucy,' I whispered.

She beamed at me. 'You felt that, right?'

I nodded my head and stared at the camera. *It didn't feel like this last time.*

'What did you do, Luce?' Devin asked.

'I just tweaked the spell and used Acionna's blood as the ignition key. It settled into place, so the app should actually work now. Hunt, did you want to check that it's still working okay?'

'Sure can. Do you have your phone on you?' Hunter asked me, and I blinked, realising it wasn't on me.

'Yeah. Sorry, it's on my bedside table. Give me a second,' I said, getting my thoughts back. The magickal overflow was different from anything I'd ever felt. Undersea magick was different, lighter, but there was a succinctness to this. Like it was always there.

I turned on my heel and walked over to my bed to grab my phone. I unlocked it and walked back to the balcony. It didn't take long—maybe a whole minute. I handed the phone to Hunter, and he tapped away at it.

The warning alarm buzzed, and I stepped up to the camera out of habit, but Hunter quickly finished tapping on the screen of my phone before he handed it back to me.

'Okay. It should work this time. You'll just need to press this button, and it'll take the image for you. You won't have to touch the camera at all.'

'This sounds vaguely like yesterday.'

'I know, but I promise we fixed it,' Hunter said.

I wanted to believe him without the proof, but I was sceptical.

Lucy stood back and out of the way, and Hunter did the same. We were all waiting for the moment my phone would beep to signal that it was time to take the photo. A hush settled around us. I wanted to say something, but I was lost for words.

The alarm buzzed, and I clicked the button on the phone. Collectively, we held our breaths as the shutter snapped the picture. I could see it come up on the phone, and I looked, waited for the pain—the one like the day before. I closed my eyes so I couldn't watch it fail.

I couldn't watch their disappointment at the attempt to help free me. But when no pain came, we all waited so it would tick over to the next minute, and then we waited another minute. Last time, the pain had been immediate. As soon as that minute ticked over, I opened my eyes, and tears welled.

'Holy shit,' I whispered. 'It worked. There's no pain.'

'Holy cow, Hunt, you did it,' Devin said, and hugged his best friend. I didn't know what to say.

'Luce, you definitely had something right,' Hunter said, and picked her up in his arms and twirled. She squealed, and I couldn't help but smile at the display of affection.

'Put me down, Hunt,' she said with a laugh.

I almost waited for more pain, just like last time, but still, it didn't come through.

It meant that I could do so much more without needing to rush home. I could have some freedom for the first time in months.

'I can have my life back,' I whispered to Devin, who pulled me in close and held me tight. I hadn't realised tears had started to roll down my cheeks until I noticed that his shirt was wet from them.

He had made a promise to help me, and he had.

'Dev, you followed through. Now I want to help *you*.'

How will I be able to repay him for this? I didn't know, but I was going to make sure he got out of the whole assassin job thing. He needed to.

'You are here helping me every day,' he said.

'We should probably go now,' Lucy said. I pulled myself away from Devin and walked over and wrapped my arms around her.

'Thank you. You have no idea how much you have just helped me.'

'No, thank you,' she whispered. 'You have brought my brother back to life. I can't even begin to repay that.'

After the revelation of being able to take a picture by pushing the button on my phone, I felt so much relief, but also fear. *What happens if it fails tonight? What if it was all just a one-time thing?*

Devin had to go and do some family things with Lucy, and I didn't question it. I just told him to go because his sister was important, and I wanted to make sure she knew that—that she knew she still came first regardless of whatever Devin and I were.

He also told me he'd be back before I had to take the picture in case the same thing happened. I told him he didn't need to, but he insisted, and who was I to deny him that?

I wrapped my cardigan around my body a little tighter as I walked across the sand. The space between was such a liminal place; I was half in the world of the humans and half in a world where I didn't fit.

194 days was too long to be away from home, from everything that I held dear, and I didn't see that it was going to change any time soon. We had the location of the witch, but the ranges were huge. We had to narrow it down, or there was no way we were going to find her. I held onto hope that we would.

The autumn sun shone down on the ocean, sparkling with the soft movement of the water. There was a break in the surface, and I saw a creature crash through the water. I blinked and stared at the ocean again before I looked from side to side and behind me. *Did anyone else see that?*

Everyone else on the beach—most had their dogs or a coffee in hand as they walked the shore—was too involved in their conversations.

I stepped closer to the water's edge and watched to see if I could see it again. This time, when it bobbed out, I recognised the face. His dark skin, turquoise eyes, darker hair. Eain was so striking against the crystal blue of the water—he always had been.

I stared at him for a second, my mouth ajar ever so slightly.

His seal skin folded out, and now that Eain was closer, I saw the small patch of pelt he had wrapped around his wrist. That was all that we needed to start the transition to our seal-like form. On the outside, it was the smallest of patches.

'Eain,' I called out, and his eyes caught mine. A huge smile took over his whole face, and I shook my head. He was naked, and I felt the attention of all of the people around. They stopped their conversations and movements. Anyone else would have thought it was weird, but not Eain. He was used to the attention. It was always the same whenever he came to shore.

'Acionna! I was hoping to see you,' he said, and as soon as he stood directly in front of me, he held out his arms for me. I beamed and wrapped my arms around him. He was wet, but it wouldn't last long. He would dry up soon.

'You were hoping?' I teased.

'It's been a long time. I thought you would have forgotten about me,' he said.

Those words were ridiculous, and I shook my head.

'What do you take me for?' He pulled back, and his hands grabbed my face and guided it up. If he tried to kiss me, I was going to kick him in the balls, but instead, his eyes searched mine.

'You look like you're fatigued. Where is your pelt? Let's go back. We can fix this right now.'

Straight to the pelt. I frowned and stepped back. The way he said that so easily was like he knew exactly where it was. Or what had happened.

'I can't. I don't know where it is,' I said.

'You what?' Surprised clouded his gaze. 'What do you mean, you don't know where it is? Surely, that's not the case.'

His words sounded foreign in his mouth, like he didn't believe himself.

'Eain, do you know where it is?'

He was silent. 'What? That's ridiculous.'

'I don't know,' I said as I stepped back further away from him.

'Acionna …' he said, reaching out to me.

For the first time in months, I saw it. I saw what I had missed at the Matching ceremony. There was more to who he was. It didn't matter that we had known each other our whole lives or that he was the natural choice after all of that. Eain wanted something that only I could give.

'Don't "Acionna" me. You know where it is. What did you do, Eain? Why are you here?'

He rubbed the back of his neck with his hand and looked past me. 'We should take this discussion elsewhere. There are many wandering eyes.'

'I don't care. You are the one who is here. You're the one who made this a thing,' I said angrily.

Is he the reason I am landlocked? Cursed to take the stupid photo day in and day out? Does he know where the witch is?

'Acionna, you have to come back home. Everything is falling apart. Your mother …'

'My mother is what? Missing a daughter? Yeah, I know. I'm here. I can't go back without my pelt.'

'She's missing two,' he said.

'Wh-what?' I stammered.

'Ariel is missing too.'

The way that she looked at me that last time, the paleness of her skin, the anger. She was landlocked too. How—

'You're lying. I saw her the other day.'

'You did? When? This is imperative.' There was more concern for her than there was for me.

The pit of my stomach dropped, and I realised what I had done at the Matching. I had picked the man who had been easy, but he had been Ariel's because they had concocted a plan to take the throne from me. Eain didn't care about me, and the words he had said didn't mean anything.

'Eain, what did you do?' I asked, my whole body threatened to give me away. I was furious that I had trusted him.

'Nothing. It wasn't supposed to go on for so long.'

'What. Did. You. Do?' I asked again.

'Ariel said she knew of someone ... All she needed was for you to sleep with someone on shore so she could take your pelt.'

An invisible knife stabbed into my heart and twisted so hard at those words. I scrambled away from Eain, making sure I was far away from him.

'Get away from me. Go back home. And when I get my pelt back, I'll deal with you accordingly. Our Matching is undone, and I don't want to see you again.'

'Whatever you say on land won't stick. You're compromised.'

'The only compromise I have is that I let myself trust you when I shouldn't have.'

He rubbed his nose and chuckled. 'You were the easiest one to get to after Ariel. I just knew she wouldn't be queen, and I wanted to be with the queen.'

I narrowed my eyes and wished I could punish him the same way he had me. My eyes flicked to his wrist where his pelt lay warped around it, and he clicked his tongue and laughed.

'Don't do anything stupid, now. You're already in so much trouble,' he said.

'With who?' After the death of Devin's dad and the funeral, I had a few photographers stalking me, but there wasn't much they could get from me. *They could get this from me now.* Talking to a naked man. But Devin wouldn't believe it.

'The powers that be.'

'Do me a favour, Eain. Go back home and steer clear of me. It took you this long to find me, and you did it because you're looking for Ariel. Whatever you did warped her brain, and she is in pain. When I'm back, I will change the rules, and you will wish that you never even thought about me.'

Eain laughed again. 'I'm shaking in my fur. You won't be back for a very long time,' he said.

This time, I closed the distance between us. Eain was nearly a head taller than me, but he was a roane, and they were weaker than selkies. I looked up at him and balled my hands into fists at my side.

'Mark my words, Eain, you'll be sorry you did this.'

My knee connected with his stomach. He bent over, and I threw a punch to his face. My fist connected, and I heard a crack.

'And if you think you will be welcome ever again, you are mistaken. Go and spread your rumours, but remember that it was me who hurt you first.'

And with that, I turned on my heel and walked away from Eain. I needed to find Ariel. She was pitted against me because of that man, and I would fix it. No matter the cost.

I stared at the screen, my fingers tapping over the keyboard as I tried to find anything on Ariel. *Has she been in the news? Are there any weird seal sightings?*

Selkies were myths, so it was no surprise that I couldn't find anything.

'Ash, you know when you texted me and said you had met with the man you were supposed to marry, and that he was naked? I didn't expect to see pictures of him in the wild.'

I tore my eyes away from the screen and to Devin, who walked through the front door, his grey eyes staring back at me with amusement. He had a bag of food. I could smell it without even glancing at it.

'Did you see the pictures of me kicking his arse?' They'd surfaced about ten minutes earlier, and I wanted to hide.

'Yes! They are my favourites. He looks like he deserved it.'

'He did.' I chewed on my nail and closed the laptop, realising I wasn't going to get any closer to finding Ariel.

'Are you okay?' Devin asked as he put the bag down on the table and slid into the seat next to me. He took my hands and pulled me over to him gently. The bench seat made it easier than it looked.

'I think so. I just ... He's the one behind me missing my pelt, and Ariel too. We need to find her. She's out there alone, and knowing she doesn't have hers, makes me nervous. Ariel was so weak.'

He hugged me tighter. 'She seemed pretty upset when you saw her on the beach. What makes you think she wants the help?'

I licked my lips and shrugged. 'I know that if I were in her position, I would want the help, so I'm banking on her wanting it too.'

'Okay. Where do we start?'

I shook my head. 'I don't know. I've searched for any sign of her, and I can't find anything. I don't want to rely on magick, but it might have to go there.'

'You're lucky I have some of the best witches in the state.' He chuckled.

'I can't ask Lucy and Hunter again.'

'Yeah, you can. They'll gladly help out.'

'This wasn't on my bingo card,' I said, and leant back. His eyes searched mine, and I took his face in my hand. 'You weren't either, but I like you on it. Most men would have lost it at the thought of their lover with a naked guy, but you kept your cool.'

Devin smiled. It went all the way up to his eyes, and I couldn't help but smile softly.

'Ash, you're a selkie. Nudity is second nature. The fact that it was on the beach and not in your bedroom or somewhere else made it easier not to care. I'm proud of you. I know you are stronger than you look and tougher than you say. Eain deserved every bit of what was handed to him. You don't need to tell me otherwise. I'd rather you tell me if you are going to do something to ruin what we have.'

'And what do we have?' I asked.

'We're a team. I think that's pretty evident. I feel like we've known each other for so long, and it's natural. Plus, you're really good at sex. I think that's a plus.' He grinned, and I swatted his shoulder.

'Technically, we have known each other for longer than in the flesh.'

'Dreams definitely do count,' he said.

'Only when you're at the helm of them.'

'Look, call Lucy and Hunter. We can have them come over tomorrow and try a locator spell. But I want to make sure that your decision is firmly me and not Eain,' Devin said, and he pressed his lips to mine, an arm wrapped around my body, pulling me in close. I moaned into his mouth as I kissed him back. The way his body felt pressed against mine felt so right, and after seeing Eain and missing home, it was nothing.

Devin is my home now.

CHAPTER THIRTY-ONE

Devin
Parthmuthi 2016
Somewhere in the desert

DREAMING HAD NEVER BEEN simple for me. It had always been a meditative state, something I would slowly slip back into—like I could take a breath to keep going and repeat. Most got enough sleep to keep going, but not me. Dreaming was a conscious state of mind thing, but it was the time where I couldn't sleep. Dreamless sleep was a pipe dream, so when there were no dreams, that's when the bliss happened. Sleepless dreams were a rarity in life because they meant that I could heal my body and fix the aches. But it was also when things happened. Just when I didn't want them to. Dreamless sleep was hard to find, and a voice—one that plagued my dreams but had been so far away for so very long—broke through that sleep. I jolted awake.

'Devin,' she whispered.

The voice from my childhood—the one I bickered with, that I loved and most of all, cared about above all else. She was the reason I was still going, even when she tried not to go on. I shook myself awake and looked up at the ceiling. The stars were high up, the roofing clear enough to ensure I could see that.

'Devin?' she whispered again, this time a little louder. Lucy got closer. I could hear her footsteps to the right. She was navigating through the cabin, trying to find me. Lucy was so close, and after Karrept nearly killed me, I couldn't afford to lose her.

'In here,' I whispered back. With nothing but a pair of boxers on, I jumped off the top bunk. I hoped she wasn't alone. We would need the backup to get out. But regardless, I didn't want to be half naked. She didn't need to see the scars that covered my body. I pulled a brown T-shirt over my head, and was grateful the cabin was empty save for me, everyone off on an assignment while I had a week off. Finally.

'Dev!' she whispered through the door excitedly. I shoved my legs into a pair of jeans and grabbed a pair of socks, ready to slip them on when I heard the door. I looked to see her, my twin sister with her wavy brown hair, grey eyes not unlike mine and a smile from one ear to the other. I wished I could be as happy as she was, if not more so, but it was impossible. Our lives were too different then. The things I had done to survive made us so different.

I would have still made the same choice, though, if it meant I saved her again and again.

'Luce,' I whispered, and before I knew it, she bounded into my arms and clung to me. The sound of her sobs was muffled against my chest, and I had to force myself not to shiver and recoil. *She may be my sister, but is she really? Is it an illusion? What is real? What isn't?* After all of the training, I had everyone held at an arm's length. Even my baby sister.

Shit.

'Are you alone?' I asked Lucy.

'Like I would let her go anywhere without me.' I looked past my sister and saw Hunter and breathed a huge sigh. He was someone I could relax with. I untangled myself from Luce—her sobs had dwindled down to hiccups—and without thinking, hugged him. He hugged me back tightly, and it was like we could do it. I would be getting out of there alive. That was ... I didn't expect a lot of people to miss me.

Hunter was the man I wanted to be there to help Luce, though, and I was grateful for him.

'Good. It's not safe here. What are you doing anyway?' I asked, but I already knew they were there to get me out.

'We're breaking you out,' Lucy chimed. 'Wow, a glass ceiling. That would get intense when it rains.'

'You have no idea.' But that wasn't what my mind was on. *Who cares about the ceiling. How are we going to get through without them knowing that I'm going?*

'Luce ... How are we—' I asked, and just as I did so, Hunter whipped out a bracelet. I could see that they were both wearing one too. He slipped it on my wrist, securing it tightly, and a charge ran up my arm and down my spine. 'Whoa ... What was that?'

'Magick. To be exact, a heavy glamour that'll keep you and whatever you touch invisible. But you have to keep quiet. It doesn't hide our voices,' Hunter said in a hushed tone.

'You guys are too much.' I grabbed my duffle bag from under the bunk. In it were clothes and rations. It was the bag I'd had ready for weeks, hidden away in plain sight. I knew that Lucy was going to come for me, but she never said when. I didn't want to scramble around, knowing we would only have a small window to get out in one piece.

'You're ready?' she asked, surprised. I nodded. 'You're Mr Prepared now. That's new.'

There was a lot Lucy didn't know, and I didn't know if I would be ever able to put it into words for her. She wasn't ready for the things I had to say or the things I'd had to do to even be there. I just smiled at her. 'Before we leave, I need to stop to get some weapons.'

'Weapons?' Lucy asked, and Hunter stared at me. He could see that I was different and knew something was up. I would tell him before I told Lucy. Again, she wouldn't be ready for the truth. There would be so much guilt too.

'Yeah, just in case we have to fight our way out. It's not going to be as easy as it seems, Luce. Not now.'

Her mouth opened and then closed like she wanted to say something but didn't know how. Luce stepped back from me to give me space, but she was uncomfortable. She wasn't a fighter, not unless she absolutely needed to be. Lucy knew enough self-defence to help herself, and from the scars, I could see she had done enough fighting to get hurt. I wished she hadn't needed to.

Lucy slipped her fingers between Hunter's, and he squeezed them. I looked between them and grinned. *It's real this time.* 'You guys are finally all good, then? It only took you how many years.'

'Shut up. You know how your sister is.' Hunter grinned back.

'If anything, I'm glad. She needs it.' I patted him on the back because he was still my best friend, and I was happy for him.

'I'm right here,' Lucy said.

'I know. Let's go.' I dropped the duffel bag and shoved my feet into the socks and the shit-kicking boots that were right beside the bed. I laced them up fast. It was time. *Now.*

I opened the door to see if anyone was around. Even though most were out, there were still people around The Camp, and because of that, I was still cautious. I held up a hand to keep the two of them back, just in case there was someone, but the coast was clear. I stepped out of the room, holding the door open for them. They both walked through it, and I knew it was going to be harder with them there. Alone, I could have done it in half the time, probably not getting noticed. But three people instead of one? I was internally begging for them to get through it unscathed. I knew the easiest way to get out was past the main guard house, and I knew where all of the alarms were—we had to. If we weren't trained to avoid that shit in our own backyard, how were we going to avoid it in the real world? They might have even tripped the silent alarm breaking in to get to me. *Fuck.*

In silence, I made sure they were close behind me. Hunter still had Lucy's hand, and I think I preferred that. We skulked along the facade of the building to the weapons shelter. All I needed was my bow and arrows, and I had left them just inside the entrance. As I stepped into the shelter, I turned to look at Lucy and Hunter, their eyes wide with shock. But I didn't have the capacity to hold their hand through it. I motioned for them to stay put, and opened the door and slipped inside the room. I grabbed my bow and quiver of arrows, swinging the bag over the shoulder that had my duffle bag, and took hold of the bow with a firm grip. I motioned for Lucy and Hunter to turn around and, with two fingers, also motioned for them to keep a lookout, then held a hand up to make them wait. I wished they knew the signals that the guys knew—it would have made it so much easier.

I knew that, after that, it would be all or nothing. After spending close to four years at The Camp, I knew what my place was there. There was nothing out in the world for me—at least, not anymore. And the bond Lucy and I had? It would never be the same. There was too much she didn't know—that she couldn't know. It would break her to know the number of kills I had to my name or how I did them.

I was about to open the door and slip out when I heard voices—and they weren't coming from Lucy and Hunter. *Fuck.* My body automatically went into fight mode, and I pressed myself against the wall, trying to make myself as invisible as possible. Just because the bracelet was on my wrist didn't mean that I wasn't still hesitant. Magick was fickle, and if I had learnt nothing else while away, it was that. Sometimes, things that were meant to be hidden and stay that way came flooding out. If one looked too hard through a glamour, it all crumbled away.

'Is D-Man on shift tomorrow?' Henrik's voice floated past the room. *Fuck ... Of course the best hand-to-hand combat person is up now. Why are they back already?*

'Yeah. He should be getting some sleep, so he'll be ready,' Jarrad said.

'Does he really sleep, though? I mean, he seems to be half here, half in the dreams,' Henrik muttered.

'You and I both know that even with that, he's the best we've had. You're jealous that he's knocked your arse unconscious more times than not, Rik,' Jarrad said.

Anger vibrated in my chest, and it took everything in me to not storm out and run Henrik's head through the glass door. Jarrad sticking up for me made me wonder how many times he'd had to do that. I didn't think I was cocky, but to hear the praise out of Jarrad's mouth was worth it.

Does he know I am here?

God, I hope not. I needed to move and make sure that my sister and best friend didn't get caught in anything. I couldn't risk getting them hurt. I was numb to a lot of feelings, but the fierce protectiveness of making sure my twin got out alive and well was truly there. It kept me sane.

The voices outside petered off, and I opened the door. Hunter and Lucy pressed themselves up against the building, their intertwined hands gripped together hard, their chests barely rising. I knew they were scared.

I wondered what she was like then, what her powers were like, or if she even remembered any other self-defence. She was my sister, but so much time had passed. Could she still hold her own? Or were she and Hunter going to be the death of me? They were practically strangers, and I was going to have to relearn how to talk to them again. Or even what they were like. I was so out of touch with the people who were my people.

Both of their eyes stayed on me, and I motioned for them to keep a hold of each other's hands. Lucy and Hunter both nodded and almost tightened their grip on each other. It reminded me of when they first started going out. They had refused to hold hands because they were scared of what I would say—or at least, that's what Lucy did. She was always too worried about things she shouldn't be.

'Come on,' I mouthed and motioned for them to follow me. They were fast on their feet, which was good because we only had one shot at it. I crouched low, and they followed suit; if we could stay low enough, we would avoid the windows and anyone who would see us. The gates were open, thankfully. Soldiers would be returning from their shifts very soon, but with the end so near, I knew it was too good to be true.

'D-Man. You wouldn't be trying to get away, would you?' Lucy and Hunter stiffened, both of them stopping in their tracks. I turned to find Jarrad looking right at me. Ian and Henrik were to the side and looked puzzled. They couldn't see me, but Jarrad could.

Fuck.

I swallowed hard and turned to face him. Hunter and Lucy were just off to the left, and I kept my gaze firmly on Jarrad, not anywhere near them. If he could see me and not them, I wanted it to stay that way. Jarrad's eyes glowed, but they were just a normal human shade of green. He never, *never* let anyone see what his true being was.

'It depends on what your definition of getting away is. There are many,' I said.

Jarrad just smiled at me while Ian and Henrik moved closer. I pulled out an arrow and set it in the quiver, pulling it back fast and hard. The glamour dropped on me, and they both stopped dead in their tracks. They knew that if I let go of the arrow, they would be dead. I shifted it from them and pointed it at Jarrad's forehead, and the two of them froze.

'Come on, D-Man, you're not really going to let go of that arrow. We're buddies. We've been through too much for you to follow through with it.' Jarrad's eyes didn't leave mine, but his smile turned into a shit-eating grin, and he took his eyes off me.

His gaze shifted to where I knew Lucy and Hunter were standing. 'Oh, hello there, you pretty little thing. You must be his other sister. She's gorgeous, D-Man. You've been holding out on us.'

I stood up straighter as Henrik moved. I let go of the arrow in a motion that he hardly saw. It thunked into his bicep, and he screamed. Ian moved in front of him to stop another attack. I pulled another arrow out and pointed it back at Jarrad. 'I would watch your mouth if I were you. The next one goes between your eyes, Jar. I'm not playing around here.'

'I know you aren't, but where do you think you're going to go? You're one of us now. You can run, but we will find you.' He said it without a single hint of emotion, which wasn't new.

He took a step closer.

'Jar, come on now. You need to stop looking at my sister like that.'

'I'll be seeing you real soon, cutie.' He winked at her, and I shifted my aim ever so slightly. I let go of the arrow, and it flew past Jarrad, but not before it scraped his cheek. He hissed at me and touched his face, but was distracted. It was deep and would scar, but it would keep him occupied. I grabbed Lucy's wrist and pulled her away from The Camp. Hunter followed without a word. The trek to somewhere we could get reception would be long, but I knew I was going to pay for marking Jarrad.

He would make sure of it.

Choiak 2015
Somewhere in the desert

'So why are we Karrept's army?' I asked as I took a swig of beer from the glass that had just been placed down on the table. Jarrad, Harry, Friar and I were all sitting at a table in a pub not far from the training camp. It was the first time I'd seen beer in a long time. It was also my birthday, but no one knew that. I wanted to take a peek and see what Lucy was doing, but I couldn't do it with everyone around. I missed her. I missed being able to see into my twin's dreams, and lately, she hadn't been dreaming a lot, which could mean that she was stressing out a lot or that she was doing really badly. I hated to let her down too.

My strength was divided between training and Destiny. I had to find the right time to get to Luce. I couldn't fuck it up.

'It's all top secret, dude. Like, only a handful know, but there's some sort of prophecy,' Jarrad said, leaning in. I rolled my eyes.

'Prophecies are bullshit. You can't give us that sort of shit. What's the real deal?'

He shrugged, and Friar slapped his hand on the table. 'This is bullshit. I'm away from my family for this shit? We don't even know what we're doing here, and you expect us to follow you blindly? Karrept's army? Are we all getting brainwashed so one day we wake up as sleeper agents and kill off humanity?' He was an incubus and had a wife—go figure—but he was still strong as shit.

'Something like that,' Jarrad said.

He was doing some sort of deflection thing. It was starting to get really annoying.

'Listen, I don't have time for your avoidance bullshit. You owe us an explanation. I was kidnapped from my family, separated from my sister, and now I don't know what's going on with them. And you're training me to kill supernatural beings. There is something going on. What is it? And deflecting and saying some half-arsed commentary is not going to make it better. Trust me. I know. I want to get back to my family, and with every passing day, I know I'm not going to get there. Am I?'

Everyone looked at Jarrad. He tried to flinch away from the questions, but someone needed to tell us what was happening, and no one else was game enough to tell us shit. Jarrad was training our team, and he knew more than we did.

'There's shit coming. A war that will crescendo at some point in our lifetimes. And Karrept's army is supposed to be the ones to stop it. They're going to break down the barriers between the good and evil in the world and unite everyone, but before they do, they have to cleanse it. It's why you're all being trained to kill. You need to be the ones to cleanse the world of the bad people. Or maybe the good, depending on the hits.'

I threw my drink at him, and everyone at the table stood up, chairs scraping against the dirty floor.

'What the fuck, D-Man?'

'That's fucking crap. *Cleanse the world.* Do you know what that sounds like? Like he's fucking Hitler. We're in the middle of nowhere in a place where no one knows us, and everyone in this bar is going to forget we were even here. It's what always happens, but you spin us some shitty lie that is all about cleansing the world. The world is always going to be full of bad people, we know that, but that doesn't give you the right to kidnap us and make us kill against our will. I never wanted to be a killer. I wanted to finish high school, have fun, meet the woman of my dreams and get married. Do you know what it's like not to have that? Everyone else in The Camp is older than me. Much older. I'm the baby, and I get treated the worst.'

Jarrad crossed the short distance between us and gripped my shirt. His eyes hardened, and something flickered in them.

'Are you telling me you don't want to be here?'

'I never wanted to be here, Jar. Karrept kidnapped me, and you know that. He hand-picked me because I picked up a stupid book. How is that fair?'

'Friar, back up,' Jarrad said, and I flicked my attention from Jarrad to Friar. He was trying to stick up for me. I could see it in the way he bunched his hand into a fist and unflexed it. *Whoa.*

'Friar, it's okay. I've got this.' I hadn't realised I had any friends. I always worked on being alone, and it just worked better that way. No one would ever be able to have the bond that Hunter and I had, so I never really tried with anyone. But to know that Friar, a man who was scary as fuck, was willing to stand up for me was something I was actually really grateful for.

'Jar, why can't we go home? Why won't they even let us contact our loved ones? What's so secret about this?'

His grip tightened on my shirt, and I could feel the slip of material straining against his strength. Any tighter and he was going to rip a hole in one of the only shirts I really liked. *What is he doing? What is he?* Jarrad had to be some supernatural being, but we never knew what. He wouldn't be in charge if he wasn't.

'Because family is a distraction. Do you think we do this for fun? We're training you to be perfect soldiers, and perfect soldiers don't have family. They don't even have names. We give you nicknames for a reason.'

Friar took a step forward, and Harry put himself between Jarrad's back and Friar's front. 'What are you doing?' Harry growled softly, but somehow, it was loud enough for all of us to hear.

'He's going to *hurt* him,' Friar reasoned.

'Jarrad will not hurt Devin. There's a reason why we're all here,

Friar. Rein in those emotions, or your wife is going to be mourning a man she is willing to come back to her.'

Jarrad let go of me as he listened to the exchange, too, and caught my eyes. He was trying to figure me out. 'D-Man, have you been dreaming lately?'

I blinked and nodded.

'About what?'

'Not much.'

I was lying … Kind of.

'Don't lie to me, D-Man. I know you're not. Where's your head at? You've been missing drills, and when you are there, your energy hasn't been the same. What have you been doing?'

I forced my breath to stay even. That was the hardest part of lying. It was what we were all learning. We had to be good liars because if not, our covers would be blown whenever we were out on our own. No one could afford that, so they were training us to be such good liars that even a werewolf couldn't smell it on us. We hadn't come across one yet, so it would be interesting when we did.

'Why does it matter? I'm still passing and doing what is being asked of me.'

'You've dropped down.' He pulled back and, out of nowhere, slugged me. I tasted blood in my mouth, and Friar was there, decking Jarrad right back.

He smirked as he licked at the blood from his split lip.

'That's a hell of a punch, Friar. I'm impressed, but you're hitting me for no reason. D-Man knows what he's doing, and he's got to pick the right answer.'

I knew better than to spit the blood in my mouth out. It was DNA that could be used against me, and it was a bad idea to let that happen. I swallowed it and ignored the metallic taste.

'I'm doing what I need to. Why I'm doing it? You don't need to know. Stop being such a jackarse about it all. I bet there's someone you care about whom you'd be willing to help out no matter what. I don't want you to say there isn't because that would be a lie. You're not some poor lonely man. You've got friends and family who probably cared for you at some point, but you didn't care for them.'

Jarrad started to wind up again, but Harry caught him. 'Jar, seriously, he's egging you on. Just let it go. Whoever he's helping is probably desperate. It's not worth it.'

My sister wasn't desperate.

Without thinking, I broke a half-full bottle of beer and held it to Harry's eye. It happened in a heartbeat, and I hadn't realised just how fast I had moved.

'Jar, get your boy away from my eyes before I take his from him.'

Jarrad just laughed. 'That's all it took for him to step up? Call whoever he's helping desperate? That's all that we had to do? Well, fuck. Harry, you're a genius.'

I inched the bottle closer to Harry's eyeball. 'You don't need to see, right, Harry? You do all the talking.'

'Jarrad! Call him off.'

'D-Man, take a deep breath. He doesn't need to lose an eye.'

'She is not desperate,' I growled and backed off, the bottle dropping from my hand and shattering on the ground.

'Your sister. That's who you're helping.'

'Karrept doesn't care about her. He broke her and now plays with her for fun. I can't let her die. She's my sister,' I said, and looked at Jarrad. He nodded, and I was still surprised that he hadn't tried to kill me or something. Maybe I was doing the right thing. Or maybe he was just feeling nostalgic or something.

'He doesn't care, but you can't keep doing this.'

'I. Won't. Let. Her. Die.'

'I know, man, but you might have to.'

'I'll just find a necromancer. Surely, there is someone here who can help. Someone will help me even if I have to kill them. This is not the end.'

I turned and left the bar. I was done with their shit and everything right then. My sister was a priority, and even if they stripped me of my emotions, they were not going to strip me of my brotherly duty.

I'd made a promise to my dad when I was a boy, and I was going to keep it, no matter what.

My sisters were all that mattered to me, and they couldn't stop that.

Payni 2017
Melbourne

Everything felt so off. I hadn't had a hit in over a month. Maybe they were waiting out of respect, but I felt like it went deeper than that. The feelings that ran through me were raw, unmatched. I'd forgotten what it was like to feel such strong emotions. Any time I'd shown any at The Camp, I had been punished. That was the norm. I got so used to hiding them.

But now? I felt less like I was a shell of a being and more like a human. I wasn't sure if that was the best thing in the world, exactly, but it was enough for the moment. Acionna was the reason for that change.

In the kitchen, I puttered around with some food. It was a basic sandwich, but I wanted something quick and easy.

The chef in the kitchen was clicking his tongue at me because I wouldn't let him cook for me. After not being able to for over four years, I liked to craft my own food creations. One of the maids came in with something in her hand.

'That for me?' I asked between a bite of what I thought was the most delicious sandwich I'd had in my life.

'Yes. You have to sign this.' She whipped out a pad, I scribbled my name on it, and she hustled off.

It was a yellow envelope with my name on it—pretty standard in those days, but the thing that got me was that it was bigger than the normal envelopes with my name on them. *Weird.*

'Hans, it's okay. I promise, I'll eat this and be gone. Go and take a break.' He muttered something under his breath and left the kitchen. I grinned and licked my fingers before I grabbed a knife and sliced the top of the envelope. I dropped the blade and pulled out the document. I froze. It was a hit.

I held my breath as I opened the manilla folder and saw a face so familiar to me that I dropped the file open. My jaw dropped open. *What the actual hell? No, hell no.*

'Devin, Hans said you were in here ruining his food. What are you doing?' Before I could close the folder, Lucy snatched it from me, horrified.

My stomach churned, and I met her eyes. Lucy wasn't supposed to see it. I couldn't hide it anymore.

'Devin, what is this? Why is this Acionna? Why is there a bullseye around her head? What the hell?'

My stomach dropped further. *My girlfriend, my love, is my next hit. They know about us, and they want her out of my life because they know she's compromising my job, my life.* My fingers itched to take the file out of Lucy's hand, snatch it back, burn it and pretend I'd never seen it in my life. But I knew it was not that simple.

'Devin. Answer me.'

Lucy was using her authoritative voice that always made me cringe.

'Because I have to kill her.' No other words could describe the pain in my chest right then. That delicious sandwich suddenly felt like dead weight in my stomach.

'Kill her? Why would you do that? She's your girlfriend. Is this some stupid-arse joke? Because I'd like you to take it back right now.' Lucy waved the file in my face, and there was a part of me that really just wanted to go and die. *How could this happen?*

Greg was going to die. After Jarrad. *Fuck.*

'I kill people for a living, Luce.' I looked at her, and it killed me because my baby sister was not supposed to know those things about me. I wanted to keep her safe from it.

Her eyes dropped away from me, and I could see the hurt.

'W-what?' she stammered and dropped the file like it was hot. I scooped it off the ground and tucked it under my arm. 'How? When? When you were taken?'

I nodded. It wasn't how I wanted to tell her, but there we were.

'I was trained to be a killer at the camp you rescued me from. We're assassins for hire. We kill supernatural beings, Luce.' Her face paled because she knew we were alone. My worst nightmare was to have to kill my sister. Having to kill my girlfriend was a very close second. *Fuck.*

'But Acionna ...' She trailed off, her hands motioning wildly to the folder under my arm.

'Is a selkie. That's why they want her gone,' I said, but Lucy knew she was a selkie. That wasn't a mystery.

'No, I know she's a selkie, but why *her*?' Lucy was so innocent sometimes. I liked that about her. She wasn't hardened by the world. Not like I was.

'Because she's too close to me, Luce. She's opening up a part of me that no one else has, and it's terrifying. I cried. Me. For the first time in years, at her house, after the circle. They know things like that. They can sense it without needing to witness things. Don't you understand? You're in danger too. Every day that we get our relationship back is another day you climb higher on their kill sheet.'

'Kill sheet?'

I nodded. 'Mum's on there. Hunt, too, and probably Kali. Dad ...' I was about to say he was, too, but Lucy didn't need to know that I knew his killer. That was too much for her too soon.

'Dad what?' *Oops.* I forgot that she was like a bull at times. 'Dad *what*, Devin? Answer me.'

'He was probably on it too. I don't know. I don't want to kill Acionna. I'm trying to think of a way out of it.'

Lucy turned around to leave, and I exhaled a soft sigh before she turned back around. 'Was Dad murdered?' And I closed my eyes and took a deep breath before I nodded.

'Yes.'

'Do you know who murdered him?'

'Yes.'

'Find him and kill him. But don't you dare kill Acionna. She's the best thing that's happened to you. Ever.'

I sighed again and put the file on the bench. I walked over to Lucy and folded her into my arms. 'Luce, you don't have to tell me that. I know she is. I'm so lucky to have her, but I'm also lucky to have you as a sister. Someone who didn't stop hoping and looking for me. And I love you for it. This is all going to be okay.' I held her tightly.

'Do you promise?' she said, her voice muffled into my chest.

My heart ached, but I knew I couldn't not promise.

'I promise, Luce. Trust me, okay?'

She nodded, and I held her closer. *This is going to be a rough time.*

CHAPTER THIRTY-TWO

Acionna
Payni 2017
Melbourne

POUNDING at the door pulled me from my sleep. Devin wasn't there—he didn't stay the night. He was being all secretive about that too. He didn't give me a reason, but I didn't think anything of it.

I grabbed a robe and wrapped it around my body. There was no way Devin would be at the door—he knew where the spare key was.

The kitten scrambled under the bed at the noise, and I saw Janice at the base of the stairs. Her bleary eyes were concerned, but I shook my head and motioned for her to go back into her room. 'Stay out of sight,' I mouthed to her.

'Who is there?' I asked.

'Open up, Princess.' The voice was foreign, and I swallowed hard. *Who the fuck is it?*

'I think you have the wrong house,' I said, and took three steps back. The door shook with the force of the pounding.

'Right house. Right time.'

'It's the middle of the night. The neighbours are going to call the police.'

There was a laugh on the other side, and then the door shattered. I covered my face to protect it from shards of glass and shattered pieces of wood.

'You're ready for us,' the masked man said. He had broad shoulders, big, muscled arms and I could see the hint of a tattoo on his wrist. I could take just one goon.

He stepped out of the way, and two more were behind him.

Okay, that was a plot twist I didn't see coming.

'Who are you?'

'Not important.'

'Might not be for you, but I don't let a lot of strangers into my house, and seeing as you just broke in ...' I was stalling. If I could get more out of them, it would make it easier to relay the details. Or at least for Janice to relay the details. I didn't look behind me for her because I wanted their attention on me.

The goon came at me, and I blocked his advance, kicking my leg out and hitting him in the balls. He went down hard, and I smiled.

'Strangers are a problem.'

A gun was cocked, and I looked from the groaning goon to the second man with a gun. He ripped his mask off. He was good-looking, had green eyes and brown hair. He also had stubble, like he was three days behind shaving.

'You are a bit problematic, aren't you?' His voice was rough, like he didn't want to do what he was doing but had no choice.

Or it was a ruse.

'What can I say? I don't play by the rules.'

'That's a bit of a problem for us, then, isn't it?'

'Not sure if that matters so much,' I said and backed up. My bare feet were careful of the glass. Or at least, that's what I hoped, because I didn't step on any as I did so.

'You're going to need to come with us. And I'm not really asking.'

'Well, if you're not really asking, I guess I don't have to come then.'

He gave an inhuman growl and stepped closer, the gun still pointed at me.

'Is that supposed to scare me?' I said, and stopped moving backwards as I put the dining table between us. I felt a little safer—not by much, but it was enough.

'No, that's my angry growl. You should see what it sounds like when I'm trying to scare someone.'

He was a regular comedian, and while I loved banter as much as the next person, the situation wasn't ideal.

'What are you?' I asked. 'You're some sort of shifter, that much I can tell. You move like liquid. They all do.'

'You're smart. Not a lot of people pick up on that.'

'Helps when you move like liquid, too, you can pick out those. So, tell me your flavour? Because if you're here, you already know mine.'

His eyes flashed purple before they were back to their usual green.

'Werewolf ... Interesting. Do they know?'

He bared his teeth.

'I'm guessing that's a no.'

'You're a smart fishy, aren't you?'

'Seal, actually. Don't get it mixed up. Do you have a name? I mean, if we're on a first-name basis, it could be a little easier to negotiate.'

He chuckled. 'I can see why he likes you.'

I stopped dead cold. He was talking about Devin. 'What?'

'We sent your file to him. To kill you. Normally, he's pretty prompt, but this doesn't seem to be a priority for him. D-Man is slipping.'

'Your. Name,' I said through gritted teeth.

'Jarrad.'

'Jarrad. Sounds like a dumb name.'

'It's what I was birthed with. You could come quietly with me, or I could make it hurt.'

I grinned. 'I've never gone quietly in my life.'

'I was hoping you would say something like that.' He shot the gun, the loud crack draining out all of the other noise before pain spread through my shoulder. I glanced down, expecting to see blood, but instead, there was a dart.

My eyes widened before everything went black.

The room was not as dingy as I expected it to be. In fact, it was quite nice. There was a bed to the right of me, a couch to the left and a table directly in front of me. My hands and legs were tied to the chair, and I felt exposed. I sat in my sports bra and jeans—thankfully, I'd had them on and wasn't flouncing around naked.

'Are you comfortable?' Jarrad asked as he sat next to me. He crossed his hands over one another and stared at me. Jarrad seemed to be waiting to see if I would spit in his face or something. I didn't do anything. I sat patiently. I'd learnt, long before that trying to bargain with captors didn't work. And time passed slowly, but it was worth it.

'Are you going to talk to me?' Jarrad asked. It was like he was a friend who wanted to know why I was silent. I didn't deserve that tone.

'What do you want me to say?' I asked—the first words I'd uttered since they took me.

'Something. You've been oddly quiet, and the guys are getting antsy.' Jarrad leant back in the chair and clasped his hands behind his head. He was just resting, comfortable with what was going on and what would happen. It was weird. I was tied to a chair, and I almost wanted to be where he was, so I didn't have the rope cutting into my skin.

'Why? Are they used to their women begging for them?' The venom that dripped in my voice was not going to go undetected, and Jarrad raised an eyebrow at me.

'Something like that. You know, Devin was my best soldier. He was the one I knew wouldn't crack. He would stay strong. Even when his sister rescued him. I knew, even then, that he wouldn't crack, but then you came along and things changed. What is it about you?' Jarrad pushed the chair back and stood up. It was like he had ants in his pants, like he was trying to get the hit on me.

'What can I say? I have charm,' I said. It sounded way smarter coming out of my mouth than it did in my head. I was a little surprised about that. I hadn't meant for it to sound like that. *Oops.*

'Your fucking pussy is what swayed him. I can smell him all over you, and I could smell you all over him. You, stupid woman, turned him.' He was right in my face, but I looked past him. It was weird, but even when Jarrad was trying to intimidate me, all I wanted to do was laugh at him. 'You keep silent now? You spread your legs, he comes willingly and you break him down.'

Jarrad's hands gripped my chin hard, pain radiating, and he made me look at him. 'He had years on him. His father would have been safe too. It was a warning. And when you hit the table, I thought he could have killed you. It would have been so Devin-like if he had, but he came running into the office and refused to do it. Refused. Do you know how rare that is?'

I wanted to tear my jaw away from Jarrad, but his thumb and forefinger were holding me tightly. If he kept it up, my eyes would start to water. It was starting to really hurt, but I refused to whimper. Maybe he was waiting for that. I could feel him waiting for me to crack.

'Rare for Devin. So rare, in fact, he had never done it once. Not even when he had a broken arm and had to shoot with a gun versus a bow and arrows. He was the one who did me proud, and then you came along and fucked it all up.'

He let go of my chin, and my head hit the chair. For an instant, I was blinded by spots, and it took everything in me not to close my eyes. Jarrad paced, his fingers running through his hair, and I could feel the beast that was just under the skin. Werewolves were notoriously angry animals. They didn't have a lot of control over their beasts, not if they were new. If they were born into it, their control was excellent. Everyone knew that—even selkies.

'You selkies are all the same. You fuck men and women and then leave them hanging. You make them want more, you make them need you, and then you leave them.'

Ahhhh. 'She was a selkie, wasn't she?' I said. Suddenly, it all made sense to me.

'What? Who?' He whirled around to look at me.

'The woman who scorned you. She was a selkie, wasn't she? What did she do?'

His hand, closed fist and all, hit the table hard enough to make it rattle. That was some power he had. If he hit me hard enough with that fist, I was sure he would shatter my skull. I was really hoping it didn't get to that point. That would be a really bad point.

'She *left* me. I was in love with her, and she left me, and then I was taken away, made to pick up the pieces with her gone. Why?' He stared at me again, and his eyes burnt purple. They made me wish that I had more abilities than I had. I was better in the water. In my playground, I could use anything as a weapon, but on land … I was useless.

'I don't know. Sometimes, we just leave. We need freedom.'

'Freedom is for the *weak*,' he spat out at me, and I had to hold my breath. I had to tiptoe around it because I was going to get hit. I could feel it. I could see it in the way he moved. *Shit.* 'I loved her. She was my one. And since then, all I've done is fuck people, waiting to find her again so I could fuck her again and then leave her like she had left me. Sometimes, karma is the best medicine you can offer someone. Do you know her?'

'What's her name?' I asked cautiously. I didn't think I should be asking, but I had to know. If it was one of my sisters, I was as good as dead, which was a strong possibility. It couldn't have been me because I had never seen him in my life.

'Gracia,' he said. The name rolled his tongue like a lover. I knew he loved her still in that very sentence, and no matter how much smack he spoke about her, he wouldn't be able to hurt her. He couldn't.

I shook my head. 'I don't know a Gracia. Where are you from?'

He shook suddenly. Clearly, I had given him the wrong answer. 'Ireland,' he said. But he could have fooled me. He had no accent. Not even when he was getting upset. Sometimes, accents became more prevalent when someone was upset, but that was not happening.

'I knew some from the Irish coast, but no Gracia. I'm sorry.' I wasn't really, but I was being damn well polite.

Jarrad growled and flipped the table. It crashed to the floor with a loud bang and made me jump in my chair. He turned around, his eyes brighter than before. He was huffing, and I knew he was losing control quickly. I could see his teeth lengthening and his nails growing. One scrape with those nails, and I would be done for. Not even a selkie was immune to the poison of a werewolf scratch.

'That's not good enough,' he growled.

'Jarrad!' someone's voice came, and he tore his eyes away from me to someone in the background.

'Go away,' he grumbled.

'Step away from the lady, or I will be forced to take matters into my own hands. You know I don't like getting my hands dirty. That's what all of you are for.'

He was huffing, and slowly, he took a step back. I held my breath as I waited to see if he would charge at me. I really didn't want him to do that.

'Hello, Acionna. Do you have a last name? I always liked addressing people with their last names. A lot better than using their first.'

A man in a suit came into my view, and I shook my head. 'No last name. Selkies have no use for them.' The human I used didn't matter here.

'Such a shame. I think you'd have a lovely last name if you did. I hope that Mr Frows here didn't scare you too much. He has a bad temper. We were working on finding a way to calm him down, but he isn't very good at sharing.'

He was so eloquent and nice. I was in shock. I didn't expect a man who seemed to be a criminal mastermind to be so kind. *Don't movies show them to be sleazes?*

I blinked at him, afraid of what I could say at that moment. In the corner of my eye, I watched Jarrad get a hold of himself. He rubbed a hand over his face and sniffed. And he was back to playing human.

'That's better, Mr Frows. You can go now. I'm not sure if keeping you with Acionna is a good idea right now.'

'But I wasn't finished with her.' Jarrad seemed to have lost his place too. The man in the suit looked at him, and I saw a flicker of anger before it was gone. He threw him across the room, and Jarrad hit the wall hard, his head hitting the wall with an almost sickening crack. Werewolves were notoriously hard to kill. One could injure them to the edge of the world and back, but it didn't mean shit. They just got back up and walked away, which was exactly what Jarrad did—he got up and brushed himself off.

'You have finished with her, and you will go and get a hold of yourself. Go have a shower or go for a run. I will call for you when I need you again, but trust me, it won't be for a while. Now go.'

Jarrad looked like a dog who had been told off and was walking out of the room with his tail between his legs. The image made me snort, and both men looked at me. I swallowed the laugh and blinked, wiping the laughter from my eyes. *Shit. That wasn't a good move.*

'What is so funny?' Jarrad growled.

'Nothing,' I said quickly, and he leapt forward. The man in the suit held up his hand, and Jarrad was hit with an invisible wall.

'Go and cool off, Mr Frows. I will not ask you again.' The man in the suit was putting a little more emphasis into his words, and Jarrad left in a huff. When the door shut behind him, the man in the suit turned back to me.

'It's in your best interest if you don't antagonise the wolf in him. He's normally a very good soldier, but he's becoming a little unhinged. Now, what was so funny?'

He wanted to know, and I suddenly wanted to run out. I could feel the power in the room. It made me dizzy, and I gasped for air—he was literally pulling it out from the room. I closed my eyes, my head starting to droop, but before I got there, the room snapped back and I was awake and up again.

'I can keep going,' he said, and by the tone, I already knew he wasn't a patient man. *Fuck.*

'Jarrad looked like he was leaving with his tail between his legs, which is funnier because he's a werewolf.'

The man in the suit seemed amused. 'I'm terribly rude, aren't I? My name's Mr Dovev. I'm the one in charge of Mr Ryder's position, and I was the one who put the hit out on you.'

I swallowed hard. He was so calm, so collected about the words that came out of his mouth. I knew that I was in trouble. Some deep trouble. *Fuck.* 'Hi,' I said. *What else can I say there? I mean, knowing the man in front of you is the one who put the price on your head ... Not scary at all, right?*

'Hello,' he said pleasantly. 'Now, you and I have some business to talk about. I hope you don't mind.' Dovev gestured to the seat, and I shook my head. 'Good,' he said as he pulled the chair up in front of me and sat down. He unbuttoned his jacket and leant forward. His hair was jet black, his eyes crystal blue, his skin unmarred and slightly tanned, his cheekbones high and his lips almost kissable. He was a good-looking man. There was no denying that, but I didn't think I could handle it anymore. I averted my eyes as soon as I was done studying him, and he laughed.

'You are a pretty thing,' he said as he trailed a finger across my jaw and down my collarbone. He slowly pried the robe apart.

'Can you not? Unless you want to untie my hands. Then it's fair game.' The words were out of my mouth before I could stop them. *How could that have happened?*

'What? Do this?' He pulled the robe apart a little more, and my breasts were on show. I hated that my hands were behind my back. 'I think I can. You have beautiful skin. I wonder what the rest of you is like.'

I spat in his face. He pulled back and took a handkerchief out from his inner pocket and flapped it open, wiping my spit off his face.

'That was uncalled for.' He finished cleaning his face and slapped me. My whole head vibrated with the shock. 'That was the only warning you get. Do you understand?'

My eyes watered, and I nodded. 'I understand,' I said, and Mr

Dobrev leant back, crossing his legs at the ankles and clasping his hands against his stomach.

'You are very pretty. I can definitely see what Mr Ryder saw in you, but you know it has to stop, right? We need him to kill you. But I feel like, now that we have you, we can do one better.'

I was afraid to ask who 'we' was. The kick would be one of his sisters—that would break him. I knew it would, and I really hoped they weren't that cruel.

'His family is safe. For now, anyway. So, you understand, right? You have to break up with him for things to be okay, and you won't be able to get out of here until you do or he comes to find you. Although I'm not sure if he will find you. He doesn't know about his place, and I'm sure that even if he did, he would be too busy trying to hit his mark to care about you.'

'It's not up to me. I wasn't even the one who decided it was all in or nothing. That was Devin. So if you want someone to end it, you need to find him and talk to him because I'm not going to do a thing.' I wouldn't be put in that situation.

'Oh, but that's where you're wrong. I can get you to do whatever I want. I know about your deal. I bet that now you're about to miss your first shot, you're going to end up stuck on land. How disappointing that would be for you, especially since I know the ocean is your home. I could find the witch for you and destroy her before she can touch your pelt.'

I stiffened. That was not something I was bargaining for. Part of me wanted to take up that option because I could get my pelt back and be free, but I would miss Devin too much. I needed him, and even if Mr Dovev didn't believe me, I was going to stick with him. No matter what.

'Try again tomorrow,' I told him, and that's when I pressed my lips tighter. As far as I was concerned, that would be the last word.

He stood up and clicked his tongue before he backhanded me. My cheek throbbed and I whimpered. 'Remember that, because tomorrow I'll ask the same thing, and until you give me exactly what I want, I won't stop. Until then ...' With that, he left the room, and the sob that had been stuck in my throat came scrambling out, the pain of my cheek more severe than I'd first thought.

CHAPTER THIRTY-THREE

Devin
Payni 2017
Melbourne

The shrill noise of my phone was grating in my brain, ripping me from my sleep. I patted around for the phone and knocked it off the bedside.

'Fuck.'

I scrambled to pick it up because it. Wasn't. Going. To. Stop.

'Hello?'

'That was a little too long of a wait, D-Man.'

'Jar?'

Silence from the other end.

'What the hell?'

'That's no way to talk to your best friend.'

I rubbed my eyes with my free hand and checked the time: 3:33 a.m. *What the fuck?*

'You and I both know what that really means.'

He chuckled on the other end. 'Was worth a try, yeah?'

'What do you want?' I asked this time.

He wouldn't call me at that time without a reason, and I knew it wasn't for a hit. It couldn't be. I would have gotten a text and an email with the information.

'I wanted to check that you were awake.'

It was weird to have him say that. He knew it wasn't the easiest to get me, but when I was awake, I was up.

'What did you do?' I sat up.

'Good, you're listening.'

I sat up in bed and stared at the time. It was the middle of the fucking night.

'You got your latest hit, didn't you? It was marked as urgent, and it hasn't been fulfilled yet, has it?'

Did I get through the file? No. After Lucy saw it, I shoved it in my room and ignored it. Urgent hits were near and far in between. They weren't all that odd, but that one could wait. I wasn't going to kill Acionna.

Not when I was finally getting a life with her.

'Where is she?' I knew that he had her.

'For now, not so safe, but alive. I don't know for how long.'

'You know that when I come for her, I'm going to kill you.'

'I know. I look forward to it. You might want to check her home first.'

Jarrad ended the call, and I climbed out of bed so fast I nearly went headfirst into the post of my bed. He had her. I needed her back.

I picked up the phone and called Hunter. He was always the first call.

'What's wrong?' he asked without any hint of sleepiness in his voice.

'They took Ash. I need help. Can you meet me at her place?'

'Do you need Luce?'

'No, I'd prefer for her not to come.'

'Got it. I'll meet you there.'

I got dressed—black jeans, black T-shirt and a black cap. Sometimes, night stealth needed a little bit of hiding. I grabbed my leather jacket. It wasn't cold enough, but if I had to fight someone and they had a knife, it would slash the leather first.

I grabbed my keys and legged it out of there. From the time I hung up with Jarrad and called Hunter, it had been less than ten minutes. I had to hope for no traffic at 4 a.m.

I slammed the car into park and screamed up the pathway to her front door. The door was shattered, and I was careful as I stepped over the threshold.

'Janice? It's me, Devin. Are you here?'

There was blood on the floor. I hoped it wasn't Acionna's, but I wasn't sure.

'Mr Devin?' I heard her voice and looked at the end of the stairs. She had the kitten in her hands, and they both looked shocked.

'You're okay?'

She nodded. 'Miss Acionna was taken. Three guys came all dressed in black. One of them was named Jarrad. He had a gun pointed at her.'

'Wait, you're sure it was Jarrad?' I asked.

'Positive, Mr Devin. Miss Acionna made sure she repeated his name.'

'Fuck,' I cursed and turned around to look at the damage. It was just the door, but it was enough. 'I'll have someone over as soon as it's light to fix the door. Can you keep the kitten and yourself safe until then?'

She nodded.

'Dev. Holy cow,' Hunter said as he walked through the door. 'This is ugly. Is that all that was broken?'

I looked over my shoulder. 'I think so. I'm about to go and check upstairs. Can you stay with Janice and put up some wards? In case they feel like they want to come back?'

'Yeah, I can do that.'

I nodded and ran up the stairs. The first place I went to was Lucy's bedroom. I needed to see if they touched anything. As I got to the top of the stairs and covered the short distance to her bedroom, I saw the bed was a mess. But it was just a normal mess, like Acionna had thrown the covers off. Nothing else looked out of place … except her phone. *Fuck.* It was there.

I picked it up, hoping there was no passcode, but I was disappointed.

'Fuck.' If I couldn't get into it, her pelt would be toast. Maybe Janice would know the code. It was wishful thinking, but I had to hope. Satisfied with the state of the room, I left and closed the door so it was slightly ajar. The kitten loved to sleep on Acionna's bed, and who was I to rob her of that?

I jogged down the stairs. 'Janice, do you know Acionna's passcode for her phone?' I asked and held up the device. She paled at the sight of it and nodded.

'I only know it by chance. It's 11117.'

I put the code in and it unlocked. I breathed a sigh. 'Hunt, what is the app I need for the camera?' He came up beside me and took the phone, swiping twice and handing it back to me.

'The one with the purple lens. That's what you need to make sure that the image is shot in time.'

I checked the alarms; they were in place. *Thank fuck.*

'Oh, Miss Acionna said Jarrad was a werewolf.'

I froze and turned to her.

'What?'

'Yes, said he moved like liquid.'

He's a motherfucking werewolf. And that means …

I pulled my phone out of my back pocket and dialled the only other werewolf I knew. Travis' name blinked across the screen, and I brought the phone to my ear as I listened to it ringing.

Hi, you've called Travis Matthews. I can't get to the phone right now, but if you leave your name, number and your preferred drink, I'll get back to you as soon as I can.

'Travis. It's Devin. Call me back as soon as you hear this. I need information.'

Werewolves didn't need a lot of sleep. It explained so much about Jarrad.

'If he doesn't call me back, I'm going over there to haul his arse out of bed.'

'I can help,' Hunter said. He wiped his hands on his pants. 'The wards are good to go. They should keep anyone away who isn't supposed to be here.'

'Thank you. I really mean it, Hunt,' I said.

'You would do the same for me if the roles were reversed.'

'I'd do worse because it would mean they had Lucy.'

'I'm glad the roles aren't reversed.'

CHAPTER THIRTY-FOUR

Acionna
Payni 2017
Melbourne

My cheek throbbed, and in front of me was a vodka soda. I was pretty sure I wasn't allowed to have alcohol with the pills they gave me for the pain, but if I was going to stand in the room with Mr Dovev, I was going to make sure I was hopped up on something. The dress I was wearing was blue and clung to my curves. It was just the right size, which was surprising because I didn't think they would be able to get it just by looking at me. They even got the lingerie right, despite cheating when they felt me up, but it was the right stuff to go under the dress.

I was seated at a table. The cheekbone that was fractured was throbbing, and I resisted the urge to throw my drink at Dovev's face. It was really, really tempting, and I had to keep distracting myself to make sure I didn't.

'You look lovely,' he said as he tipped his glass at me. I wasn't sure what to make of that compliment.

I picked up my fork and shoved food into my mouth—it stopped me from saying anything. I already wished to be tied back up to the chair. Anything was better than that dinner I didn't want to happen. It was a dinner that shouldn't have happened. *Why am I so special?*

'You know, on a date, the woman is supposed to ask questions and engage in small talk, not just eat her way through everything on the menu.'

Well, geez. Date or no date, it was against my will. I took a deep breath before I put down my fork. 'A date also gets a chance to choose whether or not they want to come, not be dressed in something that isn't theirs in the first place and dined with. Thanks to you, I'm here in clothes that aren't mine, eating a dinner that is only partially satisfying.'

It would have been more satisfying if I had been bathing in his blood. Anything was better than sitting there and watching his smug face as he tried to actually make conversation.

'You're not a very nice lady, are you?' he asked, bringing the tumbler to his lips and taking a sip.

'No, I'm not. But I'm particularly not nice when people threaten those I love and try to make me have some sort of'—I gestured to the table—'whatever this is.'

'It's a date. I'm trying to woo you.'

'You want me dead.'

'That, too, but if I can get you away from Devin, you won't end up dead.'

I swallowed and took a second to compose myself before speaking. 'I love him. I'm not sure how that is going to change in the span of a dinner.'

'Easy. I'm offering you your pelt for him.'

I held my breath. *No, he can't have my pelt.* 'Where is it?' I breathed. I wouldn't believe he had it, not until I saw it in front of me. I knew my pelt. I knew it so well that whatever he brought out, I'd instantly know if it was mine.

'Here,' Dovev said. He motioned to someone, and they left the room, returning with something. A package. I felt for it, but in my gut, I already knew it wasn't it. *He thinks that he can get it that easily?* I had tried for months, and he thought he was strong enough to beat a witch who had it already? I didn't think so.

I smiled at him—or did my best to. 'Not mine. Although whoever's it is, you might want to run it by Jarrad. I hear he's looking for someone who matches that description.'

Dovev slammed his fist into the table, and I jumped. 'This is yours. I know it.'

I shook my head. 'Doesn't feel like mine, and if it was, I would have been instantly drawn to it. Not going to happen.'

I was going to make sure that witch was good and properly dead when all was said and done. But I had to give it to her, she was one crafty woman.

Dovev shook with anger. *Does this mean I pushed him too far?* I sure hoped so. He glared at me across the table, and I held his gaze, but part of me wanted to turn away and pretend I couldn't stand his glare.

'Are you sure? This is your pelt. I found the witch. I decimated her, and she is now gone. How is this not your pelt?' He stood up this time.

'I am as sure as a bright day that it is not my pelt. I don't know whose it is, but it's not mine.'

He threw it to the floor, disgusted, and while it wasn't mine, the lack of respect was appalling. Before I could help myself, words left my lips.

'You should pick that up. A pelt deserves respect, and you're not giving it.'

He turned to look at me, his eyes glowing with anger. I was waiting to see what he would do, and I knew it wouldn't be fun. 'How dare you!' He was losing his composure fast, and part of me was jumping for joy at the way he lost a little more of his decorum. 'You can't talk to me like that!'

'Why? Why can't I talk to you like that?' Bold—even too bold for me.

'Because you're a prisoner. You're nothing.' He stormed around, the food forgotten, and I really wished that Devin was there to help me.

'Are they all like that?' I asked. All of his assassins were prisoners in their own skin, and he made sure they were on a tight leash.

'Who?' he asked as he stopped in front of me. Slowly, I stood on my two feet. He easily towered over me, which was weird because I was tall for a human, but he was taller.

'Your men and women. Do they know that they're prisoners?'

His hands came up to hit, and I kept my face cautiously blank. He stopped his hand before it came to my face and growled before turning away. 'I can see how you're making him break. You're good, selkie, but I'm not sure you're good enough. Did you know I used to have a wife who had a selkie friend? No one can find her. And a little tip? No one ever will.' I swallowed hard, giving him the reaction I knew he wanted. He grinned before he backed away. 'You need to understand that you're a wanted woman. I can have you killed, but I'm waiting to see if Mr Ryder will fill out his end of the bargain. If he doesn't, that's going to be bad for him. Very bad.'

'What are you going to do?' I couldn't help myself. I didn't want to really know what the deal was, but I knew I had to know something.

'What happens to the hunter when he becomes the hunted, Acionna?'

Fuck. He was going to have Devin killed.

Thwack. Thwack.

I jolted awake and scrambled up.

'What the fuck? Oh my god.' The pain in my head was immediate. My pulse pounded and my ears rang.

'Good, you're awake!' I heard a voice from the adjourning room. I blinked to clear my vision and noticed the bars. They were shiny. Then, I looked up at the ceiling and found the room was dingy. It wasn't a room, though. It was a jail cell.

'Ariel?' I whispered. 'Are you okay?'

'Yes and no. I'm … I had to have dinner with that creep, and he tried to do things to me. He has my pelt.'

It was Ariel's pelt. My heart ached.

'Why are you here, Air? I thought you were safe. What did you do?'

She sobbed, and I got up out of the bunk and went over to the bar.

'Careful. It's silver,' Ariel said.

It didn't matter. 'What did you do?'

'I was so mad at you. You took Eain, and then you slept with Ben. You took everything.'

'Ariel …'

'But then Eain kept talking about you, and he said it would be easy to do. He knew a witch who could take your pelt and hold it hostage. It wouldn't be for very long. Just long enough for you to feel what it was like to hurt as much as I did. But it went all wrong.'

I pressed my lips together and reached through the bars to her. I held out my hand, and she took it. Her dry hand was cold and rough, like she had pulled something heavy for too long.

'The witch took my pelt too. I've been stuck here for as long as you have.'

'Air. How could you?' I asked.

The lies Eain had spun to get to her to think like that were starting to unravel.

'He made a good case. He said I could be on the throne, that I would be better at it than you, and all I had to do was play my part. Act jealous, let him get Matched with you. He would take care of it all.'

'You know he lied?' I asked and squeezed her hand.

'I know that now. I need to get out of here. *We* need to get out of here.'

I suddenly realised I still had my pelt intact. It wasn't destroyed. I pulled my hand back rapidly, pressing my hands all over my body.

'My pelt is still around. It hasn't been destroyed,' I said incredulously.

'What?' Ariel asked.

Devin must have gotten my phone. It was the only thing I could think of that had saved me.

'I … It's too hard to explain, but I met someone, Air, and he's unlike anyone in the Undersea ever. He may have saved my pelt.'

'I guess that's something.' She exhaled hard and leant back against the chair she sat in. 'I don't know how to get mine back. Dovev has it, and I want to kill him for it.'

'So why don't we?' I asked.

'What? How? We are locked in a jail cell, with silver and probably magick. We can't get out of here.'

'We can,' I said.

'How can you be so optimistic? Especially after everything that has happened. Everything I put you through?'

I looked at my sister and knew she would never get it. She was selfish and only wanted for herself. 'Because, Ariel, to be a good leader, you have to have hope. You need to look out for others. It's what all of Mother's training was about. It's never been about me or about you. Or even her. Being a ruler is to be selfless and worry about others before yourself. This is why you were never a contender. You only think about yourself.'

It was harsh, the words just slipping from my lips, but I wasn't going to placate her. I wasn't going to make it easy for her. Ariel deserved to hear it all. Every last bit of it.

'I do not,' she countered.

'You thought about yourself when you wanted to Eain, the throne. Even Ben. The fact that you wanted me to hurt just as much as you is damaging. Were you planning on getting any of our siblings to shore?'

I watched Ariel get up from the chair, and she refused to look at me. I was right.

'Who was next?'

'Adella,' she mumbled.

'The most innocent of us. You should be ashamed of yourself. Was it so hard to live with us?'

'No … I just wanted more attention.'

'Of course you did. I should just leave you here. Let you find your own way out or rot.'

Ariel gasped. 'You wouldn't dare.'

'Wouldn't I? I want to so badly.'

She would deserve it. But I wasn't that mean. I wanted my sister to be safe and to find happiness, but I wanted to get her back. Ariel looked way more rough around the edges than I did. She didn't have a Janice looking after her.

'Oh, lookie, you're awake.' I heard a voice, and Ariel scampered into the corner to make herself as small as possible. I turned on my heel, still in the dress Dovev had put me in when I dined with him. It was gross. But the voice didn't belong to either Dovev or Jarrad. I saw the tattoo on his hand, and put two and two together—it was the man I'd kneed in the balls.

'I get to take you for your next outing with the bosses.' I heard the key click into the lock and he turned it. As he did, the door unlocked and it swung open. I stepped back into the cell and kept going until my back hit the wall. The man grinned and grabbed my arm. He pulled me out of the cell, and did it with such force that I cried out. Pain shot through my arm. I tried to rip it back, but it felt like jelly. *Did he just break my arm?*

'I love it when you scream. It's so endearing.'

'I think you dislocated my shoulder,' I whimpered.

'Good. That's for my balls.'

I looked over my shoulder at Ariel, who was still in the corner of the room, cowering like it wasn't happening. I walked with the goon. If it saved her, I would do it, but we would have to wait and see what it brought.

CHAPTER THIRTY-FIVE

Devin
Payni 2017
Melbourne

'Do you have her location yet?' I asked Hunter. I paced back and forth in my bedroom, which probably bugged him. He was sitting on the floor crossed-legged with a pendulum and a map. Lucy was right next to him, but didn't touch him. She was careful not to distract him and break his concentration. Except I didn't have that sort of boundary. The pendulum kept swinging, not locking on a location. I hated waiting for pendulum magick to work—sometimes, it could lead one down a dark alley, and sometimes, it led them to where you needed to go.

'You need to stop asking, or I'm going to get Lucy to put you in time out,' Hunter called.

'And I'll do it,' she spoke up.

I paced back and forth, about to open my mouth again. Lucy glared and I shut my mouth. It had been three days since she was taken, and I had taken three pictures. It was nerve-wracking because I didn't know what the image was meant to look like. I didn't have Acionna's eye.

And I missed her. I missed her like crazy. Her voice, her scent, the taste of her lips. All of it. I hadn't realised just how much I would miss her until she was gone.

I needed her back, and I needed her back now.

Hunter let out a big *a-ha* and I got down to his level to look at the pendulum and the map.

'Where did you find her?' I asked.

'I have them at the abandoned District in Docklands,' he said.

'You're shitting me? He was there the whole time?'

'It looks like it. I can't tell you which building yet, just that she is definitely there.'

'I don't care. Pack it up. Let's go. We're finding out in the car where her direct location is.'

'Dev, we don't even know if it's real.'

'We do. Come on. Worry about the rest later.'

'Wolves. We don't have them,' Lucy said. I was surprised that she wanted to wait for them, but it made sense to have some muscle on our side so we weren't relying on Lucy, Hunter and their offensive powers.

'I don't want to wait for them. If they're not here now, we go without them.'

Hunter kept the pendulum swinging as I spoke, and he held up his hand to me. 'Costco ... It looks like they're at Costco.'

'Now, can we go?' I asked.

The wolves would have to wait. Travis never called me back, and Lucy said she had spoken to him through their bond but heard nothing back.

He had never been so flaky before, but he was going through some things, or so Lucy said. If he were around, I would have grilled him about Jarrad and what he knew. He was the son of the alpha of one of the major packs in the world. He would know information about him for sure.

'Luce, I know he's your friend, and you have that weird as shit bond with him, but I need to go now. I don't want to waste any more time.'

'Fine. Grab what you need. Let's go.'

She didn't need to tell me twice. I got my bow, arrows and keys.

Acionna was coming home, and no one was going to stop us.

The drive could have killed me on the freeway and through the throng of traffic. It was peak hour, but Hunter refused to go above the speed limit. He said it was because he couldn't risk getting caught, but I didn't care about that. I needed to get to her.

We pulled into the abandoned park. It was eerie. The place would have thrived if they had done it right. But instead, they put it in an awkward position just off the freeway and called it The District.

'Can you see where they are?' I asked Lucy. She had her eyes closed, and she tapped into the magick of a crystal ball—an object she assured me had changed with practice. The ball had a live image of Acionna; her hair was tousled, there was a cut on her cheek and her shoulder looked messed up. It took everything in me to not storm the place.

She was tied to a chair, and Jarrad was talking to her. We couldn't hear what was being said, but she looked like she was out of it.

'I can't wait any longer,' I said, and ran off to the door.

'Dev!' Hunter hissed, but it was too late. I was there.

I kicked the door once, twice, three times before it shattered, and pulled an arrow out of the quiver, locking it in place. I aimed it at Jarrad's chest, not sorry for what was to come.

'You need to let her go,' I cried out.

Jarrad turned to face me, the purple in his eyes evident as he stared back at me.

'You know, she is a little firecracker. She didn't crack once, except when Dovev tried to put his hands on her in a way she didn't like. Her shoulder got dislocated, but I think that was from Harry, actually. I pushed it back in place, but it's probably hurting like a bitch. Selkies are human-like with their healing when they don't have their pelt,' Jarrad rambled.

'Why is she untied?' I asked.

'She's your girl, Dev. As much as she fucked up everything, there is still a part of me that wants to see you happy.'

'What are you doing? You never talk so much,' I said.

'Stalling. Is it working? But also, your girl likes to pull at things. Unravel them so they can make some sense, doesn't she? She's good.'

Jarrad put his hands in the air in a defensive position, almost as if it would stop him from getting hit.

'Why did you have to betray me?' I asked. This time, it was about Dad and not about Acionna.

'Do you remember what I told you all those years ago, Dev? If I had to be the one to kill the family, it's a last resort and a message. Your dad was a good sport. He knew what was coming and accepted it. He didn't beg.'

If I was a wolf, a film of purple would settle over my eyesight and it would be the only colour I saw until I got the bloodlust under control.

'What are you trying to achieve here? I'm taking Acionna with me, whether you like it or not. But you're not leaving here alive.'

'You were the best, you know? Out of all of them, it was always you. I pushed you the hardest because of it, D-Man.'

Hunter covered me. I felt him rather than saw him, and he moved towards Acionna without a word.

'You hide behind your bow because you know that without it, I'd beat you,' Jarrad egged. I looked at the arrow tip. He wasn't wrong, but I didn't want him to know that.

'I hide behind the bow because I'm good at it. What's your excuse?' I thought about lowering the weapon, but Jarrad was a werewolf, and in hand-to-hand, he would demolish me. I was human, and he was not.

'Smart. You know I had to do it.'

'You could have denied the request. Given it to someone else.

Given me warning,' I shouted. Fury pumped through my blood, and I wanted nothing more than to finish Jarrad.

To put the arrow through his heart and finish him off. But I wanted to know why.

'You always said Karrept was at the helm, but who is Dovev?'

'An alley of Karrept's. Very interesting man—potentially a descendant of Karrept,' he said. I hated that name.

'I have one of those on my side. He's standing right there.' I motioned in Hunter's direction.

'Direct descendent, yes. This one is murky.'

Acionna groaned and came to. 'Ash, love, are you hurt?'

Jarrad moved, and I let go of the arrow. It sliced the top of his shoulder, and before he could react, I had another one out—pointed at his head this time.

'Uncalled for,' he growled.

'I'm okay. My shoulder fucking kills, but what is more pain?'

'Hunter is going to grab you. Let him, yeah?' I said as I saw Hunter move in my peripherals. He got to Acionna and carefully picked her up. She leant on him, her bad arm hugged close to her body.

I moved the arrow down and let go of it. It sailed through the air and sank into Jarrad's chest. The velocity of the arrow dragged him to the ground, and I ran at him, this time with another arrow in hand.

'You were the best. You're the only one who is left to kill them. But be careful. They know a lot about you. More than you ever gave away. Karrept knew everything about you before you came to us, and he made sure to pass on that information. You have to ...' I stopped him and slammed the arrow between his eyes.

Breathing hard, I stared at him. It was over. He was dead. The one man who had been there through the most traumatic part of my life was dead. He'd helped mould and shape that version of me, and to have to kill him was bittersweet, but we were no closer to getting Ash's pelt back.

I stared at him for a fraction longer before Ash groaned. I got to my feet and crossed the distance between us, taking her out of

Hunter's arms. I held her tightly and pressed a soft kiss against her hair.

'I'm not letting you out of my sight without good reason ever again,' I whispered. Acionna choked back tears.

'I don't plan on going anywhere soon,' she murmured.

'Good.'

I held her tight before I pulled her away. 'We aren't any closer to finding your pelt.'

'Ariel. She's behind bars. She knows where to go.'

Her sister is here? She saw her? And she knows the location of the witch?

'How do you know?'

She smiled. It was sad and didn't quite meet her eyes. 'She said it without saying it. She'd been trying to get more of my sisters to hand over their pelts to the witch.'

'Shit.'

A gunshot exploded in the room, and we all ducked.

'Just a warning to everyone. Good luck.' The words rang through the abandoned supermarket and were gone just as quickly as they had sounded.

'We have to find the bastard,' Hunter said, and I shook my head. There was no way we would find Dovev in time. He would have to wait.

CHAPTER THIRTY-SIX

Acionna
Payni 2017
Melbourne

I COULD FEEL ARIEL—SHE was right *there*, her body weak, but her pelt was not far away—just like mine, but they'd taken her and I had to find her. I felt my pelt pulse. That was the only way we could find it. I could feel it somewhere in the house. Wherever that stupid witch was, my pelt was with her too—and Ariel. It was waiting for me, calling me closer, but I was afraid of what she had done to it. The guy in the main room hadn't said anything I hadn't figured out already, but my mind swam with different ideas. *Has she stitched it to someone else? Does she really think that it will fly over with me?* I needed it back. My body ached to feel lit again. Five months was too long to go without it. I needed it.

'Ash, wait, you can't just go in there with nothing. You have to wait,' Devin called out behind me, but I was done waiting. I was so done with waiting. All I wanted was to get it. I had to feel it in my hands again, and if I had to get through everybody to do it, I was going to make that happen.

My fingers pushed the door open, and what I saw was stairs

leading into a dark and dank basement. I felt like I was about to walk into a bad horror movie cliché. As I took a step, I felt hands wrap around my waist and pull me away. I thrashed against them until I heard Devin's voice.

'Please, let me go first. I can't handle it if anything happens to you,' he whispers, and even though it soothed me, I didn't want him to go first. I wanted to see it all myself. My pelt was right there, ready and waiting for me, calling me home. I longed to feel it moulding against my skin as my body changed and shifted. I waited to feel the skin envelope my body and let me swim through the water until we were one. I didn't want to wait any longer.

I let my body go loose, and Devin breathed a sigh. If it were anyone else and I didn't love and trust him, I wouldn't have relaxed and kept fighting.

'Thank you,' he whispered, and kissed my cheek before spinning us around. He pivoted on the ball of his foot and started down the stairs. I watched the darkness swallow him before I followed, one step at time. It felt like it was taking forever. My body was heavy with anticipation, waiting and willing time to hurry up.

'I've been waiting for you,' a voice said. It was familiar, and I knew it was the witch. I practically jumped down the last few steps and was ready to run at her, but Devin's strong arms wrapped around my torso and held me against him. *Damn him and his quicker thinking.* I wanted out.

'Your sister said you were a firecracker. Speaking of which, have you spoken to Ariel? I think she's missing something.' Candlelight flickered around the room. Hundreds of jars filled with things I couldn't name lined the walls. Shrunken heads lay in many, and the witch had an evil grin on her face. 'Cat got your tongue? Or perhaps the Dreamwalking Assassin does? I know who you are. Dovev was very clear on keeping you around. Such a shame that he had to die. I liked my husband.'

I felt Devin stiffen in my arms, and that's when it all fell into place. The witch was the one who was in charge of everything, but together with Dovev, they were a team. I hadn't expected that.

'You are the one who was setting out the hits?' Devin asked.

'One of the many. Want to know how I did it?'

'Who are you?' I asked. There was no way to get to my sister without making Devin let go, and something told me there was no way in hell he was actually going to do that.

'Esmerelda is what everyone likes to call me, but that's because Grinda was too nice.' She laughed at me. 'Honestly, my name isn't important. What is important is your sister's. I want a full collection of selkies, and you're going to help me. Both of you are.'

Devin held me tighter. I knew that if he didn't have his arm around me, I would have fallen to the floor, my knees weak. How stupid. 'You do know there is no way in hell that they're actually going to help you. You haven't given them a reason to.'

She smiled at us, and I wanted to rip that smile right off her face. If only I could. I would. 'Oh, dear, but they will. You see, I have their pelts. I can do whatever I like with them because they know I will destroy them if they don't do as I ask. You wouldn't want to see that, would you?'

'Devin. I need an arrow.' He stiffened at my back.

'Ash,' he murmured into my ear. That should have been the first indication that he wasn't going to give it to me without a fight, and part of me was ready for it. I didn't want to do it, but if I had to, I would. 'No.'

'Yes, no, Acionna. You don't want to do that. Or your sister will lose the one thing that matters the most to her.'

Ariel looked at me. Her eyes widened, and words started to tumble out of her mouth. 'Acionna, please, no. No. I can't live without it. I'm sorry. I'm so sorry for what I did. I shouldn't have, but I was angry, and I know it was the wrong thing to do now. But don't let me get the end of it. Don't let her take away my lifeline.'

Devin held me tightly, and I slowly niggled out of his grasp. 'It's okay,' I murmured to him. The witch watched us. I wasn't sure if she could do anything much but stare. Devin slowly unfolded his arms from around me, and I squeezed his bicep before walking over to

Ariel. I knelt by her and a sob erupts from her lips. 'Can you forgive me?' she asked.

I smiled at her. *How many times have I imagined this? How many times have I wanted her to feel her way through what it would feel like?* I remembered how, for so long, I wanted her to pay. But watching as she got weaker instead of stronger made me sad that it had all happened. She needed someone to teach her a lesson, and maybe this was supposed to be it. Instead of wanting to forgive her, I wanted to wring her neck for letting us get into that position.

'Let her go,' I told the witch, who laughed at me.

'Oh, but dear, this is so much fun.'

'Devin killed your husband, and he won't hesitate to kill you either. We have wolves and witches. You hide inside this pitiful house to keep away the outside, and you steal what isn't yours. Didn't your mother ever tell you it is rude to steal?'

'I didn't have a mother, so no.'

Well, then, that explains a lot of things.

Just as I was about to say something more, bright light flashed in front of me, and I had to cover my eyes.

I don't know how much time passed, but as I tried to blink to clear my vision, I heard grunting, fighting, and my eyes struggled to put things into focus. I couldn't see a damn thing. *What is happening? Who is fighting?*

'Hello?' I murmured, reaching out. I felt a hand grasp mine. It was a woman, familiar.

'I'm here, Acionna. I can't see what's going on either,' Ariel said. I clung to her hand and hoped that, by listening to her and holding on, I'd be able to actually get up and move.

'I don't think I like this.'

'Who is the guy?' she asks.

'I don't think that's the right thing to be asking right now, Ariel. Let's think of something else.'

'He's cute.' The same smug tone that she'd always had leapt into her voice, and I rolled my eyes.

'He's off-limits to you. My boyfriend. *Mine*,' I said. I heard her growl and dig her nails into my arm.

'Just like when you slept with the man I wanted? How do you think I feel? I deserve to have him too. Give him up.'

I ripped my arm out of her hand and looked in the direction I thought she was in. 'You haven't changed. Even with the witch taking your pelt, you never learn. I thought something like that would have made you appreciate family and forgive, but you're still the same. No wonder she got you. You're exactly the same. I should leave you here. Let her do whatever she likes with your pelt, it doesn't faze me in the least.'

She gasped. 'You wouldn't dare.'

'I would. You're selfish enough to deserve it.'

'Ash? Can you hear me?' Devin's voice broke through, and I blinked, trying to find where it was coming from. The light was still there in my eyes.

'Dev? I can. What's going on? Are the witches at it? I can't see shit.'

'Yeah, something like that. Stay there. Keep talking to me. I'm going to come to you,' he said, and I heard shuffling off to the side. It wasn't that far, but I knew that without my eyes, my other senses were trying to make up for that fact. Everything else became more intense.

'You can see me? How is that fair? Why can't I see you? I want to see you. Let me see you.'

'Soon, love. Just keep talking. I'm nearly there. By the way, that dress is not the right colour for you.'

I heard a squelching sound and a scream. 'Dev, what was that?' There was silence, and my mind raced. 'Devin … talk to me. What was that?'

'Lucy. It was Lucy killing the witch,' Devin said in my ear. I sobbed, and something inside me broke. I was free. Free to have my pelt back, and free of that stupid curse. Free to go places, free to swim in the ocean.

The white light slid away from my eyes, and I could see Devin. He was beaming at me. I hugged him, holding on tightly. He was so perfect. I looked past him and saw the witch in a mess on the floor. I was about to say something when a sharp pain stabbed my side. I cried out and looked down. A knife had been thrust through my back, barely nicking Devin. His eyes were wide, and my legs gave out on me.

'Acionna!' he screamed and caught me before I fell. 'Lucy, finish her.' *Who is her? Why is she 'finishing' me?*

The pain was white-hot. 'That really hurts,' I whispered, and Devin was shushing me, his hand lovingly stroking my face. I could feel the blood draining from my body, and it was like I had floated up to watch over what was happening.

'Hunter,' I heard Devin sob, and he slid under me. 'We have to do it.'

'Do what? Don't cry, Devin. You're too pretty to cry. Did anyone ever tell you that? Because it's true.'

He was crying a little harder, and I knew that he was crying not just for me, but for Jarrad and for his dad. Because things come in threes and if I was going to die, at least I helped free him of the shackles that held him down.

'Hold her still, Dev,' Hunter said.

'Huuunter. What are you doing? Give Devin a hug. My arms aren't working, and I can't get there. Help him,' I said in a sing-song voice. It was hard to sound serious, the pain making my body throb.

'I've got her,' Devin said in a tone I couldn't quite make out. Then I felt it. It was like the hot poker was ripped from my body, and my scream cut through the silence.

The pain was excruciating. It tingled up my spine, through my arms and down my legs. I started to shake, and Devin held me tight.

'Hunter,' he said calmly. 'Hunter! She's losing too much blood. Fix it. You have to fix her. She can't leave me.'

Leave him? I wouldn't do that. But I could feel my body getting heavier, my body colder.

'I think I need to sleep,' I said, and Devin shook his head. His eyes were a mess, and his nose was red. It made me want to kiss it, it was so sweet.

'Don't you dare sleep, Ash. Stay with me.'

'I'll see you when I wake up, Dev,' I said and shut my eyes. Everything was black, and nothing mattered anymore.

CHAPTER THIRTY-SEVEN

Devin
Payni 2017
Melbourne

ACIONNA HAD HER PELT BACK, and she was frolicking in the ocean like a seal. And alive. She was alive. After she had passed out, Hunter had patched her up as best as he could. Kali met us halfway, using magick to help kick start Acionna's healing, and it was lucky that the lackey who stabbed her missed anything of importance. Lucy finished her, and I knew it added to her nightmares, but she was closer than I had been.

I watched from the shore, and it made me beam with joy. Acionna was back in her native state—the one she had grown up in, been raised in. Ariel was with her, and together, they were giving everyone a rare look at what seals playing together looked like. Or that's what they thought.

I couldn't pull my eyes away from them, almost scared that Acionna would slip away without a word. She had promised she wouldn't do that, that going back would help cement what she needed to do, but she was going to come right back and make sure I was supported. It had been a week since I'd killed Jarrad, and I had a decision to make—would I continue in the shadows or step into the light and take control?

'They're completely amazing,' Lucy said as she sat down next to me.

'I know. I can't imagine what it was like to not be able to do that for close to seven months. Luce, knowing you had to live without me for so many years. I'm sorry. It was our fault. We opened that damn book.'

She shook her head and placed a hand on my knee. 'I'm as much at fault as you are. But we couldn't stop The Illuminate Year. That stupid timeline Karrept and Nefertiti put on my life, on all of our lives.'

Lucy was silent as she watched Acionna and Ariel play.

'We didn't kill Nefertiti.'

'What?' I asked and turned to her. 'What do you mean?'

'We had to split her up. She had merged with Lili, and it was to the point that if we tried to separate them, we would lose Lili.'

'Who is "we?"' I asked, already afraid of the answer.

'Me, Kali, Lili and Destiny.'

'You did what?!' Destiny not wanting to find a necromancer suddenly made sense. She was battling Nefertiti's voice, and that was just as bad as having Karrept's in my head.

'We didn't have a choice. We need a fourth person for the elemental spell. I wish I could have taken it back, but it was the only way.'

'Lucy, Destiny is undead. She can't keep taking energy from everyone. Destiny needs a necromancer, and she doesn't have the will to live as a result.'

'I *know*. I feel horrible, but I couldn't lose my best friend and my sister in the same breath.' She looked down at the sand and drew shapes in it to distract herself.

'We have to find her a necromancer or she is not going to be here. She'll die permanently, and we won't be able to do anything about it.'

'What is their importance? They're a myth,' she said.

I shook my head. 'Not a myth. They're real. They are just harder to find because no one believes they exist.'

'What will they do?' she asked.

'Keep her alive so she can function, keep her hair vibrant and, well ... look alive.'

Destiny was headstrong, and even after all of the trauma she had faced at the hands of Karrept, she was still there—barely, but she was there.

'She always loved you, you know,' I said. Even when Destiny was hard on Luce, it was because she wanted to make sure she could withstand all that would come.

'I know. She had a weird way of showing it, but after Egypt nearly three years ago, things have changed. She's different. I know she's undead, but, like, her whole demeanour changed.'

'She realised that life was too short.' I smiled.

Acionna and Ariel splashed about before they both dived under the water. I expected them both to come up, but they didn't. I looked around, and people waited with bated breath to see them come to shore, but there was no sign of them. People started to mill away from the beach, taking their blankets, snacks and kids with them.

'Are you going to be okay?' Lucy asked.

'Why wouldn't he be?' Acionna asked as she came ashore. Her pelt was wrapped around her wrist like a cuff, and I stood up to greet her. I grabbed a towel and wrapped it around her shoulders. She took it with a smile.

'This is a weird situation,' Lucy said.

'It is, but I promise to come back as often as I can. And he won't be alone at big meetings or anything of importance. I just have some things to take care of.'

Like she had to fix a kingdom in disarray after everything that's happened. I pulled her into my arms and kissed her. Acionna laughed against my lips, and I sighed. She was perfect because she didn't expect; she just wanted and loved.

CHAPTER THIRTY-EIGHT

Acionna
Payni 2017
Melbourne

I KISSED Devin goodbye and walked into the water, my pelt firmly attached to my wrist as I let it envelop my body—first my legs, then my arms all turned into flippers before I dived under and my body transformed into that of a seal. The water felt heavenly on my skin. I would never take it for granted again. My pelt would go everywhere with me—I would make sure of it.

I'd never had a human who accepted me for my pelt and kept it safe like he did. I mourned that Devin couldn't come Undersea with me, but that was the nature of my people. If we fell in love with humans, they stayed on shore for us.

As I swam deeper than I had in months, the water felt foreign, like I didn't quite fit in anymore.

The way home was familiar; it was the same way I had swam time and time again, and I knew it off by heart. *Go right down, turn to the left, then right and down again.* And there it was.

The kingdom was surrounded by colourful coral and sea plants. It was my favourite view to see the castle among the reeds and coral.

As I swam towards the castle, my body transformed from seal to that which was humanoid with seal qualities—the only way we were in the kingdom.

It was where we were safest.

I swam into the castle and past the selkies, merpeople and fish working in the town centre. Whispered words would make their way to my mother before I did, but I was there now, and I intended to make it right.

As I hit the inner castle, Adella raced out and barrelled into me. 'Acionna!!' Her excited energy made me laugh.

'Della, hi! That was fast.'

'You're home. Are you here to stay? What happened? Ariel said it was bad.'

Ariel had already been back two days, at least, but I made sure I spent time with Devin before I went back. But I was there now, and that was all that mattered.

'Back in action, but I have to talk to Mother first. Is she …?'

'Acionna.' As if she knew we were talking about her, Mother appeared, her brown locks floating in the water, her darker eyes staring at me. She was not emotional or at all maternal—it wasn't in her nature—but she held open her arms for me, and I untangled myself from Adella to take her up on that offer. She held me tightly, and I let her. The last time she'd embraced me, I was but a little pup, so I'd take it—and then some.

'Mother. I'm so sorry.'

'Hush. You aren't at fault. Ariel has already told me it was her, but I heard there is someone else at fault too.'

How much did Ariel tell her? Did she leave any of it for me to say?

'Yes. Eain. I am Unmatched with him as of this moment, and he will need to be prosecuted. I want his head. Or even his pelt as revenge.'

'You are entitled to it. I accept the Unmatching. You are free of it.'

The blessing was all I needed, and a weight lifted off my shoulders

—a weight I hadn't realised I had been carrying. It had been there since the day of the Matching, and suddenly, it was gone.

'I need an audience. I want to do this publicly once and then never again.'

'I'll organise it,' she said, and pulled herself away from me. Mother straightened herself up and stared at me. It was the first hint of any sort of motherly nature that she had shown in all my years. I couldn't tell if I should be excited or terrified.

And why did it take me being away for so long for it to come out? Is it because she is the queen, or that was how her mother brought her up?

'One more thing before you go and freshen up for it. Is there a man?'

Devin. I pressed my lips together.

'Yes, and he's wonderful. And human.'

She nodded, turned on her fin and shimmied out of the hallway.

'That went a lot better than I thought, but who was that woman?' Adella asked.

I stared after her and shook my head. 'I have no idea, but I don't know what to do with it. Do we take it or leave it?'

'I think we go with it because this is the happiest I've ever seen Mother, and that is saying something.'

'I know.'

I would have taken it, but if we stayed in the hallway much longer, I'd get waylaid by other sisters and people. I needed to get to my room to freshen up and take control of my destiny.

It was no different from Devin taking control of the hotel and announcing his plans. I could do the same and punish the man who was supposed to be my partner.

A heavy feeling settled in my gut. It wasn't natural for me to have to do that, and it would be the first of many things I would have to do that I didn't like.

The auditorium was full. Selkies, roanes, merpeople and fish all gathered, hushed whispers and looks thrown in my direction. The prodigal daughter had returned, and that was the biggest news around.

Mother waited for the hush to die down, but I didn't think it would. There was too much going on. As I looked out, I saw Eain leaning against the pillar at the back of the room, an easy smile on his face. It took everything in me not to storm over to him and rip it from his face. He wouldn't be smiling after I was done with him.

'Hush, everyone. We have some important news.' There was a quiet that settled as everyone stopped simultaneously. 'As many of you can see, Acionna is back. She is back after a very unfortunate event, but we gathered here today to listen. Acionna.' Mother gestured towards me, and I hid all signs of my nerves.

I can do this.

Eain was the descendant of an important line of roanes, and I was about to make some serious enemies. Did I care? A little, but that man needed to be out of the kingdom.

'I'm back after being landlocked.' An audible gasp ripped through the room. 'An orchestrated event to make my step to the throne more difficult. One that was calculated and forced in a pact with one of my very own sisters, who was also landlocked as a result.' My eyes found Eain, and he straightened, his eyes wide. He hadn't believed me when I'd told him to stay away. Eain was going to see what happened when he didn't listen to his future queen.

'As of this very instant, I am Unmatched with Eain. He is shunned from this community and exiled, effective immediately. He was the one at the helm of this elaborate plot to take over the throne and rule in his image.'

Eain tried to run, but the guardians that looked after the throne seized him.

'You're a liar, Acionna. Tell them the truth. It was all you wanted.'

'Take him away,' I shouted. And they did.

'Anyone who is a known associate of his will be banished from the kingdom. We don't support those who want to crumble our reign. I will not stand for it. I will be queen in no time, and when I am, I will demolish Matching ceremonies, allowing humans to have a part in our lives and making sure there is no one who will challenge my rule. I may be young, I may not be the people's choice, but I am your queen when the time comes.'

Silence echoed in the room, and I searched the faces in the crowd. Many were shocked by what had happened, and others beamed. It would be a totally new rule—one that was different from my mother's.

She slid next to me and murmured, 'You can't get rid of the Matchings.'

I turned to her. 'I can and have. They are no longer a part of finding a mate. It was barbaric to have to choose someone and have no chance at love. You were never in love, or you would agree.'

She shook her head. 'Love grows with time.'

'I don't want the time. I want heart-beating, head-dizzying love. I have it with a human.'

'And he feels the same?'

Not in so many words. 'Yes. He does.'

'Then Matchings are disbanded. On one condition.' She paused. 'You are to work on a way to make sure that the bloodlines are kept pure. That you have a method to keep the next generation thriving.'

There was a loud roar throughout the room. Everyone was excited about the exit of Matchings. Which said a lot about the process in itself. But I was going to make sure there was a better way.

It was hard to love someone you just met, and expect them to be everything they need.

CHAPTER THIRTY-NINE

Devin
Payni 2017
Melbourne

THE CITY WAS quiet as I woke up. Lying next to me, Acionna snuggled deeper into the covers, her face peaceful and childlike. I realised then that I was in too deep. Even if she didn't push back, I wouldn't have left. She was too beautiful, too much to lose. I forgot how much it hurt to love someone so much I can't eat or sleep because all I want to do is drink them in. I slipped deeper into the covers and pulled her petite body against me. Waking up from the hazy sleep, she blinked, those intense green eyes opening slowly.

'Dev?' she whispered huskily.

'Shh. I just want to embrace this.' I watched as her eyes widened. Acionna knew what I meant.

'What time is it?' she murmured, resting her head on my shoulder. I wrapped my arms around her body and smoothed my hands over her back.

'Dawn o'clock,' I murmured, inhaling her scent.

It was the day I would sign the official contracts in front of the media and have my first big meeting. There would only be more of those moments.

'Oh, god. Come on, Dev, back to sleep.' Her sleep haze voice was enough to seriously make me stay in bed a little longer, but I knew I couldn't. The meeting was that important. It was going to shape who I was and who people saw me as.

'I wish, but I just wanted a cuddle before I got up for work,' I whispered, pressing a soft kiss against her temple before I rolled her over and slid out of bed. Naked, I walked across to my bathroom. Normally, I wouldn't look over my shoulder, but things were different now. She knew who I was, what I did, and she was not running away. I looked over at her, and she was on her side, her hand propping her head up, and the covers barely covering her chest. I stopped for a moment. Flashes of her skin pressed against mine and sliding over mine were enough to make me desperately want to slide back between the sheets to be with her.

'Keep walking, Mr Ryder. You have an important meeting, don't you, now?'

I groaned and walked into the bathroom. *Mr Ryder. I'm going to be Mr Ryder for the entire day.*

After the shower, I padded into my room with a towel wrapped around my waist. Acionna, on the other hand, was walking around in a bra, panties and thigh-highs. Instantly, my brain sparked into gear, and I balled my hands into fists to stop myself from going over to her and shoving her against the table to have my way with her. If I did that, I would be late. Late for my first day as CEO of Ryder Hotel. *Fuck.*

'Put some clothes on, Acionna,' I whispered.

She looked at me and smiled wickedly, the temptress in her out in full force. 'Am I distracting you?'

Acionna held my gaze, her smile widening as she watched me struggle with the words.

'Yes. If I didn't have to be there on time, I would do you on the table there, and then maybe against the wardrobe.' I groaned at the imagery in my head. 'Put some clothes on, Ash, I beg of you.'

'You beg of me, hey?' she said as she slipped into a pencil skirt, and I knew it was a pencil skirt because of Lucy and Lili—they liked educating me on women's clothing.

'Shirt,' I choked out. She looked so sexy. If I could only force my attention off her.

'Pants, put some on. It'll help,' she murmured.

I looked down and frowned. *I don't think so, but I'm going to have to try, or neither of us is getting out of the room.*

Everything was laid out on my bed, and I knew that Acionna carefully picked the right suit, the shirt, tie and cufflinks. First underwear, always briefs with suits because there was nothing more awkward than wearing perfectly tailored pants and having a line from the boxer briefs. It also makes zipping up easier too. Acionna just smirked and did up the buttons of her shirt. It was a soft green colour that brought out her eyes and the natural tan of her skin. She simply beamed.

It was cold so I slipped on a white singlet that hung to all of the right muscles. Two years before, it would have hung off me weirdly, but luckily, I had put on weight. I buttoned up the shirt slowly, this time watching myself do it in the mirror. It was almost like I was a passenger in my life, watching myself button up the armour that would be mine during the day. I pushed the shirt beneath the waistband of my pants and made sure it sat smoothly before I picked up the tie. Dad had taught me how to tie a tie when I was at school. *First, you cross it over and make sure that the skinner part of the tie is shorter than the thicker part of the tie. Then, you loop the bigger part of it around the short part twice.* A Windsor knot was always more appropriate than whatever else there was. Some of the knots at school were horrible. *Next, you wrap the thicker part over the folded part of the tie and pass the arrow through the junction and pull, slowly and adjusting the tie as you go. And lastly, you slide the skinnier part of the tie into the hole that's there—normally with the washing instructions—and you are done.*

Acionna walked over to me, heels and everything, and adjusted my tie before clipping a tie clip to keep it in place. 'Thanks,' I murmured.

'You really do look fantastic in a suit. Arms.' She held a cufflink in her hand. I did as I was told, lifting an arm up for her. Acionna played with the cuff before she slid the cufflink into place and adjusted it. It sparkled in the rising sun, and it was only then that I realised there was an *R* on it—the logo for the hotel.

'Acionna, those … I can't wear these. They're my …'

'Your dad's. I know. Your mum said you have to wear them. She came in while you were in the shower.' I blinked at her. Mum never came into my room, not anymore. 'She said your dad wore them for his first meeting when he signed the very first contract, and has worn them on every important business venture since. It's for luck.'

Tears clouded my vision before I had a chance to catch my breath. 'Acio—'

'Don't, it's okay. I get it.' She slipped the other cufflink into my shirt, and I had time to take a deep breath. 'You look good in Armani. Shoes.' She picked them up and handed them to me. I sat on the edge of the bed and slipped my feet into the Italian loafers that were well worn but didn't show it. I'd been to enough charity balls in the past year or so to wear them in properly. I stood up and bounced on the balls of my feet before I stopped rocking and sighed.

'Stop,' I murmured to Acionna, lipstick in hand.

'What?' She actually stopped, and I grinned at her. I crossed the room, closing the distance between us before I grabbed her hips and pulled her in. I kissed her hard and fast. Acionna moaned, and before she could sink into the kiss, I pulled back. 'There. You look flushed enough.'

'Tease,' she threw out, tapping her fingers against my cheek. Ash untangled herself from me and I watched as she slid colour on her lips.

The ride to the hotel was going to be hell, but worth it. She would be there to help me sign my first document, but she had to go before the press conference, and that was okay. I could do that alone. Lucy,

Dest and Mum were going to be there. When I was flanked by Ryder women, nothing could go wrong. Or at least, that was what I hoped.

The room was full of reporters from all of the heavy hitters. *The Age, The Herald Sun, Nine, Ten, Seven, ABC* and *SBS* all had representatives that would record it live and beam it across the country. It would reach the nation by the end of the day, and that would be it. I would be in charge. The podium was at the front, and with my cue cards, I ran over what I would say, announcing to the world that I was taking over. A year earlier, I had been deep at a camp, learning how to kill people, and now I was about to take over my dad's company.

Who the hell am I?

'Dev, are you okay?' Mum asked.

Her grey eyes were lined with black, and she stared at me.

'I'm okay. I just want to get this over with. Are Dest and Lucy here?'

'We're here. We're here. Sorry, Destiny had an accident,' Lucy said. I looked at Destiny. She wore a long-sleeved shirt and slacks while Lucy had on a skirt and a light, flowy blouse.

'What happened?' I asked and moved to Destiny. She backed up and held her hands behind her back.

'I tripped and hurt myself. It's nothing, I promise,' she said.

Lucy gave me a look that said more than what Destiny words could say. *Fuck. It was on purpose.* Not what I wanted to know, but it wouldn't matter. I had to do the thing. I would deal with it after.

Rhea came up to me and smiled. It was an easy smile, but there was nothing easy about what was to come.

'You've got this. They're ready for you, Dev. Just stick to the speech, and you'll be okay.'

I nodded and walked into the room, Mum, Lucy and Destiny flanking me, and Rhea bringing up the rear.

I put the card down on the podium and adjusted the microphones.

'Hello, everyone. Thank you for taking the time to come along. As many of you know, I'm Devin Ryder, the only son of the late Matthew Ryder. I'm here to make an exciting announcement.' I paused for effect and searched the crowd.

There was no one familiar, but that was okay. New journalists were a good thing.

'As of this morning, I signed official documents to be the owner of Ryder Hotel. I will continue the legacy my father built with his bare hands. I can't wait to take Ryder Hotel to the next-level and see how much growth we can achieve.' The room erupted with applause, and I nodded in appreciation.

'Are there any questions?'

Rhea was in charge of the section, and she pointed to a woman in a blue suit.

'Any news on the cause of death for Matthew?'

Ooph. Not the time to talk about that. 'We, as a family, know, and that is all we are comfortable saying. Death is a pretty ceremony these days.'

'Will there be any name changes?' another asked.

'My last name is Ryder—my dad's last name—so it stays.' I looked at Rhea, and she was signing off with a cute sign against her note.

I was happy to stop it there.

'Thank you for coming. We appreciate it, and hope that you can enjoy your stay at Ryder Hotel the next time you visit.'

I waved, walked away from the podium and back into the foyer. 'How was that?' I asked.

'Sharp, sweet, perfect,' Mum said.

'Of course you'd say that, Mum. What else am I supposed to say? "Good luck, losers?"'

'Devin!' Mum said.

'I know, I know. Keep it appropriate.'

'Remember for next time.'

Too many rules to be this high up. Why didn't they tell me?

Oh, wait, they probably did, and I forgot.

Dusk slipped into the sky with the change in weather. Acionna was due back, and I padded across the cold sand to wait at the water's edge for her. She'd only been gone a few days, but those days felt like weeks, even months. I didn't know what was wrong with me, but since she started going home regularly, all I wanted to do was take her in my arms and never let her leave. But there was also the joy of being there when she broke the surface.

I focused on trying to find the rest of the operation here that Dovev had set up. It was deeper than just the skin level of what happened and why he was now dead. I knew there was more to it. So far, he was like a ghost. There was no trace of him. Not even at his place.

In my hands was a towel and a robe. No one was going to be looking at Acionna naked if I had anything to say about that. A splash pulled me from my thoughts, and a seal peeked up through the surf.

Acionna.

I opened the towel and waited for her to make her way over to me. Every time I saw her shed her pelt and become human, it was fascinating.

That day was no different. She came to a spot where she could stand. Her legs were first, then her arms, face and body.

The fur would recede into her body, and all that would be left was a small square. She'd taken to wrapping it around her wrist to have it closer and keep it safe.

'Hello, Ash, love,' I said, and she smiled.

'Hi, Dev,' Acionna said softly, taking the towel from me. She wrapped it around her body and leant up to kiss me.

'Welcome home,' I said, wrapping the robe around her shoulders. Things immediately felt like they clicked back in place with her back.

I was home.

Finally.

REFERENCE

Ancient Egyptian Months

Season 1: Akhet—Inundation
December: Choiak (Keek)
November: Athyr (Hatoor)
October: Phaophi (Babeh)
September: Thoth (Toot)

Season 2:Peret—Growing
April: Parmuthi (Bar-moodeh)
March: Phamenoth (Baram-hat)
February: Mechir (Amsheer)
January: Tybi (To-beh)

Season 3: Shemu—Harvest
August: Mesore (Mesoree)
July: Epiphi (Abib)
June: Payni (Ba-oo-neh)
May: Pachons (Beshens)

ACKNOWLEDGMENTS

I thought this would get easier with the next book, but it has gotten so much harder. This book was a therapy book, the first draft written over 10 years ago, when Dad first passed away it was the first book he didn't know about. In fact I hardly knew about it, so it feels bittersweet to publish this one. But I couldn't have done this book without some very amazing people in my life.

This book was also the beginning of the adventures of Rajah and Abu - Abu is a ginger cat I rescued (read a stray who I coerced with food to be my second inside cat) and it has been just as adventurous as stressful, but they helped me, with endless cuddles, get through this book.

Thank you to Nick, Josh, Rin, Anthimos and Sethmi for being some of the biggest cheerleaders I have had. You guys truly made writing this book so enjoyable - also I 100% appreciate you being alpha readers and helping with the fact checking, the squealing over scenes and helping keep me accountable. I appreciate you all for this so much.

Thank you Loren - our gym sessions were a haven and the gentle yet firm reminds to finish writing and finish editing never went unheard, even if I complained about doing it.

Congratulations to Elias for winning the renaming Tyler - Jarrad was the solid choice, thank you so much for making that suggestion - it fit so much better than Tyler.

To Mum, you always asking me the questions I hate answering but always support me beyond anything I can ever expect. Thank you for believing in me and my dream that comes along with writing books. I love you.

To Pete, my brother, you are an inspiration to me, you have always hit the ground running and never give up on things that drag you down. I am so grateful for the lifetime of laughter, support, help and joy you have brought me. I know I used to joke that I wanted a sister but you are all I have ever wanted. I'm so grateful to have you as a best friend and a brother.

To Andrew, who would look at me incredulously and yell 'Maaaaandiiiii' whenever I self sabotaged myself or tried to cheat myself out of doing the work. Thank you for the support.

To my editing team - Brittany at BLD Editing, you made me fall back in love with editing and helped build me up. I am so grateful to you and for helping me feel so empowered about my words. I appreciate you more than these words can do justice and I am so grateful to have worked with you. Bring on book 3 and what magick we can create together. Thank you to Ramona, who helped tidy up this manuscript. I definitely thought we had caught all the changes.

Where would I be without my husband, Dave, who picked up the slack while I was busy writing and editing. He may not be a reader (yet) but he listens to my rambling when it counts. Thank you for your support and your love.

I am also so damn lucky to have a small group of authors who helped support me while I was in the trenches, thanks to Peta, Mel, Demi, Maddy, Allison, Lex, Maz, Janice, Simone and Steph for your support, yours cheers of encouragement and banter. I don't know how I did the majority of this book without you. Not to mention the editing.

Lastly, I want to thank *you*, dear reader, I am so grateful that you are here. That you have read Faded Fragments and fallen in love with a world that has been with me for my whole life.

We're just beginning and with Destiny's book next, what do you think her side of this whole story is like?

ABOUT THE AUTHOR

Mandi Kontos is an urban fantasy writer who lives in Melbourne Australia with her husband, tuxedo cat Rajah, a plethora of plants and a collection of journals she never writes in. By day she is a buying assistant, by night a writing mindset mentor and word wrangler.

She has a Bachelor of Arts, Bachelor of Writing and Publishing and a Masters in Creative Writing. She is a perpetual student and loves to learn.

Mandi loves to take the supernatural and blend it with the mundane things of life, taking mythology and spinning it on its head.

Her debut novel *Faded Fragments* has been a labour of love and is the first in *The Nexus Series.*

Join her newsletter to get updates about her writing and books to come.

instagram.com/mandikont
tiktok.com/mandikont
amazon.com/author/mandikont
threads.net/@mandikont

SIGN UP FOR BOOK UPDATES

If you loved Fractured Pieces, sign up to the email list to get sneak peak behind the scenes at the next book and the others coming in the series. It's your best bet to get a chance to access to special bonuses and pre-orders before anyone else does.

Scan the QR code to sign up today.

FRACTURED PIECES PLAYLIST

Want to listen along to the playlist that inspired the book? This is your chance. It's a mixture off hyper fixation, sexy tunes and everything in between.

Scan the QR code to be led to the playlist that I used to write the whole book.